DEATH COMES LAST

The Rest of the 1950s

Gil Brewer

Edited by David Rachels

Stark House Press • Eureka California
www.starkhousepress.com

DEATH COMES LAST: THE REST OF THE 1950s

Published by Stark House Press
1315 H Street
Eureka, CA 95501
griffinskye3@sbcglobal.net
www.starkhousepress.com

DEATH COMES LAST copyright ©2021 by Stark House Press

"The Golden Scheme" reprinted by permission of the Estate of Gil Brewer. All rights reserved under International and Pan-American Copyright Conventions.

Introductory material and "Complete Index of Gil Brewer's Short Stories," copyright ©2021 by David Rachels.

ISBN-13: 978-1-951473-61-7

Cover design by Jeff Vorzimmer, ¡caliente!design, Austin, Texas
Cover illustration by Robert Stanley

PUBLISHER'S NOTE:
This is a work of fiction. Names, characters, places and incidents are either the products of the author's imagination or used fictionally, and any resemblance to actual persons, living or dead, events or locales, is entirely coincidental.

Without limiting the rights under copyright reserved above, no part of this publication may be reproduced, stored, or introduced into a retrieval system or transmitted in any form or by any means (electronic, mechanical, photocopying, recording or otherwise) without the prior written permission of both the copyright owner and the above publisher of the book.

First Stark House Press Edition: November 2021

Praise for *Redheads Die Quickly and Other Stories: Expanded Edition:*

"Brewer's short stories, published from the early 1950s through the 1970s, still have the power to shock. And they might even be better than his novels. They are certainly wilder and more intense."
—Woody Haut's Blog

"Never one for dull moments, Brewer wastes no time grabbing his readers, pulling them right into the thick of a seedy, titillating plot, and keeping up an exhilarating pace from climax through conclusion."
—*The Florida Bookshelf*

"Brewer masterfully hooks readers with the opening sentence of each story. Once hooked it is nearly impossible not to continue reading."
—Alan Cranis, *Bookgasm*

"Not a dud in the bunch, all of them featuring the classic Gil Brewer themes of sexual lust, booze and dangerous women."
— Kurt Reichenbaugh, *The Ringer Files*

"If you're a Gil Brewer fan, this is a must-buy!"
—George Kelley

"Brewer's stories linger in the reader's mind like extreme public indecency."
—*Los Angeles Review of Books*

"Brewer's fevered Florida noirs throbbed with sultry, sexy tropic heat years before John D. MacDonald's Travis McGee weighed anchor in Bahia Mar."
—*The Seattle Times*

". . . each tale delivers a delectable slice of darkness . . ."
—Ben Boulden, *Mystery Scene*

"Every self-respecting pulp noir fan should read these stories."
—Paul Burke, *NB*

Contents

Editor's Note 6

Prelude: Gil and Gil 7

A Note on the Texts 8

Two Stories by Gil Brewer pére
    Caught with the Goods 11
    Just Plain Dumb 16

The Rest of the 1950s
    Final Appearance 21
    Motive for Murder 31
    Gigolo 37
    The Screamer 46
    Death Comes Last 78
    I Saw Her Die 97
    Teen-Age Casanova 103
    Fog 113
    Midnight 120
    Alligator 128
    Goodbye, Jeannie 135
    Short Go 138
    Return to Yesterday 145
    The Golden Scheme 152
    Somebody Knew Her 166
    The Tormentors 170
    Renegade 177
    "Beeg Fool" 189
    Love Me, Baby 198
    Stop Off 205
    I'll Be in the Bedroom 210
    The Price of Pride 216
    That Damned Piper 224
    Old Timers 234
    High Heels and Kisses 239
    The Glass Eye 245
    This Petty Pace 251

Complete Index of Gil Brewer's Short Stories 259

Editor's Note

This is the fourth collection of Gil Brewer's short stories I have edited for Stark House Press. In review:

Redheads Die Quickly and Other Stories collects about half of Brewer's short fiction from the 1950s. This collection was originally published by the University Press of Florida in 2012 and was reissued in an "Expanded Edition" (with five additional stories) by Stark House Press in 2019.

Death Is a Private Eye: Unpublished Stories of Gil Brewer collects 22 stories from Brewer's manuscripts at the University of Wyoming. These stories are mostly from the 1970s, but the two longest stories in the collection are from much earlier: "Death Is a Private Eye" (c. 1950) and "A Present for Cleo" (1956).

Die Once—Die Twice: More Unpublished Stories of Gil Brewer collects 24 additional stories from the Wyoming manuscripts. Whereas *Death Is a Private Eye* gathers stories mostly in Brewer's classic noir vein, *Die Once—Die Twice* casts a wider net, not only in terms of genre (noir, science fiction, romantic confession, and so on), but also in terms of Brewer's forays into explicit sexuality.

Finally, we have the present collection, *Death Comes Last: The Rest of the 1950s*. Taken together, *Death Comes Last* and the expanded *Redheads Die Quickly* contain all of Brewer's short fiction published between 1951 and 1959. Additionally, *Death Comes Last* features:

- "The Golden Scheme," Brewer's last remaining unpublished story from the 1950s;
- a pair of crime stories published in 1929 and 1930 by Gil Brewer's father (who, confusingly, also published under the name Gil Brewer); and
- the first-ever catalog of every Gil Brewer short story known to exist, including everything published thus far (with complete publication histories) as well as everything still unpublished.

There are, perhaps, two more Brewer story collections still to be published, though not by me. One would collect stories that Brewer published after the 1950s, and the other would gather more material from his papers in Wyoming. And, just maybe, there might be a third: Jeff Vorzimmer has begun stylometric work to identify unattributed noir stories of the 1950s, and he has already homed in on two stories that appear to be Brewer's. In any case, my hope is that the index of Brewer's stories that concludes this book will give potential editors a sense of the possibilities.

Prelude: Gil and Gil

The two Gil Brewers—Gilbert *Thomas*, father, and Gilbert *John*, son—were both alcoholic pulp writers. The father did not make his living from pulp writing, or if he did, he did not do so for long. The 50 stories that Gilbert Thomas Brewer is known to have published all appeared between 1928 and 1933. The elder Brewer was most successful with air adventure stories, though he dabbled in other genres as well, including hardboiled crime.

In 1931, Gilbert *John* Brewer turned nine years old, and this was the age, by his own account, when he wrote his first short story and began dreaming of becoming a writer. In interviews about his beginnings as a writer, the younger Brewer never mentioned his father, but it is difficult not to see a connection: The son's ambition to write took hold when his father's pulp career peaked.

Though the younger Brewer wrote (again, by his own account) hundreds of short stories over the course of his teenaged years, when the twenty-year-old joined the army in 1943, he was still unpublished. After World War II, when he got out of the army and returned stateside, he settled in Florida because his family had moved there, and his easiest path forward as a writer was to let his parents support him while he continued to develop his craft. He wanted to be a better writer than his father had been. He wanted to write Literature, not pulp.

Gilbert Thomas Brewer   Gilbert John Brewer

But Gil senior's wife and Gil junior's mother, Ruth Wilhelmina Olschewske, was not happy about her son's freeloading and—to make matters worse—Gil junior was already an alcoholic. When he refused to get a paying job, his mother kicked him out of the house. By doing this, Ruth caused her son to follow in her husband's writerly footsteps. Having to support himself, Gil junior no longer had the luxury of writing what he wanted to write. To make money, he turned to the sort of popular writing that his father had done. Like his father, he dabbled in various genres, but crime writing paid the bills.

The younger Brewer did not become a pulp writer in the purest sense, as pulp magazines were mostly gone by the time he turned professional, and he published only a few stories in actual pulps. But he found his home in the pulps' spiritual descendants: the cheap digest magazines and paperback novels of the 1950s. As a professional writer, the younger Brewer was, for a time, fantastically successful. He had a million-selling paperback and an agent who wanted him to return to his pursuit of Literature. But after that agent died, he ended up with an agent who wanted only merchandise, and his drinking continued to be a problem.

But the younger Brewer wrote some great stories and novels all the same, and his devotees might even argue that some of them are Literature. At the least, he surpassed his father, both financially and artistically, though his father's crime stories are still fun to read. Readers are not likely to confuse stories by the two Brewers, mainly because of the older Brewer's dated style. The father's stories with their loftier diction, hardboiled patois, and avoidance of the verb "said" are amusing today even when they do not mean to be. The younger Brewer may have been inspired by his father to write, but he learned a few things from Hemingway, too.

We begin, then, with a taste of Gilbert *Thomas* Brewer, a pair of short hardboiled tales from *The Underworld Magazine* and *Detective Fiction Weekly*, both true pulps. After this, we have 27 stories from Gilbert *John* Brewer, which comprise his previously uncollected short stories from his glory decade of the 1950s. Death comes last, but writing lives on.

A Note on the Texts

"The Golden Scheme" is printed as it appears in Gil Brewer's original typewritten manuscript, which is held at the American Heritage Center at the University of Wyoming. The rest of the stories in this collection are reprinted as they appeared in their first published forms with one exception: "'Beeg Fool'" first appeared in *Salvo*, which used boldface type in place of italics, a practice that is not replicated here. Beyond this, typographical errors have been silently corrected, and idiosyncrasies of punctuation have been altered when necessary to clarify confusing sentences.

Two Stories by Gil Brewer pére

Caught with the Goods

The Underworld Magazine
April 1929

"Thought that hick was easy pickin's, didn't ya? But he was too quick for ya—an' I was handy. Caught with the goods, eh, Slippy? You'll take a nice long train ride this time, believe me."

Patrolman Burke of the Fourth Precinct was in a garrulous, almost an exuberant mood, as with careful hold he propelled his charge towards the Station. Nor was his cheerfulness without cause, for he had captured the long elusive Slippy O'Day, one of the cleverest dips that ever lifted a wallet—had caught him with the goods.

There also walked beside Patrolman Burke a tall, lean-visaged man, an alien to the bustling city with its jostling, hurrying crowds; he who had caught in a firm grasp the slender wrist of the wily Slippy even as a fat wallet had been lifted stealthily from a commodious hip-pocket.

Burke had insisted upon the stranger's appearance at the Station where he might identify both the thief and the evidence—especially the evidence, which he had carefully secreted upon his uniformed person. He was taking no chances, for he had captured a rich prize whose clever evasions of the law had long irked police.

Steadily the strange trio made their way through the seething mass of pedestrians, the bulking form of the officer cleaving a passage through the eddying crowds. Time and again, his companions were buffeted about and against him, but Patrolman Burke minded it not at all as he strode grimly toward the Fourth Precinct Station, already visioning the cloud of glory that would envelope him as he surrendered his charge to the law.

At one stage in their journey a slender girl in mounting the curb had ostensibly tripped, had clung for a moment upon Burke and his captive while regaining her equilibrium; then with a confused apology had hurried on her way.

To Patrolman Burke the incident gave occasion for nothing more than a growled warning for Slippy to watch his step. He failed to note the swift grin that lighted the pinched and wizened features of Slippy O'Day, or the new jauntiness in his captive's manner.

Thus it was with supreme confidence in the honor about to be bestowed upon him that he entered the Fourth Precinct Station and presented himself before the desk of Lieutenant Mortison.

Mortison was a veteran of the old days of Tong warfare and the *Tenderloin*. Coolly he surveyed the impudently smiling face of Slippy O'Day, an eager light gleaming for a second from piercing eyes, only to be swiftly diffused in bleak, gray depths of boredom.

"Humph! In again, Slippy," said Mortison.

"Yessir," replied the indomitable Slippy. "I was interrupted in me duties by this officer"—a finger pointed toward Patrolman Burke—"who insisted that I pay yer honor this visit. He's accusin' me o' pinchin' a roll, and—"

"That's enough, Slippy," interrupted the Lieutenant. "What about it, Burke?"

Gravely clearing his throat preparatory to the indictment of his prisoner, the dull rosy flush born of Slippy's audacity, gradually receded from the face of Patrolman Burke.

"It's an air-tight case, Lieutenant. I've got the wallet in my possession as evidence, and this gentleman, the owner, will testify. That's what I brought him along for."

• • •

Hope vied with skepticism in the glance Mortison fixed upon the disillusioned visitor to the city as he proceeded to gather in all the evidence.

"What's your name?" queried the Lieutenant.

"Barton, sir, Joel Barton."

"Where from?"

"Orville, up-state, sir."

"You say this man," indicating Slippy O'Day, "tried to pick your pocket?"

"Yes, sir," asserted Barton, who was beginning to realize the importance of his position. "I was standin' on the corner, lookin' up at one o' them movin' signs, when I felt a twitch like around my back-pocket where I carry my money. I reached around and grabbed this feller by the wrist an' derned if he didn't have my wallet right in his hand; ready to make off with it, I'll betcha."

"You saw this, Burke?" asked the now confident Lieutenant.

"No, I didn't see it, but I heard the commotion, so I stepped right over an' collared him."

"Yup," burst out anew the excited stranger, "he come right over in the nick o' time. That feller must be pretty slick; dipped right under my coat." Barton favored the region of his hip-pocket with a demonstrative slap, paused with a startled air; then digging his hand in his pocket brought forth a fat, leather-bound packet.

"Why—why, dern me, if it ain't come back!" gasped the startled suburbanite as he stared at the wallet reposing in his hand.

Patrolman Burke darted a hand beneath his tunic, groped wildly for a moment in the throes of consternation, then glared venomously at his recent charge. Slippy stood with arms folded, lips pursed, brows creased and with meditative glance bent toward the ceiling as he murmured: "Wallet, wallet, who's got the wallet? Officer Burke is it."

Then dropping his pose and bowing with an impish grin, Slippy addressed the lieutenant: "Beg pardon, yer honor, but havin' important business on the avinyoo, maybe I'd better beat it."

"Yes, you can go," growled Mortison. "But watch out. You're gettin' clumsy, and we'll have you yet. Remember, we're watchin' you."

"I'm watchin' you," roared the enraged Burke, who felt keenly the irony in his superior's glance as Slippy trod jauntily toward the Station door and freedom. "I'm watchin' you, an' I'm gonna get you with the goods." The door snapped closed, and Slippy, wearing a mocking grin, was lost to view.

It was almost a month later that news of Slippy O'Day reached Lieutenant Mortison, coming from one of the police reporters who dropped in to glean from the blotter the happenings of the night before.

"Well, you've lost your chance of nabbing Slippy O'Day," announced the scribe.

"Eh! Slippy—what's up? Has he been knocked off?"

"Not him," laughed the reporter. "You couldn't guess, so read it and weep." A late edition, folded to the item in question, was tossed on the desk.

• • •

Mortison read, stolidly chewing the ends of his bristling gray mustache. Upon completing his perusal of the article, he exclaimed: "Well, I'll be jugged! So he's got religion, eh? And has joined the Mission class! Well, I'd never have thought it of a little heller like Slippy. But I'm mighty glad of it, if it only stays with him. Lordy, he's been a corker!"

It was at this juncture that the Station door swung open, admitting Patrolman Burke.

"Mornin' Burke," greeted Mortison. "Heard the news? Slippy O'Day's got religion."

"Just met him. Said he thought he'd tell me he couldn't play tag anymore."

"Do you think he's on the level, Burke?"

"Well, I don't know. He seemed different somehow. Not so fresh and brassy. But I'm not forgettin' Spike Dooley. You remember he got religion for about three months while he stacked things for the Lansberg cleanup. I think Slippy'll bear watchin'."

But could the guardians of the law have overheard the conference that took place about two hours later in the back room of a more or less popular bowery resort, any doubt they held regarding Slippy's regeneration would have been dispelled.

"I tell yer, Tess, we're quits. The game's goofy an' I'm cuttin' it. If yer don't wanna listen to me, yer kin do as yer like. But I'm through snatchin' an' we're quits."

"I've been listenin' to ya long enough, Slippy," replied the girl called Tess. There was a cold glitter in her eyes. I thought ya was havin' a spell, at first; that you'd got hold of some bum dago red, or somethin'. But I guessed wrong.

"So you're turnin' me down cold, eh?" continued the girl, her anger kindling. "You're goin' straight, huh? You'll go straight, all right—straight to hell. Blackie Dawson'll fix you; he says he will. Him an' me's teamin' up from now on." There was a dangerous snarl in the girl's voice.

"You know what happened to Cox, Slippy? an' Bennett? Well, Blackie says you're number three, so watch out. You won't starve to death in your new business—you won't live long enough." With a disdainful glance, the girl swept from the room. The converted Slippy was left alone in deep contemplation of a future heavily shadowed.

That Dawson would try to kill him, Slippy believed without question. But luck, a smooth-running, infallible streak of luck had always favored him, and he was willing to lay it evenly against Dawson's vindictiveness.

There were other things to think about, however, for with the decision to change one's vocation, there is always the new one to select. Slippy's decision had come about rather abruptly when curiosity at a time of flush pockets had led him to look in at a meeting in the Mission. Once there, he with a few others, had felt the call to better things; had stayed for a talk with Father Dougherty, and had gone forth with a new vision of life.

Still, in order to live, one must eat. And in order to eat while one lived in the way Father Dougherty counseled, meant, for the Slippy O'Days, work. But what sort of work? And where obtainable?

Such was the problem, with the spectre of Blackie Dawson hovering in the background, that Slippy pondered throughout the day. And as night fell he mentally bade his problem wait and started for the Mission.

It was still early, and he seemed almost alone as he walked swiftly toward his destination. Above the deserted streets, an occasional elevated train roared through the night; the sooty smoke of the East River boats blended aromatically with the peculiar odor of delicatessen shops and the tang of roasting peanuts. The old familiar sounds seemed to hold a new significance—the click of pool balls resounding from doors through which he had often passed; the ribald hilarity from the chop suey joint over what had once been Brady's saloon, and where drinks, both soft and otherwise, were still served.

• • •

Just a block from the Mission, Slippy found Patrolman Burke making the rounds of his beat.

"A business engagement, tonight, Slippy?"

"Social," was the quick correction. "I'm out of business as I told yer this mornin'. Haven't found a new line yet."

"Just curious, ya know," rejoined the policeman. "Spike Dooley went out of business, too—for a while."

"Yer standin' on yer foot," came the enigmatical reply, in a tone of resentment. "I'm not Spike Dooley."

"Just the same," blustered Burke, "don't forget I'm watchin' you. And if ya break out again, I'll get ya, an' I'll get ya with the goods."

"Yer wanna lay off the pipe, Burke. Yer gettin' wild. I could work the old game forever, an' you'd never get me right. Why? Because outside of other little gifts, I'm lucky. That's somethin' you cops ain't got—luck."

It was a dark scowl that Patrolman Burke sent after Slippy O'Day as he strolled down the street.

"A hard egg," muttered Slippy to himself as he neared the Mission. "But his shell is chipped."

Then hearing a peculiar clicking sound emanating from a darkened, old tenement, he paused and faced the doorway. For a brief moment he peered into the gloom of the darkened hall, then flashed his right hand to his gun-pocket. But it was empty—he had been converted.

Immediately there issued a stream of flame, a quick succession of shots, and Slippy swayed for a second or two upright, then slumped to the sidewalk.

Racing to the scene with pistol in hand and whistle shrilling, Patrolman Burke was the first to reach the side of the stricken man. Slippy was hit hard and going fast. There was a queer little smile hovering around his mouth and a surprised look in his eyes that was swiftly fading, as he was carried into the Mission and stretched out on the floor.

Reading aright the signs of ebbing life, the policeman nodded to Father Dougherty, who knelt beside the dying man and proceeded to administer the last rites of the Church.

Once Slippy began to mumble a little and his eyes fluttered as though it were all over. But a second later they opened wide, fixed on the heavy gold watch-chain Father Dougherty always wore suspended between the lower pockets of his vest. Almost too quickly for the eye to follow, there was a flicker of trained fingers—a flash of gold.

Slippy's lips twitched; barely audible came the words: "You've got me—Burke—with the goods. But—I'm luck—lucky."

There was a gasp, and Slippy O'Day lay dead on the Mission floor with Father Dougherty's watch in his hand.

Just Plain Dumb

Detective Fiction Weekly
14 June 1930

"If yuh freeze ontuh me, Mag," growled Spanner Kelley importantly, "yuh won't be worryin' about *this* daddy leavin' yuh fur the Big House."

"No?" Maggie Guinan was palpably skeptical. "That's the line Kid Grogan was handin' me when the dicks come along an' muzzled 'im."

"Uh-huh!" grunted Spanner Kelley. He flipped the ash from his cigarette with a disdainful gesture. "An d'yuh know why so many o' them amachoor prowlers get the rap?" he queried with a knowing scowl. "I'll tell yuh why. Because they're dumb!"

"Dumb, eh?" Maggie Guinan's smile was an amused challenge.

"Soitenly. Just plain dumb, that's all. But me—I use the ol' bean."

"Yuh fox the coppers, eh, Spanner?" The girl's smile was taunting, but friendly. She admired self-confidence in any man.

Spanner Kelley chuckled derisively. "Lemme tell yuh somethin', Mag. Any mug can fox a flatfoot. It ain't that. It's bein' careful not tuh get foxed yourself."

"Yeah. How do yuh mean?"

Spanner grimaced thoughtfully and paused to light a cigarette. Looking up suddenly, he said, "Here's the dope, Mag. Moseyin' a prowl is just like playin' tag with the law, see. An' if yuh don't wanna get slapped in the clink, yuh gotta outguess the dick that's called in tuh lamp your tracks. Yuh gotta be scientific."

"Scientific?"

"Soitenly. Now get this. It's the big brag of every dick that the crook ain't livin' who don't furget somethin'. Maybe it's only some measly little thing yuh don't even stop tuh think about, see. But that's just what the dick looks fur. An' when he finds it, he's got your ticket all ready fur a train ride up the river. So, me—I don't furget nothin'. That's what I'm tryin' tuh tell yuh. D'yuh get me?"

"I got yuh, Spanner." Duly impressed, Maggie capitulated and flashed her companion a smile.

"That's the chatter, Mag," growled Spanner cheerfully. Then under the flush of victory, he conceived a brilliant idea. "I'll tell yuh what," he said eagerly. "How'd yuh like tuh see me work? I'm figurin' on coppin' a swell string of ice to-night. Wanna come along?"

Maggie considered the invitation while adjusting her garters and tucking a vagrant curl back under her scarlet beret. "Why not!" she agreed finally. "Seein's believin', eh, Spanner?" She laughed throatily.

II

Two hours later, Spanner Kelley and Maggie Guinan faced each other across the darkened bedroom of a ground floor apartment in West End Avenue. But for the fact that they had made surreptitious entry through an areaway window, their casual air might have proclaimed them as homecoming tenants.

Spanner surveyed the room with a swift, roving glance, grinning confidently. "Here's where we lift a bunch o' white rocks that'll keep us in velvet from now on," he announced in a hoarse whisper.

He stepped to the dressing table and selected an old-fashioned, silver jewel casket. Holding it in the ray of light from a street lamp, he stirred its contents with a bony finger, glimpsing an antique brooch, two nondescript rings, some glass beads, a thimble and a few pins and needles.

"Junk!" he scoffed. He tossed it back in place and expertly probed the drawers of the dressing table, bureau and chiffonier. But without success.

"One o' these wise dames, eh!" growled Spanner. He straightened up and turned for another careful scrutiny of the room. His eyes lighted with the sight of a tall black vase gracing a small reading desk. He picked it up, shook it experimentally, then turned it up over in his broad palm.

An instant later he held up a necklace of exquisitely matched diamonds. Maggie's eyes sparkled brilliantly. She favored her companion with a look of admiration as she watched him casually lift the flap to a side pocket of his top coat—as the glittering gems flashed from sight.

"Wise?" Spanner chuckled contemptuously. "Dumb!" he declared.

He strolled jauntily through the living room and into the dining room. Pausing before the buffet he slid open a drawer and inspected the silverware. "Just cheap triple-plate," he scoffed.

With Maggie trailing behind him, he swaggered back into the bedroom. His heroic air was exhilarating, almost intoxicating. Approaching a closet he swung open the door for a scrutiny of shelf and hangers. A pearl gray fedora caught his eye. He tried it on; then tossed it back. It was too large.

There was a light top coat of exceptionally fine texture. After examining it at arm's length, he slipped nimbly out of his own vestment and donned the other.

It felt smoothly comfortable. In a mirror lighted by a convenient street lamp he saw that it imbued his lithe figure with a flattering air of elegance.

"It's a swell rag, Spanner!" exclaimed Maggie. "Yuh look grand in it."

"Betcher life, Mag," declared Spanner, patting the lapels and grinning at his reflection. "An' it's mine."

In the next instant, however, his grin vanished, his eyes hardened. Whirling on his heel, he rasped, "Quick, Mag! We gotta sneak. Out yuh go!"

The headlights of an automobile, halting outside, also had been reflected in the mirror.

When Mrs. James Barrington reached home with her husband shortly before midnight, she made ready to retire immediately. But she never failed to make sure of the contents of the tall black vase. All of which accounted for the screams which echoed through West End Avenue, Mr. James Barrington's frantic telephoning to the police, and the subsequent arrival of Detective Forbush and Officer Terhune.

"Don't you worry none, madam," advised Detective Forbush with heavy reassurance. "We'll have your necklace back in no time. An' we'll nab the crook that grabbed it. Anything else taken?"

"Oh, dear! Oh, dear!" moaned the anguished Mrs. Barrington. "I don't know. I don't care. Just find my necklace. That's all—just my necklace." Nevertheless she bustled about through the various rooms in a hectic search for further losses.

Meanwhile Detective Forbush and Officer Terhune went through the prescribed formula for picking up the trail of a wanted criminal. But at the end of a quarter of an hour they had achieved nothing but a high state of exasperation.

"Damme, now!" growled the detective. "There ain't a crook livin' that don't forget somethin' or other. This is puzzlin'!"

A muffled groan sounded from the depths of the bedroom closet. Mr. James Barrington appeared, his face livid.

"Damned if my new top coat isn't gone, too," he growled. "And this rag left in its place." He kicked the discarded garment of Spanner Kelley half way across the room.

Detective Forbush pounced upon the rumpled top coat and snatched it up. He glanced eagerly at the collar band, seeking a label that might lead him to the manufacturer and on to the wearer. With a black scowl of disappointment he thrust a hand into the inside breast pocket. Nothing there. Close to profanity, he dipped a hand into one of the side pockets.

His thick-set body tensed. A look of utter incredulity spread over his face. But when he withdrew his hand he stared at the scintillating beauty of the lost Barrington necklace.

"And he forgot that!" exclaimed the detective dully.

"Dumb!" declared Officer Terhune. "Just plain dumb!"

The Rest of the 1950s

Final Appearance

Detective Tales
October 1951

He kept looking at me, waiting for me to say something. He hadn't told me what he wanted yet. He just perched there on the edge of the bed in his hotel room, and looked. Brown eyes big and bland behind horn-rimmed glasses, while he watched me twist and curl up inside. "You're all tense, Eddie. Anybody'd think I was trying to get you in trouble. Nothing like that, boy. . . ." Licking his lips, his voice gentle as a baby lamb's first bleat.

Yesterday on the street it had been Sam Dell, in plain clothes, with his big flat feet. Loud-mouthed, loud-mannered, skinny as a crowbar, only maybe harder. Crowbars bend if you've got the weight. "Watch it, Eddie. You're in my book."

Cooney shoved himself off the bed. "You got a wife, Eddie. Nice. What you call a job with that construction company, building houses for other people. Maybe you'd like some cash?"

"You can stop right there," I said. "I won't buy any of it." I turned, started toward the door.

Cooney cleared his throat the way he does. "A nice wife," he said quietly. "You rent your home, but after all, it is a house with a roof on it and windows without bars."

I stopped with my hand on the doorknob, finally let go and faced him again.

"The boys are counting on you. Lyttle, Springer and Hines. We're sort of together."

"I see."

Cooney smiled. "I knew you would." That was the rest of it. The fire behind the smoke—hoods, all three, with Cooney playing brains. Waiting, while Cooney fixed it. Those three couldn't show themselves without drawing a police congregation. Cooney could.

It's like that, lots of time. You're fighting every minute, fighting fear. You step outside those gates, you start dodging shadows. Shadows can pop up. "Eddie, we got it all cased. You're in. What? Not interested, Eddie? Well, we'll pull it without you. Can we help it if somebody tips the cops Eddie Reynolds pulled this caper? You know how the parole board is, Eddie. Sure, that's better."

"Why'd you pick this town?" I said. "Why do you want me?"

"A neat little deal, Eddie. In no time it's all over."

• • •

Cooney sat on the bed again, spread his hands, dropped them to his knees. He wore a fawn-colored suit, with red suspenders over a starched white shirt. Blue polka-dot tie. Straw hat on the bedpost. That was Cooney. After six years, he'd only changed skin deep. Smiling, smiling. With as much hair on his round, pink skull as there was honesty in his chromium-plated heart.

"I was never a crook, Cooney," I said. "I did time for something that was a mistake. I'm straight."

Cooney said, "Aren't we all? Bum raps, every one."

"You wouldn't know."

"Maybe you're right. Do we talk yet, Eddie? Or do we play tag some more?"

He blinked—a man growing old, the veins stringing purple across his hands, his belly a kind of big mush melon bulging his trouser-tops. Smiling blandly with his mouth and his eyes behind those glasses.

It felt as if somebody had laid a cold knife blade along the back of my neck. I could almost feel my heart squeeze the blood, the way you'd wring a sponge.

Sam Dell's ghost was beside Cooney on the bed, his voice loud: "You were there when my brother was killed, Eddie. He was a cop. You know what that means? Do you? It means I'll get you. You so much as spit on the sidewalk, I'll get you. You say you can't talk because you don't know. You know."

And me between them now.

Cooney, with Lyttle, Springer and Hines. "We were all together once, Eddie. Together on that warehouse job, the furs, remember? What's his name, Dell? Shot dead, while you loaded the furs. And they could never prove a thing. None of us had a gun, time they cracked down. Buzz Lyttle ripped open the gas tank on that truck, jammed the guns in, then set fire to the truck. We fell. But they never found the gun, Eddie."

I watched him and all the time these cold waves kept sweeping over me, as if somebody was spraying me with ice water. I'd forgot about the guns.

Cooney killed Sam Dell's brother. But the gun stayed hidden for ten years.

A long, long time.

Time for the World War, and a mock peace. Time for me to get paroled six years before Alvin Cooney and the others. Time to get married and have a daughter of five.

But not time to forget.

Forgetting wasn't allowed.

I wanted to pick Cooney up by the throat and twist him in two. Punch his face in. I wanted to go home through the early evening and tell Mary.

I couldn't do any of those things. If I did, something would happen. A whisper on the telephone and Sam Dell would have me breaking rock behind bars—maybe worse.

Cooney sighed. "Eddie, stop playing Atlas. You haven't got the world on your shoulders. A few days, it's all over."

"I need time to think." My voice was muddy.

"Sure."

"Tomorrow night, same time, here." I eyed his left shoulder. "I see you got a gun."

Cooney blinked, moved his bony hand. Abruptly it was full of snub-nosed .38. "Always." He stood, clamped the gun back into the spring holster, patted his middle.

"Suppose you fail?" I said.

"We won't," Cooney said. "They'll never take me again, though, alive. When you think, Eddie, figure all the angles. See you tomorrow. You got a car, haven't you?"

"Tomorrow," I said, and walked out.

• • •

The streets were quiet. The night was black. Suppertime. Down on Central by the First National, the town clock boomed seven slow times. It rang out the rhythm of my heels against the pavement.

It rang out the fact that I had twenty-four hours to make up my mind. Cooney wouldn't be recognized in town, if nobody looked hard. Ten years at his age changed a man. Stir did it.

The grey coupé I knew so well swung into the curb as I crossed Ninth under the street light.

"Reynolds. Eddie Reynolds." Sam Dell stared at me from the car window, his eyes flat, his thin face like chipped stone against the pale dash-lights.

"Quit riding me," I said.

He filled his pipe, lit up. Smoke gushed away from the car. There wasn't a sound on the street. He turned the motor off, and I could hear him breathe, see his face like a death's head.

"What do you want?" I said.

He smoked his pipe, watched me as I stood there under the street light.

Pretty soon he belched, knocked his pipe out, turned away from me, started the car and drove off. I watched the red taillight wink around a corner.

In a drugstore two blocks from home, I went to the phone booth, dialed Tim Tuttle, Ace Wrecking Company.

Tim's breath rasped over the wire. When I told him what I wanted, he was full of sly questions. But he finally gave, when I prodded his memory.

"That there truck ended up at the old city dump, Eddie. The police took custody, sold it to Bloomer, the junk man, and he finally had me haul it out there by the sand pit when he went out of business."

"Go on, Tim." The little hairs crawled on the back of my neck.

"Probably all gone now," Tim said. "Mebbe the scrap-metal drive picked it up when they moved the dump to Fortieth North."

I felt hollow inside, but I got him to explain right where he had dumped it. It wasn't hard. We kids used to play in the sand pit, by the city dump. Tim said, "Far's I can remember, the truck's in a dry creek bed by the old toboggan slide."

I made him give me his word to keep quiet about it. He said, "Sure, Eddie, but why?"

"I'll tell you, maybe, some day." Then I called Mary, told her not to expect me home till I got there.

She was puzzled, all right, but she said, "All right, darling."

I bought a flashlight and walked out to the old city dump. By the time I got there I was shaking all over and wringing wet. I had to find it.

I had to find those guns. Cooney's gun. I didn't know exactly why, or what I'd do if I did find it. But I had to know. When you're in the middle, you got to make a move—any move—so I had to find that truck, and the guns. Rats scurried through the darkness and I felt like one of them.

Sam Dell on one side. Cooney and the boys on the other. Me, getting the pressure. They wouldn't leave me alone, now.

I knew why Sam Dell had stopped me on the street.

He'd heard Cooney and the others were out of stir. He was waiting to pounce. I choked up inside and pushed through tall grass up onto a sandy hillock.

• • •

By moonlight and with the flash I saw that the kids still played here. The way I had once.

Paths ran through the grass. The sand pit was a series of hummocks and hills, gullies and stunted trees. A weird place at night. When the city turned it into a dump, they dumped anyplace.

I stood on top of the toboggan slide, thinking how small it was really, and how large it had looked to me when I was a kid. It had been a world then, a big one. You could get lost in it. Now I knew no world was big enough to get lost in.

The grass was thick. Things rustled and peeped down below.

My foot slipped. I went down in a hurry, stumbling and sliding in the sand. Night was a hell of a time to look for a wrecked truck ten years gone.

Everything was down there. Oil barrels, sheets of tarpaper, tin cans, bed springs, smashed car frames, and metal scraps nameless forevermore.

But no truck.

What little hope I'd had left, and despair took over. I shouldn't have expected any luck. I staggered around, started toward the toboggan slide again, tripping through the junk. It looked as if the war scrap-metal drive had overlooked the old dump.

My foot jammed in a hole. I went flat on my face, the flashlight fell from my hand. I crouched up and stared where the light was focused. At a paint-flaked, burned, rusted license plate on a half-sunk truck chassis. I stumbled over to it, scrubbed the plate with my hand. Y-11032-T, and the year, ten years ago, stamped into the bent tin.

There had been two gas tanks on the truck. One full, and a reserve, empty. Buzz Lyttle had ripped the empty tank with a jack-handle, put the guns in, and whacked it back into shape. It had been Lyttle's one crowning achievement in life. It was a pity he probably wouldn't have grandchildren to tell it to. My heart hammered and hot blood pulsed in my neck and head.

Fifteen minutes later I dug out the tank. It was buried in sand, torn half loose from the frame. The other tank had blown. Only one wheel and the rear axle remained.

Using an old Ford leaf-spring, I went to work on that tank. I found them.

There were three guns. One was a snub-nosed .38. Alvin Cooney's gun. The only type he ever carried.

I stuffed the other two in my pockets and looked at the .38. The hard-rubber buttplate had melted down over one side of the barrel and plugged the end. Rusted plenty, it had obviously been in heat, aged a lot like Cooney.

But it was the gun. One shell fired. The shell that killed Sam Dell's brother.

I stood there. I'd made my kid mistake, talked big, got in with Cooney and the rest. They'd needed me to drive the truck. I needed money, and I hadn't known what the score was. I'd done time for that mistake. And now I was in it again. All the way.

• • •

I started out of there. I didn't know what I'd do. But I had the gun and somehow that's what mattered.

"Reynolds! What've you got to say?"

I stopped short at Sam Dell's voice ahead in the darkness on the path back to the road. I jammed the .38 into my hip pocket just as his flashlight blinded me. I kept my light turned on the ground. I couldn't see him, only heard his voice.

"What the hell you doing down here?"

He had followed me. Dell, thin and hard, standing there behind that flashlight, keeping the glare in my eyes, his voice loud, demanding. "Come on, Eddie! Give out!"

Police protection. Here was the law. Hounding me, and I hated Dell; hated the loud voice, the hard unbending shape of him, saying, "You changed your pattern today, Eddie. Why?"

"Building something. Thought I'd find some hinges down here." It sounded thin.

He cursed softly, and I smelled the smoke from his pipe on the wind, heard the rats below in the dump again. Dell was sniffing around. He knew Cooney and the rest were out. He didn't have to tell me, and he knew he didn't. Detective Dell. Call your nearest precinct.

I said, "Get off me, will you?" and walked past him toward the road.

He followed, swishing through the grass.

"Drive you home?"

"I'll walk," I said. I stood there, watched him climb into his grey coupé and pull away down the macadam. The guns were like hot branding irons in my pockets. They cooled. I went home.

"Eddie," Mary said. "What's the matter?"

I looked around for my daughter, Betts. "Where's the kid?"

"She's in bed. Eddie—" I cut her words with a kiss, held her tight against me. Mary was plain and tiny in her blue pajamas and I loved her.

"I'm going to be busy for a couple days," I said. "No questions, honey. None at all."

"No questions," Mary agreed. "All right, Eddie."

"Go to bed." I tapped her with my palm, where she could feel it. She went obediently to bed.

I went out to the garage and blew the dust off my work bench. I looked for a long time at my car. A blue sedan. Then I dropped two of the guns into a box and laid the .38 out on the work bench.

Seven hours later the sun winked through the garage window and glinted on the barrel of the .38. I had chipped off the melted buttplates. The barrel was pretty clean. I stripped the gun, filed it clean, used emery paper, and polished all the parts. I oiled it, got it right. Then I built new plates, and fixed them on. I cleaned the corroded cartridges, the dead one as well as the good ones, and put them all back in the cylinder.

The gun was ready. But I still didn't know what it was ready for. I could have given it to Sam Dell, back there. And right now I'd be on my way to the little green room.

I had saved the gun.

It could be I'd dug my own grave.

Back in the house, I called my boss at the construction company and got three days off on account of grippe. Then I went to bed.

Mary pretended to be asleep. But I knew she'd lain there all night, waiting. I held her close and whispered, "No questions. It's something that'll soon be over."

She squeezed my hand. I was asleep when she got up.

• • •

Cooney was perched on the bed, that night in his hotel, wearing the same clothes and the same bland look. "I called you at your house, just so you wouldn't forget," he told me. "Not that you would, boy."

"Sure." I stared at his feet. He had little feet in tight, brown, crepe-soled shoes. "Tell it to me."

Cooney cleared his throat, and I felt again how old he was for this business. "Okay," he said. "It figures. You want to know what you're getting into. You wouldn't sing on a friend. We stick together."

"Tell me."

"Tomorrow, ten o'clock in the morning. All you do is drive your car by at precisely ten-ten—*exactly*. You stop. I get in. You take me to Allenville, a two-hour drive, where Buzz Lyttle and the others are waiting. You get your cut."

"No cut. Where's the place?"

"Holland Real Estate, on Central. I told you it was neat. An old guy's paying off in cash. Forty thousand, for a home. Inside job, all the way." Cooney made a circle with his thumb and forefinger, dropped it over the bedpost. "Like that. Neat. The deal is set for ten. The old man'll be there, but I allow ten minutes. He pays in cash, because he won't deal any other way. A crank."

"It stinks."

"I keep telling you, it's perfect," Cooney said.

"Where'd you get it?"

Cooney spread his hands, shoulders high, and blinked. "His son, Eddie. His very own son."

"It stinks. It's no go."

"It's forty grand, cold. The old guy draws it from the bank next door. He walks into the real estate office, pays off—to me." Cooney's face was pale, and a fine film of perspiration showed on his skull. He splashed at it with his hand. "It's so simple it's a dream."

It was crazy. He was right about the dream part. A hundred things could happen. Forty thousand split up was nothing. But Cooney didn't see it that way. They never did. I started to tell him "No" all the way. But it came out, "Okey, I'm in," because all day I'd been thinking. Hard.

Cooney's sigh was big for his size.

He said, "You drive your car up at ten-ten, get that. I could do it all, but there'd be a hitch if I parked. You come at ten-ten, double park, with the door open." He paused. "Describe your car, Eddie. Exactly." He got out a silk handkerchief and mopped his face.

"A grey coupé," I said. The lie came out and I put fancy-work on it, and I knew why then. I hadn't known until now. If it worked, I was set. If it didn't, I was sunk. "A grey coupé, no shine to it. Black top." I told him the year, the make, described it pat. "The right front fender is ripped, smashed in. Watch for the fender, that's your cue."

"Got it, boy." He stood, mopping at his face, and poured us a drink in two water glasses from a cheap bottle of whiskey. We drank. He drank gustily to crime. I drank to a grey coupé that was sitting in front of the city hall right now—that sat there every morning until noon.

We went over it, from every angle. Ten minutes after ten. If Cooney didn't have the money by then, he'd be there anyway. But he'd have the money. The guy's son was making five thousand on the deal. The others were holding him till it was over. A rich family, Cooney said, they wouldn't miss it. The son was a bad boy.

"All right. I'll see you." I went home and to bed. Mary curled up next to me. We didn't talk. I didn't sleep. I planned my side. Something told me it wouldn't work.

• • •

Mary woke me in the morning. "Some man's on the phone."

I took it. Cooney. "Synchronize our watches," he said. "When I whistle, it's nine-two. Get that." He whistled.

I set my watch. "Nine-two and a quarter," I said.

"Right. Now, Eddie. Be there at ten-ten. Exactly." He underlined the word with a tense voice that wasn't bland any more. I could see him sweating. My own hand was wringing wet on the phone, my stomach sick. "Be there if you got to run somebody down," he said. "Be there."

"Relax," I said. "Anybody'd think it was your first go." I hung up on that. Let him stew.

I went back to the bedroom and dressed. Mary stood in the doorway, tiny and worried, trying not to show it. I felt wooden and old, tired. My eyes were stiff and my ears rang from concentration.

I could hear Sam Dell laughing in my head. Mary came over and put her hand on my arm, stood there. I looked at her, remembering corridors with bars, the *tramp-shuffle-tramp-shuffle-tramp* of weary feet. I felt rough cloth on my back and cold round bars in my hands. You come out to what? Free to get socked back in again—you live that long.

I finished dressing. My pants were heavy with the .38 in my hip pocket.

"Mary. Remember—you're mine, I love you." Saying that with Cooney and the boys out there, and Sam Dell waiting to pounce. "I'm going out for a while." I kissed her. She didn't say a word. I told her to wait here in the house for me, kissed her again and I could feel her fear soaking into me, mingling with my own.

I left.

• • •

I stood on the corner by City Hall until five minutes after ten. Cutting it close, as close as I dared—praying Dell wouldn't come out. Cooney would be there now, sweating, nervous—scared, just like me.

I crossed the lawn in front of the City Hall, glanced once in the side front window. A blue-coated back was at the window. I knew Sam Dell was in there, his voice loud. I got in the grey coupé parked at the curb, Sam Dell's car. The keys were there. This had been my chance to take. If the car hadn't been there, I'd really be gone.

I gunned the engine, let it roar. Then I leaned on the horn, hard, let in the clutch, and shot out into traffic. From now on things would add up. It would work, or it wouldn't. You cut it in the middle like that, and one side vanished. You hoped it wasn't your side.

It was close. I snaked the car in by Holland's Real Estate at ten-ten and a quarter. Cooney was coming out the front door, his face twisted, frantic, frenzied with looking for me. Then he spotted the car, ran at me.

I flipped the door open. He jumped and we were away before he was inside. He slammed the door, flopped back against the seat. "Ride it, boy. Easy!"

"Did you make it?"

He laughed. I guess it was nervous release laughter, kind of like a madman, maybe. Then he panted and emptied a brown manila envelope into his lap. Green bills in bundles. "I got it. All of it, Eddie. Forty grand, and Eddie"—he swallowed, choking, and I had to knock his hand off my arm—"I got another two grand outa the office safe." He laughed. Then he went sober, put the money back into the envelope.

We were out of the business section. Worry and regret swept over me in a bitter wave. It was going wrong. I'd expected sirens by now. I searched the rear-view mirror. Just calm traffic.

I'd tipped the law the only way I knew. But they'd missed. I knew Sam Dell had been in City Hall. They must have heard me take the car, seen me. Where were they?

We left the town behind, rode the blacktop.

"Make time, Eddie—open 'er up."

I looked at him. "You're happy now, Cooney? It's over, you made your mark?"

He lit a cigarette, took a drag, flipped it out the window. The car purred, began to whine. "Yes," Cooney said. "You were right on time, Eddie boy."

• • •

We took a curve, approached a wooded section. The road was clear ahead. I felt the sharp edge of steel in my side and Cooney's voice was dry and cracked.

"Pull up, Eddie. Pull up slow. That's right."

I stopped the car. This was it. I could read it all the way now. It had missed. I'd flunked out, muffed the brass ring. All the way. Up and down.

"Come on, Eddie. We'll take a walk into those woods. Hurry it up, boy." He was out of the car, waiting, motioning me out on his side. I went along with it.

He got behind me. We tramped into the woods, off the road. It was cool in there and a robin winked among the trees, chirping. The sky was soft and blue overhead between the green branches.

"Stop here, Eddie. Sure, boy, sure." He looked at me over the barrel of the gun, his straw hat slanted comically over his eye, crisp and starchy and old. His knuckles stuck out around the gunbutt, white. You figure a good wind would blow Cooney away, like dry leaves. But the wind blows you instead; you feel that wind inside you, cold.

You did it all wrong. You cut the stale piece of cake. The cheese was dead.

He stands there talking, the old man who pulls the trap. "You're the only one, Eddie. I could never bank on you." Shaking his head, blinking steadily behind those horn-rimmed specials of his. "You know I killed a cop named Dell. It would be taking a chance to let you go on living. I can't do it."

"Sure," I said. "I understand. A long chance."

He nodded, smiled. "I'm glad you see it my way. You're a good lad, young. I'm sorry. But I don't want to go back. We figured this clean-up, figured you in, just like this—and out. Two birds—you know the story. If you'da come with us all the way, it would've been all right, Eddie. But you won't stick. I can't let you loose. See?"

"Sure, I see." There wasn't much of anything now. Just emptiness. Mary waiting back there, and Betts without a father now, growing up with it hanging over her head; something she'd never know, never understand.

"Over here, Eddie. A little bit. By this ditch." He moved to the ditch. I moved, and thought, if I was going to die, why not make it good and hard? So I dove at him. He dodged, firing, an old man with stumbling legs. Three times the gun spat. I heard them back in my subconscious. We went down fighting into the ditch.

He was an old man, and tigerish, spitting and cursing. I took the gun away like you'd pick a bunch of grapes off a vine. Easier. Cooney was a dry vine. He came at me, his mouth twisted up.

His hat had fallen off and he trampled it, yelling at me. I slammed his face and his glasses broke. He was vicious, screaking in a high, crazy old man's voice. I batted him with the gun and he crumpled, bubbling.

I felt sick, stared down at him. He watched me, his eyes rheumy in his head, and I heard Sam Dell's voice.

"That's enough, Eddie." They came through the woods, must have been ten of them, with Sam Dell the only one in plain clothes.

Cooney tried to scamper away like an animal, on his hands and knees. I jammed my foot on his leg and he kept tearing at it with brittle fingers.

"I didn't think you'd come," I said. "I thought you missed it, too."

Dell moved close. The others stayed back. Three of them carried sub-machine guns. "No," Dell said loudly. He was stringy-thin, the muscles in his drawn jaws working spasmodically as he looked down at Cooney who made noises in his throat, plucking and plucking at my leg.

"I was afraid you didn't get it," I said. "I couldn't do it any other way."

"I saw you take my car," Dell said. "It got me hot, but then I thought, why? Things clicked. We knew he was in town, Eddie. We had to wait. We watched you on the corner this morning. We followed you through town, saw it all, parked back on that curve in the road when we saw your car stop. Two and two began to add. We came as fast as we could." He paused. "I heard what he said, Eddie. There won't be any more trouble. We'll pick up the others in Allenville."

He knew it all. I worked Cooney's gun into my pocket, palmed the old .38 off my hip. "This is the gun that killed your brother, Sam." I told him all about it, handed it to him, took my foot off Cooney. "Ballistics will add the score. You've got him cold."

I stepped back. Cooney shrieked some blasphemy, and yelled, "You'll never take me!" He scrambled into the ditch. He ran for the car on the road. He was under good cover beneath the edge of the sloping ditch.

I looked at Sam Dell. He was patient, thin, his eyes hard and very still. He topped his thin lips with is tongue. Cooney's head bobbed up as the ditch went shallow.

Sam Dell lifted the .38, aimed carefully and fired.

Cooney sprawled in dry leaves. Dell turned to me. He didn't smile. "It's all right, Eddie. You're a knuckle-head, but it's all right. Go on home to your wife. Take my car. I'll pick it up when I get back."

I glanced at the others waiting among the trees. Then I walked back toward the road. All I could think was, Ten years. That gun hadn't been fired in ten years. It had waited, like that for ten years. Cooney's own gun.

As I drove off, I looked back toward the woods. I couldn't see anything. But I knew they were standing around a vicious old man, dead, on the ground. The brown envelope was beside me, on the seat. Dell had allowed that, too, so I could hold it for him. It was all right. It was okay. All the way. Up and down.

Motive for Murder

Man to Man
June 1955

Vinnie knew something was troubling him when he came home from the office that night. He closed the front door a shade more carefully than usual.

Then he stood there, banging the newspaper into the palm of his hand, and stared absently at the floor. And all the time she was right across the room, waiting for her kiss.

"You going to stand there all night?" she said. "I thought you checked your thinking in a box at the office."

"Still working, I guess." He came to her and kissed her lightly on the forehead.

Well, she'd let it go, this time. She took his hat off for him, uncovering all that black hair, and straightened his blue tie. The knot was on a level with her eyes.

She left him standing there, went to the hall closet with his hat. When she returned to the living room, he still hadn't moved. He held the newspaper in one hand and blinked at the wall.

He was handsome, she decided, even when he worried. Probably something at the office. "The Office" was a name, to Vinnie. She had never seen it.

"If you're hungry, mister," she said, "we're having steak tonight." She waited for *this* to take hold, because if there was one thing Bill really went for, it was steak.

"Steak?" he said stupidly.

O.K. She jammed her small hands into the flimsy pockets of her red-and-white polka-dot apron, and ambled back down the hall into the kitchen.

She'd never seen Bill act this way. He had an occasional office problem, but usually he cursed, paced the floor, called people up and snarled at them, and everything was all right again. He never just stood. He never, no matter what, ignored steak.

• • •

Supper was pretty dismal. Bill didn't say a word about the steak. He ate it as if it were canned beans and it got Vinnie's goat.

She didn't say anything. She was beginning to feel sorry for him. He was like a big bear, worried and befuddled.

"Vinnie," he said, after he'd waved aside a large slab of deep-dish apple pie, "I've got to go out tonight."

"Oh?"

"Meeting. Won't be back till around eleven-thirty, or so." He took a half slice of bread, dipped it into the last of the steak gravy. She was thunderstruck when he forgot all about it, and left it there. It was his choicest finishing morsel.

She rose, went over by his chair and put one hand on his shoulder. "Tell mama," she said. "What's the matter, hon?"

"Oh—nothing." He lit a cigarette and blew smoke at his plate.

"Come on," she said. "I know something's got you down, Bill. If you tell me, maybe I can help."

He tightened his lips and butted the cigarette in the steak gravy, beside the bread. "Really, Vinnie!"

* * *

"It isn't Aunt Martha again, is it, Bill?" She didn't like to bring this matter up, but there had been a time . . .

He looked at her straightforwardly. "No, Vinnie. I've given that up. Forgot all about it. Screwy, anyway. It's best the way you think, about that."

This made her feel better. She'd had enough bother about Aunt Martha.

When Vinnie's Aunt Martha died, she had left her twenty thousand dollars, which seemed a terrible lot of money. She and Bill tried to decide what to do with it and there was trouble right away.

Bill wanted to quit his job and go to Tibet. When he first told her, she laughed outright. She'd thought it was just a kind of hobby.

But he was serious. Ever since he was a kid, he had lived in Tibet, in his mind. He studied, he read, he even drew maps. If Vinnie saw another map, or heard of another mountain pass, she figured she'd scream.

He planned how much it would cost to get there and live ten years.

Ten years in Tibet. He told her he had discovered something. Lost people. Degrees of mentality that would astound our modern thinkers. His life's desire. He wanted the money for that.

Vinnie was troubled for a while, the way he talked. He said he was the only man who knew certain things because of his life-long study.

He insisted. He tried to persuade. He even raved some.

But she wouldn't hear of it and she told him never to mention it to their friends.

She told him to earn twenty-thousand to go with her money. They'd buy a house, invest carefully. Then he could go, maybe.

Vinnie knew that by then he would forget about the whole childish notion.

Once he got so mad he stayed overnight at a hotel.

She finally made him see it her way and he hadn't mentioned Tibet since. That was over a year ago. Vinnie was glad it wasn't Aunt Martha. The money was still in the bank.

* * *

"Please?" She kissed the top of his head. "You've got to tell me what's bothering you."

"All right." He bunched his fists beside his plate, then relaxed. "A man said he was going to kill me."

Vinnie's hand went away from his shoulder, dropped to her side.

"Don't worry," Bill said. He took her hand and patted it. "He's somebody you don't know. I knew him a long while back. He told me yesterday he was going to kill me."

"But—Bill—"

"I know, I know." He rose, looked down at her. She felt terribly small and the tight feeling grew a little worse. He meant what he'd said. The fright showed in his eyes.

She swallowed. "What did you do to this man?"

"Nothing. It's some crazy war psychosis. He believes he's got to kill me. Persecution—something-or-other." He paused wearily. "I talked with a psychiatrist."

Excitement touched her lightly. "The police—you'd better go to the police."

He smiled. She noticed how strained it was. "They'd just laugh, Vinnie. There's no proof of anything. He's just a crank."

For a moment she stood perfectly still, then she ran to him, her throat all choked up, her heart rocking. She felt tiny and lost and afraid.

He turned as she came up to him. "Don't tell anybody, Vinnie."

She put her arms around him. "No, no," she said. "Don't worry."

She didn't know what to do. It was something so big and terrible and ugly, it just didn't seem real.

"If you go out tonight, Vinnie," he said, scowling at her, "be sure to lock the door."

"Oh, Bill!" She wanted to cry, but she wouldn't let herself. "You mean he might come here?"

"No telling." He took her hands. "Now, don't fret."

Her voice was shrill. "How can I help?"

"He probably won't do anything," Bill said. "Two to one, he's just talking."

Then she remembered. "Bill, you're not going out tonight."

"I have to, Vinnie." He smiled in that strained way of smiling he had now. "It'd be kind of silly if I just sat here, waiting—wouldn't it?"

She couldn't trust her voice, so she nodded.

He dropped her hands, walked into the hall and returned with his hat.

She flung herself at him. "Bill, you can't!"

He unwrapped himself. "I've got to. Are you going out?"

"I don't know." She shook her head. "No, I couldn't."

"If you do, don't forget to lock the door. You know how these nuts are. Better lock it anyway, even if you stay in."

"Oh, Bill." She clung to him and he kissed her. He kissed her right this time. But she could tell by the tightness of his lips that he was bothered much more than he would say.

• • •

Then, somehow, although she tried to hold him, he was gone. She heard him whistle as he walked up the block toward the bus stop. Then she was alone.

She locked the door.

She stood there, remembering all the things she should have asked him. It was always that way with her, it seemed. She never remembered until too late.

The house was very quiet.

She could smell the stale supper, and a car hissed by out on the dark street.

An instant later she was at the telephone, calling her sister, Betty. She had to tell somebody. He couldn't expect her not to.

She told Betty and got the horse laugh. Betty was like that; instead of cheering her up, it only made Vinnie feel worse.

"If it was me," Betty said, "I'd have the cocktail shaker ready. Get some sweet music on the radio. Maybe he's handsome."

Betty wasn't married. Vinnie hung up and sat there on the little stool, by the telephone stand, staring at the door.

Of course, whoever it was, he didn't want *her*. The threat was to Bill. But if this person came and wanted to wait for Bill here . . . he might, he just might . . .

"You know how these nuts are."

• • •

Vinnie rose and stumbled out into the dining room. She forced herself to collect the dishes and wash them. She didn't let herself think during the process.

The telephone rang. She ran into the living room, reached for it, then snapped her head back. Suppose. She lit it ring.

Finally she picked it up, but whoever it was had waited as long as he intended. The instrument clicked in her ear. She put the phone down with a kind of terrific slow motion, her teeth gnawing at the inside of her lower lip.

She went out to the kitchen again and hung her apron on the towel rack. Then she moved around the house, straightening things. She found three books that were due at the library.

All right, she would return them and draw a couple, and come home and read.

• • •

She locked the house carefully, then swung along up the dark street and the wind was playful in the trees. It was dark and there were two blocks to the bus stop.

She reached the corner where the bus stopped and she was panting. She had been running a little, the last part of the way.

Once on the bus, there were people, and most of the fear left her. It was remarkable, really. It had been silly of her to be so scared. She'd been like a child, afraid of the dark.

She smiled brightly at the bus driver when she got off.

She walked through the park, braving the shadows without a qualm. The library was absolutely dead and she returned the books, found two others to her liking. It was eight-thirty by the library clock.

She got a drink of cold water at the library fountain, waved to one of the librarians she knew, and left.

• • •

She was a half block away when she sensed she was being followed.

All the former fear and anxiety, the rushing pulse, the perspiration, returned. No matter what she did, she knew she must not look behind her.

She forced herself to walk slowly toward the business section of town. It was grueling, because impulse told her to run.

Vinnie tried hard to see behind her by looking into store windows, but she didn't see anything. She began to lose the feeling that she was followed.

She turned into a theater, bought a ticket and for one hour, she sat through a pirate drama. She didn't understand a single thing about it, finally rose and hurriedly left.

She hurried to the bus terminal, and her bus had just come in. She got on, paid the driver and sat down. The bus was empty.

Her mind was whirling now and it was hard to fight off the fear. She was weak with it and tried peering out the side window, counting cars that went by.

Then she heard somebody get on the bus, heard the coin drop into the box, heard a man walk by. But she turned too late to see him.

The doors wooshed closed, the lights went out, the bus started again.

A newspaper crinkled. She tried to look around, but she couldn't. All she could see was the edge of the newspaper. How silly. Somebody reading by the street-lights.

Nobody else got on the bus. Vinnie walked up front and sat down by the driver, nearly dropping her books because her hands were slippery with sweat now.

She could feel the eyes of that person sitting back there. She wanted to scream. Where was Bill? Oh, God, she thought, make him be home.

• • •

There were three blocks to go to her corner. She would leave by the front bus door, quickly. Two blocks. Where was that man getting off—the one sitting back there, reading a newspaper in the dark? One block.

She grabbed for the cord above her head, the buzzer buzzed. The bus slowed with a rumble and she was crowding the front door. The lights came on, the door opened, and she was outside, running. Then she paused, forced herself to look back.

Tremendous relief streamed through her. She thought she would collapse with it, because the bus had started up. The man wasn't getting off here.

Then she was wildly sick inside. The bus had jerked to a stop at the far corner and the doors opened and the shadow of a man detached itself from the bus and melted into the shadows of the trees. The bus moved off.

She ran. One of the books slipped from her fingers. She grabbed for it and missed. Forget it. Run, she told herself. She held her skirts up high and ran. She lost the other book just as she turned up her own front walk.

She raced up the porch steps with the key already in her hand, but she couldn't get it into the lock. Finally she managed. She slammed the door, ran straight for the telephone, slumped onto the stool.

Panting and sick all over, she dialed the operator, got police headquarters and told them stridently the whole story. She hung up, her body convulsed with sobs.

• • •

Then she heard footsteps on the porch. The door—good Lord, she'd forgotten to lock the door. She leaped up and the door opened.

"I told you to lock the door, Vinnie."

It was Bill. Her hands clenched to her face, bursting with relief, her shoulders shaking.

"Did you call your sister, Vinnie?"

She nodded, searching his face, unable to speak. He was very pale and his eyes were black, his lips almost cruel.

Then she knew it had been Bill following her. She knew that calling her sister had given him an alibi.

"I'm going to Tibet, Vinnie," he said softly. "I must."

He stepped toward her. She tried to scream, but the sound never escaped her throat.

Gigolo

Pursuit Detective Story Magazine
July 1955

He turned the corner, spotted me, and lumbered toward me, the morning sun bright on his Panama hat. His mouth got grim and he flagged his arm.

"Jackson!" he called.

I turned back the other way, shoving against the hunched forms and rigid faces of early shoppers. What in hell was I going to do now? I'd known it would happen sooner or later. But not now.

"Jackson," he said. His heels smacked the cement. "Wait up. A word with you."

I cut between two old ladies, made it to the curb and moved quickly through traffic to the other side of the street. I tried to catch a glimpse of him in the window of a store. He'd made it, too. His heels racked hard behind me.

"See, here—" he called. "Jackson!"

The hell with it. What can you do? I turned into the bar of the Hotel Floridian. It was dark and cool. The place was empty save for the barman polishing glasses.

"Beer," I said. "Small draft."

A lot of heavy breathing moved in on my left.

"All right, Jackson."

I didn't turn and look at him. He grunted, climbing onto the stool next to mine. There was a fine trembling in his voice.

"Shall we talk here?" he said.

I took my beer, paid for it, and looked at him.

"We'd better go to a booth," he said. "I want to talk to you, Jackson."

"What'll it be?" the barman said, blinking tired eyes.

He waved the barman away.

"I hardly know you," I said.

He nodded. It was one of those flat-faced, don't-pull-that-one-on-me nods. His face was very white and when he smiled it was sick. Short and heavy-set, he wore a pearl gray tropical suit and a plain blue tie. In this weather. A sheen of perspiration highlighted his face. His nose was something like a golf ball, new and white.

"You tried to duck me, didn't you, Jackson?"

"Why should I?"

He laughed nervously. One of these *heh-heh-heh* laughs.

"Don't try to get away," he said. "I won't have it."

I looked at him a little more carefully. The eyes had it. You know? Glazed and afraid and a little crazy.

"All right," I said. "Let's sit in a booth."

In the booth he stared at me across the small table. I sipped my beer, watching the fear and nervousness in him. I knew what he wanted. I didn't like it. There was nothing to do about it.

"I suppose your wife thinks you're at work?" he said.

I watched him, not feeling so hot.

"That what you do?" he said. "Every morning? Tell her, 'G'bye, honey. Gotta get to work. Late now. See you tonight.' You kiss her and whistle down the walk. That the way it is, Jackson?"

I still didn't say anything. The way his voice shook, it wasn't good.

"Only you don't go to work," he said.

I waited.

"Every morning, you come downtown and hang around. Just long enough—so you're sure I'm out of the house. Because I *do* go to work, don't I, Jackson?"

"So I've heard."

"So you've heard. You're something, Jackson. Waiting until you know I've cleared out, then you spend the day with Lorna. Don't you, Jackson?"

"Watch what you say."

He made a sniff with his nose, tilting his head back. He was still plenty scared. His head bobbed just a little and he couldn't control it. His mouth worked at the corners and this thing was in his eyes.

I was scared, too. I didn't dare leave. He might have a gun. You read about it that way in the papers. Sometimes they have a gun. They go off half-cracked. They don't know what they're doing. He was on the edge.

"Because you got fired, didn't you, Jackson? Three months ago from the part-time job your wife knew nothing about. And it's over six months since you worked at the job she thinks you're working at now. You're a liar and a cheat, Jackson. A sneak. A gigolo. My wife. She's my wife, I tell you. Lorna," he said. "You hear?"

"Don't talk so loud."

He lowered his voice. It burst out of his throat in that wild whispering way they get. He had his hands on the table, working them together like he had a ball of clay, mangling it. I watched those hands, let me tell you.

"You crud," he said.

"Where did you pick all this junk up?" I said.

He slammed his hands on the table, rising a little, then settling back again. "Liar!" he whispered harshly. "I got suspicious. A few days, I've been watching you. I followed you—know every move you've made. I took some time off work. How you think I caught up with you this morning? You crumb!"

I finished my beer, wishing to hell my hand wouldn't shake like that.

"You leave her alone, hear?" he said.

I didn't say anything.

"This is a warning," he said. "Damn you, Jackson." He looked at me and his voice rose. "I'll tell your wife. How do you like that?"

"Look, Waugh," I said. "You don't know what you're talking about."

"I'll kill you," he whispered. He was breathing hard and his eyes were lit up. The words raced past his lips. "You stay away from my wife, Jackson, or, by God, I'll kill you. I'll tell your wife. I'll get the cops. This can't go on. Don't you know what you're doing?"

I stood up. "Is that all?"

I thought he was going to cry. He was all worked up. Maybe he did have a gun, but he couldn't make it. He was a mess. He had always been a mess.

I turned and walked toward the doorway full of sunshine.

"Jackson," he said.

I kept on walking.

"Jackson, come back here, you—Jackson!"

On the street, I started down toward where I'd parked my car. Only I knew I had to contact Lorna. There was no sign of Waugh back there. I cut across the block and down an alley toward the rear entrance of a drugstore.

It was a fine mess. But he wasn't going to stop it. It was too good. I had to see Lorna. This was pay day; something Waugh didn't know about Lorna and me. Something nobody knew.

There was a soft, nauseous core inside me, from the way Waugh had looked and acted. He wasn't the type to do anything. But sometimes they go berserk.

• • •

In the drugstore, I found an empty phone booth and slid the door shut. I stood there, trying to calm down.

I thought of Shirley, at home—of how I'd left her this morning. Down inside me someplace, I still loved her. And she loved me.

Sure. Only there was Lorna. Lorna with the jet black hair that smelled so good; the body that could send a man crazy. And the money that made life so easy. She had the money; loaded with it. Waugh only worked to keep up appearances. He was that way. She had told me all about it.

The four of us had met at a country club dance. They were out of our class, even though they lived in the same section of town. They owned a large home four blocks from our place. But so far as Shirley was concerned, we'd never seen the Waughs since that night at the dance.

Then one day I took off from work, went out to the beaches, trying to drown a hangover in the Gulf of Mexico. Lorna Waugh was out there, drinking sunshine. Alone. In a tight two-piece black swim suit and she was hungry for fun.

"My husband's a bore," she told me. She was always very frank.

Two weeks later, I was wearing a path across her back yard each day after Waugh went to work. I worried about it. But Lorna was too much woman to forget.

"Ken, honey," Lorna said to me one hot afternoon. "This is silly. You ditching work this way—worrying about it. Why worry? Do you really like that silly job of yours?"

I hated it. A shipping clerk, under a mean-eyed grandmother of a boss in a plant that manufactured farm implements; cultivators, tractors, harrows, mowing machines.

"You know what I like," I told her.

"Yes," she said. "I do. And it's underhanded and sneaky—but it's nice. I like sneaky things, Ken—and so do you. You're weak. So am I. We're a good pair, only we can never go any further than this, right now. Herbert would fight a divorce. But we can work it another way. And someday, we'll have it just right."

"How?"

So she told me. Quit my job, she said. And play with her. She'd pay me my salary to keep Shirley calm.

It took me at least half an hour to agree. I knew the spot it would put me in. I remembered Shirley's hopes for our future. I thought of a lot of things.

Only Lorna Waugh was that close.

I took a part-time job to appease what conscience I had left—then Lorna laughed me out of that and we stayed on a beautiful picnic.

The phone booth was hot. I dialed her number and waited and then she was there, breathing what we had across the wire; making me feel what we had.

"That's a laugh," she said, when I told her about what had happened. "He's a bag of wind, Ken. Don't let it bother you. He'll bring it up tonight, maybe—I'll get it out of him. Then I'll make him forget he ever thought such a thing."

"I don't like that, either," I said.

She chuckled. "Relax," she said. "He'll only have a bite of the cake—you've got the icing."

"Think I should see you today?"

"You'd better."

I swallowed, thinking of how she looked right now. Maybe wearing those white knitted shorts and a strap bra to match, stretched out on the couch, talking with me. Her wealth of shining black hair flowing over her shoulders, touching the floor. I liked her hair long, so she kept it that way for me. And her eyes, like dark sin—her red, red mouth.

I had to see her.

"All right," I told her. "I'll run home first, tell Shirley I took the day off—tell her I wasn't feeling so hot. It won't be a lie."

"I'll fix that," she said. "But why go home?"

"Gotta find out if he went to Shirley."

"He wouldn't."

"He's in bad shape."

She chuckled. "You don't know the half of it, Ken. But quit worrying about Herb. He's a dead onion."

I swallowed again.

"Honey," she said, "make it as soon as you can, huh?"

I told her, "Sure," went back to my car and drove home.

• • •

Shirley wasn't home. I got caught in a kind of web of confusion, pacing the house. Finally I made a pot of coffee, and was in the kitchen finishing a third cup when Shirley returned. She came in the kitchen door, looking as beautiful as ever, her ash-blonde hair bringing the sunshine along from outside.

"Ken! Whatever are you doing home?"

I told her I wasn't feeling well, had taken the day off. She had been to a neighbor's, having a gab-fest.

"Did you—did you get paid?" she asked.

"They pay off this afternoon. I'm going to drop around and pick mine up."

"Oh. That's good." She grinned. "We're broke again, Ken."

She went over by the sink and got herself a drink of water. I stared at her, wondering how I'd ever gotten away from her the way I had. One of those things, I guess. Shirley was a knockout. No getting around it. She was wearing black slacks this morning, with a clinging white terry cloth jacket, a little black ribbon tied around her neck.

She stood there, sipping from the glass of water, eyeing me over the edge. She held the glass with both hands, like always. Shirley was the snuggly type.

I stared down into my coffee cup. I heard her go into the other room and I got to remembering again, and wondering. Funny, how things worked out.

I remembered how happy we'd been. And how the heat of our love had never been supposed to die. I remembered some of the little things we'd had, the secret things, the good things. Like the wink. When we were out someplace together and either one of us wanted the other, only there was no way to pass the word, we would wink. Twice. Shirley would wink twice with her right eye, and I'd return it with my left. Then we'd make a bee-line for home.

The good things.

That wink had been our big secret. It had been so long since we'd used it, I'd almost forgotten about it.

I wondered why it was all gone? Then I remembered Lorna. The feeling I got, just thinking of Lorna Waugh told me all I had to know.

Some things you don't count on. Some things just happen. Some things you can't fight too hard.

So quit stewing about her husband. It isn't going to matter, because nothing can stop you, Jackson.

"You feeling better?" Shirley said from behind my chair.

I stiffened. Her hand touched my shoulder. I stood up, glanced at her, moved into the living room.

"Yeah. Maybe it's just I didn't want to work today."

"But you will pick up your pay, Ken?"

I nodded. "I'll go do that now. Couple things I have to attend to. Might be a little late."

"That won't be unusual."

I looked at her. There was no expression, though her eyes were watchful. For a moment I wondered if Waugh had gotten to her. It wasn't that. Shirley was the type who would speak out.

"What do you mean?" I said.

She shrugged, stepped closer and looked at me, her eyes narrowing slightly.

"Things aren't like they used to be, Ken."

"Why, that's foolish."

"Foolish or not, it's true." She turned, moved across the room, sank down in a lounge chair, crossed her legs on the ottoman. "Everything all right, Ken?"

"Why, sure."

"If that job's getting you down, why don't you get another?"

"It is," I said. "I hadn't wanted to tell you. I don't like the work. Maybe I'll start looking around."

She seemed to brighten. She stood up, came across the room to me and put her arms around my waist. She kissed me on the chin. I stood there like a board. I couldn't bring myself to kiss her back. She shrugged away.

"All right, Ken," she said. "Go get your pay. I've got a lot of shopping to do."

"I wish you wouldn't act like this."

She didn't say anything. She kept her back to me and there was a rigidness to her shoulders that I didn't like.

"You hear me?"

"I heard you." She turned, smiling, her hair swirling around her shoulders. "I'm not acting any way, Ken—really. Hurry back, O. K.?"

"Sure," I said. "Sure."

• • •

I drove around a while, still wary of the Waugh house. Maybe he would be hanging around. It bothered me. But I got to thinking of Lorna, waiting for me. It was too much. Besides, I had to have that money. Shirley would ask questions. I couldn't return without it.

I parked in the street by a vacant, wooded lot, and checked to see if anybody was nearby, maybe watching. Everything was clear. I skipped from the car into the woods that led directly into the Waugh back yard.

Climbing the fence behind their place, I was already aching for her. It was always this way. It was a damned queer way to live, dodging around like I was. But you only live once. Lorna Waugh was a lot of living.

Crossing the thick turf of her yard, between heavy-laden fronds of royal palms, and blood-red hibiscus blossoms, I asked myself an important question. Would I be doing this if Lorna wasn't paying the way?

I decided I would. Only the future would have a narrower aspect.

No sign of Waugh's convertible Olds. It wasn't in the garage. If it had been parked out front, and he was home, her Ford would have been in the drive to warn me. It was in the garage, looking lonely. I thought how it would be nice to spend the afternoon at the beach, maybe up at Redington. After a while.

By the time I reached the back door on the rear gallery, anticipation had me anxious. She would be up there in her bedroom, waiting. She never answered the door for me.

I went on in, through the big house, down the heavily carpeted hall. I could smell her perfume.

"Lorna?"

She didn't answer. I hurried upstairs—and she was waiting, all right.

• • •

She would wait a long time. I stood there in the doorway, and the silence was deadly thick, broken only by the rocking tick-tock of a clock somewhere downstairs.

"Lorna," I said. I heard myself say it. Then again.

I went over by the bed, staring—not wanting to even see what was much too obvious.

She was sprawled across the bed, head hanging, her black hair fanning to the floor. She wore the knitted white shorts and the strap bra. I took another step, then recoiled at the sight. My heel touched on something that rolled. I tried to catch myself, went headlong toward the bed, half on the body.

My knee splashed in a spreading puddle of Lorna's blood, on the floor. My hand smashed down on her head.

I gagged, flung myself away, staring at the blood on my hand. I went crazy with it. I heard the words coming out of my throat, trying to wipe my hand clean on the bedspread, staring at the thing on the bed.

It was soaking through my trousers. It trickled into my shoe. I grabbed a small throw rug, wiped at the blood, sobbing a little now.

I'd stepped on an empty gin bottle. The odor of gin was stupefying in the room. The bottle had been used to shatter her skull.

I came to my feet, stepping back away from the bed. Her eyes were half open and they seemed to watch me, her face upside down over the edge of the bed, her upper lip hanging loose from her teeth.

I turned and ran.

I ran down through the house. I knew I had to get rid of my clothes. I was scared and still a little crazy. I kept trying to wipe my hand, not caring—wiping my hand on my trousers.

I pounded through the kitchen, out the back door.

There were two of them in the yard.

"Hold it right there," one of them said.

I whirled, cutting toward the drive and ran full into a big one with a sunburnt face, the shining black bill of his cap pulled low over unkind eyes.

"Listen," I said. "This is wrong. You got it wrong!"

"Put your hands behind you."

"No. I tell you! I just—"

"What?"

I heard one of them call from an upstairs window.

"It was a woman, all right," he called down. "She's dead."

"The hands," one said.

The cuffs bit into my wrists. It was blurred. What they kept saying was all jammed up with my knowing it was all wrong.

"You've got to listen," I kept saying. I kept saying it all the way downtown, between two cops in the back of a patrol car. I was still saying it when they took off the handcuffs and closed the steel, barred door to the cell.

"Let him quiet down," one of them said to another, as they walked away from the cell. "Wouldn't be any good, questioning him now. Give him ten minutes, then bring him into the detention room."

"Lord," the other said. "Lord, did you see her?"

"I saw her."

"Call my wife!" I yelled. "Call my wife!"

"We did, Jackson," one of them said softly. "We did call your wife. Just quiet down."

I heard myself yelling her name. "Shirley—Shirley!"

Then I heard myself begin to cry.

• • •

"You're crazy, I tell you. Crazy. I wouldn't kill her. What reason would I have for killing her?"

"Sure, Jackson."

"I found her that way, I tell you."

"You went to see her," one of them said. "You were plenty scared, too, because her husband warned you about it this morning. But you went anyway. She told you it was all over. Because she knew when a thing was over with, Jackson. But you couldn't stand that, could you? Losing her—and the money she was giving you?"

"Money?"

"He knew about that, too."

"Where's my wife?"

"She's here. We're trying to get her to see you. She's afraid of seeing you, Jackson. I don't blame her."

"I didn't do it."

There were two of them in the room with me. One of them shrugged. The other was smoking a cigarette. He dropped it on the floor, stepped on it, lit another.

"It would help if you'd confess," one of them said. "But it really doesn't matter."

I tried to say something. So many thoughts tried to come out, I just kind of babbled. It made me sick to hear it.

"A neighbor tipped us off," one of them said. "Said she heard a woman scream. Said she'd seen somebody climb Waugh's back fence a number of times lately. Said she hadn't wanted to say anything. But when she heard a woman scream—"

He left it that way.

"Shirley," I said. "I want to see my wife."

"I told you," the other one said. "We're trying to get her to talk with you, Jackson."

• • •

She would speak to me from the corridor, through the cell door. She stood there, about two feet away from the bars, watching me. She looked wonderful, but strange. Her hair was beautiful. She did not smile.

I thought of how people might look to animals in a zoo.

"Shirley, please—believe me."

"Yes."

"Nobody will listen. I know I've done wrong. But I didn't kill her, Shirley."

"Yes."

"For God's sake. Say something."

"Yes." She backed away, watching me. "Yes, Ken," she said. "Yes." She turned and walked swiftly out of sight. I tried to see her, calling to her, pressing my face against the bars. Her heels clicked and clicked and the steel door down there clanked and grated.

• • •

You know how it is?

No.

They appointed a defense counsel. Nobody wanted this case. In a small town, like this, it's different. The big-time criminal lawyers live in the big towns, where the big things happen. Nobody would listen.

My lawyer listened. He listened and nodded and said, "Yes, Jackson."

In court, he couldn't find his tongue. From the witness stand I tried to catch Shirley's eye. She was sitting two rows away from Herbert Waugh. She wouldn't look at me. Not while I looked at her.

They had the barman from the Hotel Floridian in there, too. He had heard everything.

"Waugh warned him. Yes, sir. He gave him every chance. Why would a guy do a thing—"

• • •

The jury was out fifteen minutes. I thought my heart would burst through my shirt. The blood kept filling my head and I kept remembering Lorna in the knitted white shorts and the way her eyes had watched me as I left the bedroom that day two weeks before.

"We find the defendant guilty—"

Of murder. With clemency. Twenty years to life at the state prison, in Raiford. Court adjourned.

• • •

I sat there.

"Please, Mr. Jackson. Stand up again."

"I can't."

"You've got to. It's all over now."

Waugh was watching me. I stared at him.

Shirley met him in the center aisle.

Then I saw it and I knew. I went out of my head.

Shirley and Waugh looked at each other. Then she smiled. Then she winked twice with her right eye. Waugh winked twice with his left.

"They winked!" I yelled. I tried to break away, pulling toward them. Two guards clung to my arms.

Waugh took Shirley's elbow. They walked out of the room.

For days I kept trying to tell people about that. Nobody would listen. It didn't mean anything to them that I knew he had killed his wife. That he and my wife had planned the whole thing. He would get Lorna's money. He and Shirley had been together all the time I'd been with Lorna. I knew it. She was the neighbor who tipped the police. Waugh had framed me himself. From the first preparation in the hotel bar.

"They winked at each other," I kept telling them. "Don't you see what that means? It was our secret. Shirley's and mine."

They never did listen.

The Screamer

Pursuit Detective Story Magazine
September 1955

She was late meeting me tonight. I parked the coupe down the block, and waited. Palm fronds stirred in the saffron glow of a streetlight on the corner and I sat there smoking, and musing on how rough it could be when the woman you loved was married to somebody else. I saw her coming then, and the way she was running, I knew something was up. I held the door open and she jumped in beside me, her white dress swirling about her legs.

"Get going, Cliff!"

"Sure." We took off, heading across town, toward the beaches. "What's the matter, Evelyn?"

"I'm scared." She came over next to me, held to my arm. "Edward's found out about us."

I felt a touch of excitement. I'd known this had to come sometime.

"Oh, Cliff," she said. "He's awful!"

"He would be. Take it easy, now."

"He warned me not to see you."

I tried to relax. It was difficult. Edward Thayer was a prominent lawyer and he could cause plenty of trouble. But Evelyn and I loved each other and there wasn't much you could do about that, either.

"He won't give me a divorce," she said. Her voice was a little shrill. "Says the scandal would ruin him."

"Look," I said. "It's a nice night. Let's save it. We can talk it over when we get out to the beach. Everything's going to be all right."

"But, Cliff. It's such a mess!"

"I know." I patted her knee, looked over at her and grinned. She tried to smile back, without much success. Then she moved still closer to me. Neither of us said anything for a while.

I drove on through town across the causeway and we came down the main beach road. It was one of these deep blue star-studded Florida nights, when headlight on the highway sparkle wickedly bright, and pleasing music from nowhere layers the wind like delicate icing on a cake of nostalgia.

Pretty soon we reached the spot where we turned off, along a stretch of white sand. The tires hissed, and long, sear grass dryly finger-tipped the fenders. I pulled the car over beside a stand of six raddled cabbage palms, turned the ignition off and set the hand brake. We were in the shadow of the palms and the ceaseless chatter of near-rigid fronds was loud. Back on the highway, gleaming cars wooshed, zoomed and honked toward festivity.

We sat in the darkness and listened to all of this. The car creaked. On the other side of us, the ground leveled out and tall Australian pines bent moaning. Straight ahead, between low-lying dunes, was the beach and the Gulf, and the tiny place in eternity where we could be together without having to dodge behind Venetian blinds at the sound of footsteps.

"Well?" she said.

I grabbed the folded blanket and the thermos of martinis and we went on down to the beach. We sat on the blanket in the moonlight, with the Gulf quietly lapping the sands. You could smell the salt and the wind was cottony and it might have been perfect. I started opening the thermos.

"Wait, Cliff."

She was sitting with her legs under her, propped on one hand, the moonlight bright on her thick blonde hair, shining in her eyes. Her white dress looked somehow whiter and she was still trying to smile. Normally Evelyn was able to believe we were doing the right thing, but I knew her husband had gotten to her.

"I'm sick, Cliff—sick," she said. "I didn't want anything to spoil it here tonight."

"Nothing's going to spoil it," I told her. "It's just coming out into the open, the way it should be."

We watched each other for a time.

"He's mad," she said. "Real mad. He knows everything. He caught on to where we meet, followed me the other evening. He got the license number on your car and had it checked. He knows all about you."

"That makes us even."

"He knows how you used to be a cop. And how you rent out boats for fishing, now. You should have heard him laugh at that. He knows how you saved that Andy Leonard's life two years ago, when you and Leonard were sent after that escaped convict from Raiford. How you got shot in the arm—and because your arm won't straighten out just right, they won't let you back on the force. He said he wished you'd got shot in the stomach."

I didn't say anything. Even Evelyn would never know how much being a cop meant to me. When people joked about it, I'd always begin to sweat.

"I tried to tell him we've known each other a long time," she said. "That we can't help what's happened. But he's not human. It's no use." She hesitated. "He told me he'd figure a way to stop you for good, if we keep it up. He hates you. He's thinking of himself, though—not me. He doesn't want his name sullied. He's hopping mad, Cliff."

A large motor launch was coming along the shore, close in. It's engine was loud, sputtering and thumping as it crept past us.

"Cliff," she said. "What are we going to do?"

I pressed her back on the blanket and our mouths came together and I held her down that way until she began to respond. She twisted sharply, writhing, then her arms tightened and she moaned a little and the current was re-established. I began to realize more and more just how much I loved her.

She started to say something about sand-spurs, when we both stiffened. Somebody was running across sand, from the highway. Whoever it was was getting close; they were back there by the dunes. I heard other footsteps then, pounding, and hoarse breathing, and somebody grunted.

A woman screamed, the scream stridently repeated; a crazed shriek of fear.

I kneed myself up and started over the shelf of sand into the grass above the beach.

"What is it?" Evelyn whispered. She came up beside me.

Somebody moaned.

A flashlight splayed blindingly straight at our faces, then went out.

"What's going on?" I called.

I heard a hard thud, and then more running footsteps, going away now, over toward the Australian pines. I started after the footsteps. There was a bounding shadow up there, but there were yellow and red dots in my eyes from the flashlight and I couldn't see right. The shadow vanished around the cabbage palms by our car. I heard the pounding feet heading toward the highway. I tripped on something, sprawled in the sand on my face, my mouth full of sand, my eyes gritting with it.

"Cliff!" Evelyn called.

A car door slammed out there. The car gunned away and I heard the tires shrill as it turned on the highway.

"Cliff," Evelyn said. "Are you all right?" Then she kind of held her breath and I got my eyes clear enough of sand so I could see again. She was standing up there against the paler sky, looking down into the grass. "Cliff," she said.

I got up and went over by her.

"God, Cliff."

I had tripped over the sprawled body of a young girl.

Then Evelyn said something I didn't get. She stepped close to the figure in the grass and knelt down. All the good opinions I had of her soared a little more.

"Don't," I said. "Stay away."

"I'm all right, Cliff."

The light color of the girl's hair, her twisted skirt in the moonlight, touched off memories inside me. I had seen them like this before.

Evelyn reached out, took the girl's shoulder, turned her over. The body moved loosely, as if it were oiled at the joints. Then the young face looked vacantly up into the moonlight, eyes half open, shining, staring with that stare they have, the red mouth twisted in death so you could see the bright white tips of teeth.

Evelyn made a sound in her throat, drew away, cringing toward me. I saw the slow shaping of horror in her face.

"Easy, now," I said. "Ever seen her?"

"No—no."

I thrust her aside, knelt down. The kid was dead, all right. The fine blonde hair of her head was matted darkly where she'd been struck. Full of energy in life, in death this seemed hard to imagine.

"You'd better go back to the car," I told Evelyn. She was standing there, perfectly straight, her arms flat against her sides, staring.

"I saw him, Cliff. I got a good look at him."

"Good girl." I waited. I hadn't seen a thing and some of the sand still pained in my eyes. "Describe him," I said. "Quick, now."

She started to speak, then stopped.

"I can't describe him," she said. "He sounds too much like a description of any man. Only he was young." Evelyn pointed to the body. "Young, like she was young. I could tell the way he moved, the way he looked back. He stopped on the road and stared back here. A car's lights shone on his face." She paused, looked at me. "Cliff," she said. "If I ever see him again, I'll know him. The lights were right on his face."

"What was he wearing?"

"A—a jacket, of some sort. Open. He wasn't wearing a tie."

I went over to her, looked into her eyes and held both of her hands. "Listen," I said. "You doing all right?"

"Yes—fine."

"Go back to the beach. Get the blanket and thermos. Take them to the car. I want to have a look around."

"What are you going to do?"

"I'm taking you home," I said. "Then I'm going to report it."

"All right, Cliff." She turned away without looking down, and walked across the dunes toward the beach.

Something shining on the sands, had taken my eye. It was a long, five-cell flashlight. The lens and lens-housing were broken, bent. I didn't touch it. That's what she'd been struck with. It could be a nasty weapon swung by a strong man. I prowled around and found a purse about fifteen yards off on the sand toward the road. It was a white, straw bag. I kicked it, so the contents spilled out. There was a letter. I picked it up and held the envelope in the moonlight. The writing was readable. It was addressed to Jinny Foster, 219 Palm Drive. There was no return address. I put it in my pants pocket.

I turned and watched Evelyn cross the dunes carrying the blanket and thermos. "You coming?" she called.

"Yeah." I went over by the body again. The moonlight was terribly bright. This kid was terribly dead. It got me, seeing her there in the grass like that.

You wonder why it happened. You want to know why; how anybody could do a thing like this to such a pretty young kid.

I had no way of finding out, except by reading the papers. I'd already made too many enemies, trying to get back on the force. All I could do was report it and sit and wait. And I'd have to report it anonymously—because what was I doing out here? How did I happen to find this body? Did I know the kid? No? Prove it. She's a nice-looking kid, isn't she? Built real solid; lots of stuff. There's a full moon tonight, too, isn't there?

2.

Driving Evelyn home, neither of us said much. She was frightened. She pressed close against me and I could feel the taut smoothness of her body beneath the light dress. I wanted to ask her something, but I hated to scare her more than she was. Only I had to ask her.

"Listen. You think maybe he knows you got a good look at him?"

"That's what I've been thinking about," she said.

I sensed worry behind the flat tone of her voice.

"He looked right at me," she said. "And I was looking at him. I wasn't paying any attention to myself—but the car lights were bright on him and they might have been on me, too."

"Well," I said.

"Cliff," she said. "You think he might—might try something?"

"If he saw you, he might," I told her. "But ten to one he's banking on the fact that you didn't really see him—and sure as hell didn't know him. He might be in Georgia by now."

"You don't believe that, though, do you?"

"No."

I swung the car past her house, and came to a stop down the block. Then she was in my arms. She shivered a little and I held her as tight as I could, wanting more than this. Her mouth was soft and hot and it was good, but I could sense the nervousness.

"You get in the house and stay there," I said. "I'll call you."

"All right."

We kissed again and then I made her go. She started down the walk. I waited a moment, watching her. Then the porch light went on back there and the front lawn lighted up with yellow, the trees and shrubbery in dark shadow. I saw her husband coming running down across the lawn. He was a big man, but soft big, heavy big. The way he ran, you could see his heels sink into the turf. You could almost hear him pant. He had on a robe of some kind, and he kept waving his arms.

I watched Evelyn stride up the walk, past him. He kept rumbling along beside her, waving his arms. I couldn't hear him, but his mouth was flapping. I heard the front door slam back there, as loud as a shot.

He came running down the lawn. He hit the sidewalk, his shoes flapping on the cement like boards banged together. I threw the car in gear and got out of there.

I needed gas, and I had to find a pay phone. I could have phoned at home, but I wanted to get it over with right away. The boys had to get on this. I wished I were one of them; able to be on this. I couldn't get her out of my head; the way she looked, lying there in the grass, her eyes half-lidded in the moonlight. There was something tenderly horrible about it and I thought how it would be to have whoever did it beside me in the car, right then. How I could stop the car, drag him out on the street and tear his face off.

I stopped at an all-night drug store on the edge of town, and put in the call. It was eight-fifteen by the clock on the wall over the soda fountain.

"That's right," I said. "Six hundred yards past the Sunny Shores Hotel. Turn right on the sand by a row of Australian pines."

"If you'll just give us your name and—"

I hung up. Al Calvin had taken the call from the desk. He was one of the boys who was so nice after I got out of the hospital. He'd helped prove to the chief and everybody else, that with my arm the way it was, I couldn't draw a gun fast. He also proved I was right-handed and couldn't learn to use my left. For my own good, of course. Calvin always did it for everybody's own good. They hadn't needed proof. You have to be fit to be a cop. Only he'd stuck his pale snout in anyway. Calvin. Mama's little helper boy.

I went on outside and drove on down the road to the gas station where I always take my car, told Howard to fill her up and check the oil and water.

It came to five, even. I reached for my wallet and it wasn't in my hip pocket. Howard took his cap off and scratched into his thatch of black hair and watched me as I remembered.

"Bill me," I said, and drove off, heading for the beach.

I could see myself taking that spill over the body of the girl, landing in the sand. I could see the wallet slide from my pocket, drop on the sand with the moonlight on it. Identification papers. Three snapshots of Evelyn. A letter from her. All hell.

These things happen, I told myself. It's going to be all right, boy. They won't find it. You'll beat them out there, anyway. You'll know right where to look. They won't be looking for your wallet. No, I thought. But they'll be looking for something, anything. Sure. But the wallet's probably covered with sand. That's why you didn't notice it. Sure. Only one of them will stumble on it. They always do. Yes, but you're going to be there first—remember?

It was a nice thought. It didn't work out that way. Coming down the beach highway, I saw two patrol cars parked on the shoulder. As I rode past, I saw still another police car in there on the sand and the spotlight was focused on a patch of grass and you knew what was there.

They'd nailed me up good and solid, by being on the ball. I drove on up the road, made a U turn, and came back, heading for town. There wasn't much to do now.

I might have lost my wallet someplace else. Only I knew damned well it hadn't been that way. The thing to do now, was work with the knowledge in my mind that they had already found the wallet, knew I'd been there.

Whether I liked it or not, I was becoming involved in the killing of a young girl named Jinny Foster.

I drove around a while. I drove on up the beach road to Indian Rocks, wondering what I was supposed to do now, and getting no place. Then I came back to town. I had it pretty well worked out in my mind, but I cursed myself for taking the long drive.

I stopped at another drugstore, put a call in to Evelyn from a booth. I hoped she would answer the phone. She did.

I told her everything. "So, listen. There's a good chance they'll find the wallet. It's a stinking thing," I said. "If they do, we're in a mess. You, too. I want you to take a train somewhere. Have you got a friend in some other town?"

She'd been trying to interrupt me. I ceased talking when I realized she was ready to break at the other end.

"They did," she said. "They found it."

"Oh."

"They found it and they've already called here, Cliff." She didn't say anything for a moment and I could tell she was on the verge of tears. "They're coming here. They want to ask me some questions. They didn't say anything about the murder, just that they found this wallet. Edward's fit to be tied. He doesn't know what it's all about, of course. He's thinking of himself, again. He almost cried."

"I'll bet. Listen, Evelyn—don't tell them a thing. Nothing, you understand? Insist you took a walk tonight—alone. You hear?"

"But, Cliff—you know how they are."

"I'm asking you to do this. I've got good reasons. You don't know a thing. Everything they tell you is news."

"Well, all right."

"They won't hurt you. Just take it easy."

"They implied you did something."

"Sure. They think I killed that kid."

"Edward's yelling his head off for me. I've got the door locked."

"I'll keep in touch," I said. "Love you."

I went on outside and stood on the sidewalk. A wind trailed down the avenue, dusting along the curb. A cool-looking girl in a tight red shirt bridled past, her sharp high heels rapping, her chin very determined. I went over to the coupe and opened the door and leaned on it.

So far, I had a head start. Maybe. If I got a move on. But I had to really move, because they would be hot on this one. If I was going to come out on top, I had to stay ahead of the law. I had to find who killed Jinny Foster.

Jinny must have been a nice name for her.

I stepped it fast over onto the North side of town, parked the car in a vacant lot and started walking. There was only one man I could go to, and he might not be home. I had to have a car. Andy Leonard collected cars and he was a cop, and I hoped he was still my friend.

"Cliff," he said. He stood in the door. He looked at me and blinked, then turned and looked at his wife. She was sitting in the living room, her legs crossed. A cute little redhead, with a frown. "Stepping outside for a minute," he told her. He came out and closed the door and looked at me and nodded.

"All right, Cliff," he said. "What is it?"

I watched him and I knew he knew. Andy was a tall, thin wretch, with droopy eyes and a sad mouth. His clothes never fit properly. Just now he was wearing a pair of pajamas, red ones. His hair stood up like brown fingers. Actually, he was as tough as telephone cable. He was a good cop.

"What have you heard?" I said.

"Maybe we'd better not talk about it."

"Do I have to remind you of anything?"

"Like what?"

"Like I saved your life once?"

"You don't have to, no."

We watched each other. He turned and looked back into the living room.

"Come on," he said. He started down off the porch. I followed him around the side of the house past some shrubbery. We came to his garage. It was really an old barn. He slid the door open and we stepped just inside. We stood there, with the moonlight paling through the doors. He didn't turn on the lights. I could see bits of metal gleaming and glinting in the shadows.

"I've got to have a car," I said. "Have you got a spare you aren't tinkering with?"

"Where's yours?"

"Best you don't know."

"Cliff," he said. "Did you do this thing?"

"No."

"They notified me. I may be put on the case. How did the wallet get out there? They're really hot on this, because she was just a high school kid. Some of the boys are saying you were headed for something like this."

I told him everything.

"That's it?" he asked.

"Andy, I've got to have that car. A few dollars, too. I can't go home. They'll be there, waiting. What in hell would I tell them? They'd get no place, and neither would I. Meanwhile, whoever did this is maybe putting miles—"

He held up one hand and blinked. "If you did it," he said, "I'm one of the guys who's going to get you, Cliff."

"Now that's settled. How about the car? I've got to move fast, Andy."

"I can give you a forty-nine Merc convertible. She isn't hopped up. I got it for the body. Haven't done anything with it yet. There's no top, though."

"Who wants a top?"

"If you did this," he said, "you know where it'll put me."

He showed me the Merc. While I drove it out into the driveway, he went back to the house and returned, holding a bill in one hand. He gave it to me. It was a ten.

"That's the best I can do."

I sat there, idling the engine and we stared at each other some more. The Merc rattled like hell.

"I bought it for fifty bucks," Andy said, rapping the hood with his knuckles. Then he stood there and his hair waved around on top of his head and he looked sad as hell.

"So long, Andy."

He just looked at me as I let her roll out of the drive, into the street.

3.

The Foster home, at 219 Palm Drive, was lit up, but no police cars were around. I parked the car a few houses down and came back and rang the bell.

Jinny's father answered the door. He was a thick-set man, wearing a wrinkled gray uniform and I recognized it as a mailman's outfit. His lips were drawn tight, and his deep-set eyes were a little shiny. I took the chance that he'd been notified. I had to work very fast.

"I'm from the police," I said. "Hate to do this, Mister Foster, but I'll have to ask you a few questions. Make it as quick as I can."

"I told you over the phone I'd do all I can," he said. "Come in." He stepped away from the door. There was a small hallway, and a small living room to the right, with a woman sitting over there in a chair beside a goldfish bowl, wiping her eyes with a handkerchief. Her face was red-blotched and she avoided my eyes.

"Could we go out in the kitchen?" Foster asked.

I tipped my head toward the woman in there.

"All right," he said. We went into the living room and he slumped into a chair. I perched on the edge of a couch and looked at him. The woman didn't say anything. She kept sniffing and swallowing behind the handkerchief.

"They said they'd send somebody right over," he said. "I didn't think it would be this quick. They didn't really tell us anything. Just that Jinny is—was—" He put his hands together and cracked his knuckles and stared at the floor.

The woman broke into tears again, loudly.

I knew they were in a rush to get started, but they could have waited to tell these folks in person. Sometimes it's rougher over a phone. It sounded like something Al Calvin would do, to hurry things along.

I told Foster what I knew, making it sound as if I'd gone out there in one of the patrol cars. "Now," I said. "All I'd like, as quickly as possible, is the name of your daughter's closest girl friend."

"What will we do?" Jinny's mother said. "Frank's supposed to be at work. Jinny's our only child. We were just sitting here." Her sobs ran up and up and up. She caught her breath and sighed. She swallowed several times. "She didn't—I won't—how could . . . ?" she said. She put her head down in her hands and rocked her shoulders and began to really cry.

Foster rose and went over to her. He patted her back, then looked at the palm of his hand.

"She was seventeen," he said. "She was a senior. Her best friend is Inez, I guess—huh, Martha?"

Mrs. Foster rocked her head up and down. I felt sorry for the both of them, but I wished they would hurry it up. I knew you couldn't hurry them. The house was neat and they looked like good people; not the kind that these things are supposed to happen to. Often that's the way it is.

"Inez what?" I said.

"She hasn't got a phone," Foster said. "Harrington."

"Inez Harrington," Mrs. Foster said.

"What's her address, Martha?"

Mrs. Foster waved one hand toward the rear of the house.

"She lives out—out on Melbourne Boulevard."

"Kind of in the country," Foster said.

"It's the first house past the Melbourne Drive-in theater," Mrs. Foster said. "You won't miss it. The name's on the mail box. Same side as the drive-in."

"What could have happened?" Foster said softly. "What could she have done to have this happen?"

Mrs. Foster looked accusingly at her husband and sobbed.

I shook my head and stared at the floor, then stood up, and moved into the center of the room. I had to get going, yet I couldn't appear too rushed. In the back of my mind I kept thinking of what Evelyn had said about seeing that guy. And not knowing whether he saw her watching him. It kept rapping me, and the sweat was beginning to pop like pins under my shirt. "There anything else you could tell me that might help?"

They both shook their heads.

There were lots of things I wanted to ask them about Jinny. There was no time. I had to somehow stay ahead of the boys with the sirens. It would take maybe an hour to get anything out of these people. Jinny's girl friend would know more about the inside.

"Officer," Foster said. He stepped across the living room to me. "Could I go with you?" His eyes were a little wild. He kept wadding his hands together, cracking his knuckles. "I would like very much to get close to whoever did this," he said slowly. His mouth jerked and twisted.

"I'm sorry, you can't do that," I said. "We'd like the same thing."

Out on the street again, I hurried for the car. I headed for Melbourne, pushing the old convertible. It really rolled, but somebody had beat the hell out of it. Melbourne Boulevard was rough and full of pot-holes and the car wobbled all over the road. I didn't like thinking about those two people back there and what they would think when they found I wasn't with the police, was, in fact, a chief suspect in the murder of their daughter.

Then I remembered the letter I'd picked up out on the beach. I drew up on the shoulder of the road, under a streetlight and got the letter out of my pants pocket. It was badly crumpled.

"Honey-Baby," I read.

"How long you going to keep this up? You know how it is with me, baby, damn it. Quit making me ache. Seeing you wiggle down the hall will drive me to drink. Everybody but me, now, and don't try to kid me

because it's all around what's going on and I'm not forgetting last summer. How could you forget? Ha-ha. I can't stand it. How's about us having a little party? I'll see you in study hall. I'm drunk right now, so see what you're doing to me? Hic-hic! Please, doll—I want some candy, too!
"Burn this."

There was a PS.
"I've got a new car. It isn't broken in yet!"
It was signed, "Waiting, Tal."

I sat there a moment, thinking it over and not liking any of it. You hear these stories about high school kids, and you read about them, and then you have something like this in your hand. Innocent, of course. I thought about Jinny Foster's home and her parents, then I put the letter back in the envelope. Finally, I put it in my pocket again.

4.

She was a tall girl in a yellow sweater and very tight dungarees. Her hair was black and wild and short and her eyes were blacker than her hair. She stood in the doorway, with the light shining from the hall, across her shoulders, and jammed her hands into the waistband of her dungarees.

"Nobody's home," she said. She said it with a finality that told me nobody walked over her. Her voice was low, and slightly affected, each syllable carefully pronounced. Her eyes were very wide, bold. "You can't come in? Who are you?"

I grinned at her.
"You a friend of Jinny Foster's?" I asked.
"She send you over here?"
"Not exactly."
"What did she send you over here for?" She didn't move a muscle. There was a screen door between us.
"Could I come in?"
"No."
"I'm from the police," I said.
"That's a hot one."

I watched her take her hands out of the waistband, place them flat on the backs of her hips. She rocked up on her toes and shook her head.

"You can't come in," she said. "What's with Jinny?"
I reached over and pulled on the handle of the screen door. It didn't open. It was locked. She didn't move. Then she frowned.
"I've never met you, have I?" she said. "Or, have I?"
I decided the only way with this type was to hit hard. I gave it to her straight and told her Jinny's folks had sent me here. She blinked a lot while I told her, but that was all. "You're her friend," I said. "I need some information. I'd like the names of her boy friends."

She gave a little snicker through her nose.
We watched each other. This was great.
"How old are you?" I said.

She didn't even blink, now.

"I can wait all night," I said. "I can go back and bring some uniformed officers with me, if that's what you want. They'll be along soon, probably. I'm working on this case in plain clothes. Jinny Foster is dead—Now, what do you want to do?"

She apparently didn't want to do anything. The way she kept looking at me was fierce.

"You could help us a lot," I said. "Only the quicker you act, the quicker we can act. We can locate other friends, of course, but Mrs. Foster said you were her best friend."

"What's Mrs. Foster's first name?"

I sighed. "Martha," I said. "Her father's name is Frank. They live at 219 Palm Drive. Mrs. Foster is badly broken up about this."

"Let's see your credentials."

I cleared my throat. There was a slight cramp in my neck. "I told you, I'm working in plain clothes. We don't carry credentials sometimes."

"Where's your buzzer?"

The hell with her. She was a beaut. I let her know it, the way I looked at her, and something must have clicked, because she reached out and flipped the hook loose, gave the screen door a nudge with her knee.

"Come on in."

We stood in the hallway. From somewhere at the back of the house, soft music was playing. It was very sweet, sickly, slop.

"I appreciate this," I said. "Now, if you'll just answer a few questions, Miss Harrington."

She changed now. She moved very close to me and looked at me just as closely.

"Is it true? Is Jinny really dead?" she asked. And the timbre of her voice changed, too. The way she said that, she was just a kid again. For a time there, she had been far removed from kiddom. If you closed your eyes and just listened, it was all right. Otherwise, the whole thing was incongruous. She wore a lot of perfume, and it was a good perfume, only it was all you could smell in the house. She must have sprayed it on the walls. Up close, you could see how really young she was; the white and pink of her cheeks and the clear whites of her eyes, the very tender lips with too much purplish lipstick on them and just a little of it on her very white teeth. The sweater she wore had probably been given to her as a birthday present about six years ago. The soft tendrils of hair at her temples were damp and Inez Harrington exuded heat and vim.

"Yes," I told her. Jinny Foster was dead.

She wanted to help then. She got me pencil and paper and we sat on a couch in the dimly lighted living room and she wrote down three names.

"They're the ones," she said. "They're her—well, I mean." She laughed and leaned against me. You could feel the stirring vitality. She was talking too damned much.

"Thanks," I said. "Now, this Talbot Swanson. Who's he?"

She leaned against me and looked at me, blinking.

I moved away. She smiled and dampened her lips, rubbing one over the other. The lipstick didn't smear.

"Would he be called Tal, maybe?"

"That's right. His daddy is filthy."

"I see."

"Filthy rich. You're cute," she said. "There's nobody home. And they aren't coming home, either. Not all night. Why don't you relax?"

The music poured softly through the house from back there someplace. She turned on the couch so she faced me, up very close, and scrunched one leg up under her. Everything she wore must have had strong seams. She must have been still taller than I'd thought, because she was wearing nylon stockings under the dungarees, and no shoes.

She snickered through her nose again.

"You don't have to kid me anymore," she said. "Where did Jinny meet you?"

I turned away and stared at the list of names on the paper in my hand. It blurred a little.

"You weren't fooling about those names?" I said.

"Nope. They're Jinny's best. Talbot isn't really, but he will be. He's got an inside track, or something." She inched herself along the couch, riding on her foot, until her legs pressed against me. She kept moving her knee. I was trapped against the arm of the couch. She leaned forward.

"You're no cop," she said. "Cops don't drive beat-up Mercs. Not *that* beat-up. I saw you park it down there. I was out in the yard. There's been a prowler. Got to watch it. But you're no prowler."

I folded the paper and tucked it in my shirt pocket.

"Honey, if Jinny sent you, it's O.K.," she whispered.

I looked into her eyes. They were very black and there was nothing behind them but now.

"She tell you to give me this line?" she whispered.

"No."

Her face became quite sober. She moved still closer and smiled. There was just the faintest trace of nervousness in the smile. Not enough to count. "Well?" she said.

I rose quickly, turned and looked at her.

"This is for the books," I said. "Remember it. I wasn't lying to you. Jinny is dead."

She leaned back against the couch and smiled broadly.

I left the place. As I turned the car around in her driveway, I saw her standing at the screen door, rocking on her toes.

5.

The first name Inez had given me was a Sam Roberson, over on Lowell Court. It took me back into town, not far from the business section. But the street was subdued and the houses were nicely kept, the lawns trimmed and mowed. The Roberson place was set well back, between two banyan trees.

I wondered if they were all like Inez? They couldn't be. I wondered if Jinny were like Inez? Somehow, I didn't think so.

I parked the car down the street a way, in the shadows again, and sat there a moment. So far, I'd been lucky in keeping ahead of the police. How long would it last? I wanted very much to know how Evelyn was making out, and I had to keep shoving her out of my mind. That she was in very grave danger, was a thought I didn't like at all.

It was a square, stucco house, circa nineteen-twenty-five.
"This where Sam Roberson lives?"
"I'm Sam Roberson."
"Must be Sam Junior I'm looking for."
"My son?"

I waited. The man at the door was holding two shirts on metal hangers and he was sweating. The house was brightly lighted, and a woman came into the hall.
"What is it, Sam?"
"Somebody wants Sam," he said.
"He's upstairs, studying."
"I'm from the police," I said. "If I could talk with your son, I'd—"
"What—what?" the woman said. The two of them crowded in the doorway.
"It's about an—" I paused. "A friend of your son's has been—" I stopped again. "A girl your son knows was killed tonight," I said. "I've been sent out to ask a few questions."
"Come inside," the man said.

I went on in and we stood in the hallway. The woman took the shirts from the man and hurried away with them. She returned and stood at the foot of the stairs, wringing her hands. I thought how easy it was for anybody posing as a cop to gain entrance into private homes.

Mr. Roberson was a short, thin individual, wearing steel-rimmed glasses. He did not know what to say. His wife was opposite; large and ham-armed, with a mouth like a clamp. They were very average people. It stuck out all over them.

After some more talking, Roberson said he'd call the boy downstairs.
"I'd like to talk with him alone," I said. "Would it be all right if I went on up?"
They looked at each other. It was all right.
"Second door on the left," Roberson said. Then he said, "I'll just run up with you—I won't stay."
"Oh, dear—whatever?" Mrs. Roberson said.

• • •

"Yes, sir. Sure. I know Jinny real well."

I leaned against the closed door. The room was that of an active young man, with an interest in sports and possibly a very sincere interest in fly fishing. A small work bench across the room was arranged with a vise for tying flies. Four beautifully hand-made fly rods hung from hooks in the ceiling. On one wall was a huge, flat, glass-enclosed case with hundreds of flies mounted on fine white batting.

Young Sam Roberson had been seated at a desk by some windows across the room, when his father showed me in and introduced us, before he left. Now Sam came across the room. He was of average build, dressed in blue slacks, and T-shirt. His blond hair was cut in a neatly square crew-cut.

"You're from the police?"
I nodded.
"Maybe you'd better tell me what this is all about."
"When did you last see Jinny Foster, Sam?"
"Why, I saw her tonight. Early tonight. Why?"
"You know Inez Harrington?"

"Sure. Say, what is all this?"

I walked across the room, over to his desk. A chemistry book was open beneath a goose-necked lamp. Night frowned through the open window, yawning drowsily among the curtains.

"Jinny's dead," I said, turning to him.

"Dead?" He sat down on the foot of his bed and stared at me. "Jinny, dead? How do you mean, dead?"

I told him. He watched me all the while, rising from the bed and stepping closer as I talked. "So, now," I said, "would you tell me all about your seeing her tonight?"

"Good night," he said. "Jinny." He stared at the floor and swallowed. He swallowed again, returned to the bed and sat down. "Good night," he said. "Good night. And I was just with her a little while ago."

"How long a little while?"

"Well, early, really. Just after supper. Just dusk, around there. I had to run downtown with the car." He paused. "We're—the family, that is—we're going up to our fishing camp on Lake Oklawachi tomorrow. The folks are packing stuff now. I had to run down to pick up a gasoline lantern we were having fixed. I saw Jinny walking along Sixteenth. I picked her up. Said she had to go to the library."

"Oh?"

He looked up at me. His face was very sober, and the way his eyes looked, he was remembering Jinny Foster.

"She had a book due at the library."

"What kind of book?"

He shrugged. "Some medical book, something. She's—was—deeply interested in medicine, lately."

"So?"

"Well, I told her I'd run her down to the library. She sure was glad. She had a date, or something."

"Who with?"

"She didn't say. I took her down there and dropped her off. She went into the library with her book and I went over and picked up the lantern and came home."

"That's all?"

He stared at me. "That's all. I asked her, maybe I could have her up to the camp for a couple days. The folks wouldn't mind. But she was busy, or something."

"How did Jinny seem, Sam?"

"You mean was she nervous, like that? No. She acted fine. Even told me a joke. But she was in a hurry, all right. Wanted to get to the library. I guess she was meeting somebody somewhere."

"Was Jinny your girl?"

"Sort of."

"Didn't it bother you, her meeting somebody else?"

He shrugged again and stared at the floor.

"You remember the name of the book she had?"

"Sure. 'The Medical Advisor,' something like that."

"This Inez Harrington. What kind of girl is she, Sam?"

"Well," he said. "She's a good scout."

I hummed a little and turned the chair by the desk around, and sat down. "How good a scout?" I said.

"I don't know what you mean, sir."

"Well, when you say she was a 'good scout,' do you mean she made fire by friction? Or is it something else?"

His face grew brick red.

"Relax," I said. "I met Inez."

"Oh, did you?"

"Now, about Jinny. Was she a good scout, too, Sam?"

"Yes, sir. I mean—*no*, sir!" He nearly broke into a grin.

I stood up. "Then the last you saw of Jinny Foster, was when she walked into the library?"

"Yes. That's right. Listen, about this good scout business."

I lifted one hand. "Who's Talbot Swanson, Sam?"

"Well, he's a guy—just—"

"And this Roy Patterson. About him. Did he go with Jinny?"

"Sometimes."

He was staring at the floor again. I began to get the feeling I should move on. Evelyn kept appearing in my mind's eye. It was foolish, maybe, but it was as if she were calling to me. I wondered what she would have thought of these high school kids. I wondered what I thought of them.

I knew a lot of time was going by and I didn't like it. I had a feeling I wasn't getting anyplace. Suppose the killer was some kind of crackpot, and suppose he *did* get a good look at Evelyn looking at him? But all I could do was keep plugging, and try to stay away from the police. Sam Roberson was a little help. Only who was it Jinny had planned to meet?

I moved toward the door.

"Sir?"

I turned to him.

"Sir, Inez and Jinny were good friends." He swallowed.

"That's nice." He had been going to say something else. "Look," I told him. "If you know something you're not telling me, why not loosen up? We'll find out everything sooner or later."

He didn't say anything.

"O.K.," I said. I watched him a moment. He was staring at the floor again. I left him that way, went on downstairs, smiled and lamely excused my way past the Robersons, and out onto the porch. I started for the convertible.

6.

It was some party. Both Roy Patterson and Talbot Swanson were at the Swanson home, over in Jungle Acres. It was a huge sprawling place, reached through a winding gravel drive. The house was enormous, with a screened porch running all around the outside. The screened porch was dark except for the occasional flash of a match, or cigarette lighter, the dim orange glow by the record player, and flaming feminine laughter. Just inside the house, shadowed against dim, faraway lamplight, somebody was playing a set of trap drums, accompanying a jazz record. When I reached the porch door, I saw it was a woman playing the drums. Glass tinkled and clanked and liquid splashed and moans and hisses and rustlings came from the darkness, between the *rappity-bam-slam-tickety-tick-clang!* of snare and too much cymbal.

"Come on in, have a drink, you old soak. Say, who are you, anyway?"

"Tal? Tal? Tal?"

"Shaddup, bag!"

"Tal! Who is it?"

"I don't know. Who are you?"

"Is your—?" I said. "Can I—"

"Talbot? Is you is or is you ain't?"

"For cryin' out loud, be quiet a minute. Mom, lay off the drums, will you?"

"Who is it, Tal?"

"Ha-ha-ha-ha-ha!"

I stood there and looked at the hair-in-the-face, slightly reeling fellow who was trying to ask me who I was.

"Listen, witch," somebody said to somebody. "You pull that again, I'll clobber ya!"

"Will you! Will you!"

"Look," Talbot Swanson said. "What you want?"

"I'd like to talk with you," I said. "I'm from the police."

He straightened carefully. "That so?"

Everybody went quiet. The drums ceased. The jazz record stopped playing. Crickets chirped.

I watched the woman stand up behind the set of drums. She picked her way around them and came stiffly forward, and a light went on. Not a bright light, just bright enough to show huddled shapes and pale faces, and loud grins.

The woman came to the door. She stood beside Talbot Swanson and scratched her thigh with a drumstick. She was a very pretty woman, wearing a tight black dress. She had blonde hair, bunched into a tail behind her head and she was rather drunk. She leered at me.

"Whoever complained this time?" she said.

"Nobody," I told her.

A tall thin fellow came through the house carrying two glasses. He veered carefully across the porch and up behind the woman. Holding the glasses away, he leaned over and kissed the woman on the back of the neck. She whirled.

"Roy!" she said.

"Who's he?" Roy said. He drank from one of the glasses.

"We're just having a little get-together," the woman said, turning to me again. Somebody put on another record.

"Are you Roy Patterson?" I said to the one with the glasses in his hands.

He nodded and sipped again.

The woman was nervous. "Would you care for a drink?" she said. When she looked at me, she narrowed her eyes a little, and let her lower lip dangle redly. Now she was jabbing her hip with both drumsticks, holding them in one hand. They made quite a dent, and it was a perfectly curved hip. She was talking loudly above the record.

I was sweating now.

"Could I talk with you two?" I said, indicating Talbot and Patterson.

"What's this all about?" the woman said.

I sighed and looked at her.

"I'm Talbot's mother," she said. "I want to know what this is all about."

I told her a little of it. After some chatter, I managed to get Roy Patterson and Talbot Swanson outside. We stood under an oak tree by some sparkling cars. I was still sweating.

They were both cocky and wound up tight.

"My old lady's going to raise hell," Talbot said.

"What about your father?" Patterson said.

"He's out cold," Talbot said. "They brought him home in a taxi." He turned to me. "Mom and Dad been doing some drinking," he said. "Sometimes they do, you know how it is? But my father passed out downtown at his club. Mom wanted me to have a little party. She likes to play the drums."

"You knew Jinny Foster?"

"What's it to you?"

"Come on, Tal," Patterson said. "The hell with this."

"You're going to monkey around with her too much," Tal said to Patterson.

Patterson snickered. It reminded me of Inez. I stood there. I looked up at the sky. It was very deep blue and the stars were real bright. The moon had looped across and was starting down the other side now.

Talbot's mother came off the porch and across toward us. She walked with a fine high-heeled slink. She had only one drumstick now. She kept jabbing herself with it, her hip, her thigh, her midriff, her cheek. As she reached us, she scratched her head with it and leered at me some more.

"Why don't you have a little drinkee," she said.

"Go on back, Mom," Talbot said.

Patterson looked at her and snickered. She avoided Patterson with quiet adroitness. She came around by me, trailing clouds of gin.

"I could tell you anything you'd like to know," she said.

Patterson snickered.

"Damnit!" Talbot said. "Mom," he said. "Get to hell back in the damned house!"

"Tal, baby," his mother said.

Patterson crept up on her and caught the other end of the drumsticks. They faced each other and pulled and yanked for a second or two.

I took Talbot's arm and steered him around two cars.

"When did you last see Jinny Foster," I said.

"Jinny? Hell, I dunno. The other day."

I told him very carefully and quietly what had happened, trying to impress it on him.

"Dead, huh? Say, that's too bad. I'm sorry. I really am sorry about that."

I looked at him.

"Roy, don't!" Talbot's mother said from over there in the shadows. "Roy, dear. My, what—Roy! Stop it!"

Talbot sucked breath between his teeth.

"I'd appreciate it if you'd try to help me," I said.

"Sure, sure." He kept hitching his shoulders and glancing over in the shadows.

"Roy!" she whispered. It was a raw, heated whisper.

I heard the drumsticks rattle on the ground.

"Damn him!" Talbot said.

Patterson snickered.

Talbot's mother ran out of the shadows, laughing. She lost a shoe. Patterson ran after her. He picked the shoe up. They reached the side of the house, by some bushes. He caught her.

They faced each other, whispering. Then, tightly clutching each other, they moved along the side of the house into darkness.

Talbot shrugged and turned to me.

"Did you know Jinny Foster?" I said.

"You kidding?"

I was so damned mad my stomach hurt.

"Just answer the question."

"You got a search warrant?" He laughed and hitched his shoulders. "Yeah, I knew her well. Who didn't?" He stepped up close to me. "Listen," he said. "I want you to leave here, see? I don't care if you are a cop. You're busting up a private party and I don't like it."

I hauled the letter out of my pocket, took it out of the envelope and waved it in front of his eyes. I held it still.

"You wrote this," I said. "You're in a tight spot, Swanson. I don't like any part of you."

He grabbed the letter from me. I grabbed it back and looked at him.

"That little—!" he said. "I told her to—!"

Patterson had heard what I'd said about Jinny, and it hadn't touched him at all. Swanson, here, looked nasty enough to do anything, but I couldn't reach any of these people. I was getting no place very fast.

Talbot's mother came along the side of the house, carrying her shoe. She straightened her dress and brushed at her skirt, then lifted one long leg and put her shoe on. She moved toward us and she seemed a lot more sober, now.

"All right, Tal," she said. "In the house. Break up the party. It's all over. Everybody goes home."

"What?"

"That's what I said. Shall I repeat it?"

I saw Roy Patterson lurch around the side of the house. He paused and looked over our way, his face flashing whitely, then he went over to the porch entrance and on inside. The screen door whammed.

"I'm sorry, officer," Mrs. Swanson said. "Things seem to have gotten out of hand." She coughed gently through her fingers.

"Go on away, Mom."

She lifted her eyebrows at me and sighed. Children were such a problem, honestly.

"You got anything you'd like to tell me?" I said to Talbot.

"Tell you? No." He turned to his mother. "You think I'm busting up the party, you're nuts."

"That'll be just about enough of that," she said.

I turned and walked away from there. It was hopeless. I had to do some thinking. If I were really a cop, I'd have been able to do something. As it was, I was stopped.

"Well," I heard her say. "I guess that's that."

I felt real nice inside, after meeting those folks. I walked on down to where I'd parked the car in a kind of daze, carrying the letter in my hand. Finally, I put the letter into my pocket again.

7.

Andy Leonard tried to get rid of me the minute he saw me at the door. He came out onto the porch again, still wearing the red pajamas. He closed the door.

"Leave the car and get going," he said. "Now."

"Take it easy."

"I mean it, Cliff. I don't want to talk with you. Don't make me. It'll only put things in a worse light than they are already. If I see you again, I'll run you in—I'm on the case now. Just going to get dressed. No sleep tonight."

"What in hell do you mean?" I backed away from him, down the front walk. "You can't work tonight."

"We'll be on duty, though. You know that."

"What's up?"

He waved his arm, pointing down the street. "And don't take the car. I'm taking a chance, just talking to you."

"How else can I find out what's going on?"

"You can't. You aren't supposed to. . . . All right, you're the chief suspect, Cliff. And they think the girl was pregnant. They're not sure yet, but the report'll be in pretty quick."

I whistled softly.

"Now, get a move on."

"Thanks, Andy."

"Don't thank me."

I started away. "Listen," he said, jogging across the lawn. "I know you wouldn't do a thing like this, Cliff."

"Thanks, again."

"But you better stay low. Everything about what you've been doing smells. This Evelyn Thayer business. The boys are onto that."

"I'll get going."

I walked off. Once I looked back. He was still standing there on the lawn, looking wretched. I knew he hated to act the way he did. But it was his job, and he didn't want to lose his job. He could lose a lot more than that if they found out he was talking with me and had loaned me that car. He flagged his arm at me, turned, and moved toward the house.

I went on down the street. At the corner, I waited for a bus. Everything was fixed just fine, now—all tied up into a neat bundle with a fancy knot, and I was in the bundle.

It was getting late. The night was cool. Standing there, I let one bus pass me by, thinking things over. I decided to take a stab at trying to see Evelyn. I had to know how she was, there was no use trying to get around that. Sooner or later, I'd end up hanging around her place. So I took a bus over that way and, sitting there in the flashing darkness, listening to the squeaks and squawks as we lurched along over boom-day brick, I thought about Edward Thayer. He'd been in my mind a lot lately, for one reason and another.

Thayer was a pompous old fool. Not old in years, maybe, but pompous, for sure. And foolish, for damned certain. I hadn't figured he would come through with a divorce. He thought about his reputation, imagined what reputation he had hinged on the fact that no familial scandal revolved around his life. I wondered what he was bucking for. He wasn't a particularly good lawyer, although he thought he was. They talked about him behind his back down at city hall; they said he was a pompous old fool. He was a blunderer. In court, he was even worse than that.

He wore black, horn-rimmed glasses, and walking along the street with a briefcase under one arm, he held his head cocked a little to one side, and kept chewing the corner of his lip. Very impressive. He had no ideas. A lawyer without ideas is dead, done before he starts. Thayer knew his level, but he wouldn't admit it. He was frightened to death of legal procedure. He was frightened. He was scared of himself and the world and of his wife, and he didn't love his wife and never had. He loved himself. Once he told her he had married her because she knew how to mix martinis so well. He did this because he thought it was the right thing to do; kid her like that. He was really kidding himself. He didn't even like martinis, but he wished he did; he tried valiantly to like them, because it seemed some of the politically powerful individuals in town—necessary to Edward Thayer's mental welfare and monetary well-being—enjoyed martinis. This was the way of it with Attorney Thayer. He talked of this and that, and of State's Attorney, hintingly, at odd moments. Only he had no ideas. He could cock his head. He could chew his lip. He could kid his wife about martinis. He could wear expensive suits and walk grandly down the street. But he might just as well have been dead. And he knew it.

I got off the bus a block away from Evelyn's house.

She said it was awful, how he tried to memorize just a little something in the law books. He spent days and nights at the County Building, up in the library. She said that when he was in school, he hadn't even been able to memorize "The Spires of Oxford," or whatever the hell.

He's riding you, I thought. Get him the hell out of your head. You probably need some food. A good cup of coffee would be the thing. A good something.

• • •

I came down the street. The lights were out, except for the upstairs bedroom, where Edward was ensconced. He would be sitting up in bed, probably wearing steel-rimmed glasses, since nobody could see him—or maybe he went right on kidding himself in private, God knows—biting his fingernails and vainly studying things he couldn't get.

Her bedroom, downstairs, was blacked out. I followed a hedge of Turk's cap along the side of the house, then cut over toward her windows between some softly singing cedars.

"Hey!" I whispered, rapping on the sill under the screens. The windows were open and I could see her in there. She was undressing in the dark, standing in front of the mirror on her closet door.

"Oh, God!" She came over to the window. "You scared me. Cliff. What are you doing here? They just left, fifteen minutes ago."

"Take it easy. You look swell—good enough to nibble and chew."

"Cliff."

She'd had on a pair of stockings. Now she had on a thin dressing gown. A streetlight down the block found its way inside her room, paling the darkness, making it just right. That intimate coziness, conducive to contrary conduct. I knew I needed that coffee.

Then I saw she meant it. She was trembling and her face was as white as the sheets on the bed behind her. I could hear her breathe and it was the kind of breathing that goes hand in hand with panic.

"He phoned, Cliff."

"What?"

"He—*him*—the guy who killed Jinny Foster."

I plucked at the screens. They twanged. I sat on the outside sill, and leaned my face against the screen. She put her head against the screen on the other side and her palm was cold and damp.

"What'd he say?"

"He warned me not to say anything about seeing him. The police were right here, when I answered the phone. I told them it was a friend. I didn't know what to do. You said—"

"I know what I said."

"He said he'd get me."

"You look sweet, sweet."

"Cliff, what am I going to do?"

"Thinking about yourself, eh?"

"Cliff, it's no joke. He sounded kind of—well, nutty. He said nutty things. Insinuations about me, Cliff. He sounded, well—not right, or something."

"Imagination," I said, wondering what in hell to do.

"What are we going to do?"

"Everything's all right," I told her. "Don't worry."

"I'll scream, if you don't stop, Cliff. You should hear Edward! He cried, Cliff."

"Well, I'm sorry. I mean it. I really am sorry, damn it."

"Something's the matter with Edward."

I rapped lightly on the screen, and when she was silent, I told her everything, up to date.

"It's no help at all," she said. "You haven't been able to do a thing."

I stared down at the flower bed I was standing on. "I know it," I said. "A fine cop, I am."

"You're a good cop. Nobody could do anything. How could anybody do anything."

"You're getting hysterical," I said. "Take it easy."

"Yes."

"Now. How did this guy sound?"

She sat on the inside window sill and pressed against me. The screen bulged and bent, but it didn't give.

"Loosen the screen," I said. "Take it off."

She did. I climbed through the window and held her, kissing her, and she kissed me back, and shuddered and pressed against me and ran her hands up and down my arms. It was very good, holding her again, knowing she was all right. It was better than ever before. We stood there, hanging on to each other.

"How did he sound?" I said.

"Mushy—potato-mouthed. Like he was chewing shredded carrots."

"Handkerchief," I said. "Trying to disguise his voice. Silly, because you don't know him."

"He said he recognized me because I was so well known—because of Edward. Big monkey-monk, he said. He sounded scared, Cliff. Panicked."

I hoped she didn't sense what saying these things did to me. "Believe me, he *is* scared. Whoever he is, he's all alone, and frightened."

"And maybe desperate, Cliff."

"Yeah. All right. I'd better go."

She grinned at me.

"You do as he said. Now, how did you make out with the law?" I asked.

"All right. I insisted I took a walk. They insisted I didn't. They said I was with you, maybe. They added the maybe, and Edward gasped. I stuck to it. After they left, he smashed a vase against the wall and began to cry."

"Don't talk about him anymore. It's making me uncomfortable. You just keep on the way you're doing. I'll let you know in the morning. Something's got to break. If I can stay away from the police long enough, they'll get a lead—find out something. They'll be on the job, at least. If they have me, they won't be doing a damned thing. Without me, they can't touch you."

"Poor Cliff."

"I'm getting out of here," I said. "Before I—" I kissed her quickly, and thrust her away, and climbed out of the window into the flower bed. "Fair Juliet," I said, sweating. Flowers crisped beneath my feet.

I looked back at her.

She moved to the window and teased me.

"You'll be sorry," I said. "Wait and see."

"That's what you think. Cliff, be careful."

"You stay in the house, hear? Don't go out for anything."

"All right."

She did that again. It wasn't fair. I moved away. Out on the sidewalk, I started down toward town. I had to find a place to sleep. Nothing else could be done tonight and the way it looked, I'd just have to lay low tomorrow. Maybe I could come up with something. Maybe lying in a bed, somewhere, I could sort out everything I'd met with tonight. I wasn't much satisfied, though.

I got a room in a guest house, about eight blocks from Evelyn, climbed between the sheets and lay there thinking about her. I tried to think about other things, but it didn't work very well. Finally, I got up and took a bath, and went back to bed again.

That crazy household, out in Jungle Acres, kept coming back to me. I hadn't got much out of them, except for impressions. I needed something tangible to go on.

I lit the bed light, pawed for my pants, got out the letter to Jinny Foster, and lay there reading it over. It was what it was. Talbot Swanson could have done this thing.

Hell, so could anybody.

I thought of Inez Harrington. It seemed as if I could smell her. I went to sleep with the letter in my hand, and woke up late in the morning with the letter crumpled under my face, on the pillow. It was ten o'clock. I woke up with a resolution.

8.

Sometimes, the first thing in the morning before you're fully awake, your mind is the clearest it will be during the day; unencumbered by blocks, mental wars, the perpetually insistent troublesome trivialities which age you without your knowing it; in a nutshell, living. So, I woke up like that, knowing I was going to get dressed and walk over to Evelyn's and in at the front door and face Edward Thayer and tell him I loved his wife, and, man-to-man, have it out with the guy. It was senseless for either of us to continue the way we were. Thayer was a human being. Maybe the whole trouble was, he didn't understand.

It was so neat and clean that way. They employed a maid, and I visioned myself—as I hurriedly dressed—asking her to fix me some breakfast, while I discussed marital problems with Thayer.

On the way over, I thought how it was Saturday and a lot of men would be going fishing. They would be driving to my place out there on the bay. The police would greet them. No, they couldn't rent a boat. What did they know about Cliff Merritt? There would be talk of little girls sunk on anchors out in the bay. The boathouse would become haunted. They would wander around and stare at the house of The Fiend.

I waited at the end of the block, while a police car pulled away from the front of the house. Then I came on along the sidewalk, and turned bravely in at the front door. Maybe the sun was too bright. Maybe the bed I'd slept in had been soaked in tincture of opium. Anyway, it seemed the right thing to do.

The front door was wide open. A light was burning in the hall. As I rang the bell, looking inside, the maid came tearing through the house, with her hat in one hand, a coat half on, and a white apron slipping down her knees.

The phone was ringing.

The maid looked at me and screamed. She turned in mid-stride, started back where she had come. Her hat fell off. The apron slipped and she tripped, sprawling headlong in the hall. She was making little screams now. The phone stopped ringing and I went over and grabbed her hand. She nearly fainted.

"Come on," I said. "What's the matter?"

"Oh, oh!"

"Come on!" I knelt down beside her and looked her in the eye. "You've got something wrong," I said. "Somebody's been filling you with Mother Goose stories. Where's Mrs. Thayer?"

She kept looking at me and she began to calm down. She must have seen something in my eyes that assured her she was all right. I helped her up and she stood there looking at me.

"They said you're a—a—"

"Please," I said. "They're wrong."

"Mrs. Thayer's gone. They said you did it—you! She vanished from her bedroom, last night."

I held myself down. "Where's Mr. Thayer?"

"He—he went over to the Foster home." She kept shrinking away from me. I tried to talk with her. It's very difficult changing a person's opinion, once somebody else has made it up for them.

Turning, I went over to the telephone and yanked the wires out of the wall. I looked at the maid. She was quite young, and her eyes rounded. I grinned and that did it. She turned and ran out of the house, the apron flapping on one leg.

By the time she had reached the street, I was standing in Evelyn's bedroom. The Venetian blinds were torn off the window. The screen she'd taken out for me was on the floor, twisted and the mesh torn. That was all.

I went on through the window and out to the garage. Thayer's Cadillac was gone. Evelyn's red Buick convertible was there, so I took that and headed for the Foster place. I must still have had it in my head that I wanted to see Thayer.

Wouldn't it be grand, I thought, driving across town, if little Edward had conceived this whole thing?

9.

The Cadillac was parked in front of the Foster place and no police cars were in sight. If the law only knew. I parked the Buick behind the Cad, and ran up the front walk.

Thayer met me on the porch. He acted as if he were in training for ballet, the way he pranced around, waving his arms. He was dressed in a gray business suit, wearing his black horn-rimmed glasses. He kept dancing around, pointing at me, chopping his teeth up and down.

"You!" Thayer said, as I came up onto the porch. "You!"

"Take it easy," I told him. "Let's go inside."

"Ruined!" Thayer said. "I'm ruined—absolutely!"

I looked at him, gave him a shove. We went into the hallway and I saw the Fosters standing there. She was still crying and he had his arm around her. He released her and came toward me and there was a sick look in his eyes.

"Wait," I said. "You've got it wrong, I'm warning you. I wouldn't come here, if what you've heard is right."

"Oh, God, Frank," Mrs. Foster said.

Frank stopped and looked at me.

"I'm here to talk with Mr. Thayer," I said. "I'd appreciate it if you wouldn't try to use the phone. I have no gun, but I'll sure raise some hell, if you try something." I looked particularly at Frank Foster and knew how he felt. Only he wasn't sure about it, either.

"What have you done with Evelyn?" Thayer said. His voice was peculiarly even-toned.

"Please, Frank," Mrs. Foster said. "Don't try to do anything. The police will be here."

Foster stood there and stared at me, breathing rawly.

Thayer kept plucking at my arm. "I'll break you," he said. "I'll fix you in this town, Merritt. Scandal around my name. My wife."

"Let's not get too personal," I said, keeping an eye on Foster and hoping he wouldn't break. He looked tired and I knew what he'd been through. This didn't help any.

I turned to the Fosters. "Please," I said. "Let's sit down in there."

They looked at me, then turned and went into the living room and sat down on the couch. Thayer lumbered in and I looked at him and then at a chair. He went over and slumped in it, leaned back and fixed his gaze on me. I stood in front of him, with my back to the Fosters. Then I moved a little, so I could see the top of Frank Foster's head in a mirror up over Thayer's chair. There was no use pushing your opinion of a man too far.

"Now," I said. "Tell me how you found Evelyn was missing."

"You've ruined me," he said. "You've dragged my name through the mire." His shoulders dragged downward as he looked at me. "Evelyn and you."

"How did you find she was missing?"

"The police came. They wanted to talk with her again. I asked the maid to call her. My wife was gone."

"Your wife," I said softly.

He kept looking at me from behind the glasses.

"You heard nothing last night?" I said.

"No." He rose up a little in his chair. "Behind my back. You and her. I know, don't think I don't. All this. They'll get you, Merritt."

"Why don't you get me?"

"Don't think they won't," he said. "And I'm not finished with you, either. Her, either. I'll do something, by God. I'll have some satisfaction out of this. Evelyn can stay away, now—"

"You ever think she has no choice?" I said.

"Bah! You aren't kidding me for a minute, Merritt."

"That's the trouble with you," I said. "One of the troubles. You have no imagination."

"You can keep her wherever you took her," Thayer said. "The police will take care of that. That's not for me to decide. She needn't come back!"

"Ever think maybe she couldn't come back?"

He chewed the corner of his lip. "You aren't fooling me a minute," he said. "I've seen your kind in court."

I glanced at Frank Foster. He was frowning at Thayer.

"I'm going to divorce her now, by God," Thayer said. "She'll get what she asked for. Too late for anything else. Dirty, vile, wretched people."

"I'm going to tell you something," I said. "I didn't take Evelyn away and I had nothing to do with the Foster child." I turned and looked at them there on the couch. "That's the truth," I said. "You can believe that!"

"Liar!" Thayer said.

I looked back at him, feeling a little sore now.

"She's no damned good," Thayer said. "I know all about you. I know what you two have been doing. You think you've been kidding me, Merritt?"

"We weren't trying to kid you. Evelyn's in danger, can't you see that?"

"Serves her right. I'm sick and tired—"

"Stand up."

"What?"

I reached down and grabbed the front of his shirt and tie and mangled them up and lifted him to his feet and held him there. "Take your glasses off," I said.

"What?"

"You heard me." I tightened my grip a little, twisting.

He did not move.

I reached up and took his glasses off, folded them and plopped them into the breast pocket of his suit.

"Hold it right there," Andy Leonard said from the hall.

• • •

I turned and looked at him.

Thayer broke away and sat down again, smiling up at me.

Andy came into the room, followed by two uniformed cops. They were very young cops, with that fresh, pink look under their black-billed caps. Andy was wearing a sport jacket over the open throat of a white shirt.

"Sit down, Cliff," he said. "Over there." He gestured toward a chair on the other side of the couch. The Fosters sat there on the couch and watched silently.

Leonard turned to the two cops. "You two run back to headquarters and tell them I've got him," he said. "Everything's all right, now."

"Hadn't we better stay here?"

"It's all right," Andy said. He looked at me. "Isn't it, Cliff?"

I didn't say anything. He told them again to leave. One of them didn't want to. The other one tilted his head and shrugged his shoulders. Andy gave them the thumb. They sighed and left.

Andy looked at me. His coat was open and I could see his revolver sheathed on his belt on the left side where he always carried it. It was enough to make anybody sick.

Outside, I saw the police car go past the house. They had parked down a couple houses, playing it cagey.

"Well," Thayer said. "You got him. The dirty no good son of—"

Andy lifted his eyebrows at Thayer and Thayer shut up.

"Well?" Andy said,.

I walked past him into the hallway. He followed me. We stood there and looked at each other. There wasn't anything to say, that was the hell of it. He was doing his job. He had to keep on doing his job.

"We could talk about it," he said.

"What's the use?"

"I want to talk about it—before I take you downtown. That's why I sent them away."

"Nothing to say. What in hell can I say?"

Mrs. Foster came through the hall, moving toward the rear of the house. Her husband followed her. He didn't look at either of us. A moment later, Mrs. Foster returned and brushed past us, smelling of tears and sleeplessness. She stood by the front door and I saw why. The mailman was tinkling along on his bicycle. He turned up the walk, set the standard, and moved up the porch, sorting letters, walking quietly with his eyes turned down.

"Something," he said, handing her something. He turned and walked back to his bike, sorting letters. He rode away, tinkling.

Mrs. Foster turned and stood there, looking at the something in her hand. She sighed and laid it on a hall table.

"A library card," she said. "Oh, Jinny!" She began to cry. She hurried past us. Her husband poked his head out of a door at the end of the hall, and she ran into his arms. They closed the door.

"I wish you'd at least say something," Andy said.

I was on my way to the hall table. I picked up the card, my palms sweating, and read it. *"First notice,"* it said. *"Just to remind you that your book—THE MEDICAL ADVISOR—is overdue. Please return this book at your earliest convenience, as there are others waiting who also desire this book. Don't be selfish! Thank you kindly."* It was signed, *"Mary Robbins, Chief Librarian, Public Library."* It was postmarked this morning. It had been mailed only a few hours ago.

Jinny Foster never went to the library. If she started for the library, she never made it.

I laid the card down and looked at Andy. Somehow, I knew he wasn't going to believe this. He wouldn't listen and there was no time to lose, because I could see it and it was bad. Andy's face was expressionless, his eyes coldly accusing.

"Andy," I said. "There's something—listen—"

"You going to tell me all about it, now?" He stepped up to me. "I had you pegged for a friend," he said softly. "But you're a rat. I've been watching you and I don't like you. You almost got away with this, in my mind. But pulling this stunt with the Thayer woman touches off the spark, Cliff. I just want you to know how I feel, see?"

Thayer stretched around in his chair. "Tell him officer," he said.

I hit Andy on the jaw with everything I had. He stood there looking at me and I hit him again. I had never hit anybody that hard and I felt it all the way to the shoulder, like white hot wire along my arm. My knuckles were bright with pain as he went down. Thayer started to rise from his chair, then thought better of it, watching me.

I moved over to the telephone on a stand by the wall and ripped the wires out. I'd never done this before this morning. They had come loose easily, both times.

Turning, I glanced at Thayer. He was trembling, his jaw jiggling. The Fosters hadn't heard me, apparently. I got out of there, running for Evelyn's red convertible.

As I drove off, I heard Thayer yelling inside the house. He came out onto the porch, waving his arms. Then he went back inside and Frank Foster came out.

10.

I parked the car in front of the Roberson place and hurried up to the door. Mrs. Roberson answered the door and when she saw it was me, she gave a little shout in her throat, and tried to close the door.

"I just want to ask a question," I said. "Where's your son?"

"Go away!"

"Your husband isn't home?"

"Go away," she pleaded, pushing the door. I gave it a hard thrust and it slammed open. She ran down the hall. I caught her and held her. She had tremendous arms, very soft.

"My husband will be right back," she warned me. "He just went to the store."

"Where is your son?"

She shivered and her eyes were pools of fright.

"Come on," I said. "It's a matter of life and death, Mrs. Roberson. I'll leave, if you'll just tell me that. He upstairs?"

She shook her head. Her voice was a whisper. "He went up to the lake, to the camp. He took the bags up. We can't go till tonight."

"When did he leave?"

She shook her head, twisting to free herself now.

"Please," I said. "It's very important, believe me."

"The police told us who you are!" she said. Her voice was near to screaming.

"When did he leave?"

"He left a note. We found it this morning. He—he must have left very early."

"Thanks." I left her standing in the hall.

I had to take a big gamble. But if what I'd figured out about the library card was true, then young Sam Roberson had killed Jinny Foster and might even now be preparing to do the same thing to Evelyn. Or worse. Or maybe it was already done.

Heading along Route 19, I expected any minute to hear sirens approaching behind me. I let that Buick do whatever it could, which was plenty.

Lake Oklawachi lay inland, far from the main northern route, about an hour and a half drive from town. I wound in and out on dirt roads, and because I'd never before been over this way, had difficulty in finding the place. Eventually I came along a stretch of macadam and saw a string of signs advertising a hamburger stand on the lake.

The country was wild. The hamburger stand no longer existed. The lake nestled in the midst of dark, thriving jungle, the black waters reflecting the sky as brightly as a mirror. Festoons of Spanish moss dribbled and waved from tremendous oaks along the road, brushing the car's top as I drove along. I spotted a cabin near the shore. There was a tall, gray-haired, overall-clad man out back, sawing pine logs on a small trestle. I stopped the car and went up to him.

"Could you tell me where the Roberson place is?"

"Over there. Sam Roberson?"

"That's right."

"Over there." He pointed with the saw across the lake. He was middle-aged, with a paunch, and he was interested in sawing his wood. "Follow the dirt road as far as you can. When that quits, follow the path. Only cabin that side of the lake. Young Sam's up there, though. Wife seen him breeze by just about daylight this morning."

"She did?"

"Uh-huh. That's right. Was young Sam's Ford, all right, too. Ain't seen hide or hair of him out fishin', though, either. Should of been out by now, for sure. Usually is, generally."

"Thanks." I was already on my way back to the car.

"See him, say 'Howdy from Bill,' hey? I'm Bill, hear?"

I waved and started the Buick. He was sawing again.

Big rambling-limbed oaks and moss and tangled snarls of undergrowth hid the road now from the far side of the lake. The road went on into jungle, running up and down over sloping hillocks. I drove through a short stretch of hub-high swamp without miring, and came out on sand and curved around through denser jungle. There was the Ford.

It was parked in the undergrowth, driven into it as far is it would go. The road just quit. Beyond the road, a path took over, vanishing into vines and greenery.

I got out and went over to the Ford and had a look. All I could think about was Evelyn—Evelyn, and then I found the book. It was down under the front seat of the two-door sedan, so you wouldn't see it unless you were looking—or remembered. Sam Roberson hadn't remembered; at least not last night.

It was "The Medical Advisor."

11.

I went over the rest of the car quickly. There was a woman's shoe on the floor in back. The shoe was green alligator and I recognized it as Evelyn's.

I was already running along the path, vines and branches whipping at my face. Sam Roberson was a killer. He had flunked out. And Evelyn was with him.

I broke out of the path into well-mowed lawn, sun beating down on a large cabin close against the woods. The lawn was mowed clear to the lake. Another shack stood down by the water's edge and a boat bobbed, tied to an ancient wooden pier.

I crossed the lawn, came onto the cabin porch. Young Sam Roberson was sweeping out the front room. He had the door propped open with a brick and he looked up, saw me, and grinned.

"Hello, there," he said. "What you doing way out here?"

I swallowed and stepped inside. The dust was thick. He leaned on the broom. He was wearing a pair of khaki shorts and acting fine, only I saw the glimmer behind his eyes—the tight glimmer of confusion. He was a case. Sometimes you don't know how to deal with a case. This lad was prime.

"Just sweeping up," he said. "Clean up for the folks. They couldn't make it till tonight. Thought I'd get an early start. They tell you I'd come up?"

He was talking too much, and he knew that, too.

"Yes," I said. "Your mother said you'd brought their luggage up."

"That's right. How about a Coke? I brought Cokes and ice, too."

"No, thanks."

"Better have one. They're real cold."

"Thanks, no."

"Guess I'll have one. Excuse me." He started for the kitchen, carrying the broom. I went along with it. He stopped in the kitchen doorway. "The heck with it," he said. "I'll save it till I finish sweeping. Appreciate it more, that way. This dust!"

"Sure is dusty."

"Sure is."

We looked at each other. He made a few swipes with the broom. He was swallowing a lot and he was thinking to beat the band. The sweat was popping all over him, like young pearls. Sweat trickled down the sides of his face, out of his blond crew-cut. He kept making weak passes with the broom, missing the spots he should be sweeping.

"How come you're up here?" he said. "Glad to have you. Get in some good fishing."

"Lots of fish, eh?"

He propped the broom against the wall, and wiped his hands on his shorts and looked at me. He was a big guy, and he was in top condition, and he was letting me know it. Just in case. His eyes were bloodshot, not at all like the clear whites they should have been. He took out a handkerchief and blew his nose.

"I found Jinny's book in your car, Sam. She didn't go to the library. You took her out there and killed her. It isn't going to work."

He paused, blowing his nose, then went on. He wiped his nose and rammed the handkerchief into his back pocket, and looked at me. His face was without expression, his mouth relaxed.

"Where's Evelyn Thayer?" I said. "Where is she, Sam?"

"What are you talking about?"

His eyes began to move from one corner of the room to the other. The room was sparsely furnished, with tough, rustic furniture.

"How does a kid like you get this way?" I said.

"Kid like me?" His voice was very mild.

"If you've harmed her," I said, "I'm going to kill you, Sam. I mean it very sincerely. Kid or no kid."

He thrust his jaw out, holding that way, the tendons in his neck standing out like rope. A muscle in his shoulder began to jump---jump—jump. Then he jumped.

He came at me like a bullet, dashed to the side and headed for the door. I tackled him in the doorway and we sprawled out onto the porch. He was soaking wet, slippery as a greased rag. He began to curse steadily, scrabbling across the porch toward the brick that held the door open. That brick had been in his mind ever since I'd entered the cabin, I was sure.

He got out from under me and got the brick and turned, bringing it down on my arm. Like a trip-hammer. I went right into the brick, beating at me, and grabbed him by the throat, lifting. I slung him back across the porch and he lost the brick. I dove at him. He wasn't there.

"You're an old man, mister," he said.

I looked up. He came at me, leaping, both feet ramming for my face. I sat up into that, too, grabbing the feet. I caught his feet, slung them upward and he crashed onto his back.

He began to laugh and I saw the knife. The switchblade was in his hand, from one of his pockets, and he came at me across the porch, moving on his knees.

"Yeah," he said. "I killed her. She was going to say it was our kid. She and me, we were going to do an abortion. But she got scared, see?"

I listened and watched. The kid was out of his head.

"She got scared and said she'd tell."

He came at me, running on his knees, then diving, with the knife like a spear.

I let him get in close with the knife on a long stab, then came up on his arm. I got his wrist and I was mad. I stood up with the wrist, holding his arm with the knife out there and looked down into his eyes. I bent him over backward, using my leg and knee. Then I looked into his eyes again.

"Don't," he said. "Don't."

I brought his arm down across my knee and the knife clattered on the porch floor. He gave a kick and a twist, under me. I went up and I grabbed him and flung him. We both went over the porch railing of the cabin and hit the ground and he screamed.

He screamed again, groveling in the dirt.

"My arm!" he yelled. "My arm's busted!"

I got up and looked down at him. His right arm had two elbows. You could see the bright bloody bone.

"Where is she?" I said.

"In the boathouse—don't touch me."

"On your feet."

"Don't touch me—you busted my damned arm."

I grabbed him, yanked him to his feet and sent him reeling and stumbling down the slope of lawn toward the boathouse. He tried to turn, stumbling, so he could watch me. His mouth was open and he kept moaning, and then he started to become really conscious of his arm. He flung it around and it looked very odd, the way it flipped and flopped. He began to moan and grunt again with the pain.

I gave him another shove. We reached the boathouse and he tripped and fell through the door onto the floor, moaning. It was a shack, really, filled with fishing paraphernalia, and when the door swung inward, I saw Evelyn lying on a rolled-out mass of fish net.

12.

I moved quickly over to her, holding my breath a little, hoping she was all right. He had jammed a cork from one of the nets into her mouth and tied it around her face and head with rope. Her hands and feet were tied and tangled in the fish net.

All I could see was the horror in her eyes.

I untied the gag. Her eyes were bright and sick with the kind of terror that might take time to go away. If he'd hurt her, I knew what I'd do to him.

"Evelyn," I said. "Evelyn."

She tried to speak but the tears welled in her eyes.

"It's all right," I said. "Everything's all right now."

She shivered and nodded and kept staring at him over there on the floor, as I released her from the viciously knotted tangle of the net. Her pallor had me scared and I didn't like the way she kept trembling and trying to speak.

"Oh, Cliff," she said finally. "Thank God, Cliff."

We both stiffened as he laughed a little, then moaned some more. He just lay there with his arm beside him—a young kid, staring at his arm with the two elbows.

I gripped her shoulders. "Did he hurt you in the car?"

She shook her head, watching me. I could feel her tense shuddering and I hated to think of what she'd been through.

"No," she said. Her voice was weak. "But he's far from being a kid. I mean—you know what I mean."

Things blurred a little.

She clutched at me as I knelt beside her, her fingers biting sharply into my arms. Then I could feel her growing calmer.

"He tried," she said. "He tried plenty, but I'm no kid, either, Cliff."

He moaned again over there.

"He—he just came right through the bedroom window and I saw him. I was in bed," she said.

I helped her to her feet. Her dress, an aqua evening gown, was ripped down the skirt and covered with dirt. Her soft hair was full of cobwebs, but otherwise she seemed unharmed. At least on the outside. But I didn't like the look in her eyes, the frightened way she still clung to me. Then she seemed to relax a bit more. She stood there, looking over at Sam Roberson with a peculiar twist to her lips—as if she might like to spit.

"He had this knife," she said. "He told me he'd kill me if I said anything. He panicked, Cliff. When you went and saw him, he told me he knew then that he had to get me. He recognized you—and he knew I'd seen him; at least he thought I had. Time kept running short and he worried himself into it. He made me put this on—holding the knife point against me. Cliff, it was awful!"

I waited, and she got hold of herself. She moved closer to me, watching him. He was still looking at his arm, sweating there on the floor.

"We were nearly up here when he stopped the car. I figured, this is it. He made me get into the back seat and then he told me about Jinny Foster. How she was—what she was doing with all the high school boys and that she was going to have a baby. He was the father. He told me that's what prompted her to act like she did with the other kids. They read up on abortions, trying to find how. But after they planned that, she wouldn't let him."

"He told me."

"She was going to tell on him. So he picked her up and took her out to the beach. When he stopped the car, she ran. Then he killed her."

"In the car," I said. *"Did he hurt you?"*

"We'll just go away," she said. "Won't we, Cliff?"

She looked down at Roberson again, then moved into my arms. He kept watching her with his bright bloodshot eyes.

"You sure he didn't hurt you?" I asked again.

She turned in my arms and looked at him once more. Then she looked at me.

"No," she said. "I'm fine, Cliff. Really."

She began to cry, very softly.

Death Comes Last

Hunted Detective Story Magazine
October 1955

They stood up there on the sea wall and looked at me. I stepped off the stern onto the pier. There wasn't a damned thing you could do. They had what you call a legit beef. Even if it wasn't, it would look that way. The one, Armbruster, was already out by the slip gate.

"It's tough, Howe. We sympathize, but you can see our side, can't you? You can't expect us to pay you when we didn't even catch a fish. Not one."

"Sometimes it's that way," I said.

"Let's go," the fat one said. "Let's go, Rudy."

"Hell," Rudy said. "I feel sorry for him."

"If it's the wrist watch," I said. "I'm sorry it happened. I told you I'd dive for it."

"Who do you think you are? Beebe?"

"No," the one called Rudy said. "It's the idea of the whole thing, Howe. We chartered your boat. We were out there three days. We didn't catch anything. We're all sunburned—look at us."

I looked at them. I wanted to laugh. They were a fine trio of lobsters, for a fact.

"I would have brought you in," I said. "Any time. You wanted to stay nights and all."

"You lost Holly's watch," Rudy said. "Armbruster's been sick. It's a mess. The watch cost over seven hundred dollars. You figure it."

"Yeah," Armbruster said. "You figure it. Nuts. Let's go, guys."

"But, look—listen," I said.

They turned and went. The slip gate slapped. They went up to their Cadillac parked by the curb. There was a blonde in it, waiting. There wasn't a thing I could do. The blonde was laughing at them. Laugh, blonde.

I went back aboard and sat down on one of the deck chairs in the stern. Armbruster had ripped the canvas. It was fine, all right. Just perfect.

Well, the hell with that. They'd given me twenty-five dollars to start. I had that. Deadbeats. You get them. I went inside the cabin and down into the galley and looked in the cracker tin. Yeah. I had the twenty-five.

I came back up by the wheel and started her, then went out and flung the lines, and backed her, and cut over toward the gas dock. I spent the twenty-five on gas, and headed out into Tampa Bay for the channel.

Jean would be waiting. Well, great.

Coming along the channel, I swung the boat south and kept myself from thinking until we were past the Sunshine Skyway bridge. Then I headed her for Pass-a-Grille.

She was running nice. The twin Gray Marines were like old thunder and she was pretty clean, too. They hadn't done any fishing. Just sat out there soaking up gin and beer, talking about last year in the Keys. Until I lost that damned watch overboard.

I should have gone over after it. I could have made it. I watched it twinkle, going down. Why in hell did he ever ask me to hold his damned watch?

Jean, I thought. The ball's off.

Well, maybe we could have a sort of ball. So I got to thinking about her. How she was. How it was with us. How we ought to get married—and to hell with that, too. Not the marriage. The waiting and not having the dough, and all.

I brought the boat in past the sun-blasted fingers they're putting out on the bayside of Pass-a-Grille, thinking how they've gone and ruined all the fine spearing and fishing.

What a mess. It had been a good spot. Pretty, too.

The folks without riparian rights would sure be yelling. Nice homes for years, with their own piers and docks on the channel, looking out on the green keys. So now they dredge and come along and dump sand and crushed shell in the front yards.

I was avoiding thinking of Jean. I brought the boat in by my pier and looked at the shack. They hadn't got up this far yet with their stinking scows.

I flipped the stern line over the piling, shut her off, cut along the outside deck and grabbed the bowline. I jumped for the pier, and tied her.

The hell with it. Three lousy days. And I thought I'd had something good. The rich ones from up North.

• • •

I came down the Gulf beach, walking fast. I wanted to see her bad. She wasn't out on the beach. The house back there looked quiet. There's a look about an empty house. You know? It wasn't empty, though.

I cut up the path. Her folks had left her the house. She wanted to get married, anyway. It was me, old Earl, holding out.

The screen door was locked. It was a big place for down here. Three stories. I could see the grandfather's clock in the hall.

Two-thirty. She should have been out swimming.

"Oh, Jean!"

No answer.

"Jean? The door—it's locked."

I rattled the door. It had rained this morning. You'd never know it now. It was hot, let me tell you.

"Earl?"

"Yeah."

She was like whispering, coming down the hall. I looked at her. She looked good. Damned fine. Wonderful. She was wearing her green bathing suit, the skimpy one-piece outfit with the ruffled top, like a flower opening up. My legs got watery, like always. Jean's small, real tiny, but with that kind of body—you know—soft. Lush. Nice.

Black hair. The blackest. And long, down over the shoulders, like now, coming along the hall, whispering.

"Earl?"

"Unlock the door. I been gone three days."

She didn't say anything. She stood there on the other side of the door and looked at me. It was a bad look. I could tell. It was like she was shutting the door. It's the damnedest way they have.

"You're back."

Ordinarily I would have clowned it up. You know, looking around, saying, "Who? Me back?," only not the way she was looking at me.

"Listen," I said. "I've been thinking about you for three days and two-and-a-half nights, or something like that. A long time." I put my palms against the screen door, watching her. "You going to open the door?"

"No."

"I break in?"

"Don't touch the door, Earl."

I took my hands down and looked at her real carefully. There was this look, all right. The one they get. When they close down shop.

I'd thought I was through with that look.

"Honey," I said. "It's me. Earl. Your ever-lovin'. Remember? I love you, baby. Me. Earl. I been out there." I pointed out on the Gulf. "Thinking about you. With three hamburgers. I had six bottles of beer. They did me out of my money. I lost a seven-hundred-dollar wrist watch. We never had a bite. I got four dollars and sixty cents. Me. Earl. Huh?"

"Go away."

"Huh?"

"I said—you heard me."

We watched each other. She had some cotton stuck on the screen to keep the mosquitos off. I yanked two of the cotton balls and dropped them on the porch. She watched me. The hell.

"I don't want to see you, Earl."

Cold. Freezing. I kept on looking at her. I stood real still. There's no way to fight it. Everything's perfect for a long time. Then they pull the shade, like. It's all over, lover—go home.

Not Jean. For gosh sakes. Not her.

I loved her. I honest to God did love this girl.

"You're joking," I said. "I can't take it. I'm tired or something. Maybe it's because I'm hungry. Open the door and kiss me and fix me some eggs, will you? Huh?"

She just stood there in that tight green suit, kind of batting her knees in and out. Her tan was the golden kind, always that way. Full and rich and soft and tan and warm. She had big eyes. Black, too. They were shiny.

"You been drinking, honey?"

"No, Earl."

"Do I rate an explanation?"

"There's nothing to explain. I just want you to go away. Don't come back. I don't want to see you."

"Baby," I said. "Hang on, will you—get a grip? You're all I've got. I love you. I don't dig this."

She tightened her lips. It was like squeezing two ripe cherries together. The way she looked made me want to cry. She was holding something back. She'd look at me and the bad business would fade and brighten in her eyes. Under the tan, she was pale.

"In three days you've found Sir Galahad on a white raft and floated to Paradise? That it? Somebody else?"

She watched me. She began to rub one hand up and down her arm, standing real stiff.

Back there in the house something banged on the floor. A man coughed. Down inside my chest it was as if the whole world went to pot in one gorgeous bang.

She began to nod. "Yes," she said. "Yes, Earl. That's right."

We stared at each other. The grandfather's clock ticked.

"You got to let me in there!"

She slammed the door. I heard the lock click.

I heard her walk away down the hall.

"Jean—!"

A beaut of a gust of wind came in off the Gulf. Sand swirled across the porch, eddying around my feet, sifting softly and leaving a fine trail.

Some other guy. In three days she'd forgotten something it took two and a half years to build.

It eats the hell right out of you.

I went on down the porch and out to the beach. For maybe fifteen minutes I stood out there, watching the Gulf. When I looked at the house, there was no sign of life. Oh, but there'd be life inside the house. I knew Jean.

I tell you, it's rough. Somebody said when they get you this hard, you better run. I didn't want to run. Didn't she know what she was doing?

She knew. Goodbye, Earl. You lunkhead.

I started down the beach. When they pull the shade, it doesn't do any good knocking your head against the wall.

I began to get mad.

• • •

"Oh, say—excuse me!"

I looked over there. A girl was kneeling on a big red beach towel, motioning to me as I walked along. She was on the beach in front of some cabanas and the only other person around was a fat guy attempting some surf fishing about twenty-five yards off. He had his line tangled.

"Do you have a match?" she said. "I've come out and forgot my matches."

I walked over and looked at her. I reached for my lighter and our hands touched as she took it from me. She leaned back on one hip and lit her cigarette, kind of eyeing me. Well, now—I don't know. There she was on a red towel as big as a living room rug. She wore a two-piece red swim-suit, and she was chocolate-milk brown from the sun, with lips to match the suit, and fingernails and toenails to match the lips, and pale blue eyes that kind of bleared when you looked at them. And the cream was the pale blonde hair, all thick swirls and curls.

This one had the longest legs I'd ever seen on any girl, and they were fine legs, and the rest of her was fine.

"Thanks," she said. "Care for a drink? Justice in return, all that?"

She hauled a big thermos bottle from behind her and started to stand up. Then she looked at me and patted the towel, smiling.

You could smell the sun-tan lotion and the perfume, not strong, just right. Elusive. Tantalizing.

And Jean was back there, after three days, with a guy.

"Sure. I could go a drink." I grinned at her.

"Sit down, friend."

I sat down. I felt funny, me dressed and her nearly naked. Worse than naked. And when she smiled her teeth were milk-white and even between the lips.

She leaned toward me and smiled. "I've been drinking all alone," she said. She put one hand on my arm, holding the thermos on her thigh. I stared out at the Gulf. The guy was tangled up with his line worse than ever.

"I don't want you to get the wrong impression," she said.

"You dropped your cigarette." I picked it off the towel and rubbed the burnt spot.

"You don't mind having a drink with me?"

"Hell, why should I?"

"That's the way to talk." She had a nice way of speaking, even if she had been at that thermos a bit hard. Her words came out with precision, and her voice was soft. All of this was extremely unlikely, so I looked at her again, trying to find some flaw. There wasn't any.

"Here." She handed me the tin cup off the top of the thermos. "It's nice and cold. Martinis. Like?"

I tasted. It was delicious and icy cold.

"I suppose you think I'm forward," she said.

"Certainly not."

"Liar." She took the cup and had one herself, then poured me another and corked the bottle and sat up with her arms clasped around her knees. The line of her thigh was softly aggressive. I watched the Gulf determinedly.

She said, "I've made up my mind. The next man who came along, I'd ask him for a match." She touched my arm. "I have matches, you know?"

"I know."

"Probably you don't, really. It's that I'm very lonely. Maybe that's difficult to understand. For five days I've been here and I don't know a soul."

Damn Jean. "You know me," I said.

"Thanks. I'm Lucille Warren. I'm from New York, on vacation. I'm a stenographer and it took me a long time to save up for this, and now look. Frankly, I'm lonely." She chuckled and eyed me that way, sideways. She brushed a curl of hair out of the way and grinned. "You mind?"

I told her my name. She looked at me and swallowed and said, "Let's have another drink, Earl? O. K.?"

Well, we sure as hell did that. The more I drank, the worse I felt about Jean over there in the house with that guy. And guilty about being with this girl in the red bathing suit, too—which made no sense. Two could play; all that stuff. And Lucille lay back on the red towel and watched me. Everywhere soft gold and red and cream and with all that leg she had, and all the rest, and the eyes, too.

"Earl," she said. She said it very quietly.

I leaned down to hear her better. Her eyes were pale.

"Kiss me, will you?"

I kissed her and she kissed back hard and hot, and she rolled over on her side and it was like a steam bath, flavored sweetly, and like no steam bath you ever heard of, either.

"Thanks, Earl."

I stared at her. Jean, I said to myself, I didn't mean anything. There's something screwy about this one, Jean.

The thermos was empty and she insisted I come to her cabana, where she claimed to have a fresh supply. She did.

"The chance of being lonely, Earl."

Here in the cabana, her smile was a bit more personal, and when she moved, it was toward you. She knew how I was looking at her and trying not to. Because I'd be mad about Jean and that guy, then not mad.

"Lucille, how's about me running over to my place and putting on a pair of shorts? The way you are, and all?"

"How am I, daddy?"

I didn't say anything. She grinned and slapped her thigh. I looked out the front window. The guy was still out there. As I looked, he tripped on his line and fell sprawling into the drink. Lucille slapped her thigh again.

"Where do you live, Earl?"

I told her and she had to come along. We crossed the beach road and entered Pass-a-Grille, under the thick shade, and cut down to my lot. Fifty by seventy-five, but that was all right because I had it hedged with Australian pine.

"It's small, Earl—but it's cozy."

"It'll only be a minute."

I stared at my Ford coupe, parked against the side of the shack. She was moving toward the pier.

"Oh, what a pretty boat. Yours, Earl?"

"Yeah." So she went on down to the pier. I went inside and stripped and got my shorts on. I was tanked up more than I thought. I was rushing. I was nervous as a cat. I couldn't get my breath. Jean. Damnit.

"Your boat's swell," Lucille said. She was lying on the couch in the deck cabin, with her long legs folded over the back, her head hanging down. She looked at me and winked.

"Listen," I said. "Look—Lucille—"

"Yes, daddy?"

I went down into the galley and stood there, braced against the sink. I shut my eyes tight. Red bathing suit.

"What were you trying to say, Earl?" she called.

"Nothing. Want a drink?"

"Yes, daddy. Make eet beeg wan, hey?"

• • •

Sometime during the crazy mixed-up night, I was pounding on Jean's door again. There were lights inside there, and the radio was playing real loud. "Jean, Jean!" No answer. Around the side. I looked through the window. She was still in the green bathing suit, standing by the fireplace with a drink in her hand. Jean wasn't much for drinking, but when she moved I could tell she was tight. Everybody was. I was sick all over. A man called her name. "Jeannie?" It sent me nuts. I beat on the window. She turned and veered across the room and looked out at me. Her lips said, "Go away!" She pulled the blinds. A man laughed.

I went away. Like the crow. To Lucille.

2.

"Good morning, daddy!"

I looked at her. My head ached. She was sitting on the edge of the bed, leaning over, rumpling my hair.

"You slept late, Earl."

I sat up like I was sprung, remembering. She didn't move. "Here," she said, handing me a tall, cool-looking glass. It tinkled. "Hurry up, Earl. Lots to do. Drink it down."

I set it carefully on the night stand and kept staring at her. "Where are we?"

"Oh, you've forgotten. We're at my place."

She had on tight black shorts, let me tell you, and a skimpy black bra around topside. She looked like a million. I was wearing a sheet up to my waist and the bed smelled of her perfume.

I thought of Jean and wanted out of there. Now.

"All right, Earl," Lucille said. "I'm laying my cards on the table. We've taken care of everything else."

"What?"

"All right," she said. She reached over and took the drink and drank half of it, watching me over the rim of the glass. "I'm going to be as frank as we've been with each other all along, Earl. You told me everything. All your secret aches and pains."

"What are you getting at?"

"Jean. Little Jean, remember?"

I watched her. I tossed the sheet off, got up. She watched me. I felt plenty bad.

"The guy over there, too," Lucille said. "Well, buster. You want money." She stood up, tall and terrific, and drank the rest of the drink and set the glass down. "I want money, too. Didn't you wonder why I was so easy?"

"What?"

She chuckled. "You're nice, though, daddy. Only there's more to it. Straight out, Earl—you're going to help me get some money. I'm not answering questions. But if you don't help me, I'm going to little Jean."

We watched each other and she stepped up to me. "It doesn't have to change anything, Earl."

I backed toward the door.

She grinned and shook her head. "The guy, Earl. He's loaded, and it's with him. Him and your Jean. And you're going to get it for us. See?"

"You're pickled in that stuff," I said.

"Not so much I couldn't tell Jean about last night."

I got hold of the doorknob, and twisted. The door came open. She went back across the room and flopped on the bed on her back, propped up on her elbows. Grinning. She brushed a wave of that soft, pale hair out of one eye.

I opened the door and started out.

"You'll be back, Earl. Think it over."

I got outside and closed the door. She didn't speak from in there. Then I heard the clink of glass against glass. I kept trying to remember last night. It was all a blank, after I returned to her place from Jean's. All I remembered was that red bathing suit and the way her teeth shone between her lips.

What had she been trying to say?

Jean and a guy—with money? So what? Oh, sure—only who was Lucille?

So then I knew I was going to see Jean and talk to her. No matter what. I started up the beach toward her place. It was a fine bright morning. The palms were limber and green against the clear blue sky. I felt so sick I could hardly walk. I was in my bare feet.

* * *

Jean opened the door and looked at me through the screen.

"Open the screen door," I said, "or it comes off the hinges."

"What, Earl? What are you talking about?" She reached out, unlocked the door, and gave it a shove with her knee. It opened and she stood there looking at me, wide-eyed and smiling. She moved her legs beneath the tight white skirt, and tucked the tails of her white blouse beneath the waist. Her thick black hair shone in the sunlight that slammed across the porch.

Right away there was that old feeling. I always got it with Jean. Wanting to touch the leaning softness of her.

"Well, come in, Earl. What's the matter."

"Matter? You know damned well what's the matter."

I stepped in and she stepped back until I was over the threshold. Then she moved against me and it was like yesterday should have been. The door slammed. Right away I wondered why I'd ever stopped to give Lucille a match. Because what Jean did to me, Lucille couldn't approach.

She got her mouth on mine and her body swung tight, her arms up, circling my neck. I pulled them down and held her off. "Where is he?"

"Earl, don't! Honey—!"

"I'm right here," some guy said.

I looked over the top of Jean's head down the hall, and there he was, all right.

"Oh, Kurt," Jean said. She kind of clung to me a minute, then drifted over against the wall, watching him.

"Come on," Kurt said. "Close the door, and lock it and come on in here." He was holding a gun in his hand, and he was a tough-looking baby, right enough. They don't come looking any tougher than this Kurt. The gun was an automatic, and a big one. It looked like a forty-five. It was steady.

I just stood there staring. Jean went and locked the screen door, and closed the inside door and locked that, too.

"What's going on?" I said.

"Come along," Kurt said.

I still didn't move.

"You better, Earl," Jean said. "You better do like Kurt says, Earl. Honest."

He was big, maybe six-three. He had plenty of shoulder under the dirty white net sports shirt, and there was a tear down the front of the shirt. He had great big gobs of red hair, like red Georgia clay bunched on top of his head, and he needed a shave, and as he spoke, he grinned and his teeth looked like they'd been whittled out of sugar lumps, they were that white and even. You could have hung a suitcase on the thrust of his jaw.

"Get rid of that thing," I told him. "Put it away. Jean and I been together for over two years. You step in, you got to expect—"

"Shut your yap!"

"—you got to expect I won't feel too happy about it. Now, just put that—"

"Did you hear me?" He stepped down the hall, walking like a cat, and stopped about two feet away.

"Please, Earl," Jean said in a small voice.

"This is nutty," I said. "What do you intend—"

"Shut up!"

"Yeah?" I said. "Nuts to you."

The gun whipped out, flashing upward. It raked along the side of my jaw and the blood got hot and streamed down onto my bare chest. It trickled into the beltline of my shorts. I stood there watching him. He jammed the gun barrel into my gut with a sock. I doubled with pain. He lifted the barrel up neatly and caught me smack on the forehead. He'd marked me good again.

"Kurt, stop," Jean said.

"Thanks for opening the door," I said to her. "You're accommodating. How long did it take you two to figure this one out?"

Kurt made a move again.

"No, Kurt," Jean said.

"Sorry," Kurt said. "But, honey—you've got to let them know quickly. You see? You should know that. Now we won't have any trouble—will we, Earl?"

I looked at Jean. "Who is this?"

"Come on in the other room," Kurt said. "I'm tired of standing up all the time."

"He's my brother," Jean said. "Kurt's my brother."

Kurt beamed at me. "Fetch him a towel, honey. He's bleeding. And bring me my styptic pencil." Then he came over to my side and rapped the gun against my arm. We marched down the hall and turned through the alcove to the right into the living room.

"I'm sorry, Earl," Jean said. She went on down the hall and returned with a towel. I took it and started mopping.

"Sit down in that chair," Kurt said.

I went over and sat down. He came up with the styptic pencil, pushed my head back and rubbed it into my forehead and jaw. It burned like hell. He tossed the pencil on the floor, went over and slumped into a chair.

There was something about his eyes I didn't like. They had a dead look. His mouth grinned, but nothing happened to the eyes. As if they were mirrors. Kurt was a wrong guy. He was dangerous. And he was desperate as hell. The way he sat in that chair, grinning, was something to see.

Jean kept walking up and down. You could see the movement of the flesh under the tight white skirt. When she looked at me, her eyes were afraid.

"Earl," she said, "do what he says."

"She understands me," Kurt said. "Sis always understands me, don't you, Sis?"

They looked at each other. He grinned, and then she smiled at him. It was a soft smile and it was all full of tears.

Jean was his sister?

And Lucille knew him? He was supposed to have money and she was after it. She'd nailed me for some sort of game, only that was shot, too. I wondered if he knew about Lucille?

I nearly asked him. Then I thought better of it. There was no telling.

"I didn't know what I was going to do," Kurt said. "I don't like putting Sis in a spot like this."

I looked at her. She believed him. You could tell he didn't give a damn which way was up. But she trusted this guy.

"Sis and I have been real close, always—isn't that right, Sis?"

"Yes." She nodded, half looking at me. "Only Kurt's been away, Earl."

Kurt laughed over that one. "I'll say," he said. "I've been away, all right." Then his face got serious. "Now, listen. You didn't step into this, Earl, until Sis mentioned you had a boat. Right?"

"A boat?"

"I'm in a ticklish spot," he said. "I did a little thing over in Tampa, see? You don't need to know about that, though. What it was. The police are after me, Earl. Really after me. Shoot on sight; like that."

I didn't want him to tell me. I didn't like the expression on his face. He was leering behind his mask.

"You're going to get your car, Earl. You're going to drive it upstate, to a little place called Star Gap. It's on the mouth of the Oklawatchi river. Got that? You know where it is? It's not too far."

I didn't say anything. I knew where he meant.

"Kurt," Jean said. "Please. Isn't there some other way?"

"No, Sis. No, there isn't."

"Couldn't you just go?" she said.

He looked at her. "You don't want me shot down, do you, Sis? That's what'll happen." He shook his head. "Nope. We do it my way. It's the best way, Sis. I always think of the best way. Come here, Sis."

She looked at him. She was afraid of him. But there was something else. She couldn't help herself. When he spoke, she had to obey. She went over to him and he put his arm around her waist, sitting there, and looked up at her with those damned eyes. And she looked at him and smiled and patted his shoulder. It was written all over him: Doublecross. She didn't mean anything to him. It was plain, like a sign on his face. Only she didn't see it; she couldn't read that kind of a sign. He was her brother.

You could see the resemblance, now. And she loved her brother, and she couldn't help herself, even knowing what he was.

"You drive up there, Earl," he said. "Then you take a bus back. A Greyhound stops at Star Gap if there's a passenger, see?"

She was watching me, now. She was under some kind of spell with this guy. As though she couldn't help herself at all. Listening to him, watching me, and waiting.

"Then you'll get your boat, Earl," he went on. "Pick us up out in front of here. And you'll run me up to Star Gap."

He looked up at Jean and squeezed his hand on her waist.

"So there's nothing to worry about," he told her. "I got it all figured."

"Jean," I said. "You aren't going to listen to that, are you?"

She didn't say anything.

"I killed a man," Kurt said. "I'd as soon kill you."

"You mean, you'd let me go out there alone?"

"Sure, Earl."

"Suppose I go for the cops? What then?"

He grinned at me. Then he looked at Jean and squeezed her waist. Then he winked at me. "You won't," he said. "You won't do anything but what I tell you. That right, Jeannie?"

"You've got to do this for me, Earl," Jean said.

"Don't you see?" I said. "He's using you. He's threatening me with your life, Jean."

"No. He's not, Earl."

"See?" Kurt said. "Good old Sis."

I came up off the chair. I looked into her eyes and she looked back and her hand went out and smoothed her brother's shoulder.

"Jean," I said, "snap out of it!"

She looked at me. Then I thought she was going to cry. She turned away from her brother and went across the room and stood by the side window, with her back to me. You could see the stiffening of her shoulders. She had her hands together, gripped tightly in front of her. You could tell. Then she whirled and looked at me.

"You've got to do this, Earl. For me."

Kurt slumped back in his chair and raised his eyebrows at me and grinned. He bounced the automatic on his knee.

"Maybe I'd go to the cops, anyway," I said.

"No!" Jean said.

"Would you?" Kurt said. "Don't give me that."

"How low can you get?" I said. "Tell me."

"Don't," Jean said softly. "Please don't."

Kurt stood up slowly. He looked first at Jean, then at me. I got his message.

"Please, Earl," Jean said.

So I looked at her and flushed with the memory of last night. I would have to tell her about that. But now I'd have to do this other thing. I felt bad, not because of Kurt, but because of what I'd done.

Some way I had to beat this guy. Some way, somehow.

• • •

I went back to my place. It was a one-room shack and I tried not to think what I had to do. I opened the door. Lucille was stretched out on my cot, still wearing the black shorts and bra, and balancing a drink on her belly.

"Hi, daddy."

I went over to the closet, got out a pair of slacks and a shirt and some underwear.

"How'd you make out?"

She was pretty high. She lay there, watching me, slapping the glass up and down on her bare belly. Then she sat up on one elbow and took a long drink and put the glass on the floor. She looked at me. "You meet him, Earl?"

"I didn't meet anybody."

"Don't tell me little Jean did that to your face?"

I didn't say anything. I finished dressing and went into the bathroom, thinking, What's on his mind? What does he really plan to do?

In the cabinet mirror, I was a great mess. The edges of the cuts from Kurt's gun had curled in and under and I looked real bad. I washed tenderly, decided to let the air dry it, and went back into the other room and got a pack of cigarettes.

"You going to do like I say?" Lucille said, still lying there on the cot. "Huh, daddy?"

I still didn't say anything. That got her. She came up off the cot and over to me. She was holding her load pretty well. She sure was a drinking female, for a fact.

"You'd damn well better listen to me, Earl!"

"Come on," I said. "Get out of here. I'm locking up."

She stood there looking at me, blinking her pale eyes. She was as beautiful as ever and she knew it. She stepped in close, reaching for me, chuckling to herself.

I went over to the door. I turned and looked at her.

She came by me like the wind and stepped outside, trailing a rich gin aroma. She blinked at the sunlight. I locked up and started for the Ford, parked under a cabbage palm against the side of the shack.

"Earl?"

I stopped and looked at her. She stood there, frowning at me, teetering a little. I walked back over to her.

"All right," I said. "Tell me about it. What's the angle?"

"That's better, Earl. You're going to help me, aren't you?"

So I looked at her real close. And I knew that whatever it was she wanted from me, she wasn't going to get it. So it really didn't matter. I turned and went back to the Ford. Then I looked at her again.

Her face looked like it was wrung out. She whirled and ran like hell around the other side of the shack and I heard her feet pounding on the earth, out toward the road.

I got in the Ford and rolled the windows down. It was oven-hot. I started her up and headed for the highway.

This wasn't the time or place to do whatever I might be able to do with Kurt. I had to get to Star Gap, and back.

There was no sign of Lucille.

He'd told me where to leave the car, and to return with the first bus and to bring my boat around by Jean's place, no matter what time it was.

"Do it," Jean had said. *"For me, Earl. For me."*

And meanwhile, what?

• • •

They stopped me on Route 19, just past the Clearwater turn-off. There were four police cars, and a mess of cops, and the roadblock was fixed so you wouldn't see it until you were right on top of it. They were just over the brow of a hill.

"Let's see your driver's license."

"Sure. What's up?"

The cop looked at me. Another cop joined him. They looked peculiarly alike: red-faced, sweating under the black bills of their caps, their eyes tired with waiting.

I handed the one my driver's license. He read it carefully, not moving his lips much, and looked at me.

"Oh, hell," the other cop said. He took off his cap and mopped his forehead with a handkerchief.

"What's up?" I said again. A car honked behind me.

"Move along," one of them said.

"Looking for somebody?"

"Yeah," he said. "A killer. But you're not him. Doesn't that make you feel good inside?"

I drove on. So they knew. They had him bottled up and he knew they would. It couldn't be anybody else, I felt sure. Kurt—Jean's brother.

So he had figured it neat, all right. Very. Unless they checked the passengers on the bus, coming back.

Because they wouldn't check this car again, leaving the state. So you were that near the law, and you didn't do anything, I thought. Now you're what they call an accomplice—all the way.

3.

By the time I got back to my place in Pass-a-Grille, it was dusk and it was raining. A steady drizzle was coming down. They hadn't checked the passengers on the bus coming down into the southern part of the state.

I'd left the car where Kurt asked. And now came the interesting part; the part I was afraid of. I was worked up inside with worry over Jean. I wanted to get right over there.

I'd seen nothing of Lucille. As I parked the car by my shack, I got to thinking and wondered if maybe Lucille had seen Jean? That would be fine.

I hadn't had anything to eat all day. I went inside and made a peanut butter sandwich, and drank a glass of milk, trying to think of what I should do.

I came up with exactly nothing.

There was no way of delaying it any longer.

I went on out and down to the pier and got aboard. I rigged the awning from the deck cabin to the posts on the stern. She was a forty-six foot cruiser, with deck cabin, and another good-sized cabin running from amidships forward, belowdecks. I had her rigged for charter fishing, and she was a good boat. Some day she would be mine all the way, if I could keep up the payments.

I let go the bow line and started her and backed her slow, and got out onto the stern and grabbed the stern line loop off the piling. I backed her into the channel, then put her for the bite on the end of the island.

The rain was coming down good now. The sky was thick and dirty. I switched on port and starboard running lights, went down and had a look at the ship-to-shore radio, wishing I had the nerve to use it somehow.

I didn't have that nerve. There was too much Jean wrapped up in this.

Bringing the boat around the island toward the Gulf, I tried to think if Jean had ever mentioned him. No. He was the rat in the woodshed, and now he was out for lunch.

The Gulf was oily, lifting with an easy swell at the turn of the tide, and the water was black like oil. The rain sifted down and the lights from the town of Pass-a-Grille burnished the black night dull crimson above the palms.

She commenced to roll. I came along, cutting the swell. She would break up soon, and we might have some nasty seas. I didn't like that at all.

Maybe I could get him to postpone the ride.

I brought her in as close as I could along the shoreline, and passed the cabanas where Lucille was staying. They were lit up, glistening through the rain. Then pretty soon I spotted Jean's house, up on the slope between the black-fingered thrashing palms.

A yellow light was burning in one window. A candle for papa.

Well hell. There was no dock.

I anchored her on the drop off, just past the shallows, waited for the drag and she caught good. I could tell. But she would drag anyway, if the rain broke into the wind.

We'd have to act fast.

I stripped to my shorts, went over into the Gulf and swam for shore. They were just coming out on the porch as I came along the beach.

"I see you made it," Kurt said.

Jean ran stumbling down across the lawn onto the beach. She came up to me and started to put her arms around me.

"Earl," she said. "It's all right, Earl. Just do as he says."

"Don't touch him, Jeannie," Kurt said.

He came walking along. He had that damned gun, and he was carrying a small suitcase. He looked at me, with the rain pouring down and held the suitcase up and shook it. It kind of rattled heavy and loose inside.

"Know what it is?" he asked.

I watched Jean. Neither of them had changed their clothes and the water already had her hair streaming. She had her lips parted, looking at me and then at him. It was raining harder now; a cold rain that bit into you.

"It's loot," Kurt said. He laughed. He laughed like hell, throwing his head back, letting it cut up into the raining night. "I can't swim out there with this, Earl—you'll have to bring the boat in far enough so we can wade aboard."

There was plenty wrong with him. And I hoped maybe Jean was beginning to see that. She stepped a little closer to me, watching him, but that was all.

And he looked at her and kind of laughed again, and wiped his mouth with his sleeve, holding the gun, and then he laughed again. Great.

"I can't bring her in," I said.

"Do it anyway."

Jean moved in close to me and her hand touched mine, and I felt the fine trembling of her fingers. That gave me some kind of hope.

I looked down at her and she smiled at me, licking the rain off her lips. I turned and ran down into the water and swam back to the boat, thrashing, and climbed aboard and hauled anchor, and started the cruiser and brought her in, roaring like hell. It was good to hear her roar. I was mad clear down to the cold soles of my bare feet. I should have done something. I should have jumped him. Only Jean, she didn't want it that way.

She didn't know what he was.

I was mad at myself, and sick with all of it.

Kurt was a beaut. He would pull anything.

"All right," I yelled. "Come on."

I held her there, seesawing from forward to reverse, and holding her bow out. The rain was lifting spasmodically in horizontal sheets with the fresh wind, and I heard the crack of doom out there on the horizon, and saw it, bright white flashing, ripping the sky apart, and heard it again.

Thunder. Good wild thunder.

I set the wheel and locked it and went aft. I grabbed Jean's hand and lifted. She came flying aboard and landed with a splat in the stern. Then I looked down at him, into his shining white face, standing in the Gulf with the suitcase and the gun, still grinning. A wave slapped him in the teeth.

"I ought to leave you," I said, watching that gun.

"Try it," he said. He said it fine, even standing there, almost getting knocked flat, staggering plenty, but keeping the gun up and on me.

Jean reached down and got the suitcase.

"Thanks, Sis."

I looked at him and this time I grinned.

"Grab me or you're a dead man," he said.

"Earl, please!" Jean said.

I had to laugh at that. He wasn't going to kill me. I grabbed him and hauled him up, trying to whip him against the side. It didn't work. He kept grinning and he kept that gun on me every inch of the way. He was like a chimp coming aboard, I'll tell you. And then a nice bright laugh for me.

"We're drifting, Earl," Jean said.

I beat it for the wheel. I gunned the engines and headed her straight west. I turned on the cabin lights.

They came into the cabin and stood there, watching me.

"Some brother you got, honey," I said.

She went over and sat on the couch and started to cry. He didn't pay any attention to her. He snagged his suitcase and sat beside her and flung it open.

"Good thing it's not wet," he said, looking up at me. "Isn't that pretty, kid?" he said to Jean. "I'll give you a bundle to take home."

She shrank away from him, staring at him.

"You told me that wasn't money. You told me it was a mistake—an accident you killed that man in Tampa."

He laughed, snapped the suitcase shut. There had been a hell of a pile of green stuff inside. "I was lying to you, Jeannie. Out and out tale-telling."

"Kurt, you *did* rob that insurance office."

His face changed. Something came into his eyes, a kind of dim, hard glow. He reached out and took her arm in his left hand and looked at her and said, "Shut up, Jeannie! Just shut your yap."

"Brotherly love, Jean," I said. "Just a big bear, that's all Kurt is."

"You, too," he said. "Just open her up and head for Star Gap, friend."

"Then what?"

He looked at me. His face was very serious. Then he laughed again. Let me tell you, it was a damned peculiar kind of laugh.

• • •

The rain changed to a kind of heavy mist and the wind came up and started knocking at our door. I set a course and locked the wheel. To hell with it. She would take anything the Gulf could give her, always had. She was pitching and rolling to beat the devil, and the engines were roaring fine.

I looked aft, beyond the cabin door, where Kurt and Jean stood, arguing. I couldn't catch what they were saying, but now and then he yelled at her.

I opened the hatch over the engines and had a look. There was a lot of slop in the bilge, splashing around, so I closed the hatch and eased toward the stern.

"You lied to me," Jean said. "You lied, like always. You said you'd never lie again, Kurt."

"Come off it, will you?" he said.

"I won't come off anything. All my life it's been this way. You're bad, Kurt. Bad clear through."

"Oh, Sis—you trouble me deeply."

"Why did you kill that man? You told me it was self-defense, Kurt. An accident. Why did you really kill him?"

"Forget it, will you?"

"How can I forget it?"

"Maybe he needed killing."

"Kurt. My own brother. As close as we are. What would Mother and Dad have thought now?"

"They knew me."

"Yes. They died with you in prison. But you know something? All along, they thought you were good. And I did, too. So you broke out of prison, didn't you? Why did you come back? Why?"

"Because, Jeannie—I had no place else to go." He said it real nasty and I could see him bending and shoving his face close to hers, with his lips curled up. "Get it? I'm all right now. Cozy. I'll never bother you again, Sis."

A big old gray-bearded wave mashed against the portside and ripped over the top of the cabin, singing—slicing through the stern, and the awning went. I heard it go and Jean yelled. I went out there. It was flapping, ripping. I tried to catch what I could of it and drag the canvas in. No use. The wind was turning into a gale. The canvas whipped and shredded through my fingers. My thumbnail ripped off.

"Get inside," I said. I grabbed Jean and shoved her through the screen door of the cabin, and closed the door and stood there looking at Kurt.

"Hello, Earl," he said. He was trying to be at ease on the swamping deck of the boat, leaning against the cabin like it was the corner drugstore, where he'd probably spent a good part of his life.

"You're sharp, aren't you?" I said.

"That's right. Like a blade."

He was off guard and I swung. His gun came up, but it didn't fire. I connected with his jaw. He sprawled back through the cabin door and slid across the deck on his back.

I went after him.

He started laughing. He lay there and laughed, holding the gun on me. Then he quit that and said, "Hold it, Earl. I'm not going to pot you till later. But if you ask for it, I'll wing you right now. I'll pop your kneecap. It's bad, going through life without no kneecap."

"Kurt!" Jean said.

"Out of the way, Sis." He stood up and looked at her. She backed down the steps into the galley, her eyes snapping up to mine, her lips as grim and hopeless looking as they would ever get. I brushed past him and checked the compass and re-set the wheel.

"Another half-hour," I said. "Unless we swamp."

She was really rolling and bucking. I didn't give a damn.

"Can't you get any more out of this tub?"

I didn't answer him. I looked down into the galley. She was standing there beside the icebox, staring up at me with all the pain and fear and shame showing in her eyes. I didn't like looking at that. I had to figure a way. Any way at all.

• • •

We came in past the breakwater at Star Gap, out of the Gulf, and the small harbor was some change from out there. It was plenty dark, but there was a pearl-colored mist. The boat had taken a beating and so had I.

Kurt was in the stern, staring at me through the smashed cabin door.

"We're about there," I said, feeling the drag of slow water.

Jean came up from below decks and marched past me into the stern. Her clothes hung on her, dripping, and they clung against her legs as she moved. Her hair was a black mass, curling around her shoulders, like she'd just come up out of the sea. It was beginning to rain like hell again, pouring down. The wind had lessened.

"Remember," Kurt said, sticking his head in the door. "Dock her someplace where nobody'll spot us."

I didn't say anything. Nobody would spot us. I was bringing her in right where I had the car parked. There was an old splintered jetty along there. But there was a good stretch of mud flat before you could reach solid sand.

"After I tie her, you're going to have to jump for it again," I said. "The pier's all shot."

We rocked in close by the shadowed remnants of the jetty, in about two and a half feet of water. I backed her, and shut the engines, and went out and got the stern line over an old piling.

He was standing there, watching me. I went for him. Jean screamed something. I hit him hard in the chest and we went plowing overboard.

We struck in the shallow water and came up fighting.

"No, Earl!" Jean called.

The rain was really coming down. I slipped and sprawled and I heard him laugh. It was brighter out there now. He was standing up, watching me. I couldn't get free of the muck.

"Toss me the suitcase, Sis," he said.

I went at him, staggering. He turned on me.

"All right, Earl," he said. "It's time, anyway."

So I just stood there, because I saw the girl wading out slowly from behind him, with her white dress plastered to her body and her mouth a black gash in the night.

"Don't move, Kurt!"

It was Lucille. Her voice was plenty wild.

Jean said something from the stern of the boat. Kurt slowly began to turn around. You could see the hell on his face, shining in the rain.

"Don't turn around, Kurt," Lucille said. "I'm going to shoot you in the back, I promise—*I promise!*"

I didn't move, either. She licked her lips and looked at me and chuckled. I knew she was high as the moon. You could tell. She lifted one hand and slapped some of that pale blonde hair away from her face.

Kurt said, "Baby. What Are you doing here?" But he didn't turn around, and the revolver in her hand gleamed through the rain.

We stood that way for a moment, with the rain splattering and my feet sucked into the mud bottom and you could smell the salt and the stink of sulphur and dead fish. I had the damnedest thought. About that seven-hundred-dollar watch I'd lost overboard, and those three hamburgers. How if I came through this, I was going out there and dive for that watch. It was a good watch, waterproof, and it would bring something at the pawn shop. I had it coming. It was a crazy thought, but that's the way it was. For a long moment I just stood there, thinking how I'd spend the rest of the summer up to hurricane season, hunting for that watch.

"Throw Kurt's suitcase down from the boat," Lucille said. "You, Jean—little Jean. C'mon, throw it down."

"Don't do it, Sis," Kurt said.

I snapped out of it. Lucille cursed.

"Honey," I said to Jean. "Give me the suitcase."

Jean leaned over and dropped it to me. I saw her face. Her eyes were like silver dollars and she was scared all the way. "Don't let her kill him," she said.

Lucille chuckled. She'd heard her. "Earl," she said. "You pitch it to me. It won't get very wet, don't worry."

"I'll cut you in," Kurt said. "Throw it at her, not to her."

"Go ahead and move, Kurt," Lucille said. "You're going to get it in the back, see?"

I flung the suitcase. It splashed beside her in the water, skidding. She grabbed it, holding it up, grinning.

"You're going to get it in the back," Lucille said. "I followed Earl up here in my car, and I knew what was up, Kurt. It's the way you'd work it. In the back—just like you killed Herb—my husband, Kurt. Just the same damned way."

"Take it easy," Kurt said. "I didn't mean to kill him."

"He was the only good thing I ever had," Lucille said. "Maybe I didn't deserve him, but I had him. And he worked hard. He owned that insurance company, Kurt. He built it up himself. And then you came along, sniffing the way you did." She took a couple of splashing steps forward. Kurt still didn't turn. There was something in her voice that told you she was speaking the truth and that her heart was wrung out of shape and that she was going to kill him and that she didn't care.

"You'd better do some thinking about this," I said to her.

"No, Earl. You're out of it now." Then she spoke to Kurt, talking slowly and I heard Jean sob twice up there in the stern. "You worked on me, with the sweet talk—you took me away from him—and then you killed him for this." She slapped the suitcase against the water. "I could have got the police, Kurt. But I wanted to do it myself. So, now you'll know how it is—what it's like. All the way, Kurt."

"Lucille. Honey—we can still—don't—!" He turned fast, ducking and firing.

But she caught him in the back with the first slug. She yelled and I saw it rip into him. I went for her, but it was no use.

She stood there, kind of cringing, pumping them into him and I could see her face through the rain, torn with a crazy kind of grief.

I heard the cars coming down by the water's edge and a spotlight probed out over the water. Kurt was blasting her as he fell. She sank down into the water and the mud.

Her hand was still holding the suitcase.

I went over to her.

"Earl," Jean called.

Lucille wasn't dead yet. I saw the sparkle of buttons and the sheen of wet uniforms as the police splashed across the mud flats. One of them called something, but they were quite a ways off.

Lucille was dying fast. I held her up away from the water and looked down into her face.

"You tell her?" she said.

"What?"

"About us? Last night? At my place."

"No; not yet."

"Well, don't, daddy. It would bust her heart. I know. We didn't do anything, anyway. You passed out cold."

I looked at her. She was dead.

I stood there and Jean came toward me through the water. Somehow she'd got down off the boat. I kept Lucille's head up, thinking about her. I saw Jean pause by her brother and kind of bend down and then straighten and come splashing over by me.

"He was my brother," Jean said. "Can you understand that? He always came to me for help. Ever since—only this was the last time."

"Sure," I told her. "I understand. Look, I wonder how come the cops are over there?"

"I used the ship-to-shore radio," she said. "I had to. Even if he was my brother. He was going to kill you. I could tell. I had to do that, Earl."

The police moved warily toward us. About seven men, walking slow. One of them told us to drop our guns.

Jean and I stood there together. I held Lucille's head out of the water and the suitcase full of money was still gripped in her hand, floating against our legs.

The rain began to let up a little.

I Saw Her Die

Manhunt
October 1955

Lieutenant Grisson stretched a hairy hand across his desk and turned on the goose neck lamp. Outside, it was early dusk, but here in the police station it was dark. Blinding light flooded Grisson's young-old face, winked in his gray eyes. He turned the lamp away toward the desk top, settled comfortably in his chair. He took his cap off, laid it on the floor, and mopped his head and face with a wadded handkerchief in his big hand.

"God damn, it's hot," he said.

Two policemen in plain clothes stood silently smoking by a row of lockers across the room. They were both of medium build. The blond one was Halliwell, the round-faced, dark-haired one was Dibble.

The door on the far side of the room opened and a small man stepped in. He closed the door very carefully.

"Here's a customer," Halliwell said. "Grisson just gets on duty and it starts."

"We're on duty, too," Dibble said.

They shut up.

The small man stood by the door a moment, as if doubtful this was the right place. He wore overalls, the greasy straps cutting across bare, sunburned shoulders. The overalls were too large for him and they were heavy with dirt.

Grisson looked at the man, started to reach for his cap, mopped his face instead.

"Who do I talk to?" the man said. His voice was full of the Florida backwoods, fields of palmetto, snuff, and dark mossy riverbanks.

Grisson cleared his throat, glanced at Halliwell and Dibble, then back at the man.

"It depends," he said.

"I got something here. I got to tell somebody, I reckon. I got to tell a cop."

"You're in the right place."

The man moved toward the desk and Grisson waited. The overalls were so stiff with dirt it was as though the man moved inside a very large barrel. Grisson wondered if the man were drunk.

"They's been a murder," the man said. He lifted two huge, trembling, dirt-rutted hands and knotted them slowly into fists.

"Uh-huh," Grisson said.

"I seen it."

"Oh," Grisson said. "All right. Tell me about it."

"That's why I come here," the man said, lowering his fists and speaking slowly. "I reckon."

Halliwell coughed.

Grisson cleared his throat again. "Go ahead."

"Sho, now," the man said. "Just tell it?"

"Uh-huh." Grisson grabbed the book and slammed it open on the desk. He snatched a pen from the ink-well and scratched in the time and date. "What's your name?"

"Hewitt," the man said. "Marvin P. J. Hewitt. Them middle ones stand for Purdy and Juke. I don't never now use 'em, one or other."

"Where you live, Mister Hewitt?"

"Over by Lake Seminole. We got a house, there. My wife and me, and the kids. I got five kids. We used to live in Tampa. Not anymore, though."

"Relax," Grisson said. "You don't have to be nervous."

"It's what I seen, does it," Hewitt said. "Can't help twitching."

"All right. What's your work, Mister Hewitt?"

"I'm a landscaper." Hewitt didn't know what to do with his hands. "Working yonder at Oak Summit, landscaping for Mulbrock's Nursery. New development, over there. Setting out trees."

Grisson closed the book, slid it across the desk, leaned back and sneezed.

"Should I tell it, now?" Hewitt said.

"Sure."

"I was born near Ocala," Hewitt said.

Grisson waited. Dibble lit another cigarette and sat on the small bench beside the lockers. Halliwell joined him.

Hewitt began to shake under the overalls. The shaking came and went in spasms.

"Just relax," Grisson said. "You say you saw something. Go ahead and—"

"Murder!" Hewitt said.

"All right," Grisson said. "Let's take it one at a time. Where did you see this?"

Hewitt stared at Grisson. He opened and closed his mouth several times, very slowly.

"Look," Grisson said. "You'll have to calm down. Would you like a drink of water?"

"No, sir," Hewitt said. "I'm all right now. It's just what I seen, does it."

"You're all right now, then?"

"Reckon so. It was this afternoon. I was setting a palm out in this here back yard. There wasn't nobody else around, and I heard a yell from three houses down. In the Florida room, sounded like."

"I see."

"Wasn't nobody else around. Didn't pay much attention. Then I heard one more yell."

"What kind of a yell?" Halliwell asked.

Grisson lifted a hand, said, "Wait. Go on, Mister Hewitt."

"It was a woman, yelled," Hewitt said. "I cut down around the houses and came up by the Florida room and looked in. He was killing her."

"What?"

"The man, there. He had this here gal down on the floor, hitting her. He hit the hell out of her. I could tell she was dead, but he kept on."

"Kept on?"

"Hitting and hitting. She had on a red bathing suit."

"How could you tell she was dead?" Halliwell asked.

Grisson held up his hand. "Go on, Mister Hewitt."

"Well," Hewitt said. "I was watching, like I say. I was scared. I didn't know what to do."

"For hell's sake," Halliwell said.

Grisson turned slowly and looked at Halliwell.

Halliwell lit another cigarette, avoiding Grisson's eyes.

"Then he had a knife in his hand," Hewitt said. "He stood up and he bent down and drug the knife across her throat. Easy, like pie. She bled some," Hewitt said. "He wiped the knife on her leg, good and clean. Then he folded it and stuck it in his pocket, and went into the bathroom."

"How do you know this?"

"I snuck along the house," Hewitt said. "He went in there and got a bunch of rags and come back and sopped it up. Then he looked up and he seen me."

Dibble grunted.

"Let me get this straight," Grisson said. "No," he said. "Never mind. You say he saw you?"

"Looked right at me, sir. Yes, sir. We stared at each other through the window."

"Then what?"

"I lit out," Hewitt said.

"How long ago was this?"

"I come right from there."

"Did he chase you?"

"He never come out of that house. I ran through the block, got in the truck and come over here. It's a good ways."

"Oak Summit," Grisson said.

"Yes, sir."

"Wasn't there *anybody* else around?"

"Not a soul on that block but me," Hewitt said slowly. "Three blocks over they're building, but that's a long ways. Not a soul. My truck was parked across the block, like I say."

"Did you see any cars?"

"They was a car front of the house. A blue Chevvy."

"You saw that?"

"Yes, sir."

"Ever see it before?"

"There's lots of blue Chevvies. I lit out."

"Did you know these people? Have you ever seen them before?"

"Seems like the man might be a salesman. Real estate. They got a office at Oak Summit, so they can show the houses."

"But you aren't sure?"

"Couldn't swear to a thing. Just what I seen."

Grisson stared at Hewitt.

"It's a hell of a one," Hewitt said. "He saw me. I can't get that outa my head. He knows I saw him."

Grisson turned and looked at Halliwell and Dibble. They stood up and came over by the desk and stared at Hewitt.

"Take him out there and see what this is all about," Grisson said. "Phone in."

"Let's go," Halliwell said to Hewitt.

Halliwell was a cynical man. He didn't believe a word of what Hewitt said, because somehow it didn't ring true. He knew Dibble didn't believe it, either. He did not know what Grisson thought.

They drove out to Oak Summit.

"She must have been alive," Dibble said. "Or she wouldn't have bled when he cut her throat."

"Said she bled *some*," Hewitt told Dibble.

"You said he 'sopped' it up," Halliwell said.

"Sopped, mopped—what would you say?" Hewitt said.

"All right." Halliwell could tell Hewitt was very nervous. The man kept looking out of the car window into the darkness.

"Tell me where to turn," Halliwell said.

"Turn here. Just go right on down and your first right, and stop at the sixth house. That's it."

Halliwell did that. The crickets were loud. It was absolutely quiet out there, except for the crickets. It was very hot. There was no wind.

"Jesus Christ," Hewitt said. "He saw me."

"Let's go," Halliwell said. "Frank, you bring the flash."

They crunched up the driveway and across the walk to the front door of the house.

"Mostly they leave the doors open," Hewitt said. "During the daytime, that is. Sometimes they forget to lock 'em at night."

"You know everything, don't you?" Halliwell said.

"Easy, boy," Dibble said.

"How come they leave the doors unlocked?" Halliwell asked.

"So folks can look."

The door was open. They went inside. The place smelled of fresh paint and plaster and raw wood and wet cement. It was much hotter inside the house and the crickets were muted and far away after Dibble closed the door.

"Hardly breathe," Halliwell said. "All right, Hewitt. Show us the body." He turned the flashlight beam into Hewitt's eyes.

"Right through there, in the Florida room," Hewitt said.

They went into the empty Florida room. The rear door was open, leading into the back yard. Sand had blown through the door, and was drifted on the floor.

"It's gone," Hewitt said. He stood in the center of the room and looked around at the windows. "He saw me," he said.

Halliwell turned the flashlight on him again and watched him shake.

"Show us where it was, Mister Hewitt," Dibble said.

"It ain't here," Hewitt said.

"It never was here," Halliwell said. "Right, Hewitt?"

Hewitt didn't answer. He apparently was thinking about something, though. He kept looking at the windows of the Florida room. He seemed to shrink inside the overalls.

Halliwell turned to Dibble. "Go on outside," he said. "Open the front door wide. Park the car so you can train the spotlight in here across the floor. All right?"

Dibble went outside. Pretty soon a spreading beam of white light lit the Florida room like daytime. The only tracks and scuffings on the sand-blown floor had been made by them.

Dibble came back.

"Not a sign of anything," Halliwell said. "Asphalt tile floor. Perfectly dry."

Hewitt stepped up to Halliwell and touched his arm.

"He could of thrown sand in the door," Hewitt said. "The door wasn't open before."

"Hell," Halliwell said.

Dibble got down on his hands and knees. "You say about here, Mister Hewitt?"

Hewitt nodded. His mouth was open again, slowly moving, and he was watching the windows.

"I can't see a thing," Dibble said. "Not a sign. If she bled, it would have gotten into the cracks between the tile. You'd think so, anyway."

"There'd be something," Halliwell said. "Well," he said. "That's that."

"You don't believe me," Hewitt said.

"We'd better check on the car," Dibble said. "The blue Chevvy. He said something about the real estate office."

Halliwell shrugged. "All right. Go report in, I'll check the bathroom."

Dibble left and Halliwell went into the bathroom with the flashlight. He could hear Dibble at the radio in the car. There was nothing in the bathroom aside from the usual furnishings, and a bucket of dried cement.

Halliwell returned to the Florida room. Hewitt wasn't there, so he went on outside and closed the door. Hewitt was talking with Dibble.

"You've got to believe me," Hewitt said as Halliwell came up to the police car "You've *got to!* I seen him, you hear? And he seen me. Jesus Christ." Hewitt turned and looked at Halliwell and snapped his fingers three times.

"We'd better check out that car," Dibble said.

"All right." They ran down the head of the realty company and questioned him. They found him repairing a fishing rod in his garage. He told them that there had been a man working for them who was out there at Oak Summit and this man drove a Chevvy, only it was light green.

"It might have been that color—green," Hewitt said.

"Only he's in California," the realty man told them. "He left for San Francisco three weeks ago."

"What have I got to do to prove it to you?" Hewitt said as they walked back to the police car. "I tell you, I seen it! There must be some way to prove it to you."

"Sure," Halliwell said. He was mad. He could have been sitting on the bench back there at headquarters, smoking. Damn these hallucinating characters, anyway.

They drove back into town. Dibble didn't have much to say.

"You got to believe me," Hewitt said. "He could of dried the floor up, dusted it with sand, that way. Can't you see that?"

"Look," Halliwell said. "Let us worry about it. You reported it. It's off your hands. You made a mistake, that's all. We're not mad at you." He looked out the side window of the car, then continued driving carefully. "Where's your car, Hewitt?"

"I left the truck by the police station."

"All right. You get in it and drive on home. That it, up there?"

"That's it," Hewitt said. "Jesus Christ."

They parked. They walked Hewitt over to his truck. It was a truck from Mulbrock's Nursery. Hewitt climbed behind the wheel of the truck and looked down at them.

"I wish you boys would believe me," Hewitt said. He gripped the steering wheel of the truck very hard. Then he looked at them and yelled in their faces. "I seen it! You hear! I seen it!"

"All right," Halliwell said. "Go on home. Forget about it. We'll be working on it."

Halliwell and Dibble walked away. Hewitt sat there behind the wheel of the truck and watched them. He watched them pause on the steps of the police station and light cigarettes and blow smoke into the night. The awful bright sanctuary of the station made Hewitt almost sick to his stomach. He was sweating under his overalls.

He seen me, Hewitt thought. *He seen me watching him.*

He started the truck and drove off out of town. He felt dizzy and sick and he couldn't stop shaking. He was scared so badly he kept his toes pressed tight up against the tops of his shoes. He had to go home and he didn't want to go home. He wanted to go back there and just sit on those brightly lighted steps of the police station.

As he turned onto the road that led toward Lake Seminole, it seemed every car he saw turned and followed him.

One did.

• • •

Halliwell and Dibble were sent out on it. It was five days later and a family at the end of Ninth Street, near the sand pits, had complained of a bad smell.

Halliwell and Dibble stood there on a mound of sand and looked at the two bodies laid out side by side. They were in a bad state of decomposition, but the red bathing suit and the dirty overalls were in good condition.

"Somebody's going to catch hell for this," Halliwell said through his handkerchief.

"Yeah," Dibble said. "But Hewitt sure proved his point, didn't he?"

Teen-Age Casanova

Justice
October 1955

She smiled so slyly. She had such black hair. Her lips were so red. The way she spoke was different from any other girl he had ever known. Not a bit like Carol. He did not want to think about Carol. It made him feel wrong about what he was going to do. He wanted only to be with Binnie. It was funny, because he'd only known Binnie for an hour or so, and he had known Carol for three years.

He said to Binnie, "Let's walk down by the lake."

They were standing beside the raised dance pavilion. The sleepy music of Martin Towne's Zypher-Tones roofed the Florida night. Laughter and the sound of shuffling feet flooded down upon them. Beyond the shell of light cast from the pavilion, night birds and insects warred in the pine woods and tangled jungle. Now and then a car's lights went on and off, a souped-up Ford's engine roared.

"All right," Binnie said.

When she spoke, he went all to mush inside. Her voice was tender and reedy and it did things to him.

"We can sit, or something."

"Yes."

He took her arm and they moved down past the lower wall of the pavilion, fronting the lake. She brushed against him. It was a kind of sly movement, like everything else about her, and it drove him wild.

She was so pretty. Like nothing he'd ever known.

He had told Carol he was going spearing.

"It's so nice," Binnie said.

His hand moved from her arm to slide around her waist, gently pulling her to him. Her hip came against his. She glanced up at him, smiling. The moonlight paled her face and he saw her red lips, partly open. He had to look away. Her eyes were shining with the moonlight in them.

She spoke very seldom.

"We could . . ." he let it trail off.

She looked at him and smiled. There was something catlike about her walk, the way her body moved under the thin blue dress. The softness of her.

He wanted to yell.

"It's so nice, isn't it, really?" Binnie said.

He cleared his throat, leaned over and kissed her cheek. She wriggled a little, looked at him and smiled. Then she turned in his arms and stretched up on tiptoe. Her lips were parted, her eyes closed, the corners of her lips turned up in that sly smile.

Secret. Just between the two of them.

He held her as tight as he could and kissed her. He seemed to sink right through her into the ground. He wanted to crush her, his hands on her back, then snarled in her soft black hair.

They separated, panting a little. Her eyes were on him and the music flared, drifting down toward the lake, echoing back from the far shore.

He wanted to talk. Only there was nothing to say. It seemed as if they had known each other for a long while, yet with all the bright newness there. There was no need for talk.

They came along the edge of the lake, on the grass just above the shore where the mangroves had been cut away. A mullet jumped out there in the darkness. It made quite a splash.

A girl ran out of the woods over there, running toward the pavilion. Her legs flashed white in the dying light. A tall boy crashed after her, laughing.

Binnie looked at him and they smiled, knowingly.

They reached the bench he'd been heading for. It was in a copse of cabbage palms on freshly mowed grass, facing the lake, shielded entirely from the pavilion and the lights. The music reached them faintly.

He was very excited. They moved close together.

She leaned back, making a long plane of her body and the moonlight washed over her. She glanced at him from the corners of her eyes, her hand sought his and squeezed. She was holding a handkerchief in the hand. His heart rocked so hard it hurt.

"Binnie," he said. "Binnie."

"Allen," she said.

Their mouths came together and he held her close, kissing her, experiencing something new and terrible and it was something that made him want to absolutely break her, mash her. Her lips moved against his and he heard the sound in her throat. He tried to bring her over against him and she said, "Uh-uh!" still kissing him. She shook her head, still kissing him, holding herself from coming against him. He stopped the kiss.

"How long will you be down here?" he asked.

She smiled, looking out over the lake.

"Binnie," he said. "I've got to see you."

"You're seeing me, silly!"

"You know what I mean."

"But you *are* seeing me."

"Again," he said. "Again, Binnie. When can I see you—again?"

"Why, I don't know, Allen." She looked at him from the corner of her eyes and smiled. He grabbed her, kissing her mouth, her forehead, her cheeks, her throat. He held her hands against his face.

"Binnie," he said. "I love you."

She drew her head away, smiling at him, her eyes shining.

"Oh, Allen," she said, closing her eyes, moving her lips. And after that kiss, she said, "You can see me again—if you like."

He remembered Carol. But there was no feeling about Carol now. None at all. Just an animosity, kind of.

"You through school yet?" he asked.

"Last year, high."

"Me, too. Can't you stay down here—go to school here, this fall? Don't you reckon you could stay with your aunt, like now? Instead of going back North?"

"Oh, you!" she said.

"Binnie, answer me."

She shrugged. "Well, maybe."

...

He came through the woods toward home. Walking. He didn't have a car, but somehow he'd have to get one. Her aunt had come to the pavilion for her in a big Lincoln.

Binnie was in his system, running through his veins, like acid. Eating at him with a sweet burning.

After she'd gone away with her aunt, he had jogged along the dirt road toward Spanishtown. It was eight miles from where he lived, six miles in the wrong direction from home. He found the address she had given him and stood across the street by a night-blooming jasmine bush, in the midst of choking scent, and stared at the house.

Huge and very old it was, dating back to the Civil War.

A light was lit in an upstairs bedroom and he saw her in the room. She was slipping out of her dress. He was in an agony of loving her, standing there. Then she moved to the window, pulled the shade and pretty soon the light went out. For a time he stood there staring at the dark shadow of the window, behind which he knew she moved and breathed. Finally, he turned toward home.

Carol and he had long planned marriage. It had been like that. In a manner of speaking, they were already married. For the three years since they had come together, they'd been inseparable. They knew everything there was to know about each other.

Now—like *that*—it was gone. He had no more feeling for Carol than for a chunk of wood from the woodpile. Less. Wood was useful.

He had to tell her. He didn't care what happened.

He loved Binnie. She loved him, he knew it. The way she acted; the quiet, sweet way.

Funny, how you found something like this. He had lied to Carol, said he was going spearing with Al Hewitt. He had really wanted to go alone over to the dance pavilion outside Georgeton. He had. He danced twice with Binnie, who had come alone—and then the rest.

From the moment he first held her, dancing, he had known. From the way she acted. The little things she said. Her smile. Her movements.

Right now, crossing the pine woods behind his home, he burned for her. He wanted to turn and run back there; wake her up, tell her over and over again.

He was almost ill with the way he felt. He crossed the yard toward the cabin.

"Allen."

It was Carol. She'd been standing by the front gallery and now she walked along the side of the cabin.

He stopped and looked at her. She came up to him.

"Allen, where have you been?"

"No place." He yawned.

"I've been waiting for hours."

"Why?"

"I wanted to see you." She moved up close to him, lifting her arms and for an instant she was familiarly against him. It was nothing. He didn't want to be near her. He tugged her arms down and stepped back.

She looked at him, frowning, the moonlight very bright on her pale hair, her eyes very wide.

"Allen," she said. "Let's go someplace."

"Carol. We're through," he told her. "Finished. I'm sorry, I reckon—but that's the way it is. I don't want to hurt you. It wouldn't be fair, making believe."

"What?"

He nodded. "Through," he said. "Done with."

"I don't understand."

She was wearing a light-colored dress, her pale blonde hair drawn around her head and tied with a ribbon behind. She was very pretty.

"Look," he said. "Forget you ever knew me. I won't be seeing you again. Good night." He turned and started toward the back door.

"Allen!" She ran at him, grasped his arm. Her face was stricken. "What d'you mean?"

He pried her fingers loose, released her hands. He shook his head. She irritated him. Damn it, couldn't she understand? He didn't want to tell her he was tired of her. What did he have to do, draw her a picture?

"We're through. I don't want to see you again."

"There's somebody else—another girl?"

"No." He wouldn't hurt her, not that way. "Nothing. Just through. I'm not good enough for you. I've thought it all out carefully. I reckon we'll get over it."

She stood there shaking her head, staring at him. There was a kind of wild disbelief, and belief and fright, all mingled together on her face. She kept shaking her head, bending a little toward him from the waist.

"I'm just not good enough," he said. "Thought it all out."

She turned and ran. She ran along the side of the cabin, and he knew she was crying. She ran out onto the dirt road and down the road toward her home.

He stood there a moment, listening to the sound of her feet striking the ground. Then he went inside. He closed the door and sighed.

He drank a glass of milk in the dark, so the light wouldn't wake his mother and father. He ate a cold bacon sandwich. Then he went to bed.

For hours he lay there, thinking about Binnie. He couldn't bring her face to his mind's eye—and when he thought he'd succeeded . . . it was Carol's face instead.

• • •

The next few days were very bad. Carol came around and started pleading with him. His mother probably guessed what was up, but asked anyway.

He told his mother, "She won't leave me alone. What do I have to do, draw her a picture?"

His mother just looked at him. She started to say something once, thought better of it and let him alone.

His father worked at the mill in Georgeton. If he noticed anything, he kept it to himself.

Carol lurked near him wherever he went. He couldn't seem to escape her. He'd taken a part-time job at the corners, for the summer, tying meal sacks for old Hatchby, at seventy-five cents an hour. Carol kept coming into the warehouse from the back entrance by the river, running up to him, dressed in tight jeans, crying.

"I'll do anything!" she said. "Only take me back, Allen. Don't leave me like this."

He would remember her grieving eyes, the abandoned pride.

He had to walk out on the job.

She sneaked into his room one night. "I know what it is," she whispered. "I haven't been good enough to you."

By now, he had acquired a certain brutality toward her. He thought of Binnie incessantly. An obsessive dream. Carol was like a piece of furniture that stood in his way.

That was the trouble. He couldn't shove her out of his way, and it began to trouble him.

She grabbed him, kissing him.

He pushed her away.

"Will you leave me be?"

"Allen . . ."

"It's for your own good."

"No, no. How can you forget all the things—?"

He wanted to sock her. He didn't. He couldn't do that, either. She would leave him, crying. But she would always come back.

Twice he went to Spanishtown. Once he found Binnie home. She was alone in the house. He went inside with her. She spoke so very seldom, just smiled slyly at him. Many times he'd said:

"Binnie, I love you."

She would smile at him, her eyes shining, her body taut.

"What do you do all day? When can I see you?"

"You're seeing me."

He was nearly out of his mind. She would not say that she loved him. Just that sly smile.

Going home, he reeled. When he reached home, Carol was waiting. It developed into the worst scene yet. He didn't know what to do. He wanted to think about Binnie.

"Allen—you love me," insisted Carol. "You know you do."

She wouldn't go home for a long time. When she finally did, it was the usual way—crying. The next day, she was back again. Hanging around, pleading.

Something began to happen inside Allen. . . .

• • •

Two weeks went by. Whenever he tried to see Binnie, there was nobody home. She was out with her aunt, she told him later. But they were together a few times, and it was wonderful. He was in a crazy dream state now.

Then, one evening he knew Carol was following him.

He cut off through the woods and stopped.

She came up to him, surprised. "It's another girl!"

"No, Carol."

"Yes."

"Don't ever follow me like this again," he said. He churned inside over it. He never wanted them to meet. He didn't want Carol to know about Binnie.

Carol's face was very pale. "If there is," she said. "I'll kill her."

"Go back."

"I won't go back."

But he finally persuaded her, tying his feelings up inside him. He had to sneak over to Binnie's now, watching that Carol never saw him go.

He became frenzied, thinking she would follow him.

He tried every way possible to get rid of Carol.

But she trailed him. She lurked. He didn't know what to do. Everywhere he turned, Carol—pleading—watching—waiting.

One night, lying in his bed, he knew what he had to do. It was the only way.

He had to kill her.

Then he would have Binnie all to himself. The way it was supposed to be. He couldn't stand it, the way Carol was acting. Not anymore.

He tried to think of ways to kill. It had to be some way so he wouldn't get caught.

Finally, he hit on the way. He rose in the night, trimmed a bamboo pole, rigged it with a cord loop. The next day, mid-morning, he went out in the palmetto fields to hunt down a coral snake.

By now the surface of his mind was black with a white dot in the middle. The white dot was what he was doing. He moved in a kind of concentrated and contained anger, with the sweet saturation of Binnie all through him.

He found the snake, finally—small, fat, violent-hued, and deadly—in some dry grass by a slash pine. Even though he'd been born in this country of snakes, he was careful. A coral was the deadliest of snakes. One touch, the skin punctured, was enough. But he had caught snakes before, and the fear was stilled by the promise. He snagged the snake with the loop, carried it to the woodshed and boxed it.

All he could think of now was the pale taut smoothness of Binnie, the way she smiled, her shining eyes, and what she could do in that sly way of hers.

Carol was no longer a person to him. Killing her was not really killing her in the sense that it was wrong—murder, anything like that. She was a talking, walking *something* that stood in his way. Like walking into a tree every time you turned around. . . . And she *might* discover Binnie.

The next morning when Carol found him in the woodshed, he was ready.

"All right," he said.

She clung to him, sobbing.

"I thought I'd be able to hold out," he said. "Reckon I can't, honey. Been trying to kid myself."

"Allen."

"Listen," he said. "Tomorrow—tomorrow we'll take a lunch, go over by the Oklawatchi, where we used to go. All right? We'll spend the whole day." He held her very close, thinking of Binnie. "We'll take a blanket, like before—just lay around all day. Talk it all out."

She was a wreck. She didn't want to leave him. She was afraid he would change his mind again. She'd told her mother how they would be married someday. Everything was established in her mind. He was her man. That was all there was to it.

"Sure. It was for your own good, Carol. I didn't reckon I was good enough for you. I don't care anymore."

"Oh, yes—just us."

He held her close, staring over her shoulder at the side of the woodshed, blind and bitter.

"Let's go now," she said. "It's not even noon, yet. I could never wait, Allen."

"All right."

She ran home to fix a lunch. He found some thick cowhide and sewed a small sack, arranging a leather drawstring so it would close tightly.

The coral snake was very lively in the leather sack. He got his leather jacket and put the sack in the pocket, carrying the jacket.

He writhed a little every time he thought of Binnie.

• • •

It was four miles and they walked it, with Carol pulling at him, wanting to stop all along the way. He couldn't let that happen. He had chosen the spot, not because it was their old favorite place to spend a day, but because it was so far away and nobody would be around.

He carried the blanket over his shoulder, the leather jacket over one arm. She asked him about the jacket.

"Thinking of you, I reckon," he told her. "Chance it might rain, like that other time we were out there. You could wear the jacket."

They didn't talk much. She tried, but he couldn't bring himself to say much. He knew what he had to do. So what use was there wasting time talking?

He kept thinking of Binnie, remembering everything about her and he was deeply pleased at being able to bring her image to his mind's eye now. Sometimes it was still Carol, though.

Carol didn't bother him a bit. He had a job to do. He would do it—as quickly as possible, because it might take a little time. And he wanted to see Binnie tonight.

He'd told Binnie he would come to her home at eight.

Carol looked fine, but there was this desperate look in her eyes. She was wearing tight blue jeans and a white shirt, her thick blonde hair rich with sunshine.

An hour later, he sat there on the blanket with her, held her down and showed her the snake.

He held the snake just behind the bullet head, its head sticking out of the leather sack.

She screamed as he pushed it at her.

"It's for you, Carol. I couldn't stand it."

"Allen—it's a coral!"

"Yes," he said simply. He had a terrible time trying to hold her down. She screamed and her head thrashed around. The snake bit her throat.

"There," he said.

He shook the snake out of the sack. It crawled away, slithering through the folds of the rumpled blanket and off into the dry grass above the riverbank.

Carol sprang up and ran.

The sun beat down in a vicious slant. That'll hasten it, he thought. The heat, the running, the fear and action.

She came running back and sprawled on her knees beside him on the blanket. Her face was very red.

"Allen," she cried. "You've killed me!"

He wanted to tell her why he'd done this. But he couldn't. He decided he should make it as easy for her as possible. He owed her that much.

"Carol," he said. "It's something I had to do. Told you I wasn't good enough for you. You wouldn't listen."

She just lay there, with the sun beating down on her. He knew she wouldn't move anymore now. She was staring up at him, trying to talk.

Something touched him inside, lightly, just once.

He ignored it.

"I'm sorry—I reckon, I am," he said. "Good-by, Carol. Honey."

He saw the way her eyes strained at him. Her fingers hooked and clutched at the dry grass. He did not like looking at her.

He turned away, went over and picked up his jacket, brushed it, found the leather sack and started toward home.

• • •

He spoke to Sheriff Corle. The sheriff was parked in his gray Tudor sedan in front of the River Bar and Grille, in Georgeton. Allen had been lucky. He had figured he'd have to go to the sheriff's office in Spanishtown.

"Yes sir," he said. "She acted funny, like."

Corle watched him. Corle was sitting in the car. He opened the door and got out and stood there, watching him. Corle was a long, raw-boned man, wearing a dust-covered white Stetson. He was chewing tobacco. He spat beyond the fender of the car, took the chew out and flipped it away. He wiped his hand on his trousers, straightened his hat down over his eyes.

"She just ran off, you say?"

Allen nodded. "We were eating lunch, see? Don't know what got into her. 'I'll be back in a minute,' she says. She gets up an' walks off into the woods."

"Oh, well—that," the sheriff said. He grinned. "Don't you reckon—?"

Allen shook his head. "She didn't come back."

"Now, that," the sheriff said. "I reckon—"

"I looked all over for her. Can't figure it."

"She wasn't riled?"

"No."

"Did you see if she went home?"

"No. I came straight over this way."

"I reckon it's nothing to stew over," the sheriff said.

"I thought I'd better tell you."

"Fine."

"Well, then—I reckon."

The sheriff nodded. "I'll just check with her folks. I'm going down that way. Want to come along?"

He shook his head. "I'll keep looking. I'm worried."

The sheriff frowned. He turned and got into his car and drove off. The sun was gone now and already the dust seemed to lay heavy.

Allen started jogging down the road toward Spanishtown. He couldn't seem to get his breath. He couldn't get to Binnie fast enough. He was free. There was only Binnie and himself. . . .

. . .

She was beautiful. Her dress was new, a bright canary yellow and it clung to her willowy body. She came out onto the porch and closed the door. He held her close in the darkness, his face buried in her scented hair.

"Oh, Allen," she said.

They kissed. He was still damp with perspiration from the hurried way he had come to her. He drowned in a kind of delight, being with her. When she pulled her lips from his, he asked:

"Anybody home?"

She shook her head and smiled slyly at him.

"Let's sit over here," she said. She moved over to the porch swing.

They sat on the swing, there on the front gallery of the old house and the thick, powerful flowing scent of night-blooming jasmine seemed to form clouds around them.

They kissed again. Her lips were so tender, her body so taut.

"Let's go inside," he said.

The saffron glow from a streetlight down the block shone on her hair as she turned and smiled at him. She took his hand and bounced it on her leg. She raised her head and looked past him up the dark street.

"Let's go inside," he said again. He grabbed her and they kissed and the swing creaked.

"Oh, you," she said.

"Binnie," he said. He kissed her hands. She watched him, smiling.

"Couldn't wait to see you," he said.

Her eyes shone. She glanced out over the gallery railing.

"Let's go inside, Binnie."

"Wait."

A car came down the street. It was a Ford convertible with the top down. It turned in the driveway and stopped. A man was sitting behind the wheel.

She smiled at Allen, released her hand and stood up. She smiled at him again, then walked to the gallery steps.

"Just a minute, Charley," she called.

Allen rose from the swing and stood there looking at her. His mouth moved but no words came out.

She glanced at the car, then at the door of the house. She snapped her fingers. She didn't seem to know Allen was there at all. He took a step toward her.

"Binnie," he whispered.

The car out there creaked, and the man coughed. A light wind blew among the trees, trailing in the tops, touching the Spanish moss.

She snapped her fingers again and ran inside the house. Her perfume swirled about him.

Allen stood there. He couldn't think. A horrible feeling of growing, deep embarrassment came to life inside him. He didn't know what to do.

The man out there in the car lit a cigarette.

Binnie came out onto the gallery again, slammed the door. She held a light coat in one hand.

Allen tried to say something.

She looked at him and smiled slyly. "I'm going back North tomorrow," she said.

"Binnie!" He choked with it, reaching toward her.

"I've got a date," she said.

She smiled again, turned and ran off the gallery and out to the car.

"Hell," the man said, "you took long enough."

A cigarette spun out across the lawn, showering redly.

The car door slammed. Standing there on the gallery, Allen heard her laughter. The car backed swiftly out of the drive, and hissed away down the street. More laughter trickled back. Binnie's—and the man's.

Allen stood there. He was very ill. He looked at the windows of the house. A light was lit inside. He remembered the afternoon he had spent in there with her.

He stumbled off the steps and walked out into the middle of the street. He took the road toward home, walking slowly. He was blind to everything. Binnie's sweet perfume still clung to his jacket.

He was so numb he couldn't think.

Smiling, that way. . . .

"Carol," he said. "Carol!"

He started to run. . . .

• • •

The sheriff and a deputy picked him up just outside of Georgeton on the Spanishtown road. The car came to a fast, dusty stop.

"That's him."

"Hurry up," the sheriff said. "Get in the car."

"Wait'll I frisk him, Chris."

Allen stood there, trying to remember beyond the smile, the eyes and the jasmine.

"Here it is," the deputy said. "Right in his pocket."

Allen stared at the leather sack. Then he looked at the sheriff and climbed into the car. He uttered a startled cry.

Carol sat there, moaning.

She seemed to shrink away from him, lying over against the far window.

The deputy crowded in beside him.

Allen began to scream inside. He looked at Carol. The car started with a lurch.

"You can talk, mister," the deputy said. "She can't hear you. She's sick."

He didn't say anything.

"But she could talk a little while ago," the sheriff said. "We'll get her to the hospital. They'll fix her."

"She'll pull through," the deputy said.

"It was the sack," the sheriff said. "Snake must have bit most of the poison out of him on that leather sack."

"Will she live?" Allen asked.

"You better hope she will," the sheriff said.

Fog

Manhunt
February 1956

At dusk he turned into the new housing development on the far edge of town and drove slowly, craning his neck out the window, looking at street signs. He reached Wimbolton Drive, stopped looking, and drove down the palm-shaded street. The cement block houses along here were very similar to one another, assuming a sameness of color with the approach of night. Daytime the same houses were vivid blues, pinks, reds, yellows. He craned his neck again, stopped the coupé by a small, new place.

He got out, started across the newly planted lawn, glanced back once. Across the street was a small ditch, an endless roadside row of Australian pines, and beyond the ditch and the pines was a humpy, shadowy field that stretched far into the country.

His heels scraped on the raw cement porch. He was tall, dark, wearing a light-colored sport shirt. The house was already well-lighted inside, though it was not yet completely night.

He grinned, pressed the buzzer. Somebody inside the house began running across the floor, fast. Feet skidded by the door. The door was flung open.

"Oh!" a young woman said, breathing sharply. She smiled, then went sober. "Oh?"

"Uh—is Art around?"

The young woman shook her head. She was a blonde. Her hair was very thick, bursting in thick waves around her throat and shoulders. "He's not here."

"I see. Well . . ."

She smiled again, watching him with wide clear blue eyes. "It is Mr. Thompson you wanted?"

"Yes. Then you must be—"

"I'm Mrs. Thompson, yes."

"Well—you see, I'm an old friend of Art's. Haven't seen him since you and he were married. I was in town, thought I'd drop around. He wrote me where he was living—"

"You're not Bill Calders!"

He grinned. "That's right. I suppose you—"

"Why! Art's mentioned you at least a million times!"

He kept grinning at her.

"Well, come on *in!*"

"Well, only for a—"

"Don't be silly. Come on in here, Bill."

She moved aside and he stepped in and she closed the door.

"Goodness," she said. "Imagine!"

"So you're Sarah?"

She nodded, watching him. She was wearing a blue cotton house-dress. She was in her bare feet. She stood with her hands on her hips, her hips thrown forward, and her lips were very broad and red.

"Come on into the living room," she said, turning. "Sit down."

"Well, only for a minute."

He followed her into the other room from the narrow hall. She moved quickly, firmly, large-hipped under the scant blue dress. His gaze followed her. Her flesh moved and trembled under the dress. Bright glaring light from an unshaded floor lamp beside a small, bulging brown couch shone clearly through the material of the dress between her legs.

Bill turned his eyes away quickly as she faced him again.

"Peeking?" she said.

Bill's face went red.

"It's so hot," she said. "You know? I really don't like to wear anything. Nothing at all. Just naked, all the time."

He forced a sorry chuckle. She beamed at him, flopped on the couch, watching him steadily. She motioned toward a chair across from the couch.

"Sit *down*, Bill!"

He sat quietly, carefully. He glanced once back toward the doorway, then at her, then at the windows above the back of the couch. The unshaded lamplight was brilliant white, glaring on the new maroon rug, the newly painted walls, the bright new everything with scratches here and there in the new paint. She looked pale, her lips vivid in the light.

"When'll Art be along?"

"Soon, soon. What d'you know about that?"

She bounced up and down on the couch, pressed her palms together, forced the spaded hands between her thighs, pushing the dress between her thighs, squeezing her legs tightly together on her hands, watching him.

"Uh, where *is* he?"

"Oh, he had to run out for a while. Won't *he* be surprised?"

She bounced up, jumped onto the couch on her knees and leaned over the back, reaching toward the window. She lay straight up across the couch, her toes pushing at the maroon rug and her dress drew tight up past the hollows of her knees. She yanked at the shade on the windows, drew it down to the sill with a loud *Whirrrrrrr!*

"Neighbors," she said. "Nosy neighbors, you know? The houses are so close together."

She turned and flopped back on the couch, bouncing, fanning her face with her palm and with the other hand plucking at the hem of her dress.

"Hot?" he said.

"Whew!" she said. "You know it!"

He nodded, swallowed. His face was coated with a fine sheen of perspiration. He kept looking around the room, but his eyes always came back to her with a kind of jerk.

"Art's not too well," she said. "Did you know?"

"No. What's the matter?"

"Nerves. Terribly nervous. He can't sit still. Can't sleep nights. Then he comes home from work and sleeps all day." She laughed shortly, showing even glistening teeth. "Really nervous."

"Well, I'm sure sorry to hear that."

"Yes," she said. She brought her hands back and began lifting her hair up and down, away from her throat and the back of her neck, plopping it up and down.

"Guess I better run along," Bill said, glancing at his wrist watch. "Tell you what. I'm staying overnight in town. I'll drop by tomorrow. How's that?"

"Don't go," she said, watching him closely, narrowly.

He started to laugh. Something caught in his throat and he had to cough. He went into a short fit of coughing. She leaped up, came across to him, slapped his back.

"There!" she said. "Gosh, you got all red!"

"Sorry."

"Where are you staying, Bill?"

"Hotel. The Town House."

"Oh." She returned to the couch, flopped down. She took the hem of her dress in both hands and slowly began lifting it back past her knees, dragging it up her thighs, watching him. "You don't mind if I pull my dress up a little, do you, Bill?"

He stared at her. She kept on dragging it up and up, watching him. Her eyes were narrow as she watched him. She ceased, patted it down snugly, rubbed her thighs with her palms. Then she leaned back and began plopping her hair up and down again with both hands, away from the back of her neck.

"He should be right along. So don't go. He'd feel awful if he missed seeing you."

Her legs were very white in the glare of lamplight. They were smoothly curved, plump and unblemished. She began to hum, watching him, plopping her hair up and down. It was very thick hair, damp looking at the temples. There were small beads of perspiration on her upper lip.

It was very silent in the room.

Bill was not more than two and a half feet from Sarah and the lamplight was like a hot sun.

"It's raining," she said. "Hear it?"

They sat, listening. Rain drummed softly on the roof. It dripped on the screens outside the windows.

"I knew it would rain," she said. She writhed from side to side on the couch, straightening a little, watching him. "Say!" She leaped up. "How's for a cold beer? I simply forgot. There's some in the kitchen. Everything's so new, we're so unsettled here. We've been here five months—I can't get over it."

"Really, Sarah—I'll have to go. Some things I've got to attend to."

She moved up to his chair, standing close, with the lamplight behind her. She put one hand on his shoulder. "I wish you'd wait a little while, Bill."

He stood up fast.

"Won't you have just one beer?" she asked softly.

"Sorry. Thanks," he said. "Take a rain check on that, though."

She watched him, smiling, her teeth tight together. "All right," she said quickly. She turned and moved into the hall. He followed her, watching her. She whirled on him.

"Peeking again?"

He walked into the hall without speaking.

She reached the door, opened it.

"You don't want to go out in all that rain."

"Got to. You tell Art I was by, huh? See you two tomorrow."

"Well—all right."

"Sure glad to meet you, Sarah."

"Yes." She held out her hand and he took it. He looked at her and she smiled. She held to his hand. He drew his hand slightly away, but she still held to his hand. Then she let go and stepped back and he turned and went outside into the rain. She called after him, softly:

"Good-by, Bill."

He turned and flapped his hand at her, running across the wet, muddy lawn. In the car he glanced toward the doorway of the house. She was standing there, looking out at the night.

• • •

A telephone rang.

Bill reached out from his bed and turned on the light on the nightstand. He found the phone.

"Hello? . . . Sarah? Yes, but it's—it's nearly two," he said into the phone, checking his wrist watch on the night stand. "What? Art's what? Well, now just relax, take it easy. I'm sure everything's all right . . . Yes . . . I'll be right out . . . Yes, sure, Sarah." He hung up and lay there a moment, staring at the silent window of his room, rubbing his jaw.

He finally swung his feet down to the floor, scratched his shoulder, stood up and took off his pajamas. He lumbered into the bathroom, washed quickly, returned to the bedroom and dressed in dark slacks and the same white sport shirt he'd worn earlier. He stepped into a pair of brown loafers, strapped on his wrist-watch, pocketed wallet, change and cigarettes and matches from the top of his bureau.

It was very foggy outside. He had to drive slowly and after he was in the new development again, he had to stop the car and get out and check every street sign until finally he saw Wimbolton Drive.

He parked the car, started up toward the house. The living room light was on, glaring against the shade yellowly.

Fog rolled and billowed and the air was damp, dripping, tepid. His feet scraped on the cement porch. The door opened.

"Oh, Bill!"

"Now, take it easy," he said.

"Come on in."

She was still wearing the blue cotton dress. She had on a pair of beach sandals and she was very excited, her movements quick.

"Bill, something's happened to Art! I know it!"

"What?" He looked at her closely, standing in the hall.

She took hold of his hands with both of hers.

"I hated to call you. There was nobody else to call. We don't know a soul—not a soul!"

He didn't say anything. Neither did she. Finally he said, "What about the neighbors?"

"They're nosy neighbors," she said. "We have no use for them. It's better that way."

"Well, you'd better tell me about it."

"Come into the other room." She dropped his hands, turned and hurried into the living room. He followed her, watching her move. The unshaded light was exactly as it had been before.

They stood in the center of the room.

"Art came home, just after you left. I told him you were here, where you were staying. He said he was going to phone you. Then, he said there was something he had to attend to first." She stared at him. She put her hands together and held her shoulders hunched up and licked her lips.

"Go on."

"He was laughing, full of fun," she said. "He said he was going out a minute, then he'd come back and phone you. I watched him from the doorway. He went out there, across the road. Into the fog. He went into that field, over there. It was hours ago. He never came back."

Bill laughed. He reached out and patted her shoulder. She moved her shoulder toward his hand and stepped an inch closer to him. Her breathing was loud in the room.

"You're imagining things," he said. "Art can take care of himself."

She shook her head fiercely. Her hair ruffled on her shoulders. "No. He went out there into that fog and he didn't come back. I know something's happened." Her voice rose. "I know it, I tell you!"

Bill looked quickly around the room, then took her shoulder in the cup of his hand. She hunched her shoulder into his hand, looking up at him with her lips parted, making small moaning sounds. There were three buttons on the throat of her dress and the top button was undone. She reached up and unbuttoned another button and the bright light glared on the unbroken smooth white of her flesh.

"I'm afraid to go out there alone," she said. "Will you go out there with me? I've got to go out there and look for him!"

He looked at her. She moved closer.

"Yes, sure, all right. We'll go have a look."

"Oh, yes!"

They moved quickly through the house and out the front door.

"We should have a flashlight," he said. "You got a flash?"

"No," she said. "There's no time for that."

He looked at her. She kept looking at him, then over across the street at the billowing fog and the field beyond the Australian pines.

"All right. Come on," he said.

They moved down across the lawn. They passed his car, and crossed the wet street and stepped under the pines.

"There's a ditch here," Sarah said. "You'll have to help me across the ditch."

"Sure."

They moved gingerly down the side of the ditch until they stood near a three foot stream of water. She came close to him, touching him with her body.

"Can you jump?" he said.

She shook her head. "No."

There was an iridescence to the foggy night. Lights from far in the city bloomed in the fog and Sarah's face was quite plain. Everything was quite plain for a short distance. After that everything was obliterated by the fog.

"Here," he said, taking her hand. She squeezed up next to him and he took her waist in his hand. Abruptly, he bent down, placed one hand under her legs, the other along her shoulders and lifted her and stepped across the water and stood her up on the other bank.

"You're very strong," she said.

He didn't reply. They went up the bank and into the field. He turned and looked back. There was only the blooming fog and the dripping from the sky.

"It seems foolish," he said.

"Does it?"

He shouted Art's name loudly.

Sarah moved into the field. He walked behind her. The blue dress and the blonde hair and the white arms and legs were very plain against the fog. Her dress clung to her damply and perspiration coated Bill's face. He called again.

"Whatever would he come in here for?" she said softly.

He came up to her side. They walked together, silently. They moved down small hummocks into damp ground and up and over low hills. They passed trees and Bill called repeatedly.

Sarah stopped and turned and looked up at him.

"Where could he have gone?"

Bill shook his head. He stared at her. She was breathing hard, and the third button on her dress was undone, her dress flaring open. She stared at him and then she half-smiled.

"It's terrible, asking you to do all this."

"It's all right."

"It's so hot!" she said. She squeezed her hair back away from her head with both hands, watching him. She smiled at him, her teeth tight together, glistening. The moon was up there someplace. "I'd like to just take my dress right off," she said. She kept watching him, smiling. She released her hair, leaned down and pulled up the skirt of her dress. She brought it up to her hips and tied one side of it into a big knot on her left hip. "You don't mind, do you?"

He didn't say anything.

She rubbed her legs with her hands, watching him closely.

It was very quiet. Water dripped softly, steadily from nowhere and the fog drifted.

"What would I have done if you hadn't come by?" she said.

"I don't know." He spoke quickly. He looked away into the fog, scowling. Then he looked at her. She smiled at him, squeezing the knot of blue cloth at her hip above the full white columns of her legs.

They stood there watching each other.

"I don't think he's in here," Bill said.

"Don't you?"

"No."

"Maybe you're right," she said.

They breathed together, staring. Neither moved. They stood perfectly still, staring. Then she began to slowly rub her legs with her palms again, watching him steadily.

He made a vicious sound in his throat and grabbed her brutally. She cried out, her hands clawing at his shoulders. He fastened his fingers into her dress and ripped it savagely, tearing it away from her.

She clung to him frantically as they dropped to the ground, and lay back, her face very white, pale hair fanned out around her head on the wet grass. The night was loud with violence.

Finally, hunched beside her, his fingers still snarled in the torn folds of her dress, breathing with profound heaviness, he stared down at her fixed grin. Her upper lip rolled redly away from her teeth, eyes wide and steady.

"Art never came out here, did he?"

She shook her head, watching him.

"Why didn't we stay in the house, Sarah?"

She said nothing. He took her wrists, pulled her half up.

"It's all right now," she said, staring. "I don't care anymore." Her voice was curiously flat. "We fought all the time, he wouldn't give me any money. Kept me locked in the house when he was away. Said I was no good—told the neighbors that." Her voice took on a slight edge. "I couldn't stand it, Bill! I *had* to have someone. When I saw you . . . well, after all I'm human!"

"Where is Art?"

"Back at the house. I killed him—in bed. Just before I called you. I used a knife." Her eyes were defiant now. "I planned it for a long time. It's all right now."

He let go of her and stood up. She sprawled back on the tattered blue cotton dress, looking up at him. It began to rain softly through the fog.

Midnight

Hunted Detective Story Magazine
February 1956

It finally got so bad it was like an itch all through me with no way to scratch. No way at all. I'd look at my hands, feel the itch swarming, and my hands would shake, and nothing did any good. I'd harness up the mare, hitch up the stone-boat, go up into the vineyards and clean out the rocks and boulders. It got so I could take them boulders and throw them around like they was nothing at all. I cleaned the north vineyard spic and span before I knew that was no good. I got to plowing. I plowed like a crazy man and I only got stronger, watching the mare heave at the plow, watching the shiny blade slice that hard-packed ground, watching it cleave and curl like you'd cut a store cheese. She was a big saddle-black mare with a hot eye.

It even got so I could plow that damned plow without the mare. I'd get down past them willows, so they couldn't see me from the house, unhitch the mare, and take that plow and run her hell-bent at the slope. It didn't do any good, I tell you.

I just got stronger.

Stand there between them plow handles and spread 'em till they cracked right off the bolts. Hickory, too.

It didn't do any good, I tell you.

Stand up on the hill by the chestnut tree and look down there at the house. You could take a rock and hump it right smack through her bedroom window and she'd come floating out and up the hill to me under the chestnut tree. Only not really, and that was the trouble, for fair.

Her ma would be out there in the side yard feeding them new chicks a handful of corn, and her pa leaning against the hog pen, smoking his briar, watching them eat. With it summer vacation and her home from high school in town, mostly lolloping around the place in fresh white curtain cloth. Plump and damp with sweet young sweat, her yellow hair bushed out and some of it sticking in curled strands around her throat. Looking at me, too, every time I looked at her, with it busting out of her eyes like heat lightning over the pine hill, knowing and liking the same.

I knew I should leave this farm. But I'd been here twelve years, so where would I go now? I couldn't go, because she was like a white-hot branding iron rucked right up through the soles of my feet.

Hell of it was, just remembering liked to pop my skull like a smashed mushmelon. I used to help her dress back when she went to school down the valley. Comb her hair, even. Put her shoes on.

Until that day last spring I saw her for the first time.

Before that we'd even taken walks down the gulley alone, just the two of us. Me telling her about the flowers and the trees, and why night come down like it did, and how come noon was noon, and how a horse could flick his flank when a fly bit and we couldn't and us both trying and laughing, too.

Trudy Bostich. Her ma's name was 'Lizpeth, and that's what you called her. Her pa was Charley Bostich, and the farm was gone to rack and ruin and he didn't care. He never *did* care, long as I recall. I'd work the vineyards for scampy grapes. We'd dry some berries out of the patch, raise a little corn and alfalfa, and that was it. To still be farming, you see? Run down. Never mind, Lizpeth cared even less than Charley did.

Lizpeth had the money, you see. Her folks died rich and Lizpeth played it close. And I'd mow the lawn and paint the house white every two years, and nail up the barn. It was fine. Family-like. Charley maybe selling a hog or a heifer and drinking his hard cider, chewing his Red Man, watching the cars go by.

Then a few years back we didn't take walks anymore. It just stopped. Bang. One day we was walking in the gulley, not caring a switch about anything, Trudy showing her legs, and the next day it stopped.

Of course, it was Lizpeth and Charley. I didn't heed it. It didn't matter. Trudy was a skinny button.

So then last spring I went down past the henhouse, taking a walk, and there stood Trudy the other side of the early tomato patch. She had her skirt held up, plumb full with tomatoes. She looked at me, standing there, holding her dress up, and I looked at her.

It was like being cracked across the head with a hay rake. She wasn't a skinny button no longer. She was everything any woman was ever going to be. She was ripe. Lush.

"Them tomatoes are rotten," I says. "I overdone 'em under hot boxes and they got away from me."

She looked and she grinned.

"They ain't no good for eating now, Trudy. I say, they got away from me. They're no good."

I got up next to her, the shaking all through me, and her eyes like smoking cigarette ends.

"I know it, Earl."

"Then what you picking them for?"

"Don't you know, Earl?"

I tried to say something. I couldn't. I swallowed. I shook my head. We kept staring at each other.

"Earl," she says. "I knew you'd come down this way. I had to have a reason for standing here."

Well, we looked some more, with her holding her dress up with them tomatoes, telling me with her eyes and then it was like somebody shot us both with rock salt. We come together and the tomatoes went flying. We kissed and we rocked, standing there with them tomatoes squashing and mushing between us and plopping on our feet. How can I tell it? It was like being blown up and knowing you still had time to explode.

"There's Pa," she says.

She tore away from me, red in the face, her eyes dizzy, panting, them tomatoes all mashed up. Charley was by the back porch, loading his pipe. I couldn't tell if he'd seen anything.

"Oh, Earl," she says.

"Tonight," I says. "After supper. Meet me in the barn. First dark."

She nodded and swallowed and the word spilled out.

"I hate her! I hate her! I can't have any boyfriends, Earl. Now, I don't want any. I just want you. I hate her!"

"Think about tonight," I told her.

"Earl, Ma says she's going to leave me all her money when she dies. Says she won't have men around me. Not for years. Says I got years yet. I hate her!"

You could see that, all right. She had enough hate for any ten women, and she sure was a woman, for fair. I hadn't known about any of this and it might have scared me, except how I felt nothing could scare me.

Charley turned his head toward the house, and she bust away and run lolloping toward the house. She was sure messed with them tomatoes and so was I.

Charley was setting on the porch steps now, smoking his briar, and chewing Red Man, spitting in the grass.

• • •

That night it was dead quiet at supper. Trudy would look at me and get red in the face and down her arms, even. She wriggled and she fussed. I couldn't hardly set still, only it was too quiet. Lizpeth kept looking at me, and Charley would look at me and eat and eat.

I got in the barn and she never come.

I scouted around the house. They were in the front parlor, the one that's always closed off for Sunday, setting around, watching each other. I went back to the barn and waited some more.

I waited till after midnight. Then I went out front. The lights downstairs were out. There was only a light in Lizpeth's and Charley's room upstairs.

Right then Constable Burch come along in his Ford. He always made a run clear to town and back on the valley road around midnight, every night. He thought he was a state trooper. Constable Burch ran the general store at the four corners.

He saw me before I could light out.

"Evening, Earl. Taking the air?"

"Getting a breath, Constable."

"Quiet night."

He set there with the car door open, scratching his chin, the radio playing soft music. He always wore a dusty white Stetson hat, his head like a wall-eyed punkin underneath. Constable Burch was an unhappy man with an ailing wife.

"How's Charley?" he says.

"Charley's fine. We're all fine."

"Didn't see you down to the dance at the corners," he says. "You don't come down anymore. How come?"

"Seems like there's always something to do," I told him.

"Time you got married, Earl."

We looked at each other, the radio playing real soft.

"Well," he says. "I'll be shoving along. Got to check the cemetery."

"Sure."

I watched him go. She wasn't coming. I went back to the barn and got the axe and went around to the woodpile. I split close to a cord of kindling. Then, after I put the axe away, I went back to the house and inside and up to my room.

I closed the door and Charley says, "About time you got sleepy, Earl."

He was setting there in the rocker by the window.

I turned the lights on.

"Not tired tonight, Charley."

"Figured that. Earl, you move to the harness room in the barn, now. Tonight. You can take this here bed. You fix you a place out there."

"How come?"

"You know how come."

Charley set there, rocking easy. He had on his blue nightshirt. He had the window open so he could spit out, and his eyes were beady and bloodshot. I hated Charley Bostich from that minute onwards.

Charley got up and squirted an amber stream out the window. Then he hooked his chew and whipped that out, too. He closed the window and wiped his finger, and looked at me.

"I been here twelve years," I says. "It's my home."

"You figure you can move yourself?" he says. "Or should I get dressed and help you?"

"Go to bed. I'll move."

He left. I moved.

From then on Trudy and me wasn't together alone but once. That once was for about a half a minute. We was planting some tulip bulbs for Lizpeth alongside the house. Lizpeth went inside for her scissors. Trudy and me grabbed each other and like to died.

"What we going to do?" she says. "Earl," she says. "Earl!"

"We're going to do something."

"They said I'm not to go near you."

"I know."

"They said if I go near you they'll fire you. They'll run you out of the county. I'm crazy for you, Earl!"

"We'll run off."

"We can't! I thought of that. They watch me every minute, Earl. At night they lock my door. I can't even go to town. They said it's for my own good, till I grow up. Damn her! Grow up! Her with her money, and all."

"Now, now," I says.

Then Lizpeth come back.

Time to time young men stopped by, asking for Trudy. They got run off. It was wrong. It was all right, because Trudy was mine, but it was still wrong. I kept aiming to talk to Lizpeth and Charley, but somehow I couldn't do it. I'd get right ready and it was like they knew. Then I saw if I said a word, they'd run me out. One word. They were desperate ready for anything. They was both of them like sticks of dynamite, just waiting for a chance to get sparked.

Only they didn't want to lose me, neither. I kept the place up, and they wouldn't find another man like me. Hired hands didn't come so easy anymore.

I tried to figure it. I listened to how they talked, sneaking up on them. It come out what they wanted was to wait so Trudy could catch herself a rich man from town, after she got through high school. She only had a year to go. They told each other how they watched me and her, and how if I slipped once, I was a goner. They was set in their ways, them two.

Well, it got worse and worse.

It didn't tame none.

Trouble was, we saw each other all the while. Vacation time, the hot summer, long days with the sun blooming like a devil in the sky, and nothing to do but watch.

Trudy thought about it. We'd rub feet under the table. Brush hands sometimes.

Trudy ate heavy and she swelled ripe till she was beauty rotten. She got to be a regular spitfire. She was the most wild and beautiful woman I ever see. Mile a minute, loaded like a churn of thick cream.

Something had to happen.

Lolloping around.

"You got the harness room looking right peerless," Lizpeth says. "I peeked in there this morning."

"I like it fine."

"Good old Earl."

I went on a drunk off in the woods. Alone. I couldn't even make that work right. Drank it down till it wouldn't swallow and it come up and I drank it down. Tried working it out. Split wood, plowed, painted the house, trimmed the trees, stacked wood and rocks, built a rail fence. The place looked like a million. I couldn't sleep. But I just got stronger, till I could snap a hoe handle like a toothpick.

So that's when I knew I had to get Trudy and make her my wife, or I'd go crazy. *I knew that.* Come whatever come.

Two days I figured, trying to think it out straight, and the second night along come Constable Burch.

• • •

We were on the front porch. The way Burch left his car and marched across the lawn toward the porch, you could tell something was in the air.

It turned out he wanted to know had we seen anybody skulking around the place, or the fields, the last few nights.

"Why, no," Charley says. "Have you seen anybody, Earl?"

"No."

"Well," Burch says. "A man run one of them Coggins gals all the way through the orchard. Mel Coggins saw somebody on the hill. I chased a man in the cemetery. I found out there's a loony escaped from the state hospital. So keep your eyes peeled."

"I swan," Lizpeth says.

Burch went on talking, but I didn't listen to what he said because the plan jumped into my head as clear as a picture. I knew just what, for fair.

"We'll watch careful," I told Burch, and the next night about nine-thirty I went into the house and hissed at Charley.

He come on outside by the kitchen door.

"I saw somebody down by the willows," I told him. "Get your shotgun. Let's have a look."

Well, Charley'd been drinking cider all evening and he was ready for anything. He got his shotgun and we cut down past the barn, keeping to the shadows. We followed the branch, walking the bank, sometimes in the water.

"Sure you seen something?"

"Sure I'm sure."

"We'd better split up," Charley whispered.

"Wait. We'll check the willows. If he ain't there, we'll split up and cover ground."

So we came down by the willows. Wasn't anything moving. Not much moon, either. We went in under the willows and over to the pond and Charley stood on the edge of the pond. He got himself out a chew. First off, I figured to tell him. Then I knew that would be foolish, because he had the gun. Not that he'd use it on me.

Anyway, he hooked a half a chew into his cheek, then started for another scoop, holding the gun under his arm.

"We'll split up," I says. I got behind him and found the rock I knew was there. A big one. He got his chew going, swishing it around, looking over across the pond. I brought the rock down on the back of his head. It cracked. He didn't even grunt. He fell into the pond and I waited for a minute. His feet were sticking up over the edge, his head down in the pond water. The ripples quit. A bird sang. I went home.

I cut down around the field, making a good path in the wet. Then I walked the stone fence clear back to the road. Then I come down across the field and cut the branch to the willows. Then I cut back the other way to the road again. I followed Charley's and my tracks down to the branch again, and cut off towards the hogback. I hit the stone fence again, and by the time I was done, nobody'd know which was which, if they ever did try to fathom it out.

"Charley back yet?" I says to Lizpeth. She was waiting in the kitchen. "I didn't see nothing. I think Coggins dreamed it."

"Why, no. Charley's not back."

"Huh. Should've been. I better check."

I went out and circled around and finally got to the willows and found him and run back to the house.

Well, Constable Burch got up a posse from the corners, and around, but it come to naught. Lizpeth was all worried and frightened, and Burch questioned me, and looked at me queer-like and scared me a little, too. But it got by. Trudy never cared a whit. Two weeks later it was already quieting down again. There'd been no sign of the loony, and Lizpeth hadn't cried once, and Burch quit coming by every night. He'd just beep his horn.

I kind of held my breath. Charley had a nice grave. Trudy and Lizpeth and me went on out the third Sunday and put fresh flowers on it. The rain come Sunday afternoon and washed a big hole by the headstone. They filled it up. In a little while you'd of never known Charley had been here.

It made me sick, I tell you! I'd gone and killed off the wrong one. Lizpeth was the one. No matter how hard Trudy and me tried to get together, she was there. *Every minute.* Not like anything human, stone-faced, and she wasn't feeling any sorrow for Charley.

My head begun to swim in and out.

Burch come by a month later.

We were in the yard, planting a flower-bed around the ash-tree. Lizpeth had the flower-planting bug, up down and crossways.

"He was in this section again," Burch says. "He slept in Coggins' corn crib last night. Even busted into my store, stole three boxes of corn flakes and a side of bacon. We figure he's after one of them Coggins gals. See here, Earl—you watch good, will you?"

I told him I surely would. He went away, and Lizpeth got scared again, so we went into the house and sat around. Lizpeth made chocolate fudge. Without Charley spitting, it was different somehow.

Only you couldn't rush a thing like this. You had to take your time.
If only they wouldn't catch that loony.

• • •

I let three days go by. I couldn't allow any more because Lizpeth was talking about the new school year.

Well, a change come over Trudy. She got to looking at me as wild as I felt inside. And she got to fighting with Lizpeth till Lizpeth was beside herself, not knowing what to do. It was worked up fit to fly now. I figured to was keeping Lizpeth up nights, watching, and I knew I had to act. She never went anyplace, never saw anybody, never visited. Her whole world was Trudy Bostich catching herself a rich man in town.

I got it fixed in my mind good and I knew I couldn't tell Trudy about it. Just have to let it work itself out.

Then one afternoon Trudy got the mare out and rode her bareback all around the lawn. She jumped the mare onto the front porch, and busted through it in five places, and jumped her off the other end. Trudy ran that mare through the flowerbeds, yelling and cursing like an Indian. It was a sight to see. I couldn't catch her. Lizpeth just stood in the kitchen window and wrung her hands, not saying a word.

Trudy run the very hell out of that mare, then flung off her, and come raging into the house, wailing and yelling. She stormed lolloping upstairs. Lizpeth tried to get into her room. Trudy wouldn't open the door.

"Earl, Earl," Lizpeth says that night. "What am I ever to do with that girl?"

We stood there in the parlor, with one lamp lighted, and Trudy was still upstairs, locked in her room, carrying on. I knew this was going to be the night. I looked at Lizpeth's sharp black eyes and her hair the color of black loam.

"Lizpeth," I says. "We best not talk in the house. Why don't you come out to the harness room in the barn? I'll tell you what I think you should do. We can talk about it. I know you've got your hands full and I think I got the answer."

"Oh, Earl," she says. "I knew I could depend on you."

"I'll meet you out to the barn."

And she says, "All right, you wait for me. I may be a while. I've got to talk to that girl, first. I don't dare leave her alone without talking to her."

It was right quiet upstairs now. So she went up and stood by the bedroom door, knocking and talking soft, and I went on out to the barn to wait.

I laid down on my bed and just sank into the dream.

How it would be so fine with Trudy. She'd have Lizpeth's money, and we'd live here. We'd marry up, and we'd love each other forever. I loved Trudy so much the dream was real. I wanted her to be happy, that was all, and then I'd be happy.

I was happy already.

I went and got the axe and went over and sat down on the bed, waiting. I waited and waited and she didn't come. I watched the clock and it kept on getting later. The sweat stood out all over me, thinking about Trudy. It had taken all summer. There was only one week left to school, and she'd never go back to school. A woman like her, in school! It was immoral.

Instead of the wild fury that had been in me, it got calm and thick and sure, now. Lizpeth and Charley had to pay, that was all. I couldn't help that. It wasn't wrong; I couldn't see it wrong, even trying to.

It was just past midnight when I heard the kitchen door slam and heard Lizpeth coming across the yard. I run for the door and got there as she come in. I swung that axe with every bit of me, whipping it down, letting it whistle just as she stepped through and I fought the swing at the last hair, but the blade cut in like it was white pine and on down and down.

She never said a word. I split her wide.

It was Trudy.

• • •

I stood there like it was me who was dead, not her. I looked at her and touched her and then I tried to put her back together, but you couldn't put her back together. She wouldn't stay.

I kept moaning and then I saw the knife. It was the meat knife, with dark stains, and Trudy'd been carrying it in her hand. My Trudy. I went running to the house and Lizpeth was scrambled out on the stairs, carved up and plenty dead, too.

I went back to Trudy. She'd killed Lizpeth, not being able to stand it any longer, like me. Or maybe she'd heard me tell Lizpeth to meet me in the barn, and thought wrong. She'd of had that money, too.

I set down there on the barn floor with Trudy.

Burch found me there. He come by to tell me they'd got that loony over to the county seat. He'd give himself up yesterday afternoon.

Burch shined his flashlight on me down to the barn when he heard me moaning.

"Did, huh," I says. "Catched him, huh?"

"Put your hands up, Earl."

He kept that flashlight on me. It was real bright.

"Catched him, huh?"

"Earl—put your hands up!"

I just set there.

Alligator

Hunted Detective Story Magazine
April 1956

Claude climbed up out of the gulley into the white noon sunshine on the valley road and took off his shoes. Aunt Rose would be mad. They were new shoes, with the brass studs; she had given them to him yesterday, on his birthday. He felt sad about the shoes. They were what Aunt Rose would call "a mess."

He sat down on the warm, sunny macadam and looked at the shoes. He hadn't meant to slip. That stretch of shale in the gulley by the waterfall had looked sound enough. It was like in the winter though, when there were mirrors everywhere. It was bad to step on the mirrors.

The shoes were scraped and soaked through. Mud was caked all over them. The little holes were plugged, where Aunt Rose pulled the string through. The something. He squeezed hard, squinching his eyes, but he couldn't remember what Aunt Rose called that string. The string was wet and knotted and Claude had to break it on both shoes to get them off.

Somehow that wasn't right, either.

He sat there, staring at the shoes. He had this feeling about something inside him, but he couldn't think what it was. It was something good, but it was like the way dew vanished with the morning sun.

The sun would dry the shoes. But it might take all afternoon, and then it would be dark.

That was no good. He shook his head. The dark was bad.

The alligator! That was it.

For a moment he had remembered and it flooded all through him. With the shoes she had given him the wooden alligator.

Then he forgot again. He touched his feet. His socks were soaked and muddy, too. He took his socks off. He was wet clear to his arm-pits, but that didn't matter. His pants and shirt were old.

Anyway, Aunt Rose wouldn't care. There was Hardy. Hardy was new and like the horse smelled. He did the chores and sometimes he let Claude help him, only Claude didn't like Hardy.

The other smell like the bottle Hardy drank, hidden one after one with the oats in the feed trough.

Thrown high, flickering brightly in the sun.

Remembering Hardy wasn't good.

A car went by. Leaves and dust swirled. Claude watched the leaves until they lay dead.

Aunt Rose and Hardy laughed together. They laughed in the barn. Soft. They laughed in the vineyard. Loud. They laughed with the cow. They laughed up on the hill with the stone boat, gathering pig nuts.

Another car went by. Claude watched the leaves.

His feet were cold. He tried to pull his pants cuffs over his feet, but because of the wet, it didn't help. He would get some grapes and go home to Aunt Rose. Maybe she would be laughing in the barn with Hardy.

He stood up and started along the road. It curved down and up out of the depression by the gulley. He looked back at the shoes and a car came by and ran over them.

He walked back and straightened them out and stood them side by side on the sunny macadam. He draped the wet socks over the shoes. The sun would dry them. He must remember to come and get them tomorrow. One shoe was broken from the car.

The alligator!

He turned and started jogging along the road toward home, feeling the memory of the wooden alligator inside him, like candy. When you held the alligator by the tail, it moved and moved.

He came by the school. He stopped by the fence and looked inside at the schoolhouse. It was very quiet. He was there once. He heard the woman talking, her voice flying through the window.

Claude wished he could talk.

What was it? He squeezed, trying to remember.

In the vineyard on the hill above Stuttle's, his feet were cold. He ate grapes and they were cold and his hands were cold. The juice from the grapes was cold and sticky.

• • •

He left the vineyard, running through the field to the branch. He washed his face and hands and feet. The water was bright foaming gray and icy.

By the barn there was no sun.

The sun was gone and pretty soon it would be dark.

This wasn't Aunt Rose's barn. He realized where he was, down by Stuttle's. Aunt Rose's barn was over there.

"Claude?"

He looked at Stuttle.

"Claude, you better get on home, now."

He tried to tell Stuttle, but nothing happened. If only it would happen, but it never did.

"Sure, sure," Stuttle said. "I don't doubt it a bit. You're absolutely right, Claude."

It was black and choking, but there was no use.

"Say, what you doing barefooted in this weather?"

Aunt Rose. The grapes. The sun.

"See here, Claude. You get the hell on home, hear? Big as you are, wandering around like this. Claude, you'll catch your death. Now, get. I got to be about the milkin'."

Stuttle looked up at Claude and shook his head and Claude got it so bad, trying so hard, that Stuttle turned his eyes away.

"Wipe your damned chin and get on home, Claude," Stuttle said. He went away.

Stuttle's loudness reached him again.

"Claude! You run, now. It's four mile. What in tarnation you doing over here, anyways?"

He began to run. He ran out to the road and ran along the graveled shoulder, his feet hurting. The shoulder sloped and he angled onto the macadam. His feet didn't hurt. He stayed on the macadam, running.

"Claude. You best hurry up. Getting dark."

Claude looked over at Constable Thursby, standing on the porch of the General Store. The smells reached him. They tugged him toward the store.

"'Cuss you for the hind end of a bony heifer!" Constable Thursby said. "You'll never make it. Blast my eyes. You'll get lost in the dark like last July. Be damned, spend all night a-hunting you in the woods and find you under Rose's back porch with the dog."

Claude tried to push past Thursby into the smell.

"No, you don't. See, here, Claude. Durn ye!"

"Big fella, ain't he?" Lowell said from inside out of the smells. "Rose ought to put him someplace. One of these now days, he'll pull a stunt."

"Enough of that," Thursby said to Lowell.

Claude tried to push.

"Hell," Lowell said.

"Claude," Constable Thursby said. "Get—barefooted, by the Lord!"

Claude ran around Thursby and toward the dark opening where the smell was. Lowell hit him hard in the chest. He looked at Lowell and Lowell laughed and Claude remembered Hardy.

The alligator!

He whirled on Thursby, cramped and gagging, trying to tell him about the alligator.

"Have to padlock his shoes on," Lowell said.

"You ever do that again," Thursby said. "I'll lock you up."

"Ho-ho-ho!" Lowell said.

He went along with Thursby to the pick-up truck, trying to shape the alligator with this hands.

"Sure, Claude. Ain't it hell? Sure, sure. Get in there and set. I'll run you home. A sight better than spending the night in the hills."

They rode. He held his feet with his hands.

"Where'd you put your shoes?" Thursby said. "Oh, hell," he said. "What's the use?"

They rode along and Claude watched the twilight on the hills among the reds and purples and yellows of the leaves, remembering the smell, but not remembering where it came from until it was a terrible aching. And something else behind the smell, gone again.

"Stop blubbering," Thursby said. "Hang your head out the window."

Claude looked at Thursby, liking him, watching the fat man shake his head.

It was dusk. All the color was gone.

"Now, see, here, Claude. You get in the house. Your Aunt Rose will be worrying. Don't shake your head, don't mean a durned thing and I know it. Whether you nod or shake, don't mean a thing, Hardy, Claude. Hardy!"

Claude put one hand over his eyes.

"Thought so," Thursby said. "You don't like Hardy."

He stood there and watched the truck turn and rattle back down the road, winking redly, a flame, until it was gone into the dark.

Seeing the red taillight, he remembered.

Alligator.

• • •

He turned and ran under the butternut tree, feeling the dark against his shoulders, forgetting again with sudden terrible loss, running past the stone well where the mirror was way down and around the side of the house toward the back porch where the smell was. The good smell and the warmth.

"No!" Aunt Rose yelled. "Hardy—for God's sake!"

Claude stopped and looked in the side window, his chin on the sill. Where Aunt Rose slept in the bed with the old bright tent on top. He stood there watching and the dark slipped off his shoulders, waiting away in the trees.

Hardy laughed.

Claude watched them in there. He hooked his toes on the cuffs of his pants, tugging them down, working his pants down until he stood on them, damp, but somehow like the kitchen floor by the stove.

"You're drunk," Aunt Rose said. "You've hurt me."

"Drunk," Hardy said. "I'm drunk. Damn you—sure, I'm drunk. Going to get drunker. You crazy wall-eyed heifer."

"Hardy. You've done enough. I want you to leave this house. Right now."

Hardy laughed.

Claude looked at Aunt Rose. She was tied to the bed post at the foot of her bed and the tent shook like the horse.

"Have a little fun," Hardy said.

"You release me," Aunt Rose said. "Hardy," she said. "Hardy!" She screamed and Claude watched Hardy pull up Aunt Rose's dress and push the cigarette into her leg. First one leg and then the other. Aunt Rose screamed. Hardy laughed along with the screaming.

He saw the alligator. It was on the chest of drawers against the wall, the red eyes winking in the light from the kerosene lamp by the bed.

"You like that, Rose?" Hardy said. "Where you keep your loot, Rose? Where you got it hid?"

Claude strained against the window, looking. He had to do something. What could he do?

Hardy. He was something because of Hardy. Hardy was like the dark on his shoulders. Worse than that.

"I've given you everything," Aunt Rose said. "God, Hardy," she said. "Have you forgotten? What you've done to me. I thought—I gave you myself, Hardy. Stop!"

"Feel good?" Hardy said. He laughed.

Aunt Rose screamed again. Claude writhed and writhed with anxiety by the window. He saw Hardy reel across the room and fall crashing against the chest of drawers. The alligator's head swiveled, eyes winking redly.

Hardy laughed and cursed.

Claude watched Aunt Rose strain at the bed post. The bed moved on the floor. Not far. She was blubbering like Thursby said, her hair swinging across her face. It was the rope from the hayrack. Around and around. Her hands behind her.

He watched Hardy push himself off the chest of drawers. Hardy lit another cigarette and reeled over to Aunt Rose.

Claude stood there wildly now, trying to find the sunshine, so he could see. Something to do. He tried to stop blubbering, but it came and came.

Aunt Rose screamed, and then she didn't say anything.

Claude watched Hardy hit her.

The alligator looked at him, winking redly.

Aunt Rose had her head bowed and she didn't say anything.

"Passed out," Hardy said. "She's a passing-out son of a gun." He picked up one of the bottles and drank gurgling, running sparkles from his chin, and flung it down. "If that big dumb Claude could only talk." Hardy laughed. "Twenty-six years old yesterday. Even then it wouldn't make no sense."

He hit her again. Claude writhed. She looked at him.

"Where you keep the money, Rose?"

"No money."

"Don't try an' kid with *me!*"

His face roared like the bull.

"Truth."

"You know what I'll do to you? Do you know?"

"Stop!"

The alligator.

Claude saw the light appear in Hardy's hand and Aunt Rose's hair flamed up, burning brightly, her screams lifting.

Alligator!

"Wouldn't let it burn all at once," Hardy said. He kept hitting Aunt Rose around the head and the flames went out. Claude felt the dark on his shoulders.

"Just a little at a time," Hardy said. "Mebbe if I trickle a little kerosene around the place. Mebbe you'll remember then?"

"Hardy, listen," Aunt Rose said. "I'll do anything, you hear? Only stop. Hardy. Anything."

Hardy laughed.

The light was in Hardy's hand. He reeled around the room and Claude saw Aunt Rose's eyes like black bugs, like big fly-away-homes.

He saw the alligator.

Hardy took the lamp that wasn't burning and smashed the mantel against the chest of drawers. He unscrewed the wick and sloshed the kerosene around the floor.

Claude watched the light in Hardy's hand. He turned and ran and ran.

Down the road with the dark on his shoulders. He squeezed the memory of the light in his mind. Thursby. It was very dark and cars swept past him, blowing against him, his feet hurt.

He pulled at Thursby.

"I just taken you home, Claude," Thursby said.

Claude had his mouth wide open.

"Close your mouth," Thursby said.

He retched and everything went black and then bright again with trying to tell Thursby. Aunt Rose's hair flaming like in the stove. Hardy laughing. The tinkle of the crashing bottle. The light in his hand.

"Tarnation," Thursby said. "You're all wrought up, Claude."

He got hold of Thursby's coat and dragged him off the porch of the General Store.

"Stop blubbering!" Thursby said.

"Why don't you lock him up?" Lowell said.

"All right, Claude," Thursby said. "All right."

Claude pulled.

"I think something's wrong," Thursby said. "He don't act right."

Lowell laughed. *Hardy.* Claude squeezed the flames in his mind, remembering all the time now, but squeezing just the same, so he wouldn't forget.

He had to get them there.

"You come along with me, will you?" Thursby said to Lowell.

"Nobody to watch the store."

"Damn the store. Something's wrong, I tell you. He wouldn't act like he is."

"All right."

They rode in the truck.

"He's out of his head," Thursby said.

"There's a difference?" Lowell said.

"He can't sit still. He's all wrought up. Something's wrong. I know durn well something's wrong out to Rose's."

"Hell," Lowell said. "I can tell you what's wrong. This is what's wrong, setting between us, here."

They rode through the dark.

"Lord!" Thursby said. "See?"

"Fire," Lowell said. "Rose's place is on fire."

"I told you."

"I'm damned."

Claude watched the flames, trying to crawl across Lowell.

"Quit blubbering!" Thursby said.

As the truck stopped out front, Claude hurled himself through the door. Aunt Rose was screaming.

"Ain't much, yet," Thursby said. "Come on!"

"Claude!" Lowell said. "Come back here."

Claude tried to dodge past Thursby. Thursby caught him and they fell on the ground. They fought in the dirt.

Aunt Rose screamed.

"I can get in there," Lowell said. "It's the bedroom. Lord."

"Hold still, Claude," Thursby said, fighting.

He didn't want to hold still. Everything was flaming and he was remembering clearly, everything. Aunt Rose screamed.

"I got her," Lowell said, running out of the house, carrying Aunt Rose. "She's all right. I burned my damned hand. She was tied to the bed. But I got her. It's Hardy. He's drunk as a coot in there. Burning everything up. Got coal oil on the floor. She's all right, only burned some. You all right, Rose?"

"God, God," Aunt Rose said. She sat down on the ground.

"Can't get Hardy," Lowell said. "He's on the bed an' the bed's burning."

"God, let him burn—let him burn," Aunt Rose said.

Claude broke free and ran stumbling into the house, remembering.

"Stop him!" Aunt Rose said.

"Trying to save Hardy, too," Lowell said.

"He'll catch fire," Lowell said.

Claude ran into the bedroom and clutched at the alligator on top of the chest of drawers. The flames were bright and hot and he nearly screamed like Aunt Rose. But nothing came out. Nothing ever would.

He ran outside, holding the alligator by the tail. He sat down by Aunt Rose, showing her.

"Lord," Thursby said. He was panting. "We can't get Hardy."

Claude held the alligator by the tail and it moved and moved, its eyes winking.

"He just wanted that fool alligator," Lowell said. "He didn't even look toward the bed."

Aunt Rose began to cry.

Goodbye, Jeannie

Accused Detective Story Magazine
May 1956

She was driving me out of my mind. It was like beginning with the final faint diminishment of an echo and trailing it back to its source, cliff to cliff, until you faced the wide-stretched mouth, the explosion of the scream, the shuddering palate, the clenched eyes and then provoking silence.

I knew the silence. I knew the scream.

Jeannie had me nearly nuts.

"She's old," Jeannie told me. We were in my room, down the street from her house and the afternoon sunlight splashed against the drawn shade, burnishing the room, turning her yellow hair, her white dress, her soft white skin to gold. "It won't hurt, Johnny. You've got to listen. You've got to help me do this. I can't stand it. I hate her."

"She's your grandmother," I said. "You can't hate her that much."

"But I do. You don't know her, Johnny. You can't imagine how she follows me around, sneaking—saying those things."

"I've seen her. She's harmless."

Jeannie turned her back on me and I stood there watching the gentle, teasing slope of her shoulders, wishing there was something I could do. I loved her so much, but she wouldn't listen to what I tried to tell her.

I wanted her, but she would not yet allow it to happen.

I'd never imagined you could want a woman this much.

"Listen," I said. "Jeannie. I've got a good job. A good salary. I like the work at the plant, and I'll be head clerk in no time. You know that. We'll have enough money to buy a place of our own. We could have a separate room for your grandmother to live in. Why—sure, we could even build a little separate one-room house for her. We could. It wouldn't cost much."

"Stop it." She turned on me, ran up to me, pressed herself against me and beat my chest with her fists. Her face was wrung with a kind of terror. I'd seen it before and it frightened me. "I've told you. I'll never marry you while she's still alive. You've got to help me kill her, Johnny. It's the only way."

"Jeannie. . . ."

"It's not as if she hadn't lived her life. She's been alive so long it's outrageous. By rights, she should be dead. It'll be simple, Johnny—as simple as anything."

"But, Jeannie. You're just mixed up—you don't know what you're saying."

"Don't I!" She turned and flung herself on my bed. I saw the movement of her shoulders. She was crying to herself, without sound, without tears, talking wildly with her face buried in the covers. Her tone was muffled and agonized.

"Johnny, you can't understand. I don't blame you for that. Nobody could understand—yes, they could. Listen, all my life—*all my life*—she's haunted me. She's never changed. The black dress, the white hair, the black eyes—following me. 'Jean, where are you going? Jean, where were you? Jean, stop at the drugstore. Jean, who's your new boy-friend? Jean, did he kiss you? Jean, eat your supper, breakfast, lunch, dinner! Jean, help me up. Jean, fetch my book. Jean, where did you hide my glasses? Jean, you're not at all like your dear mama. Jean, I think you don't care whether I live or die. Jean, where were you all last night? Jean, *I* know what you're doing. Jean, you're a sneak! Jean, don't curse at me. Jean, you'll be sorry someday. Jean, I'm old and you're young. No," Jeannie said. "It can't go on. It's got to stop. I mean it. I'm going to make it stop." She rose from the bed and came up to me and touched my face with her hand, gently. Then she leaned against me and offered her damp red lips, I grabbed her, trying to kiss her. She thrashed in my arms, twisted away.

"No!" she said. "See? That's the way it's going to be!"

"Stop it!" I said.

"I won't stop it. All I'm asking you to do is be there. At night. When she's asleep. Just be with me, because I can't do it all alone."

I wanted her so much I shook with it. Perspiration streamed inside my clothes. She was beautiful, desirable, and she knew what she was doing with me. She lay on the bed, watching me, taunting me.

"Johnny," she said. "Just be in her bedroom with me, that's all. I'll smother her with a pillow. It won't take long, it won't take much." She turned on the bed, and her eyes lit up with a smile that made my hands tremble. "Then, Johnny—then you'll see what I can be. We'll get married. We'll have the money she has. We'll have each other and nothing will stand in our way."

I couldn't speak, watching her.

"Say you will, Johnny. Say it, or you'll never have me. There!" She came off the bed and went over by the door and turned to look at me. She thrust her head forward and her voice was tinged with bitterness. "I hate her, Johnny. She's destroyed half my life. Please, Johnny—just do it."

"All right—all right—all right!"

"Johnny!"

She ran to me and for a moment I thought she was insane.

And that night we came along the street together, under the soft buzzing yellow from the streetlights. There was evil insinuation in every movement she made. I liked it. I wanted it that way. She had my mind dancing with what would come. The promises she'd made with body and voice had me blind. I didn't care anymore than she did.

"Only a few more minutes, Johnny," she said. "And I'll be free."

We reached her house. Only a dim light burned in the living room and the soft shifting of Australian pines in the night winds was exciting.

"She's in her bed," Jeannie whispered. I touched her accidentally and it was like touching a shorted electric cord. I saw her eyes, and they were bright white coins in her head.

We entered softly. I wasn't thinking about what she would do. It didn't matter. All I saw, felt, heard, was Jeannie. Lust and lust alone held me on a kind of fleshy red plane.

"Don't talk until after," Jeannie whispered, leaning up to me, her lips flowering. "Just watch."

I followed her through the house, beyond the kitchen to the small, meager stale-smelling room with the raddled silken drapes across the door. Each footstep on the cool linoleum was a silent shout to hurry. Moonlight splayed in the windows, and I stared at Jeannie's back, impatient for what would come after—impatient and uncaring.

We were in the room.

I could hear Jeannie breathing. There was something in the breathing that warned me, that startled me. I saw the bed and the sleeping old woman, lying rail-straight and insignificant, the pale wash of mingled streetlight and moonlight bathing the entire bed.

The old woman's chin jutted straight up, like a carved spike. Her withered hands were folded across her empty breast.

Jeannie reached down and silently lifted the pillow from the opposite side of the bed. Then she abruptly turned to me and I saw her smile.

"She's got to know what's happening," Jeannie whispered. "I've got to wake her, or it's no good, Johnny."

I tried to speak—to stop her.

"Old woman," Jeannie said. "Old woman. Wake up!" She shook her grandmother, and slapped at the clasped hands. She spoke loudly, then shouted, "Grandma! Wake up! Old woman, don't lie there!" And she began to curse and beat at the old woman lying in the bed, and the old woman did not move because she was dead.

Jeannie turned and shouted it at me. "She's beat me—she's won again!"

I started toward her and she began to laugh and curse, beating at the silent bed with the pillow.

Then she knelt on the bed and began to pound and pound with her fists, swearing and cursing—shouting her hate.

Something inside me went away.

I turned and left, free of Jeannie. And as I started up the street I could still hear her frustrated cries lifting in harsh shrieks against the night.

Short Go

Hunted Detective Story Magazine
June 1956

Mr. Williams was different. You could tell it right away. The minute I walked into the office, I sensed the difference. Two of Mr. Williams' boys were in the office, but when I came in he nodded them out.

"Hello, Luke," he said. "How's it going?"

"Fine, Mr. Williams. Just fine."

"Great. Got a little thing for you."

"Yeah?"

"That's right. Little thing you been waiting on."

I grinned. "Not a contract, Mr. Williams?"

"That's right. A little contract—down in Tampa, Florida. Think you can fill it?"

"Why, hell, Mr. Williams—I been waiting for—"

"I *know* you've been waiting."

"I been mugging guys for you, all over town. I took care of two the hard way last week, down on the docks. You should know by now I'll be able to fill a contract."

Mr. Williams watched me for a long moment. Then he sighed and scratched his head. "All right," he said. "I'll just never get used to the way you act. But my two best men are out of town. And we got a rush call. It'll have to be you, Luke."

"Swell!"

He watched me again. "One thing," he said. "How about the girlie angle? I've got to know about that, Luke."

"Oh, I've got that under control perfectly."

"You're sure? I mean, I don't want to send you down there and have you get all snarled up with some blonde."

"Why, hell, no, Mr. Williams. I tell you, I've got that under control."

"Well, O. K. But I know how it is. There's some can take the women and keep a clear head. Others got to fall for 'em. It's got to be love, you know? That's bad in this business. But you know that now, don't you?"

"Perfectly," I chuckled. "I straightened that out *my* way, Mr. Williams."

He got to watching me again, and he sighed again. "Well," he said, "damned if I'll ask you what your way is. I don't want to know."

I grinned and waited. Hell, I wouldn't tell him anyway. He had a swell office, for a fact. He was a big man in every way, Mr. Williams was. Not Mr. Big, but close in line. I couldn't wait for him to set the facts.

"How're you doing with your gun lately?"

"Perfect," I told him. "I keep in practice. Shoot every day."

"What you carrying?"

"Forty-five—same as always, Mr. Williams. She's my baby. You can have your fancy numbers—baby leaves a big hole."

He looked at me and frowned and coughed. Then he folded his big hands on his desk and waggled his thumbs. I wished he'd get to the facts.

"Remember, don't write any of this down, Luke."

"Hell, no!"

"It's Tampa, Florida. Your contact will meet you in his car. He'll finger the mark."

"Good."

Then Mr. Williams told me where the finger would make contact and I felt good about the whole thing. Mr. Williams had been hearing plenty of good about me lately, he said. I'd toed the mark, as they say, and kept my schnoz clean, and I'd finally landed what I'd wanted.

"Don't try to find out the mark's name," Mr. Williams said. "You're not superstitious, are you, Luke?"

"No. None of that for me. I could know him like a buddy, it wouldn't matter."

"It might matter to me—or to somebody else. So play it straight."

"Right." I waited for him to come across with expense money. He did. Plane ticket and a hundred bucks. He said I'd get my five when I got back with the report.

"That's for ten tonight," Mr. Williams said. "You'll get into Tampa in the morning, early."

• • •

He was right. All the way down on the plane I figured and figured so I'd have at least a few days in Florida. I'd heard about the dames down here, and what I saw around the airport even that early in the morning was enough to make me scratch dirt.

But I'd been waiting for this for a long time. It meant a lot. It was my living from now on down the line. I'd be sent all over the country, filling contracts—on the regular list.

Just the same, this was Florida. What Mr. Williams didn't know wouldn't hurt him any. So I hung around at the airport restaurant until after daylight; then I got a cab and had the driver take me across this Gandy Bridge toward St. Petersburg. It was a long bridge, and damned narrow. I looked out the car window straight down to Tampa Bay. It's a big bay, damned big. It got me sweating some.

Just on the other side, I rented a motel room, dropped my bag, and had the cabbie take me back to Tampa.

The way Mr. Williams had it set up, there was no lost time—at least for the first part. After that, it was my business till I took care of the mark.

I got to wondering who the mark was. It didn't pay to wonder. You learn that early—one of the first things.

Well, I figured to gun him and get out fast. There's no fancy chess moves in this game.

The way the dames were, in those tight shorts and bathing suits and bright-colored skirts and what-nots, right on the streets, I got to thinking how I would gun that mark any damned place. Just so I could have a short go with one of those sun-tanned babes. All over the streets, marching up and down, wiggling this way and that way, bold as snakes sunning on a rock.

I scratched dirt all over town.

The contact met me outside a Spanish restaurant in Ybor City, which was an interesting side-issue all of itself, open for a return trip by me. Anyway, he came along and made with the sign, and I got into his Chevy coupe. I could tell right off it wasn't his car. He'd picked it up this morning at a used-car lot, just to play safe. He'd sell it again as soon as he got lost from me.

Guys in this game are a superstitious lot. I knew one, he'd filled maybe twenty-three contracts around the country. A real boiler boy. His marks had to be fingered at twelve noon, or it was no go. He'd fold and come home.

He came home without doing the job once too often. Mr. Williams had me meet him in an alley one night. I had to use a brick. You got to learn all ways.

"Nice country, down here," I said to the contact.

"Yep."

"Nice-looking women," I said. "Really tossing it around, huh?"

"Mebbe."

He was a regular Gary Cooper.

"You couldn't maybe fix me up with a little tid-bit for later on, could you?"

"Nope."

He was a cold fish, for a fact. He had his job and he was going to do it.

"He lives here. Comes out at nine-thirty every morning except Saturday and Sunday. The front porch. It's nearly ten, we'll catch him at the office. He comes out that front door, goes to his garage, gets his car, drives downtown."

It was a big old Spanish-style joint on a broad boulevard across from the bay. It was surrounded by big trees and a low cement wall. It looked good. I liked it.

"We'll catch him downtown," the contact said.

I smoked a cigarette and watched the contact, thinking. He was a roly-poly bird, and he wouldn't look at me. Red-faced, nearly bald, and tending to the driving.

We parked by a parking lot. The contact lit a cigarette, still not looking at me.

"Watch it," he says.

I looked up.

"Here he comes. That's him. The one walking with that dame—the big blonde. See her?"

How could I miss? She was a bomb in tight black and her spike heels pecked right past us on the sidewalk. I nearly broke a blood-vessel forcing myself to look away from her at the mark.

A real insignificant zero, that one. Big beak, thin hair, skinny as a wet rat in a short-sleeved white shirt and gray slacks, talking up a storm. His mouth was flapping like crazy and the blonde kept nodding and chewing her lip.

"O. K.," I said. "Thanks. I'll get out here."

"He works in that building on the corner."

I got out and stood beside the car. The contact gunned off into traffic and left me leaning on nothing.

• • •

I followed the blonde and the mark. The mark went into the corner building and she gave him a little pet and a peck on the cheek and started on down the street.

What a swivel she had! I couldn't stand it. I went into a bar and had a beer and sat there cooling off. I thought it through. I had to get that witch off my mind. All witches.

So I had another beer and thought about it. It would have to be tonight, that was all. At his home. I couldn't wait. There were two marks now. Wouldn't Mr. Williams like to know what I did with the dames?

It was rough. I'd get soft on them. Every damned time I got close to one, I fell in love with her, like Mr. Williams said. Been that way all my life. In the rackets, that's bad business. Any way you look at it, it's bad business. First thing you know, they've got you snowed in a deep drift. But I couldn't do anything about it—dame—love. So I hit on an angle.

When I'd meet one, we'd shack up, and before it could drift into hearts and flowers, the same night—I'd gun her. It was easier that way. It was a nasty business and it hurt plenty when I thought back on it, but it was that, or nothing. If I did it real quick, before they yapped too much, I didn't get stuck. I had to be drunk or I couldn't do it, and there's a redhead living in Yonkers who wouldn't be there except we met in the middle of a Saturday night and she was game before the bars opened on Sunday. I followed the plan pretty well, though. To each his own—live and let live, I always say.

• • •

Well, I ate in a place, and caught a bus out there late in the afternoon. I walked along slowly, and traffic was real thick on the boulevard. I was smack in front of his place when he turned in the drive. He looked right at me, too. That would have sent plenty of the boys running back home.

I just kept walking. He was alone. He parked the car in the garage and went in the house. I walked down a block and around back, through an alley. It was growing dusk and I came up by the cement wall behind his garage.

I jumped the wall and cut through his back yard. All he needed now was to be having a family reunion, or something. Hell, I'd gun him anyway, the way I felt.

The back door was unlocked, so I walked inside. The house was quiet. A big old place, for a fact, cool and quiet. Swell place to pitch a brawl. I stood in the kitchen and looked around, listening. A radio came on, some goof yapping the news.

You get to know—nobody was in the house but the mark. You know that as sure as hell. You get so you can look at a house and say, "That place is empty. They won't be back till Monday." So you bust a window and take your babe in there, and find the master bedroom and drink their liquor and play their records and eat their food. Early Monday morning, you get out, and hang around watching, just for kicks. Sure enough, along they come, laughing about all the fun they had in Schenectady.

The mark was all alone here. Could be lots of reasons, only to hell with them. And the radio was going. I walked into the dining room, and there he was.

He was sitting on a couch, over a coffee-table, listening to the radio and eating a bowl of soup. I walked in there, and over to the radio and turned it down a little. He just watched me, dribbling soup all over the front of his shirt.

"Hello," I said.

"What do you want?" he said.

"Certainly not soup. What's the blonde's name?"

"Blonde?" He was still holding the soup spoon in the same position. Then he dropped it. It fell into the soup and splashed all over his pants and the rug and everything.

"Boy," I said. "You're a messy eater."

He stood up and pointed back toward the kitchen.

"Who are you? Get out of my house!"

"Take it easy."

He began to shake; then he got scared. They all get scared.

"The blonde," I said. "The big gorgeous hunk of blonde. With you this morning on the way to work. Long legs, kind of over-done swivel to her—"

"Nina—!" he said. "Nina, what do you—?"

"Where's she live?"

"What do you want?" he said. He took a step toward me. I still hadn't drawn my gun and I let him take another step.

"Please," I said. "What I asked you. Where does this Nina live? What's her address? I'd like to meet her."

"Get out of my house!"

"Oh, for God's sake."

I took out my gun and shot him. He tripped on the coffee table and spilled the rest of the soup and died crawling toward me across the rug. He hadn't been so scared, at that. The gun had made a hell of a racket and I'd only shot once.

I went over and looked out the window behind the couch. Traffic was as busy as ever. Just another backfire. It was a big house, with no houses close to it, so it probably hadn't even been heard outside.

Back by the mark, I checked my marksmanship. Right over the heart. It had been a quick shot, too, down from the shoulder holster and kind of backhanded. I'd been practicing it that way, but hadn't had a chance to put it to real use yet.

I hadn't heard the door open, but I did hear those *clicks.*

Spike heels.

I started running like hell for the dining room, then stopped.

She hadn't heard me, even. I ducked down behind a TV set and watched. It was the blonde. She came through the hall into the living room and saw him lying there.

"Oh," she said. "Oh! No!"

She went over and kneeled down beside him. She had a big round silken knee. She touched his face with her hand and just stayed that way for a long time, until I got cramps.

I stood up and said, "Hello."

She turned, standing up. She'd been crying without making any fuss about it. Her eyes were all red and her cheeks were wet. She looked at the gun in my hand.

"You finally killed him," she said.

"Take it easy, now."

"We knew you'd try. I guess—I guess I knew you'd get him. All the good he's done and then you come along and kill him."

Her lips were very red and her chin kept bunching up. I hated to see her do that. But I didn't know how to stop her. I hated to see her cry. She was so damned beautiful and big all over, a real hunk, you know? Crying? It didn't mix. She was wearing a silvery dress with a black sash, and silver earrings with dashes of black in them, and silver and black spike-heeled shoes, and her legs were long and silken.

"Why?" she said softly, stepping toward me. "Why did you *have* to *kill* him?"

"Now, take it easy, honey—we can work this out."

"He was so good—so very, very good," she said.

"All right," I said. "We'll take that for granted. He was a great guy. Wonderful." I winked at her. "You're not so bad yourself, sister—not so bad."

Her eyes were drying and she kept looking at me. I figured if she was mixed up with a guy who could open himself to a gunning, then she wasn't so tender, either.

"He was ridding the country of persons like you," she said.

"How you know I'm so bad?"

We watched each other.

"Nina?" I said. "You got a coin to flip?"

"What?"

"Well, it's got to be this way. I thought it all through. Either you come with me, or you go with him." I nodded toward the stiffening mark on the floor, and shook my head. "It would be a real waste. Can you see it?"

She stepped a little closer to me and I put the gun away in the shoulder holster, and waited. She came real close, watching me. God, she was beautiful. I'd never in my life been so close to anything so beautiful. It gave me a terrible sick feeling in my chest and I wanted to grab her and kiss her and tell her I loved her. I did love her, from that moment. I loved her like mad. She moved with a grace that sent blood into my head and then left me pale as a sheet.

"He'd of got it sooner or later," I said. "You know that. So why did you keep fooling around with him?"

"You wouldn't understand," she said.

"Did you flip the coin yet?"

"Yes," she said. "I flipped it."

"Well?"

"What should I do?"

I nearly laughed. I held it back, though. You don't laugh right out with one like she was. She wouldn't take it right.

"Do you have a car?" I said.

She nodded. "It's outside."

"Let's go, then."

We looked at each other for a while longer. I grinned at her and stepped up to her and put my hands on her waist. She leaned her head back and smiled and all the tears were gone and her lips were so damned red and just the tip of her tongue showed. I kissed her. I couldn't stop. She kissed me and put her arms around me. Then I shoved her away.

"We'd better go right now," I said.

She didn't say anything. I took her arm and we went across the living room, stepped over the mark, and went out through the front door. It was dark out there, so it wouldn't matter about being seen.

"Nina," I said. "I've never known any girl like you."

I was getting soft already. I didn't care, though.

She kind of squeezed my arm and we went down the front walk and got into her car. It was a black Lincoln. I let her drive and told her to head across Gandy Bridge, toward St. Pete.

"Don't feel bad about the mark," I said. "Try and forget him. He's gone, see? When a thing's gone, you can't bring it back."

• • •

She drove along the boulevard. She was a good driver.

"Were you ever in love?" she asked.

"Yes." I slid up close to her in the seat and put my arm around her, and rested one hand on her knee. "I know exactly what you mean," I said. I wasn't going to tell her anymore, yet.

"Love is a very strong thing," she said. "What's your name?"

"Luke."

"Luke, I'm terribly in love."

"Me, too, honey."

She turned and looked at me and smiled, then she kind of laid her head over against mine and I could smell her perfume and I was nuts. I was out of my head with Nina.

We came along through all the lights, past all the alligator farms and the restaurants and used-car lots and motels.

When she spoke her voice was soft, like the night after a rain. I wanted to get her to stop the car, just any damned place. It didn't matter. But with her, you wouldn't be that brusque. I knew how it was with me, I loved her and wanted her so badly—but I didn't want to scare her.

"When a person's in love, Luke—he'll do anything for another person. Anything at all."

"I know, honey."

"I mean anything, Luke."

I squeezed her knee and kissed her throat and she put her hand over mine. We came along the highway, buzzing under the big oaks, and she was driving real fast. We were hitting about eighty, and we were starting across Gandy Bridge.

I got to thinking about what I'd have to do to her afterwards, and I wondered where I would leave her. Maybe in the motel.

"I don't think you understand me, Luke," she said.

"I understand everything you say, sweetheart."

"Do you?" she said. We were about in the middle of the bridge, when I felt the car sway. "Do you?" she shouted. "Do you really understand?"

"Don't!" I grabbed at the wheel.

She tramped on the gas-pedal, laughing, looking at me and laughing, and we were doing close to a hundred when we smashed through the guard rail and started flipping toward the deep waters of the ship channel way down there below.

Return to Yesterday

Pursuit Detective Story Magazine
July 1956

He drove through the town and on into the dark country, watching for signs of change. There was little difference between now and ten years ago. The town was much the same. He had supposed it would extend far into the country. It didn't. Already the pale yellow cones of light from the streetlamps were behind him and he was fast approaching his destination—the house where Lorry still lived. The house in the cedars. Their house; Lorry's and his.

It was much too dark to see far beyond the roadside. It was never too dark for death, though, and death rode with him in the car. Death had slept with him for these ten years, and waited beside him in the mess hall, and marched along with him through the endless hours of lock-step. And now he would show death to Lorry.

When he saw the house, over there on the shadowed knoll, his foot automatically lifted from the accelerator. Even after ten years there was still the remembered impulse to turn in at the drive. He didn't, though. He smiled, and kept going, driving slowly past, watching for signs of Lorry in the yard.

It wasn't late. Only shortly after eight, and Lorry used to wander on the lawn early in the evening, back then.

He wondered if she still did.

What would she say when she saw him? When he told her what he was going to do? Because he had no choice. There was compulsion. Ten years of planning and dreaming and hating was behind it, and though he detested the thought of the vengeance inside him, there was no way of denying it. Ten years was too long a time to live with a malignant growth and still be able to deny it at will.

He wanted to kill her. He wanted to see her face change, her bright blue eyes alter with confusion. Yes. To see Lorry confused. Lorry, of all people. Yes.

What would she say?

He turned his head, peering back through the rear window. He was down the road, past the house now. There was a light in the kitchen and one in the living room. Dim lights. The way Lorry liked them. He wondered if she were alone.

He wondered if she knew he had finally broken out? She probably did. He knew of at least two kites that had reached her. There hadn't been much to tell her those times, but he knew the letters had bothered her. He hadn't dared threaten her, or let her know his true feelings.

Lorry, he had said. *Won't you please believe I did not kill Mary Russo?*

"Stevens," Warden Grimes had said on a morning six years before, "your wife's worried."

"That so?"

"Come off it, Stevens. We know you're sharp. You don't have to keep in character. Relax."

"I wasn't aware of any nervousness, Warden."

"Have you been communicating with your wife? I mean, beyond your allotted letters?"

He had laughed in the warden's face.

"We know you men manage. We know there's nothing we can do to prevent it. But if you've threatened her in some way . . ."

"Did she say that?"

"No. But she came to me and she was worried."

"I'm sorry. She didn't visit me, Warden."

So for an hour they had talked, and when he left the office, the warden had been as much in the dark as before.

And she hadn't visited him either. Oh, a few times, in the beginning, to make it look good. And he had laughed inside, watching the smooth, pale column of her throat. And then she didn't come any more. It happened like that with a good many of the men. Their women found other pursuits.

Yes.

So driving along on the old familiar road, now, he felt satisfied and unhurried. He would take his time. Think about it. They might consider his returning to her, or they might not. Anyway, he wasn't out for complete escape. That was senseless. He couldn't possibly succeed at that, anyway.

Sooner or later they would get him. And the sooner or later would be hours, or at the most, days. He had no illusions about staying free.

Only he hadn't meant to kill that guard.

The guard's name was Warzcek, and Warzcek had been a damned fool. An idiot. Still, he hadn't wanted to kill the man. It only added that necessary impetus to an already hyped-up manhunt.

But—he had time. Lots of time.

He made a swift U-turn on the highway and headed back toward the house. Twice he drove past the house, looking over there at the knoll, thinking about her, remembering.

It was painful.

Then, finally, he went past for the last time and after traveling a half-mile or so up the road, he turned off into a field. He drove down through the field and into a thick copse of fir, driving in close to the steep bank of a gully, until the car was well hidden.

He wondered if he would ever return to the car. It didn't matter. He had a mission in life. God, yes. And now that it was this close, nervousness did attack him. He climbed from the car, and for a moment he had to lean there against the door. It was as if his thinking mind had turned to cheese and his chest to a laboring fury. He could actually feel the beating of his heart.

Nonsense.

He had waited so long, though—so very long.

He turned from the car and pushed through the fir trees. He remembered them from ten years ago. Small bunches of green. And now, full and beautiful and thick and smelling of clean freedom.

Nonsense again. But he had shot a rabbit by these very trees once. With a twenty-two single-shot rifle. Quite a shot. Lorry had been with him.

"You're just lucky, Jack," she'd said.

Oh, yes. So very lucky.

He turned back across the field, toward the road. Headlights slanted brightly around a curve and a car sloped past, engine hissing with speed. That hadn't changed. Just like ten years ago. Everything was the same. He ducked into the shallow ditch beside the road and waited. The slight panic inside him ebbed with the diminishing sound of the car and he stood up, looked at the sky, and grinned. He felt good.

He crossed the road, running. His feet pounded for an instant on the macadam, then crunched on gravel, and he was in the far ditch. Water seeped into his shoes and he jumped to the bank. He knew this country, every blessed inch of it. They couldn't take that away from him. He had hunted it, hiked it, lived in it, loved it.

He cut directly away from the road, uphill across a field of fragrant alfalfa. Finally he met the dense, knee-high undergrowth edging Harrow's Woods. Inside, beneath the shadowy whisper of hickory and elm and chestnut, he turned toward Lory.

He moved slowly now.

Now was when he must think. Now was when he must realize that he didn't know what he should know. But there was no way of telling if the place were surrounded. It could easily be. They might be waiting for him in the garden— Lorry's garden. Or in the shrubbery, or behind the cedars.

They could even be in the house.

It might be that Lorry wasn't even there. They might have her in town.

He refused absolutely to believe this. They had no real way of knowing he would come here. Not after all this time. And back there all those ten years, to that day, he remembered how he had never let her know his design. He had looked at her during the trial, and listened to her lie, and seen the way she looked at Russo. That had been very bad. Yes. And the way Russo looked at her, wet-eyed. Hot. Secretly. And he had known that she and Russo had killed Mary Russo. And right then he knew that he would return somehow and do the same to Lorry.

That simple. Or complex. Whichever way you chose to look at it.

It was too late now to do anything else. Too late to hope for recompense in any other way. After all, he had killed Warzcek.

What else was it that got into a man? Especially an innocent man?

Sure—well, why hadn't they believed him?

He knew why. Because of Lorry's face, that was why. Because of her guiltless eyes and her sad red mouth, and her wonderful young body, pliant, full beneath the sheer dresses. And the way she walked and talked and moved her hips and legs and smiled oh so sadly at the judge. And because of the fine mist of tears that had come into her eyes before the jury.

With Russo grinning hotly to himself.

He slammed through the woods. All of the memories ate at him, moiling in his mind like stirred ripe sewage. He wanted to kill her. To wipe the memory out forever. To have the fierce satisfaction of cutting her off. With his bare hands. To feel her throat pulse and writhe and cool.

That's why he had discarded the revolver they had sneaked behind the walls, taped to a truck axle. Anyway, he had sent four of the five slugs into Warzcek's chest.

He parted with the woods, plowed through underbrush into a corn field. The corn field was bad. He looked around carefully, picked a naked-looking row and started out.

Lorry. It didn't really matter, but he wondered which one had it been? Russo or Lorry? Which one had fired the gun that killed Russo's wife?

He halted in the corn field and stood there, overcome with that damned remembering, the sharp bite of the scene.

They had framed him for their conspired lust. Not love. He might forgive that. But lust. He could see it. For ten years he had seen it in his mind's eye, until he practically had to fake sanity.

He moved on, making the effort to think clearly, to eliminate the waste from his mind. He came through the corn field and stood there, looking off toward the house on the knoll. The kitchen light still burned, and there was a light in the living room, as before.

It looked good. Quiet. Waiting.

He moved on.

Even if they discovered the car, it would mean nothing. Ten years had gone into the plan, and the car was above-board, in a direct and meaningful way, of course. Under his assumed name, from another state.

Tick—shush—tick—shush—tick—shush, the sound of the lawn sprinkler reached him, sank into him like a blow. He stopped, listening, feeling the memories again. The ten years of yesterdays. All those myriads of nights at this hour, when he had moved around within the house, or perhaps even outside with Lorry, hearing it. *Tick—shush—tick—shush—tick—shush,* with the moist fragrance of freshly cut grass. And her perfume, too, in the night air.

He moved on again.

He came to the fence, went under it. The wire creaked. He ran, his feet moistly crunching, then soft on the lawn. He ran directly at the house and up to it, until he stood in the near flower bed, his palms pressed against the dust-roughened white painted wood.

Silence. A great silence broken only by the lawn sprinkler out there among the cedars.

Standing there, breathless, he was absurdly and abruptly stricken with intense nostalgia. It was like a wartime gas, almost—suffocating, unbelievable, but true. He nearly cried. It was plain, sharp, understandable pain. It was all the great horrible *might-have-been* of his life, of any man's life. He could not move, only stand there drowning in memory.

He was at the side of the house, just below the sill of the dining room window. This window was dark. He moved toward the kitchen window, listening all the time now, cursing a little bit inside because he'd thought that by the time he got here, memory would be done with.

At least nobody was around; they'd have had him by now.

He raised his head above the kitchen sill and stared in there and saw her and stared, unable to move, seeing her.

Lorry.

He dropped down into the flower bed, hungering, his palms dragging against the side of the house. He breathed in the rich odors of the earth and of old flowers and of new flowers and of the night.

He heard her walk from the kitchen and leaped up for another quick look. She hadn't changed, from what he could see. He remained very quiet, listening to her heels clicking through the house, and then the front door slammed out on the porch. Her feet scraped on the porch and he heard her cross the yard. He started prowling along the side of the house until he was beneath the aromatic shedding of wisteria.

She was changing the sprinklers, pulling the sprinkler itself across the heavy turf by the hose, without shutting the water off. How many times had he told her not to do that? It ripped the grass up. He watched her head back for the porch.

There was his chance and he hadn't taken it.

He wanted to wait awhile yet. He realized this now.

She was on the porch and the door slammed and he heard her in the living room and then silence.

He moved back to the first living room window and peered into the room. She was sitting in the chair by the front window, flicking through a magazine.

She was alone in the house.

Well, they hadn't been able to tell him much, and it had cost him plenty to find out that little bit. She still lived there, they told him. She wasn't working. And that was all.

That had cost him three hundred dollars. That much.

And Russo?

They didn't know about Russo. He was manager at the plant now, promoted four years ago. Still unmarried.

Standing there, he found he did not want to look at her. It was enough, just being here. More than he'd bargained for. Too much. His house. Their house. The dream. The great big wonderful dream of a balloon that had burst.

A car hissed by on the road.

He looked down off the knoll at the night.

Lorry was right in there, this close, alone. Why didn't he go in there and face her, tell her, and do it?

It was then that he smelled the cake. Almost at the same instant, he heard her leaving the living room. He looked quickly, then moved along the side of the house to the kitchen window and looked again.

She was at the oven, opening the oven door.

She was baking a cake.

Lorry? Good Lord. Impossible.

He turned and leaned against the house, refusing himself any thought whatever. He heard the oven door scrape shut. But he didn't hear her leave the room.

He looked again. She was getting a drink of water from the faucet at the kitchen sink. She stood leaning sideways against the sink, drinking from the glass. God, she hadn't changed at all. He had changed—he of the white-shot hair, and the bitter mouth. But Lorry . . .

He looked at the blonde mass of her hair that fell to her shoulders, at the trim figure beneath the colorful blue dress and the white apron.

She set the glass down on the drainboard, wiped her hands on the apron, walked over to the stove. For a moment she stood there, looking at the stove and he heard her humming to herself.

He couldn't look. He turned with his back against the house again. And the thought sneaked into his mind.

Could he have been wrong?

No. He shouted it silently at himself. Don't be a fool.

He hadn't killed Mary Russo. He hadn't shot the dark-haired woman in the throat and left her to die, writhing on the hall rug. But he had found her. They'd been friends. And he'd been caught, bending over her, calling her name, "Mary, Mary, Mary," with the gun in his hand, because he didn't believe in murder. Who did, really—until it happened to them, to somebody they knew?

And the police had come running. The police had arrived before he'd even had a chance to realize he was still holding that damning gun.

Wrong?

To have seen the look in Lorry's eyes. To have seen Russo's secret smile. This was not to be wrong.

He looked again. She was seated at the kitchen table, smilingly thumbing through a cookbook.

Another thought struck him. Damn the thoughts. But he couldn't prevent them. She must know of his escape. She had a radio, certainly. She read the newspapers. He'd made page one of every paper in the country. In small type, sure—but he'd been there, and she wouldn't have missed it. They would notify her.

Then what?

It could only be that she expected him.

So he stood there. He was utterly sick. And a man's name kept wringing his mind like a sponge. Warzcek. Warzcek.

He had killed a man.

That he had been imprisoned for life didn't matter. Up to now there hadn't been a single shred of hope in him. He was guilty in the eyes of the law, and there was no one who cared. So he didn't care. Only to kill her.

Now there was doubt. He stood there and he could not look at her and yet he had to look at her.

She was at the cupboards, bringing down ingredients to make an icing for the cake. Lorry baking a cake and icing it?

Waiting for him. To tell him that she did honestly believe him and that she had told him over and over when she visited the prison.

He looked back at those visits. He tried to remember them and see them objectively. How had *he* been?

He had been a secretly smiling, patient monster. Waiting, watchful, staring at her throat.

And how had she been? Patient and loving, trying not to show that she saw his hurt, his trapped puzzlement.

"I believe you, Jack—I believe you. We'll do something. We've got to do something."

"They think I was having an affair with her, Lorry."

"But we know different."

That's how she had been. And she had come to him, until his leering, pressured silence drove her away, never to return.

He looked, and now Lorry was stirring something in a bowl. A strand of blonde hair fell across her face and she backhanded it free.

Warzcek. He had killed the guard, out there on the road, beyond the wall. Because Warzcek would not drop the shotgun.

How could he tell her why?

He reeled in his mind, standing there. He didn't know what to do, yet he knew what he *had* to do. He was going in there and talk with her.

Ten years. Yes. He knew it. It was true.

He had been wrong. He had condemned her. Because of a look. And Alec Russo had been his friend. He had condemned Alec Russo too.

He stepped carefully away from the house, walked silently around the backyard past the shrubbery and stepped as quietly as possible onto the porch.

Warzcek. If only he hadn't done that. All of this was so futile. All the remembering, all of everything that could have been but was not.

He watched her through the door. She had paused in the stirring and was reading from the cookbook.

He opened the door and stepped into the kitchen.

"Lorry."

She turned and looked at him. Her lips parted and he stared at the bright blue of her eyes. Yes, ten years had done something to her. Her movements were not so quick now. A certain something had come into her face and the sadness of her lips was more pronounced than he recalled.

"I've come back, Lorry. I had to come back."

She did not move. She just stared at him.

He smelled something, sniffed.

"The cake's burning, Lorry. Better get it out of the oven."

"Jack," she said. Her voice was as soft as he had always remembered it. "I knew you were coming here. I've been waiting."

"Lorry—" He ceased, unable to speak now.

He heard the single footfall in the kitchen doorway behind him and turned violently, knowing.

"Go ahead, Alec!" Lorry said.

He was still turning as she spoke, and as he made the full turn to the doorway he saw Russo's pinched face with the handsome black hair and then the bright stabbing flower of the explosion as the slug tore into him. And another. And then another.

He went to his knees, staring at Russo.

He heard Lorry's heels scrape on the kitchen floor.

"Damn, I thought he'd never make up his mind," Russo said through the thickening red haze. "You'd think that after ten years, he would. Well, the waiting's over with." Russo stepped up to him, placed his foot against his face and shoved. He buckled backward and sprawled loosely on the kitchen floor, dying.

He smelled the cake burning. He tried to tell her.

"God," Lorry said. "I was scared, I tell you. Real scared. I knew he was out there. I saw you wave from the garage when he came out of the cornfield. Go call the cops, honey. Go call the cops."

"Yeah," Alec Russo said. He kicked the dead hand, turned and walked out of the kitchen toward the telephone in the hall.

The Golden Scheme

previously unpublished
October 1956

Every afternoon about two o'clock she would ride in from her house on the outskirts of San Pedro. It raised hob with every man in town.

"Here she come!"

"Thar rides Widder Holmes."

"Hold me, Bill—nail me to a tree—hit me on the head with that hammer."

"I'm a big bear! I'm a two-gun grizzly—look out, friends, I'm gonna bust loose an' row-*dee-dow!*"

On a big white stallion, bareback. And even the boys in the foothills shinnied up their ropes, and climbed the ladders out of their holes for a look across the rooftops at Widow Holmes. They had field-glasses and telescopes, and you could see them in the tops of pine and cottonwood, leaning among the branches like bug-eyed baboons.

On a big white stallion, bareback.

Everybody felt wrong about staring like that. It wasn't the thing to do. Cathy Holmes had been widowed only a month before. Gregg Holmes had been shotgun killed in an alley behind the assay office at high noon, and the murderer had escaped, unknown.

On a big white stallion, bareback.

Previous to her husband's death, Cathy Holmes was seldom seen around the streets of San Pedro, small mining town as it was. When she came in on Saturday afternoons for salt and bacon, she wore a sun bonnet, and loose calico, with lace tight around the neck; long-sleeved, long-skirted, booted, in the buckboard.

It was different now, all right.

Bareback, on a big white stallion. In white cotton that clung to her full-blown shape like split soft chamois, sprayed with warm rain. The furled skirt caught carelessly up around long plump white legs, black moccasins dangling from her toes. The golden wealth of hair flowing around her shoulders and down her back. Proud, pointed breasts bursting from the slashed V of dress-neck, buttocks heavy and strained across the stallion—riding slowly, lazily, red-lipped and yet maybe even shy above the broad, tail-switching rump of the horse.

The wives talked. Plenty.

"I swow, that woman's a chore."

"No pride."

"No pride, you say? She's got pride enough for ten—my Bill, say—I tell you, I got to take a long nap every afternoon."

"She *don't* carry on none."

"How do we *really* know?"

"She hit Long Charley over the head with a mop pail Sunday forenoon. He offered to clean house for her—you know what he had a-mind. She cut him down."

"Then why does she flaunt herself like that."

"My John, he says last night, right out of the blue—there in bed—he says, 'Mathilda, I wish you'd eat more bacon, you ain't really got enough behind.' Now, what do you think of that!"

"We do leave her alone awful much. Getting so's we don't even speak with her. It's not right. She's a good woman, always was."

"Good woman! I reckon. Look up there on the hill. Those pines. See 'em? Them's our menfolk, hangin' in the trees with their eyes popped out. I hear tell they even come out of the main shaft—got a lookout posted. I swan—here she comes now."

"She won't have no truck with 'em."

"She don't have to. All she's got to do is ride into town."

"Why she stay here? Gregg didn't leave her nothing but that old map, of his. One he drawed for his claim over in the buttes. Nobody can find it, cain't read his writing. What's she livin' on?"

"Will Stone, an' Fib Hicklbee—they tried to help her find the claim."

"Ain't all they tried to find."

"Didn't find nothing. Will Stone said it was like she knowed it all the time—that they couldn't read the map. She won't let nobody else try."

"Everybody knows that claim's lost for good."

"Traipsin' around in the desert, like that."

She rode slowly across the bridge below Albert's sluice. Gouts of dust burst under the white's hoofs. The sun was white and hot. Sheened sweat glassed her temples, and forehead, and it was as if the horse and young woman worked together, but against each other, too—walking along, strained and heavy in the sunlight. She was a pretty girl, really. But there was something behind those dark blue eyes; something patient and hotter and more impenetrable than the sun.

Down the hill, between the adobe houses, past the ramshackle store-fronts, the *Ringtail Saloon*, among the insecure, never thoroughly established, strike-up, strike-down buildings of San Pedro.

Over beneath the brow of pinon- and juniper-freckled hillside, the mining town's twin smelters hulked belching—fat and gorged on a meal of ore.

There was the raw element, too, thronged in the streets, calling to her, whistling, remarking in general terms; drunk, lecherous and abused. She rode through them boldly, passing among the jazzy ruckus of ragtime piano from the saloon, invulnerable, unapproachable and obscene.

Cathy Holmes reined the white in at *Dugsby's General Merchandise & Hardware Emporium*, slid off the stallion's side with a careless show of red pants, flipped the rope from the hackamore off the rail, and moved lazily on inside.

On the plank walks, men smashed fists into palms, burst lusty epithets toward the sky.

• • •

That night a naked red-haired girl rolled over on a bed in the *Hotel San Pedro*, and sullenly regarded a man across the room. The man stood with his back to her, knotting a white scarf around his throat, staring at himself in a small wall mirror.

"I don't like this plan of yours, Clay," the girl said.

The man went on knotting the scarf. "Who gives a damn what you like?" he said softly.

"I heard that."

"Meant you to."

The girl's face paled, the smeared red lips twisting with scorn—only there was a shadow of pain in her eyes.

The man began to whistle softly. His name was Clay Bracker. He was long and tight-muscled, black of hair and eye, with red-brown skin stretched tautly across high cheekbones. The eyes were deep-socketed, and they were the keen, sharply watchful, don't-give-a-damn eyes of the Mississippi riverboat gambler—though Bracker did not gamble with cards. He was dressed entirely in black, shirt, pants, and boots. Around slim hips, a black, heavy gunbelt clung, one hand-tooled holster thonged to his right thigh, the gunbelt ivory and silver. Silver and ivory studs gleamed in a simple aristocratic pattern on his silver-spurred boots.

He turned and looked at the girl, grinning thinly.

"You just use me," the girl said.

"It's good using."

She turned violently on the bed, flung herself face down, the thick red hair fanned out across the mashed pillow. Her pale-skinned body was taut, save for the curve of creamed flesh over her buttocks, which trembled as she came close to crying.

The grin did not leave Bracker's face. He lunged for the bed, made it in two strides and, still grinning, viciously grabbed the girl and hurled her spinning across the bed against the wall.

A scarlet-shaded lamp glowed on the bureau. Red shadows paced the walls.

Bracker grinned down at her, his jaw faintly thrust, the eyes not humorous at all. He spoke rapidly, even-toned, deep-voiced.

"You crazy bitch! You'd frog up a thing like this. I reckon you *enjoy* living this way? Do you? Is that it? Why, damn your whoring soul, do you begrudge me these clothes? That it?"

She stared at him, cramped back in an uncomfortable position against the wall, her pear-shaped breasts lifting and holding, thighs apart, red hair snarled across her shoulders. Fear snapped its fingers in her eyes.

"*Say something*," Bracker whispered, grinning.

"I earned you them clothes."

"Sure, you did. Don't you think I appreciate it?"

"If you loved me, you'd never let me earn them that way."

Bracker's head rocked back and he shot a lungful of bright laughter at the splotched ceiling. His eyes caught hers again.

"Two nights' work," he said. "Two nights lying on your back in your favorite position, and you're kicking. What the hell's got into you, gal?"

She came across the bed at him in a running crouch, spitting and clawing, red nails flashing toward him.

Bracker moved fast. He caught her wrist, flung her back on the bed, sat on her belly, leaned close and grasped her hair on either side of her head. He kissed her. Her body writhed, fingers clawing at his shoulders, legs flailing . . . then she subsided into moaning delight. The clawing hands gripped, tugging Bracker closer.

He tore away, stood up and grinned down at her. She lay there breathing heavily, a sly smile on her lips, the eyes gone hazy.

"You bastard," she breathed.

"Yes," Bracker said. "I reckon there's more truth than you think in that."

He returned to the mirror and began carefully readjusting his white scarf. The girl watched him sullenly, lying on her side, hands spaded between her legs.

"That's another new scarf. Those are expensive," she said. "You lose the one I made you?"

He began combing his hair. "Yes," he said. He spoke softly. "I'm going to get to know Widow Holmes. Get to know her good. An' you're going to cool your heels, and your behind, while I work. All I got to do is get my hands on that map, I tell you—I'll locate the mine. I knew Greg well, Lou. Nobody around here could read his writin, and obviously his wife couldn't. But I can." He faced the girl, his voice taut. "I've wanted something like this all my life, Lou! It's what I've lived for! The big strike—the chance—the break! *And now I've got it.* Nothing will stop me—nothing. We'll be stinking rich, Lou—don't you forget it. *Stinking, filthy!*"

"I seen this Widow Holmes, you."

He relaxed. "Yeah. Not bad, is she?"

"How you know the claim's worthwhile?"

"I know. It's the biggest strike in the territory. Lost—only not for long." He reached both hands out and doubled them into fists and smashed them together. He grinned again and the eyes were a little crazy, maybe.

"Clay, I wish we wouldn't. I wish we'd get out of this dirty hole of a mining town—go back to Frisco." She sat half up, her eyes pleading with him. *"I hate it here, Clay.* The dust, the mud, the filth—the smell of sweat. . . ."

"That's why I'm doing it, bitch."

"Who you think killed Holmes?"

"I don't know."

"Why would they kill him?"

"That, either. Nobody knows."

For a moment they stared at each other. He turned, snatched a flat-crowned black hat from a chair, and without looking at the girl again, left the room. The door slammed.

Lou sat there on the bed for some moments, staring at the door. Finally she lay back on the bed and began to softly cry. Between the crying, she spoke angrily into the scarlet light of the room.

"He's no good, and I love him," she said. "He's mine. And they're after him. He's killed and murdered across the whole frontier. He's bad—he's rotten! No damned good at all. That crazy Sheriff Noonty from Alveraz, he'll get him and hang him. They'll cut his heart out—" She began beating the pillow with her fists. "She's young an' ripe. Young an' beautiful—"

• • •

Outside in the hall Bracker turned and faced the door of the hotel room again. He grinned and whispered, "Get to know the Widow Holmes, Lou? That *is* a laugh. My God, woman—while you were on your back earning me these special duds, what you reckon she was doing?" He whirled and strode down the hall, walking softly. There was only the tinkle of his spurs, the faint creek of leather that was a little too new.

Downstairs, he crossed the lobby, came outside onto the plank walk that lined San Pedro's main street. A full moon hung in a black sky over the *Ringtail Saloon.*

Loud laughter and ragtime emanated from the saloon where work-worn miners fretted the dark hours away with whiskey and bed-shot dance-hall girls, awaiting morning and work in the foothills.

Bracker paused under the sign reading *Hotel San Pedro*, and rolled a cigarette. He took three or four deep drags, bleak-eyed, watchful, as bearded and torn-shirted miners crowded past him on the walk. One hulking man slowed and passed a remark as to Bracker's dandified clothes.

"Prob'ly got a pansy hint his ear."

Bracker did not move, did not speak. He looked at the man, and the fellow went abruptly silent, quickened his gait up the street.

Bracker grinned, dropped his cigarette, toed it carefully out, turned and moved slowly on along the plank walk.

He came past a saffron-glowing window, lined with black paint lettering: *Sheriff Jack C. Walters. Office.* Bracker cleared his throat and spit on the window, then moved on.

He crossed the makeshift bridge over Albert's sluice, picking his way through the last of rutted mud. The box had burst early in the evening and turned the main street into a river before men dammed the stream back to its path.

He came through smoking dust now, striding slowly into the moonshade of cottonwoods. He did not look back. Up on the hill, beyond the silent church and the graveyard, a single lamp burned in a front window of the Widow Holmes' large, comfortable cabin.

• • •

North end of town, two dusty, red-eyed riders talked wearily from saddle as their mounts pecked tenderly over the rocky entrance to the main street.

"You reckon he's here for sure, Sheriff?"

"So the Injun said."

"Why you reckon he'd come to San Pedro?"

The taller of the two riders, bearded, broad of shoulder, turned and looked at the other, took a battered hat off and wiped his sweat-muddied brow.

"Nobody's got an idee what Bracker'll do next."

"He'll kill next, that for sure."

"I'll get that son. Take him back to Alveraz—dead or alive."

"We come a long ways, Sheriff—a damned long ways."

"Patience is what you lack, Pruitt. Patience."

They rode silently into the drying mud and the mixed jumble of ragtime piano that burst from the bat-wings of the *Ringtail*.

Pruitt was barrel-built, double-chinned. He wore a buckskin shirt. "Sheriff Noonty," he said. "You reckon they got law in this here town?"

"They have now."

• • •

"I'm ashamed of myself," the woman said. "I can't help being ashamed, Clay. Gregg's dead only a month—and look at me!"

"I been looking. I been looking a lot."

They stood in the small, well-furnished parlor of the house on the edge of town, among furniture that Gregg Holmes had brought by train, by wagon, by burro and horse and by plain man-back, clear from Boston to San Pedro, just so his bright-eyed bride, Cathy, could be happy among the things she loved, while he staked his claims and gambled against the Earth—just so she could have a place to be when she heard he was shot down at high noon in the alley behind the assay office. Just so he could have a right and proper funeral, too—from *Higgens' Parlours*. Just so she could sit there and wonder who had murdered her husband—just so she could lie among the shadows and go wild-hot under another man's hands with the memories of Gregg still chuckling—or maybe frowning—in the corners.

"Funny, how we met," she said.

"When I saw you on that horse," Bracker said, "I couldn't rightly help myself. I had to follow you back home."

"What would you have done if I hadn't been nice to you? Suppose I hadn't even talked to you?"

"I'd have raped you," Bracker said.

She looked up at him. The over-ripe curves of her body pushed boldly against the sheath of black dress, breasts lushly bursting from the slashed throat of the dress, the slim curve of silken ankles revealed in an intriguing slit above spike-heeled silver shoes. There was a secret wickedness in her dark blue eyes.

"Why do you show yourself like that in town?" he said. "Riding that damned horse bareback, and all?"

"What do you mean, Clay?"

"You know damned well what I mean."

Her full red lips parted. "I like it," she said. "I like the way it feels—the sun and everything. The way men look at me." She stepped close to him, put her arms around him and shoved her hips against him. "I like it, Clay."

"Wish you wouldn't show yourself like that," Bracker said, grinning. "It raises hob."

"Does it really bother you?"

He fastened his fingers into her flowing golden hair, and pressed his mouth against her open lips. She moaned softly, her arms snaked around his neck. He kissed her throat, her back arched, and his hands slowly skinned up the back of her dress, revealing long curved calves and full round thighs, and the pink-white bare plump flesh above the biting rims of her stockings. His hands gripped her buttocks and she began to move against him. Something feverish overcame them both. Her hand came up, ripped open the front of her dress, baring swollen, rose-tipped breasts.

He said something unintelligible, grasped her under the knees, carried her into the moonlit bedroom and dropped her sprawling on the bed. She lay back, panting, eager . . . "I love you, Clay—love you!"

• • •

"I think Gregg would forgive me," Cathy said. "That's how much I love you."

Bracker lay beside her on the bed in the moonlight and shot laughter at the ceiling.

"Please, don't laugh."

"Can't help it." He turned to her, reached over and cupped one full, bulging breast with his palm, squeezing. "Can't help anything I do with you, Cathy. You're like loco-weed—only worse—hell of a lot worse." In the pale darkness, his face held a curious seriousness for a moment, then he grinned again, slapped her belly resoundingly. She reached down and held his hand there, her face turned toward him.

"I've seen you on the street with another girl," she said. "One of those—well, she just looked like one of those—"

"She was," Bracker said. His hand moved down along her thigh, squeezing the plump flesh. "You won't see me with her anymore, though."

She rolled quickly toward him, flung her arms around him, one leg across him. Her words were violent.

"I'm so crazy glad I met you!"

He grinned over her shoulder, through all the golden hair, grinning insanely into the moonshot shadows.

"I'm plumb glad you're glad," he said. Holding her, still grinning, his voice lowered with intent seriousness. "You need somebody like me around you. Way you been acting. Cathy, I love you—I've said it before to other girls, but this is the only time I ever meant it." His voice was uniquely earnest. "But I got nothing to offer you. Only enough love so maybe you'll keep off that horse, bareback, on the streets."

She said nothing. He frowned, still grinning over her shoulder. He moved one hand to her buttocks and began softly patting her.

"You never did tell me who you are, Clay."

"That's what I mean. I'm a drifter, Cathy—up till now. Never had much, just drifting—looking for somebody like you. Just a nobody from nowheres."

"In those clothes?"

He began massaging her buttocks, slowly, and she moved her leg further across him, settling.

"Bought these duds just for you," he said. "Last of my money. The others was getting ragged rount the edges, 'haps you noticed?"

"I—I noticed you, Clay. And, Clay—I won't ride bareback, like that, into town anymore."

He clenched his teeth whitely over her shoulder. Her hips moved as he rubbed her buttocks, and they bunched under his palm.

"Clay?"

He clenched his eyes, teeth clenched, too.

"Yuh?"

"I think I know where you could get some money. What I mean is, my husband staked a claim. Gold, and very rich—a strong vein, Clay. He made a map—only nobody can read it. Even I can't read it." She squirmed closer, gently moving her hips. "Would you help me find it, Clay?"

"You sure it's something good?"

"Yes—very sure. I knew Gregg wouldn't make a mistake about that. It's all around town—didn't you hear about it?"

"No. When I haven't been with you, I've been sleeping. Haven't talked with anybody." He paused, then said quietly, "I won't lie, Cathy. I'm excited."

"Two friends of Gregg's tried to read the map, but nobody can make it out. He was a terrible man with a pen. I kind of think maybe he made the map hard to read on purpose." She ceased and her hips ceased. "He never imagined he would be killed, you see?"

Bracker hitched her thigh across him, and rolled over, so she lay full on him. He held her round buttocks.

"In a little bit," he said. "You go fetch that map, Cathy. I got a hankerin' to see it. I'm pretty good at map-reading."

She stared down at him, smiling, then began the whisper things against his lips.

• • •

In Sheriff Jack C. Walters' office, on the main street of San Pedro, Sheriff Noonty, from Alveraz, and his appointed deputy, Cecil Pruitt, talked.

Walters, a long, stringy man with kind gray eyes, said, "I cain't be sure he's your man."

"He's our man, all right." Noonty's voice was strangely taut. "Where you reckon he's at now?"

"This is *my* town, Noonty."

"Yeh. Only let's not agree that point."

Walters considered. He looked sleepy, eyes red-rimmed. "Two places he might be at, more than anywheres else. Mebbe the hotel—mebbe Widder Holmes'."

"Who's this Widder Holmes?"

Walters told him. "She ain't been the same since Gregg was killed. She found him, you know? She was supposed to meet Gregg by the assay office, and she come down the alley and found him dead, shotgunned."

"How come she taken up with Bracker?"

Walters shrugged. "Bracker's a stranger. An' Cathy Holmes looks like a gal who needs her lovin'."

Noonty cleared his throat. "How we get there?" he said. "Let's go. Pruitt, you take the Widder Holmes' place, and I'll check the hotel."

"What you so all-fired hot for him for?" Walters said. "What'd he do?"

"Every blood-evil thing you can think of," Noonty said. "Hoss-thief. Kill at the drop of a eyebrow, and *has* some eighteen or more times, counted. Woman stealer. Rustler. Highwayman. And he goes in big for rape—his pet pastime. Only, hell, I even let all that go. I mean, for a fair trial. Had him in the jug, finally, at Alveraz, my son on guard while I went out for a bite of lunch. That crazy bastard broke out and killed my son—slit his throat with a bayonet, and stabbed him thirty-six times after he was dead. So Doc Foster says."

"Reckon it's pussenal, then."

"I uphold the law. But there's pussenal feelings." He turned to the fat, buckskin-shirted deputy. "Let's fan the dust, Pruitt."

Walters told them how to reach their destinations. They went outside the office, Walters with them. Walters halted, turned and frowned.

"Some son-of-a-bitch spit on my front window."

• • •

"I tell you, it's pie, Cathy," Bracker said, pouring over a thick sheet of paper. "I can read this map like nothing. We'll leave in the morning." He looked at her. "Cathy, you're a rich woman and I'm happy for you."

"We're rich, Clay. It's yours as much as mine. I want you to have it. I love you, Clay—I love you an awful lot."

He frowned down at the map. "I couldn't do that. I got nothing to give you. You don't know nothing about me."

"You heard what I said," she told him. She leaned toward him, her breasts squashing against him on the bed. Her voice was tense and urgent. "I want it this way, Clay—you do things to me no man ever did. Gregg couldn't. I love you."

His hands betrayed a fine nervousness as he touched her, looked into her eyes, not smiling now, even frowning slightly. "And I love you, Cathy—I do to Christ I do!"

She hesitated, stilled. "Clay, I heard something outside. Like somebody walking out there."

"Wind," he said. "All right. We'll leave in the morning. You got horses?"

"Two—and a burro, and kegs for water—everything. Gregg had all sorts of prospecting paraphernalia."

They held each other closely now. A dull scrape and a thump echoed from outside the house. Bracker moved slickly fast. One hand swept to the lamp by the bed, turned the wick out, and he leaped through the darkness, naked, for the chair where his pants and gunbelt lay. Instantly he had the gun in his hand and was gone from the bedroom.

He slipped through the parlor in the moonlight, toward the front door, gun ready, breathing rustily. He cracked the door, held it loose on the hinges so it wouldn't squeal, and slid around the jamb into the chill night air.

A dark form hulked above the bedroom window.

"Stand up," Bracker said.

Buckskin shirt flashed as the other whirled, crouching for his gun. Bracker fired fast three times, spaced explosions, and Cecil Pruitt's face disintegrated in the moonlight; torn blobs of blood, flesh and white boneshard. Pruitt leaped and ran bleeding, pieces of his face trailing, plopping on the cabin porch. Strangely horrible sounds erupted with gouts of blood from a gaping hole. He ran smashing into the side of the cabin and fell dead.

Bracker stood still for a second, then stepped over the man, went through his pockets quickly, and came up with a wallet. He fumbled through it, holding it to the moonlight, squinting, and sighed. He cursed, hocked and spit at the dead man as Cathy Holmes watched from the doorway.

"Clay?"

"It's all right," Bracker said. "I killed a man once, and they're after me. Maybe you don't want me now?"

Her voice was a whisper. "I want you. I love you, Clay."

"All right. Only we leave tonight 'stead of tomorrow morning."

"Who is that?"

Bracker took the man by the booted feet. "Where's your well, Cathy?"

"Well?"

"We won't be coming back here, never, I'm thinking. We'll find the claim, an' make trail for Riverforks. We can change our names, live out of there. I just killed a lawman."

• • •

The sun was a white blister in the burning sky. The man and the woman rode horses, trailing a lone burro. They were crossing desert. In the distance, foothills hazed bluely, and bursting from the ground around was a blackly violent disgorgement of volcanic rock.

"Long's we got plenty water an' food, we'll be all right," Bracker said. "You scared?"

"No. I'm not scared—I'm with you."

He nodded. "That map leads into bad country—the worst damned country I ever seen. I edged it once, and men don't do much else but edge it. But we'll make it. We'll just use this one canteen today, won't touch any water the burro's toting, till we have to."

"All right, Clay."

The woman rode the white stallion, but saddled now. She wore a hat, too. And a long-sleeved dress to shield her from the sun. But the dress was tight, and Bracker kept looking across at her. Her buttocks strained in the saddle, her thighs ripely taut under the thin dress, full breasts jouncing with each heavy movement of the horse. Now and again she glanced toward him and smiled with a flash of white teeth.

Bracker turned his horse close beside hers, and reached over to grip her left thigh. She took his hand and slid it under her dress on the hot flesh.

"I would do anything for love, Clay."

He squeezed her leg, watching her, then looking up ahead into the distance.

"Clay—could I have a tiny drink? I'm awfully thirsty."

He released her leg, rattled the canteen, handed it to her. He watched her carefully sip. But several drops ran down her chin, sopping the dress across her breasts and the nipples showed through the suddenly translucent cloth.

"I'm sorry!"

He took the canteen. "It's all right." He looked at it. His lips were cracked slightly. He capped the canteen and hung it on the saddle. "Got a hell of a long ways to go. But just think of that gold, Cathy. Think of it!"

"I am."

"It's a hellish trail," he said. "What'd Gregg do, prospecting way out here?"

"He was always gone a long time. Used to wish I had somebody like you around the house."

He grinned at her. His eyes were bloodshot from the shimmering white heat. White foam flecked the horses' mouths.

"Clay, there's some pinon over there. A little shade. Maybe the last of the shade—let's stop and rest a while."

He looked at her and she chuckled and lifted the skirt of her dress, fanning her parted thighs.

"It's so hot, Clay—I'm hot as the devil."

They paused in the scant shade of pinon. It was next to nothing, sun blazing fixedly on the sands. She came close to him, pressed against him.

"Long time since last night," she said. "Clay," she said, putting her arms around him, moving her hips against him. "Love me, Clay—the sun just makes me hot all over—inside and out."

His voice was dryly hoarse. "Damn it, Cathy—I can't help myself with you!"

She fell sprawled on the ground, on the hot sands, grinning slyly up at him as he quickly knelt with her.

• • •

"All right!" Lou screamed. "I'll tell you, you dirty bastards! If you're lying, I'll kill you—!" She broke sobbing on the hotel bed, and Sheriff Noonty nodded to Walters. The red-haired girl clutched a sheet over her nude body.

"I'm not lying, gal," Noonty said. He leaned close to her. "Your lovin' boyfriend slept with Cathy Holmes last night, and they skipped town together last night and he killed a man last night. A deputy of mine. He stuck him down a well, that's what. Now, if you got any notion where they might of went, you'd better cough it up—or you'll be getting your beauty sleep behind bars on a straw mattress, or mebbe no damned mattress at all. And it'll be sleep—all by your lonesome, gal. Get that straight."

She told them. The words burst through sobs. "I don't know where. He didn't know where when I seen him last. Just buttes, that's all—black buttes. Someplace in the desert. I know that's where he'll be. He wants gold more than anything in this world, he says—then why does he have to have her like a—"

"Buttes?" Noonty said, frowning at Walters.

Walters nodded. "Yeah. I got a notion as to the vicinity. Let's go."

The girl sprang off the bed, forgetting her sheet. She grabbed at Noonty's shirtfront. "I want to go with you. I want to see him, just once more—that dirty! Take me with you—please take me with you!"

• • •

Midmorning of the second day found Bracker and the woman walking their horses across cracked ground. Sand whistled in the hot wind. The sun was a hazed ball of white.

"Canteen's empty. We'll have to tap one of the kegs on the burro," Bracker said. They halted the horses and the burro. Bracker walked back.

"I'm afraid, Clay. It's scary out here."

He laughed, and coughed. "Take it easy," he said, reaching for the hitch-rope on the keg. His hands jerked down, then up again. He slapped the keg, tore it loose, cursing.

"It's empty," he said softly.

"What did you say, Clay?"

Sand blew on the wind. She left the horses and walked back to where Bracker was running around the burro. He frantically untied the other keg, and held it aloft.

"They're empty!"

"Empty? How could they be empty?"

"They leaked—the sun sprung 'em—oh, Jesus Christ!"

They stood together staring at the empty kegs.

"What'll we do, Clay?"

"There's not a drop of water." He looked at her, then up ahead into the white glare of sandy sunlight seething and shimmering furnacelike.

"Where are we, Clay?"

"In the middle of nowheres."

Her voice was tinged with hysteria.

"You said yesterday we could never make it back, even with the kegs of water. How can we make it back now?"

"Get on your horse," he said. "We'll have to leave the burro." He looked at her. "Something else I ain't told you, Cathy. Them horses won't last long—not long at all. They need water bad. I've known it for all day. They're about shot."

White sand rippled across his back as he moved to his mount, and the sun burned down. The girl swung astride the big white.

"We can't just leave the burro, Clay!"

He grabbed for her reins, and started riding fast, leading her horse. "We got to leave 'im!"

In the waste of sands, in the seething heat, his horse lasted nearly two hours. Then it fell, and did not move. Without speaking, he swung astride the white and ripped its sides bloody with his spurs. The white walked about two hundred yards, then stopped and stood there with Bracker fiendishly spurring the beast's sides. The horse fumed and heaved and was suddenly dead on its feet. It fell sacklike, and they sprang free. The girl yanked her carbine from the scabbard.

"Come on," Bracker said.

She looked at him and he ran to her, took her by the shoulders, and his voice was harsh and even. "Cathy, we're caught in a trap. We've got to make one stab for it, or we'll never make it. It's our only chance—backtrail. Now, come on—!"

He tugged her along. They stumbled across the hot sands, and gradually the sky cleared of blowing sands, until it was like molten glass, wetly moving, and very hot and still and dry.

"It's happened so fast, Clay," she said, coughing. "Only a few hours ago we were laughing—we were even—we stopped—"

"An' you wrung me dry!"

"Clay, are you mad with me?"

"No. You know better—let's move."

"You sure we're headed right, Clay?"

"Yeah." He unhooked his gunbelt, took his gun and jammed it into his pants' belt. He dropped the gunbelt.

They moved along. Time stretched. The day grew hotter still. Enervation streamed through them, and their heads became leaden, their legs and arms hot aching stilts.

"Please," she gasped. "Clay, don't walk so fast. I'm so thirsty. I could drink gallons. Clay, what about the gold?"

He stopped. They stood there in the endless blaze of white waste. All around them now was a vast bowl of nothingness—of white shimmering nothingness.

"Them buttes are up the other way," he said. "We can't make it. We got to keep trying for San Pedro."

"They'll catch you there."

"Got to chance it."

They moved slowly on, like tiny insignificant bugs creeping across an endless steel frying pan over a hot fire. And as the day progressed, the hours falling off into the blaze, they slowed more and more, until both were reeling on the sands, not moving—getting nowhere. Bracker knelt on the sands and said, "Cathy, this is as far as we go. We'll never even see the sun set. I know of these things."

She stood a few paces from him.

"Are you sure, Clay? Can't we keep trying?"

He shook his head, licked purling blood from his cracked lips. His eyes were festered slits, and in the morning his lips would be black—if he had lips.

He started to rise, and fell. He tried again, and stood, reeling dizzily toward her, and she began to laugh. It was a horrible screeching laughter, and Bracker ceased moving.

"You're going to die, Clay."

He stared at her, reeling, and went to his knees. She took a step, and sprawled down too, then knelt up, propping herself with the carbine.

"What do you mean, girl?"

She worked herself toward him across the stinking sand, panting heavily, dragging the carbine. She pulled her dress up across her bare body and untied something from around her waist, flashed it in front of Bracker.

"Recognize this?" she said.

He frowned, his hand went to his throat. "My scarf?"

"Not that it matters," she said. "But I saw you kill my husband. You dropped this scarf and I saved it. So I could return it—here." She held it out, still in the hot, stifling air. He only stared.

"Cathy."

"I didn't tell anyone I saw you. I wanted it all to myself. You killed him with a shotgun. It was a gamble. The way you gamble, not with cards—the whole thing. He used to tell me about you, when you were his friend, and what happened to you. How he hoped he'd never see you again. You gambled to stay away from town after the murder and come back and try to make me, and get the gold." She heaved with laughter, watching him. "Only I schemed the same thing," she said. "I changed the map, just a little—just enough so it took us 'way out here where it's empty and there's nothing. And I rode up and down the streets bareback, so when you came it would look like I was really ready—maybe a little crazy."

"You *are* crazy!"

"Maybe. But I told you—I'll do anything for love."

"Cathy. Yes—you're right. I did these things. But I love you—I honest to God love you!"

"That's too bad, because I loved my husband."

"You opened the seams in the kegs."

"The first night."

He pulled his gun, started firing at her. His eyes were insane now and she heaved with hot laughter because the gun's hammer clicked against empty chambers.

"I emptied your revolver, too."

He tried to spring at her, stumbling, and she fired the carbine into the sand at his feet. He sprawled out, trying to drag himself toward her, cursing her, but he didn't move at all.

"You'll die, too," he whispered.

"I know."

"The gold—!"

"You're practically sitting on it, right now," she said. "We passed the spot, this same spot, Clay—mid-morning today. I imagined we would go much farther. I thought we'd last another day, at least." She chuckled. "I fixed the map just right. This sand covers a rock formation that's loaded with gold!"

He began to scratch at the earth like a dog, and she crouched nearby, laughing, and the sun burned down. . . .

• • •

Late afternoon three riders topped a low rise. Noonty, Walters, and Lou, the red-haired girl. They rode swiftly to where the dead man and woman lay on the sunny sands.

"That's him," Noonty said.

"Damn if it ain't," Walters said.

The red-haired girl screamed just once and then was quiet.

Somebody Knew Her

Pursuit Detective Story Magazine
November 1956

Carmoody looked down again at the slack and awkwardly positioned nude body of the young girl lying on the kitchen floor of No. 5, *Gulfways Motel*. Nice figure, dusty black hair in sharp contrast against the white tile floor, dark blue eyes that were half-lidded and glaring in the lamplight. Her throat was cut.

"She's dead," Carmoody said. "Which is a too bad thing. But that's about all I'm certain of. How's for going into the other room?"

The young man turned away from the detective-sergeant, stepped a yard and a half past the tiny lunch bar into the combination bedroom-living room, and slumped on the couch.

Carmoody stood there a moment longer, looking down at the body of the girl. Then he sighed, turned toward the young man.

"How long have you known her, Ulrich?"

Ulrich continued to slump on the couch in the beach motel living room. Florida night winds rattled the front screen door, breathed sweetly through the rooms and left, rattling the kitchen screen door. From not far away the Gulf splashed against the sea wall. Ulrich did not look at Sergeant Carmoody. Ulrich was sick, and maybe a little crazy since returning to find his girl this way.

"About all my life," Ulrich said.

"She was *always* your girl?"

"Yes. It was like—Yes."

Carmoody flipped a strong brown hand at the inquisitive face of the harness cop showing at the front screen door. The face went away. Carmoody cleared his throat, made a helpless gesture, ran his hand across thick blond hair, then harshly down across his sunburned face.

"Ulrich?"

"Huh?"

Ulrich sat on the edge of the couch and stared at the floor between his knees, head in hands, dressed in a blue sport shirt and light tan trousers. He was a broad, husky young man and he looked dependable, even the way things were.

"It's better we talk now," Carmoody said. "Won't be long before this place'll be crawling with cops and reporters. It'll be rough. Only reason Crosswell is here, he was on beach patrol. I pulled him in off the highway. It's quite a ways to town but they'll all be along damned quick."

Ulrich did not move.

"I know you're clear," Carmoody said. "The cab driver that brought you said he picked you up at Tampa International. Aren't you interested in why I'm here? Don't you want to know something about this?"

"Does it matter?"

Carmoody ran his hand across his face again. "What you say we go outside?"

Ulrich said nothing. He stood up, turned without looking toward the girl, and marched out through the living room to the door. Crosswell, the harness cop, opened the screen, and Ulrich vanished into the night.

Carmoody cramped his lower lip tightly with forefinger and thumb, shook his head, glanced at the body, then followed Ulrich.

Ulrich had walked to the edge of sand and grass, until he stood on the sea wall. His hands were jammed deep into his pockets and the wind snapped the bottom of his untucked shirt.

"Ulrich?"

Ulrich did not speak. He stared out there.

"All right," Carmoody said. "Here's the way it is. Your girl, Virginia, called the police. This afternoon. We've had reports of a peeping tom on the beaches, out here. She said she'd seen somebody looking in the window. They put me on night duty out here." He turned, looked back toward the motel, then at Ulrich. "It happened—must have—when I was down the road for a sandwich. I checked with her when I came back—found her like she is. It was done with a knife—only there's no trace of that either."

"Why?" Ulrich said softly. "Why?"

"Easy," Carmoody said. "You may as well know. Whoever the guy was, she must have seen him. Maybe he got bold and went inside after her. Once she saw him, he couldn't let her live. He was desperate—maybe crazy, who knows?"

Ulrich had his hands over his face. He talked through his hands. "But she—her clothes . . ."

"Torn to strips. Found 'em in the kitchen garbage pail, there. He—uh—well, the doc hasn't checked her yet, of course."

"You mean—?" Ulrich began to curse quietly until he stopped for breath. He had his hands clasped in front of him.

"We'll get him," Carmoody said. "Don't worry about that. When was the last time you saw Miss Morgan?"

"Two weeks ago."

"You've been up in New York?"

"Yuh."

"Did she know you'd be back tonight? She didn't mention you to me, Ulrich. She know you planned to see her?"

Ulrich lifted one hand, made a vague motion, dropped it. "How would I know she'd be here if we hadn't planned to meet?"

Carmoody leaned down, picked up a small chip of white shell, flicked it over the rim of the sea wall. Egmont Light blinked like a far red eye.

"Cigarette?" Carmoody said, offering Ulrich the pack.

"No."

Carmoody lighted his cigarette, scowling in the glare.

"You loved her?" he said through the thick smoke.

"I loved her. She loved me. What matter?"

"She have any—er, faults? I've got to ask these things, son—it's not easy."

"I understand," Ulrich said quietly. "No faults—not really. That is, she wanted lots of money, but who doesn't? Not crazy for it, understand? I aimed to get her everything she wanted. Someday."

"Wanted money."

Ulrich stared at the night.

"I can understand that," Carmoody said. "Did you see anybody around here, maybe your place—anything at all, when you came in tonight?" Carmoody paused.

"I mean, before you came in and found Crosswell and me there. I'd only found her five minutes before you came along. It naturally looked bad, till I checked with the cab company."

Ulrich started to shake his head, stopped. "Yeah," he said. "That's right. I saw somebody walking along the front, in the drive. He went down around the rear of the motels. He was in a hurry, too—I remember now."

"Damn it. I didn't hear a thing, either. Might have been staying right here. But I checked everybody. Maybe went down by the water. Remember if he came back?"

Ulrich's voice faltered, went quiet again. "I was with you after that."

"You know anybody—disliked her enough to do something like this? In case there's another angle?"

Ulrich turned and his voice was harsh. "No!" He stepped closer to Carmoody, the voice still harsh, but with a tear in it. "Not Ginny—why do you have to ask questions like that? Nobody could hate Ginny." He turned away and stood there again, looking out over the water. "We didn't know anybody down here. Just us."

"Yeah," Carmoody said. "Only somebody knew her, that's for sure."

"That's your job."

Carmoody's voice was kind, very gentle and understanding. "Know you feel bad, Ulrich. But I've got to ask these things. How did she know you were coming tonight?"

"I phoned her."

Carmoody sucked on his cigarette. "When you talked to her—didn't she mention about calling us in? A peeping tom?"

"No," Ulrich said. "Oh. God—I can't believe she's dead—" He paused, turned to Carmoody. "You'll never know. I could never tell you how wonderful she was. Nobody'll ever know. We'd always said we would get married. Finally we ran away and came down here—maybe it was wrong, but we loved each other. Then a friend said he could get me a job up here, if I'd come right away. So I did—we had just enough money. I got the job—then came back for her." His voice was loud. "We had a whole week yet."

"Steady," Carmoody said.

Ulrich turned away.

Carmoody looked at his cigarette, held it up, dropped it. The wind carried it a little, but Carmoody was quick with his toe. He squashed the cigarette.

"Are you going to find who did it?" Ulrich said.

"She was just waiting," Carmoody said. "All alone. She didn't have a job?"

"Before. In Cincinnati." Ulrich turned and stared and started to shout, then didn't. "I was going to yell," he said. "Yell how you've got to get him. But what's the use? What use is there now?"

Carmoody laid his hand on Ulrich's shoulder. "We'll do all we can, son," he said. "Where can you be reached?"

"I'll let you know."

"Better take it easy, now," Carmoody said. "O.K.?"

"O.K. And, thanks."

"You see, these guys—these peepers—you can never tell. They're nuts, Ulrich. They can't control themselves. They see something, they've got to look—and, well—a beautiful girl like Miss Morgan—"

"Stop!" Ulrich said.

"Steady." Carmoody looked at the young man again for a time. "Stick around," he said. "I'll want to talk with you again." Then he turned and walked slowly back toward the motel, scowling. Ulrich stared out at the dark Gulf.

Carmoody motioned to the harness cop at the door of No. 5. "Be right along," he said.

He turned and walked on around the rear of the motel, past No. 7. He glanced back toward Ulrich, then vanished into some hibiscus bushes. Once out of sight, he moved rapidly, then stopped abruptly beside a small oleander. A window was open in No. 7. He stopped quickly over by the window, frowning.

• • •

A tall blonde girl, wearing a tight white dress had just entered the room and turned the lights on. She closed the door, set down a piece of luggage, and sighed. The window was open and the tips of Carmoody's fingers touched the screen. The girl reached to a small table and turned on an electric fan, then stood before the fan and lifted her dress up to her waist, so the fan could blow against her.

"You fool!" Carmoody whispered softly.

He backed away from the window, turned slowly up toward No. 5. He was breathing heavily and perspiration shone on his face. He whirled quietly back to his position by the oleander, looking in at the girl.

She stood straddle-legged before the fan, moving her hips gently, cooling off.

Carmoody's face was dead white and a strange agitation came over him. His eyes glazed as he watched the girl slowly turn around and around before the fan, enjoying the cool breeze. Then she paused, not looking quite at him, and stood perfectly rigid. But she had seen him. She let the dress fall back to her knees and turned her head until she stared at him, red lips parted—her body like a statue stilled with fear.

Carmoody pressed his hands against the windowsill, his shoulders hunched.

"I'm—" he whispered to her. "I'm—it's all right. It's me—the sergeant." He watched her, his eyes eating at her, and he began to speak in a long and continuous sentence, the words unintelligible. "Don't move," he said. "It's all right now." His right hand tore the front of his shirt open, dipped, came up with a slim-bladed hunting knife.

The girl's lips moved in shock now, but she still did not call out.

Carmoody slit the screen in a single savage swipe of the blade. He leaped to the sill, tore through the screen, stepped into the room.

"Get out," the girl said softly.

Carmoody moved his head from side to side. "Don't you see, darling? It's me—I'm here to watch over you—here to watch you. Yes," he said, "yes."

The girl made small keening sounds in her throat.

Carmoody took a step toward her. "You're a sweet beautiful baby," he whispered. "Don't scream—it's all right," and then he began speaking obscene phrases.

The girl screamed, crouched back, her face white.

Carmoody moved toward her, his face an expressionless mask of shining white.

The door of the room opened and Crosswell, the harness cop, stepped inside. His face was pink and puzzled and he held a gun in his right hand.

The Tormentors

Manhunt
November 1956

It was mid-morning when he found the knife. It was a pocket fishing knife with a five-inch blade. The knife edge was very sharp, honed to smooth moon white, and the back of the blade was a saw. The handle was black pearl, as slick as grease, and wonderful to touch. It took him a long time to touch it, though.

He stood there on the riverbank, the astonishingly thick lenses of his glasses glinting, watching the knife as though it might take a notion to leap away. Late September sun beamed brightly through the crispy leaves of elm and maple and oak and hickory, and the air was cold in his nostrils and his wrists were blue.

Mine, he thought.

The knife lay on the very edge of the mossy bank above the slow, swirling, gray-black waters of the river, twinkling.

He looked around, his eyes like enormous wet blue agates under the intense magnification of his glasses, and then he stared at the knife again. He knew one thing: it was his knife and nobody must know that he had it, not even Nana. If Nana knew, she would take it away from him, and he would let her because she would kiss him and touch his face and he liked that. More than anything in the whole world, he liked that—the cool soft damp touch of her lips, and the warm, lingering electricity of her dancing fingers.

He wiped his mouth on the ragged sleeve of his orange sweater.

He lumbered through the sunshine, leaned hugely down and picked up the knife, folded it shut and slipped it into his pocket. He kept his hand in his pocket, the knife tight in his fist, smooth and very cold, like a bar of ice.

It was almost the same as when Nana kissed him.

Not quite, though—nothing was ever *quite* like that.

He listened to the deep whisper of the river, breathing the rich smell of the river and the woods and the damp cold grass. And from the village came the pleasant, lazy odor of burning leaves.

They would be sitting on the porch at the store and he would have to pass by them, hear them shout, yell—scream, even.

It was just a thought, though. He'd mostly forgotten that a few moments before he had passed them, staring patiently at their ridiculous laughter. He wanted to get home and see Nana.

He crashed through the woods, across rotting logs, through shallow water and mud and cat-tails and knee-high grass, and a blackbird flew up in front of him and finally he came up onto the road. He had to crawl under a wire fence and it was difficult because he refused to take his hand out of his pocket.

They were on the steps, sitting, chewing, spitting, laughing—waiting.

He stumbled along the rutted dirt of the road. His feet fumbled and he staggered.

"Hey, Beans."

"There's Beans."

"Beans, get the hell over here. Where you been, Beans?"

"Beans, what you got your hand in your pocket for?"

He came past them, watching them and stopped because one of them said, "Stop, Beans."

"Where's your sister at, Beans? Where's Nana?"

He looked at them.

"Beans, you got eyes like a cockeyed owl . . . an owl with glasses."

"Wipe your mouth, Beans." He wiped his mouth with his sleeve and a long strand of dirty orange yarn unraveled from the sleeve. The strand stuck in his mouth and he spat it out. The cold air bit on his wrist, began to nibble on it like tiny mice. He felt fear, rubbed his wrist against his side. His wrist was blue.

"Beans," one of them said. "Let's hear you live up to your name."

"Leave 'im alone," somebody said.

"Ah, can it."

Beans watched them. There were five of them, leaning and sitting, and lying on the porch. The small, yellow-haired one kept laughing, throwing his head back, gasping for air.

"Listen to Beans!" the yellow-haired one shouted. "Listen at him! Oh, Lord, he busts my gut—honest to Christ, he does."

The small, skinny, yellow-haired one had a slit nostril and he always shouted and yelled and danced around, just like he was doing right now. Beans didn't feel an awful lot of anything, but he did have a yearning to do something about the yellow-haired one, maybe walk on him like Nana told him to walk on the big bugs at night on the floor—walk on the yellow-haired one's face. He kept the bugs in a jar, to watch.

"Beans, where's your sister?"

"She," Beans said. "Nana. Home."

"That's what *you* think," one of them said. "She ain't home, Beans. We know. She ain't home. She *ain't* home, Beans!"

He began to feel like running, like crying and running.

"Beans," the yellow-haired one said, "every day when you leave the house, she waits till you're out of sight. See? Then she runs out the back way. Know where she goes?"

Beans shook his head.

"She goes out into the woods. Sure as hell, she does. Ain't that right, fellas? Ain't it? Ain't Nana right out in Sackett's acre right now?"

"Damn right, sure she is, hell yes, oh-boy."

"No," Beans said. "Wash."

"Wash my eye," yellow-hair said. "How you think she makes money so's you an' her can eat?"

They all laughed.

"Answer me, Beans," yellow-hair said.

"Wash," Beans said. "Wash clothes. Take wash, make money. Wash."

"No," yellow-hair said. "You're wrong, Beans. That's cover-up. That's for you to think. She's fooling you. You wouldn't want to think about your own sister out there in Sackett's, would you?"

"Ah, lay off the poor guy, Willy. What you bums going to do when the canning factory starts up? You won't be able to yell at Beans—what'll you do? You'll be working all day."

"Shut up," Willy said. "Beans, your sister goes into the woods every day. She's layin' out there right this minute with one of the guys from Dexter."

"No!" Beans said. A horrible feeling that he couldn't control overcame him completely and he swam through it wildly. He was sick, rotten sick, and he began to run. He ran at Willy and Willy laughed and gave him a shove and said, "Your sister's a whore, Beans!"

Beans tripped and fell by the steps.

"Let's see those eye-glasses, Beans."

They snatched his glasses off. They always did and the world went dizzy and blurred and he saw them moving in bright blurs. It was as if he were underwater, swimming in the river.

Somebody helped him up, dusted him off and he turned toward whoever it was, trying to tell him that Willy was wrong about Nana. Nana was at home, doing washing, as she did every day. The man kept brushing the dust off him, not speaking, and Beans kept on loudly telling him about Nana, and he looked at the mixed-up faces of the others, feeling proud, getting brushed off.

"Give him back his glasses."

"Oh, hell."

"His eyes ain't really so big."

Beans felt them put the glasses back on and everything cleared up fine.

"There," the one who'd been brushing him off said. "You're clean, now, Beans."

"Yes," Beans said.

The hands that had brushed him shoved him reeling out into the road, and he sprawled heavily into the chilled September dust.

"Now you know what your sister is," Willy said.

They were laughing.

"You're a bunch of lousy crumbs," somebody said. "Doing a thing like that. He can't help himself, you know that. Why do you do it? Why? Tell me that?"

"What else is there to do?"

"We ain't hurting him none."

"Hey, Beans—let's hear it!"

He lumbered off down the road, but not because of what they'd done. When he'd fallen, his hands had still been on the knife, clutched tightly, and it had hurt. He wanted to get home and maybe Nana would kiss him. Happy feeling rushed through him.

Because that was a lie, about Nana. A lie! A lie!

He ran stumbling and fell and got up and ran stumbling.

"Hello, John," Nana said when he came into the kitchen. "You all right?"

He stared at her brightly, then began to weep. The tears rippled down his fat cheeks, rolling like wet diamonds from his big black eyes, flowing from the pink lids like water from a spring.

She was here. Nana. She wasn't in the woods.

"What's eating you now?"

"Nothing."

"Here," she said. She wiped his face with the hem of her skirt, then put her hands on his shoulders and looked at him. "You're putting on more weight," she said. "It's awful, John. You got to stop eating like you do. You're growing across, but you ain't growing up none."

He reached fumbling toward her with his left hand.

She took his hand and kissed it. The hot electricity jumped down through him like a bolt. She touched his face with her fingers and shook her head. "Poor old fool," she said. "Nobody gives a damn what happens to you, do they?"

He shook his head, smiling.

She leaned and kissed his forehead. He reeled slightly, clutching the knife, wanting to fling his arms around her and cry into her soapy-smelling dress.

"Run along and do something, John," she said, sighing. "I got a hell of a pile of wash, believe me. But we'll have an extra dollar. Say! We'll have pie tonight!"

He nodded happily and kept searching for her hand. She kept moving her hand, playfully, out of the way of his. It was wonderful and so good, being with Nana, and he wished he could explain to her that he wouldn't have to kill her now.

He had planned on killing Nana like the bugs.

Now he wouldn't have to, because she was his, all his, and he grinned at her, feeling the cool knife. He could kill her with the knife, but she didn't go into Sackett's woods. If she did, then he would have to kill her like the bugs, because then he could save her for himself, like the bugs in the jar. Only he would keep her in bed. She wouldn't fit in the jar.

"All right, Nana," he said.

Because she was his.

"Yeah, honey," she said. "All right."

He stumbled to his room and lay on his bed and took out the knife, shielding it with his body. He stayed there on the bed, looking at the knife, folding and unfolding the blade, for some two hours.

"John?"

He looked at her in the doorway.

"John. Think hard, now. Did you take my yellow dress?"

"Dress?"

"Yes, I can't find it. I looked everywhere I can think of. Got to wash it out. Might's well do it with the rest of this junk. You seen it, John?"

He shook his head, watching her.

"Damn," she said. "Can't find it nowheres." She looked at him, then stepped over to the side of the bed. "Listen, John, honey—I know about that dress. And it's all right. You like to feel it on me, and it's your favorite, I know that. You didn't go an' sneak it off, just so's you could feel it in private, did you?"

"No."

"What you hiding there?"

"Nothing." He showed her his hand, the knife biting into his side where he lay on it.

"O. K., hon. You see that dress, you tell me, right?"

He reached clumsily for her hand. She touched his fingers and patted them lightly.

"Damn it," she said sadly. "Damn it all, anyways."

She went away and he fell asleep and when he stumbled into the kitchen later on, holding the knife in his pocket, she was gone. It was very still and awful and he could smell the soap and ironing and feel the swift rise of panic that sent him reeling and stumbling blindly out the door.

He hurried down the road, approached the store.

"Hey, Beans! Where you going?"

"Beans, come here. Come on the hell over here."

There was something different about them now. He always came by at this time, and usually they were sleepy or drunk by now, midafternoon. They had been drinking, he knew that, but there was something different.

"Nana?" he said.

"Yeah. You may well say that, brother," one of them said. "She ain't to home, is she?"

Beans shook his head.

"Too bad," one said.

"Too bad, hell," another said. "She's right nice. I just come back from the woods, man. I can vouch for that."

He clutched the knife, watching them.

They were lying again. But where *was* Nana?

"Where's your sister, Beans?"

"Where?" he said. "Nana home."

They all shook their heads, very soberly this time, and frightened excitement began to stir Beans. He didn't know what to do because he knew Nana wasn't home. They "Ohhhed," and they "Ahhhed."

"Won't work this time, Beans. We know, see?"

He looked around for Willy, the yellow-haired one. He wasn't with them.

"Why don't you lay off him?" somebody said.

"Ah, can it."

"Beans, we got something to tell you. Now, we want you should take it like the man you are. See?"

They laughed. Beans laughed. Then he quit laughing. What did they mean? What was it about Nana?

"He's some man, that's a fact."

"Old Beans."

"You eat lots of beans, Beans?"

"Hey, you're forgetting."

"Yeah. I got carried away. Beans—your sister's drunk as a lord. She says she don't never want to see you again, Beans. Never, never, never! She's got her a roll an' she's drunk as a pig."

They chuckled, waiting. He stood there and watched them, saying, No, No, inside, way down in his belly, and feeling, No, No, too. It was all mixed up in his chest and he didn't know what to do.

"Mine," he said. "Nana. She's mine."

"Well, you go right ahead and think that, Beans. But I tell you, you're wrong. It ain't right, Beans. Because you're her brother, see? Well, she's got to have herself a man."

"Ten men," somebody said.

"She's drunk, Beans. We all been with her this afternoon an' we figured we should do you the favor of telling you. She's up there in the woods with two men from over to Dexter, right now, Beans. Earning some loot."

He looked at their faces. None of them were laughing. They were very calm and quiet and they shook their heads slowly.

"Naw," he said.

"Yes," one of them said. "Why, hell, Beans—she's only your sister. Man, you ought to catch yourself a different gal."

"Nana," he said.

"No, Beans. It's too late."

"Say, Beans," another said, stepping up to him. "Let's see those eyeglasses."

Beans tried to stop them, but they took his glasses away again and everything began to swim again, brightly, hazily.

"Beans," one said. "You know what your sister is, now. She don't like you around her, all the time falling down, getting in her way."

Then the one who was speaking suddenly pointed and laughed and said, "Look at that, will you!" Then he whirled on Beans and said, "There, Beans! By God, that oughta tell you!"

Beans peered, following the pointed finger and heard them all talking and laughing and calling out and whistling. And he saw Nana coming down the dirt road. She had on the yellow dress that he liked so much and she reeled from one side to the other, drunk and stumbling. His yellow dress.

"Hey, Nana!" one of them called. "How about a little?"

She came on, reeling, swinging her hips and Beans watched her. Something frightening came up into his throat, choking him. He watched her stagger toward them in a yellow blur and he saw her flap her yellow skirt and wave at the men on the porch.

"Hey, Nana! Atta gal!"

He knew she was drunk. She could hardly stand up. He turned blindly, running at her in a crazy stumbling rush. They were right. They hadn't lied. They were his friends and Nana had been doing this all along—up in the woods, everywhere.

He ran and got out the knife and opened it.

"Nana!" he said.

Everybody was shouting. And Nana was trying to get away from him. She turned and ran and tripped and fell on the ground.

"Nana," he said through tears.

They yelled and screamed at him, coming after him, their feet pounding, but they were too late. Much too late. He had the knife out, gleaming, and he leaped on her, thinking how he would keep her in bed beside him and he would wash the clothes now, but she would always be there. He would know she was there.

He cut her throat. One swipe of the knife, hard digging.

"Beans!" one of them shouted.

He felt the fist strike him and he gouged with the knife at Nana, but Nana was killed already. He knew that. The blood throbbed in scarlet gushes onto the yellow dress and the dirt of the road and he could see the red and the yellow.

One of them kept whispering, "What'll we do?" and he sounded like a crazy man. *"What'll we do?"*

Somebody said, "Turned out different than you thought, hey?"

"Shut up! What'll we do?"

Beans was holding Nana's hand, but it didn't feel like Nana's hand. This hand was hard and boned and her hand had been soft.

"He's killed Willy! We was only fooling with him, getting Willy to wear that yellow dress we stole. My God, he's slit Willy's throat. It's Willy's own knife, I tell you. He lost it down to the river yesterday forenoon. Willy's dead! You hear?"

"Home," Beans said, pulling at the yellow dress.

He heard the running feet and he heard the voice, too.

"John? What's going on here? John! What have these fools done to you. Oh, Lord!"

Nana was still bleeding and Beans didn't know what to do, because he had killed her. And Nana was talking to him.

He buried his face in the yellow dress, clutching the wet red cloth.

He felt an arm around him and saw the empty wash-basket that Nana used for delivering laundry.

Someone put his glasses on . . .

Renegade

Blazing Guns Western Story Magazine
December 1956

An hour before noon, while Second Lieutenant Jonathan Allan Haggard waited impatiently beside the door of his quarters, a lone rider was seen out on the yellow simmering silence of the desert, moving toward the fort at a fatigue-knotted gallop.

"Ho!" the rider called, nearing. "Ho! *Yaah!*"

The sentry climbed from his perch on the bastion, lazily spat, and with his rifle slung across his back, slowly hunched the gate open. Clattering through the gate, the horse dropped its head, stiffened in a spraddle-legged halt, and began to snort horribly. With each breath a thin jet of crimson pulsed from the animal's side onto the trampled dust of the parade ground. The rider, clothed in red-splattered rags, continued to heel his mount as if he were still at a fast canter. Just then the horse pitched onto its side, dead. The rider leaped clear, landed running in a headlong stagger across the parade ground, toward headquarters. The sentry started after him, whirled to close the gate, then walked over and stared at the fallen horse.

Lieutenant Jonathan Allan Haggard studied this picture, yet deliberately refused to consider what it might mean. There was the possibility of duty, but with his luck he would end up commanding a detail to guard the water pump. He turned and reluctantly entered his quarters. It could even be they would ask him to bury the horse.

His wife of three months, Linda, glanced up from her sewing, where she was seated across the primitively furnished room, beside their small fireplace.

"Darling," she said. "I think you misunderstand what I mean. I'm only thinking of you. You don't have to walk out on me like that."

"I'm sorry," he told her. He stood there, tall, browned and taut, beneath the blue and gray of his cavalry uniform, watching her. He loved her deeply and knew that she loved him. But there was this grave trouble between them and she was the one who did not understand.

She frowned slightly. "Why don't you go to Major Meece and tell him how you feel? Inactivity isn't good for a man." She paused, set her sewing carefully aside, turned her fine blue eyes on her husband and sudden sunlight from a near window smiled on her saffron hair. "Since you've been at this post, you've had no decent duty. It's almost as if they think you incapable of handling Indian trouble."

"That what you think?"

• • •

Her voice frowned now. "You know that's not true. It's four months since you left the academy. I simply want to see you do something worthy of your ability as an officer. I want you to have a chance to prove yourself."

"I don't need to prove anything to anybody, Linda," he said quietly. "When the time comes, I'll get my chance."

"You don't see it at all," she said. "My brother, Richard, would have gone to Meece and forced him to give him a patrol—something. He often wrote me he did things like that. Meece admired him for it. Everybody thought a lot of Richard—the things he did."

"Yes."

His wife's gentle gaze turned to the wall above the paint-cracked bureau where she had hung a wooden plaque mounted with her brother's medals and decorations. Jonathan looked too, not enviously, but patiently, as he had a hundred times, and things broke away inside him. His gaze slipped to the framed photograph of the laughing-eyed blond young man on the bureau. Richard and he had never met, but Richard had known of his sister's marriage. Linda was so young, and rough Fort Early here in the Territory of Arizona was still so very romantic to her New York mind, what with Apaches and everything. He knew she did not want him placed in danger of being killed, as they had heard her brother was killed in the battle at Little Creek, while bravely smothering a fused keg of gunpowder when the Indians under Bleeding Cloud rolled it down among his men. Richard's sacrifice was glorious, perhaps, though all the troopers had been killed anyway. An Apache brave later captured near Fort Defiance had given information about the battle. Jonathan wondered if he'd have to blow himself to smithereens to satisfy Linda. It was a bad way to think. Yet, her brother's tragic death was somehow forgotten in the midst of his overwhelming glory and Jonathan wished heartily that he'd never heard the name, Lieutenant Richard Nobel.

"For instance," Linda said. "This new fort they're building to the west, Fort Brackett. Why couldn't you, instead of Lieutenant Proud, have taken a platoon over there to furnish garrison till those volunteers come in from Ohio? Cyrus Proud certainly isn't the soldier you are."

"Maybe that's the reason," he said, gripping his calm as desperately as he might a rifle stock during skirmish. "Maybe Meece figures he needs me here, Linda."

"Pooh," she said. "And pooh, again. I tell you, Jonathan, you've got to ask for the things you get." She lifted her sewing into her lap. "Anyway, we'll see. I'm making you a shirt to lounge around in evenings, when you're not in uniform." She was silent a moment, then added wistfully, "I used to make Richard his shirts, too."

"That's very nice," he said, turning toward the door. He knew she was going to say something more and he didn't know of any further explanations, any new methods to combat her logic. He did not want to hurt her. He stepped outside, closed the door, walked along in front of the officers' quarters. It was a delicate situation, because she had convinced herself he should be like Richard. She was not yet conscious of death or Indian war. He wished he knew what to do.

• • •

The fort was very quiet. The dead horse still lay over there by the gate and the sun palmed the earth with a heavy, hot hand. From the kitchen far on the other side of the fort came a rattle of pans, and a man laughed into the vacuum-like silence of near noon.

A door slammed, he heard the rapid pound of feet, and looked up to see Private Meechum snatch his spectacles off over by headquarters, search the area, then dash toward him across the quadrangle.

"Lieutenant, sir!" Meechum called, still running. "Report to the Major, immediately, sir!"

Jonathan started to speak, watched Meechum salute, turn sharply, and run violently off toward the surgeon's quarters.

Jonathan quickened his pace, trying to deny a thick feeling of exaltation. It would seem that the dead horse was paying off and he was being selected. He wanted to break into a run himself, but forced himself to walk steadily. He had a weird feeling that the entire fort was shuddering up out of a deep slumber.

Brevet Major Hardy Meece met him at the office door, eyed him sharply inside, slammed the door, and pointed across the room to a man slumped in a chair beside the scarred desk.

Jonathan looked, thinking. It's the rider of that horse and he's dead. He continued to stare at the ragged figure with the grizzled head tipped over the back of the chair, eyes half-closed, and he saw the broken-off shaft of an arrow jutting from the man's side, just above the waist.

"Take a good look, Jonathan," Meece said. "A good long look. I want you mad, see? As mad as I am. Just mad enough so you can still think. Understand?"

Jonathan turned to the major.

"That, over there," Meece said, stomping up to his desk, and speaking with determined quietness, "is all that's left of Fort Brackett." He leaned back against the desk, the round boyishness of his face sundered by a pair of pale blue eyes that were always dry and hard, and just now very bitter. His lips were without color, as pale as his close-cropped hair. He hunched his stocky body up onto the desk and sat there, watching Jonathan.

"Fort Brackett, sir?"

"Burned to the ground, wiped out. Proud and the fifteen men of the first platoon, all dead. Ten volunteer frontiersmen, dead. Three women and five children and maybe some others unaccounted." Meece grunted, swallowed, began to pick at the edge of the desk with hard blunt fingers. "This one got away with an Apache arrow in him."

Jonathan said nothing, viewing in his mind's eye the havoc that must have been Fort Brackett.

"Short and sweet, then," the major said. "You're to take twenty-five men, the third platoon, and go out there and find Bleeding Cloud's encampment and stop them."

"Stop them, sir?"

"Fort Early, here, will be next. The Apaches know we're undermanned. They'll strike, because they've just had success. But if we break their back first, it won't work. By that time I'll get fresh troops in here if I have to build them out of cactus!"

"Yes, sir. But—twenty-five men. That leaves you only a handful. The kitchen staff, two squads from the second platoon."

• • •

Meece came down off the desk, stomped over to the door, flung it open. "We won't need them here," he said. "You're going to stop those redskins, kill every one, if need be. You hear, Lieutenant?"

"Yes, sir."

"Poor Proud," the major said. "His wife is expecting, too. They wanted a boy." He breathed heavily, stared across the room at the body in the chair. "I know something of what you're living with, Lieutenant. I know it's not easy. I'm your commanding officer, and I make it a point to know some of my men's business. Richard Nobel was a good officer, but over-anxious. Don't you be that way, just because of—well, maybe this Indian trouble will help clear your hearth."

"Yes, sir."

"All right," the major said. "Those are your orders, you have complete leeway. Horses are already saddled, rations drawn. Meechum's taking care of that, and—Lieutenant—?"

Jonathan began to feel a slow tide of anger at many things and he wondered what he was going to tell Linda.

"I would be going," Meece said. "Remember that. But I've chosen to remain with the fort. Just in case."

"Sir, how many Indians under Bleeding Cloud?"

Meece snapped his gaze up, blinked soberly. "Yes," he said. "You'll have no way of knowing. Be prepared for any number. They sacked Brackett—mostly rum, wine, powder and guns. There's no telling. If we wait, their number will run high. There's a new leader riding with the chief and word has it he's a smart, crazy Indian. They'll have a try for every fort in this section of the territory." Meece's gaze swept across the room to the dead frontiersman, then back to Jonathan. "*He* said it looked as if they were headed for Little Creek."

"Sir?"

"That's right. It's up to you, Lieutenant—move out."

Jonathan brushed by Private Meechum and Captain Niles, the post surgeon, as he stepped out into the white glare of noon. The fort was awake now, horses and men already milling on the parade ground and he saw the tipped and tiny unfurling of the guidon. He started off toward his quarters, holding down the need to yell and holler because this was his first chance and maybe it would solve a lot of things and he had no idea how he should treat this when he confronted Linda. There was a small muttering of laughter inside him someplace that wanted to say, All right, it's Little Creek, too—and Bleeding Cloud. Is that enough, or should I carry a keg of gunpowder along, just to make it perfect? Only he stifled this, as he was stifling everything else, and she met him at the door, a little pale, a touch more sober than usual, with her fingers plucking at the wicker-work of her sewing basket.

• • •

He grinned at her and pushed past, checking the top button on his blouse. He buckled on his revolver and sabre and took his hat off and put it on again and looked at Linda and then at the plaque of medals over the bureau and then at Linda again.

"Oh, Jonathan," she said, and he held her in his arms, good and tight for a minute and she dropped the sewing basket. Her hair was too soft and sweet-smelling and she felt too good for now, so he released her and went over to the door.

The trumpet sounded, racketing in the brassy heat.

"I know you'll be a captain," she said. "A full lieutenant, at least."

He stared at her.

She swallowed hard and looked sideways at her sewing basket there on the floor, with the skeins of thread spilled out among a scatter of vari-colored buttons. So he knew neither of them could ever find the right thing to say then. There was no use trying.

"Come back," she said softly.

He nodded. "All right," and went out and he knew that she was in there in the doorway, watching him, but he did not turn around.

But half an hour later and several miles from Fort Early, he was still musing painfully on the one glimpse he'd had of her as they left the gate. She'd been standing in the doorway of their quarters, one hand whitely waving at something that did not wave back and this got together with everything else inside him thick and heavy enough to choke the big buckskin he was riding. He flagged the column to a walk.

"Sergeant?"

Sergeant Harmon Gibbs reined over beside him and they moved stolidly along through the shimmering heat, ignoring the soaking chafe of sweat. Gibbs was a cracker-thin, hawk-faced cavalry derelict, originally from Ohio, but that was a long way back, so Jonathan had heard. He was a battle thief and among dead Indians always came away with bead necklaces, blood-dipped feathers, torn leggins and anything else that looked good to him. He could not break the habit. He sent these tokens home to his mother whom he hadn't seen in some eleven years. Jonathan recalled that when he'd first come to Early, Gibbs had sent an Apache scalp to his mother and she returned it with the words, "Put this back where you found it, son. I dare not think of even a Indian crossing to the campground without his hair."

"Sergeant," Jonathan said. "Do you know if Apaches drink?"

"Drink, sir?"

"Hard likker—too much, that is."

"Reckon even a Indian's human in that respect, sir."

"Let's hope so."

"Sir?"

"Send out two scouts, Sergeant. Stark and Clawbitt. I want them a quarter mile apart, straight to Little Creek, and fast. If they find Bleeding Cloud camped anywhere along the stream, Stark is to stay put and Clawbitt to return with a clean picture of the terrain. Above everything, they must not be seen, Sergeant."

• • •

Sergeant Gibbs stared at him.

"Something troubling you?" Jonathan asked.

"Well, sir—no, sir," Gibbs said, drawling it out, looking straight ahead into bright, blinding distance. The fort was gone now and they were in rough, rocky country of sand and thrusting canyon, rose-gold and orange in the afternoon.

"You might as well tell me," Jonathan said.

"Well, sir—this now Bleeding Cloud is a bugger, and I'm not questioning you, mind."

"I mind."

"An' he has another bugger with 'im, I hear tell—so between them it will be nasty pie. Since we're in this together, sir, so to speak of—can I offer a suggestion?"

"Certainly."

"I suggest they won't be where we think they will. We ain't got no idea where they be. Could be they're hulkin' over 'hind them rocks, mebbe they been trailin' us already, waitin'."

"Yes," Jonathan said. "I thought of that. But we've got to figure on them being one place or another."

Gibbs nodded and Jonathan knew he was weighing the whole matter quietly, and not questioning the fundamentals, either. He respected Gibbs for this and was glad he had the sergeant with him.

"I see how you figger," Gibbs said. "They'll likely head for water, 'specially because of the rum. An' bein' as they're het-up over sackin' forts just now, they won't head for far water. Little Creek is near water." He paused. "Sir, time Clawbitt gets back, if they do find the camp, it'll be dark." Again he paused and Jonathan waited and when Gibbs spoke now, his voice was bluntly serious. "Sir, have you got a plan?"

Jonathan said, "If they were coming for Fort Early today, we'd have known it. They don't raid at night. They might ride early dawn tomorrow. They might also still have some rum left."

"Yes, sir!" Gibbs said. "I see some of it an' it's worth the chance."

"The scouts, then," Jonathan said. "And give your glasses to Stark, he might have use for them—we won't."

An hour later, riding along, Jonathan avoided thinking of how little Gibbs really knew of what was on his mind. He did not like thinking about it himself, but the idea was like a brick stuck in his skull and he couldn't dislodge it. He wondered what the men thought? They had all been transferred to Fort Early as replacements, about the same time he came west. The difference was, while they were old campaigners, he was a shavetail green from the academy and this was his first encounter with anything serious. He got to thinking of the nerve Meece had, sending him out when he should be an Indian-trained Captain, with arrow-scars, at least. Then he no longer troubled himself about Meece, or Linda, either, because just after dusk, Clawbitt returned sweating, his mount lathered, and led them to the rock-and-sand bluff overlooking an Apache camp on Little Creek, where Stark was waiting with the field glasses plastered against his face.

• • •

They tethered the horses behind giant rocks, looking like pointed fingers in black shadow against the paler sky, then bellied on up to where Stark was stretched out.

"Stark?" Jonathan said.

"Yes, sir," Stark said. "There they are, the bloody cloud, an' all his little cloudlets."

"What?"

"It's the heat, sir."

Jonathan and the men looked off across the stream. Against the sharp slope of a cliff, ponies cropped short grass in fading darkness, and near a large spreading circle of sand by the stream, casting grotesque shadows as they moved about, were the Indians. There were three fires, bright but small, and faint from faraway came the sound of chatter and argument. Jonathan saw three wagons just in front of where the ponies were herded and knew some of Fort Brackett lay in those wagons.

"Sir, there's a hundred and nineteen of 'em."

Jonathan looked at Stark and thought about what he had planned to do, and wondered if he would go through with it.

"Yes, sir," Stark said. He hunched his stubby shoulders, grunting, and scratched himself. "A party of thirty-three lit a shuck south just before dark. They been makin' big pow-wow ever since. Only it's turned into quite a shindig, what with the rum."

"Rum."

"A good half of them redskins is whaffed like candles. Ol' Bloody Cloud's havin' a time with 'em." Stark paused, rolled over, rubbed his left shoulder and stared at Jonathan. "They's a white man down there, Lieutenant."

"A *what*?"

"Yes, sir. Seems like he's in plumb righteous soft with the ol' cloud, there, sir. He's a-settin' right there by the south fire, talkin' with the chief, a-squattin', there. He's decked out like an Injun, but he's peaked-lookin', an' he's totin' a pack." Stark stripped the leather loop from his neck and handed the glasses to Jonathan. "You can catch a look when the fire shines on his face."

Jonathan looked, adjusting the glasses carefully, staring. He did not believe it. He blamed what he saw on the darkness and on the glasses and on his imagination. He took the glasses down and looked over there.

"Sir?" Stark said.

Jonathan looked through the glasses again. The fire light shone glinting bright on the man's face down there, on the blond hair, and the man was wearing a pack, high on his shoulders.

"Am I right, sir?" Stark asked quietly.

"Yes," Jonathan said. "Sergeant?"

Gibbs scrunched over, hunkered down and waited, his eyes mirroring the distant fires with a kind of gleeful twinkling.

"Sergeant, you'll take all the men across the stream and onto that cliff. I see two breaks where you can work your horses to the floor, where the camp is. When I get over with those Indians, and they're clumping up, you bring the men in a charge."

"But, sir—!"

"Those are your orders, Sergeant. Move out."

• • •

Gibbs looked hard at Jonathan, and Stark turned his head away. Some of the men heard the order and Jonathan heard the abrupt whispers.

"You mean, sir, you're going down there?" Gibbs asked.

"In my own way, Sergeant. Take your horses downstream, cross, and come up on top of the cliff. I'll give you plenty of time." He wrapped the leather strap around the glasses, handed them to Stark. "I won't need these, I guess," he said.

So standing with his horse, he waited in the pliant darkness by the shadows of the rocks, while the men left, taking a broad curve downstream. He felt very peculiar about Linda; discovering a sensation of loss with only the comet-tail of snatched-at recovery burning impossibly a hair's breadth beyond belief. And then, finally, he just stood there for perhaps a half an hour, giving the men plenty of time, and refusing absolutely the recompense of thought, listening to the night and the faint yowling and chatter from across the stream, over the bluff. And feeling the night, too, like a sickness—like a festering shroud that hid the secret disquiet of his mind. He knew well enough that the men thought he had left his senses.

Finally, looking off toward the cliff above the Apache camp, he tried to discern movement against the skyline and found none. But they must be there by now, he thought. He mounted the big buckskin and for a long moment sat there remembering Linda in a kind of vicious moiling of blood; remembering then the things she had told him, and wishing the night completed, done, over with—one way or the other. A kind of warm rage seeped up through him then and he set his spurs hard, reining at the bluff. The stallion leaped out and by the time he crossed the bluff he was riding hard, over and down toward the stream. The bluff was steep, but not too steep and he caught back on the reins hard, the horse whinnying and scattering sand and loose gravel and rocks and a long shrill howling went up over there. It would look natural enough that he had come over the bluff, riding fast, seen the camp and tried to run for it. He was close to the stream's bank, now. He turned the horse north, upstream, and let it have its head, watching back there. Already a sprawling fan of ponies had started after him, hoofs muttering on sand.

Checking the buckskin just enough, the Apaches surrounded him far up the stream in less than a quarter of an hour. He had figured right; they did not try to kill him, they had their orders from the white man. It would be to a purpose to find what a lone and uniformed rider was doing out here.

They did not try to speak with him, but handled him brutally. They stripped him of revolver, knife, and snatched his carbine from its saddle scabbard. Grunting and chattering among themselves, they led his horse and he smelled the rum. One warrior was so drunk he couldn't sit his pony and riding back toward the camp, he was eventually left there in the desert, reeling and laughing shrilly, falling with broad efforts to mount. Jonathan did not want even a drunken Indian out here where things might be seen. He tried to tell them to bring the warrior, motioning back there. A knife-toothed brave with bad eyes whipped him twice across the face with his bow.

• • •

They came into the firelight, beyond the wagons, and Bleeding Cloud stood up, his skin gleaming oilily, his eyes bright chips of star, and then Jonathan stared hard at the other man in buckskin leggings with the haversack on his back and the blond hair, the laughing eyes—stared into the tanned, healthy face of Richard Nobel, Linda's brother. He had not allowed himself the kindness of being certain over there on the bluff, but now he could taste the brass on his tongue.

Four Apaches rushed him then, tore him from his horse, flung him to the ground. They were crazed with the rum and he heard Nobel speak and the Chief spoke and the Indians moved grumbling away, breathing hard, their shadows leaping in weird fantasies against the sands.

"They'd tear you to pieces," Nobel said. He stepped over to Jonathan and stood, looking down at him. Jonathan came to one knee, then rose.

"You know who I am, don't you," Nobel said, nodding. "Where were you going, Lieutenant?"

Jonathan said nothing, tasting blood in his mouth from where he'd been struck across the face with the Apache bow. He saw Nobel watching him and the man stepped closer and looked hard and said, "Ah." Then he said, "Who are you, Lieutenant?"

He told him and watched the expression on Nobel's face alter and the whiteness of the teeth went away as the lips closed. Bleeding Cloud began to grunt and some of the warriors began chanting back there by the wagons. Many were sprawled on the sands, motionless. Jonathan wanted to look up there by the cliff and he began to wonder why Gibbs and the men didn't appear. He was sick deep inside now, not because of a doubtful outcome, but because of the woman waiting back there at the fort and the things she must learn—and the things he alone must tell her.

"How is Linda?" Nobel said.

"She's well."

"Stop wondering about me," Nobel said. "I made a good bargain. My life for tactical information and knowledge of the forts in the territory. It's a bargain I was after, it's a life I like. I have what I want and there's promise, too."

"And this is a bargain?"

"Call it what you like," Nobel said. "I'll leave this when I'm ready. There was never enough action with the troops, not the right kind." He threw back his head and laughed softly. "Tell me, what are you doing out here?"

"Riding for Fort Brackett."

• • •

Nobel watched him. "You'll do better than that, Lieutenant. I know you know Brackett's finished, no longer standing. I'll ask you again."

"And I'll tell you the same."

"Very well. I hate killing my own dear sister's husband." He shrugged. "You'd already have been dead if it weren't for me."

They watched each other and Jonathan thought he perceived in the man that shading of difference between loyalty as a soldier and off-scale greed for the wrong kind of adventure. He was sweating plenty now, beneath the flannel and cord of his uniform. Yet there was no sound from the cliffside.

"Bleeding Cloud's my puppet," Nobel said. "I work the wires. I'm building an army who'll know this country better than any white man. Fort Brackett's the first to go. The rest will come in their time. It won't be difficult, you know?" He paused, then said, "The battle at Little Creek where I got 'blown up' was planned by me, so I could vanish, Lieutenant. Did I get posthumously decorated for that?"

Jonathan said nothing. He watched beyond Nobel to where Bleeding Cloud was mumbling to himself. The stalwart chief squatted on a folded blanket and two arms lengths from his side Jonathan saw his revolver and carbine.

Jonathan rubbed his eyes, shielding them, took a quick squint beyond the Apache ponies. He thought he saw movement at the cliff base. He knew Nobel planned to let the Indians have him; he could read it in the man's silence. Nobel was as savagely mad as the Indians.

"Well, Lieutenant," Nobel said. "It's nice to watch you think. Would you care to make talk for your life?"

The trumpet sounded the charge. Scattered carbine fire ripped the night wastes. Jonathan heard the cries of his men, the sandy whisper of their horses as they broke through toward the stream. He rushed at Nobel, head down, and caught him full in the chest, thrust him hard away and dove for the revolver. He landed on the squirming, greasy hide of Bleeding Cloud, smelling rank and wild, and for a moment they fought, twisting on the sands.

Yells purled high, shredding the night, and in flashes he saw the Apaches and the troopers meet and he saw Nobel coming at him across Bleeding Cloud.

"Lieutenant!" somebody shouted. Bleeding Cloud sprawled away, groaning. Jonathan saw Gibbs' sabre flash, and the white flash of teeth, too. Then Gibbs was gone, his horse galloping into the thick of the fight.

He saw Nobel fire the revolver, felt the explosive rake and tug in his side. He came at Nobel, trying for the gun. Then he saw Nobel turn, wide-eyed, and fire down to the left and slowly buckle at the knees and sprawl flat out. Jonathan whirled, Bleeding Cloud slumped, dying, the carbine propped in his arms.

Most of the Apaches were at the back of the stream now. Some were in the water, and some had managed to gain their ponies and ride into the night. There were many dead and a great moaning sifted into the darkness. Jonathan walked slowly over to where Gibbs was rounding up the last of the drunk or sober redskins.

・・・

As dawn painted the eastern sky rose-gold, they filed toward the gate of the fort, their horses as weary nearly as themselves. Twenty-odd Apaches paced before the column, and Jonathan knew he had to make out his report and he had to tell Linda of this thing. He rode in a kind of painful calm, not because of his wound, but because of doubt and fear of the need to make Linda understand. And what would she say, do?

Coming quickly through the gate, he saw the major and Meechum standing over there on the porch at headquarters. Then the major stepped out and started slowly across the parade ground.

He called a halt.

"Sergeant," he said. "Report to the major. Tell him I'm making out my report. I'll be along presently. Dismiss!"

He dismounted, dropped the reins, and strode swiftly for his quarters. He heard Meece call out, "Haggard!"

Linda was standing in the doorway, and they met there on the threshold. Her eyes were deep-rimmed with dark shadow, fatigue showing around her mouth and she stared at his face, then his side, and came to him.

Neither spoke and he held her very close, feeling the fierce need and the goodness and the never-ending confusion that rode inside him. He pressed her head against his chest, trying to figure it some way, breathing the softness of her hair. He looked over there at the wall above the bureau and the plaque with the medals was gone, the photograph on the bureau taken away.

He scowled, thinking of the dead man with the blond hair, stretched and roped across an Indian pony, out there on the parade ground—and he thought, too, of the other six horses with saddles, empty of life, yet bearing the weight of his own dead men.

"Linda—" he said.

"Don't," she said softly. She held tightly to him. "I only wanted you to win through to yourself," she said. "I thought what Richard had done might help spur you on. I've lived a long night, and I know now that I was wrong. Believe me, Jonathan."

"Yes," he said. "Richard." And he knew what he must do. "I have to make a report," he said. "On paper—but first . . ."

"Yes?"

• • •

They stepped away from each other, inside the room and she closed the door. He saw her force the smile and he forced himself to speak.

"Out there," he said.

"Wait—" she said, turning to run across the room. She went to her chair and held up a gray shirt with fancy white stitching, smiling freely now. "I worked all night," she said. "I was with you every minute."

He moved up to her, still over-heavy with what he had to explain. From outside on the grounds he heard men streaming toward their barracks.

"Out there," he said again. "We found a white man with the Apaches. We would call him renegade, Linda. It was he who planned the raid on Fort Brackett. He was getting ready for more of the same, this fort, even—Linda."

"Yes?"

"Whatever his reasons, they were not good."

"A white man."

"Yes. Linda, there's something I've got to try and tell you and it's very difficult." Somebody rapped loudly on the door.

Holding the shirt in one hand, Linda went to the door, opened it, and Sergeant Gibbs stood there, grinning. Jonathan stared and Linda stared and seemed to shrink into the sunlit morning.

"Sir," Gibbs said. "Ma'am, excuse me. I didn't get to show you, sir—what with all the ruckus. See what I found in that renegade's pack, rolled up neat as you please? He must have carried it a long ways. Never been worn, but it sure fits dandy."

Jonathan stared at an exact duplicate if the gray flannel shirt Linda had made for him, down to the last tiny curlicue of fancy stitching on the collar.

"We did right well, sir," Gibbs said, stretching the shirt across his chest. "I want to say the men are proud to serve under you, any time." He saluted smartly, about-faced, and strode off. Jonathan went over and closed the door.

"Richard," Linda said.

"Yes," Jonathan said. "He was young, remember—perhaps he didn't think as we do. We brought him back, Linda."

Linda stared at the gray shirt in her hands, her face quite expressionless and Jonathan knew there was nothing to do now. Suddenly, she strode across the room toward the fireplace where glowing coals from last night still breathed on the hearth.

He reached her just as she started to drop the shirt onto the coals.

"Don't," he said.

They looked at each other and both of them held the shirt, their fingers working in the smooth, fresh cloth.

"I'll be proud to wear it," he said. And something new and good passed between them, and all the grave fear washed away as they looked into each other's eyes. A new smile came to Linda's face.

"All right, Lieutenant," she said. "You'd better make out your report."

He knew the major would be waiting. But it certainly wouldn't hurt him to wait a little while longer.

"Beeg Fool"

Salvo
January 1957

I watched Marie move lazily and roll over on the blanket. I grinned at her. She stuck her tongue out, and turned her back. Her back was bare, and it was a nice back.

"You great beeg fool," she said. "Always *amour—Amour-amour-amour!*"

"Quit kidding," I said. "You love every mile."

I lit a cigarette, waiting for dark. Tonight had to be it, because the krauts were on the run, and I had a long way to go. And what with MPs crawling around, and me AWOL from the line, things weren't too hot. Anyhow, I didn't think I'd be going back to the outfit. You could make it easy, if you knew the ropes. I'd had a belly full of war, and should have had sense enough to walk out in Africa or Italy.

We were in a cellar on the outskirts of St. Lô, and you couldn't even hear the guns. You could smell it, though. You could always smell the dead.

Every time Marie tried to hang the curtains, the same thing happened. I mean, curtains would have been swell. But she'd have to stretch, and her dress pulled up, and she had some legs, this one.

Anyway, it was better than hanging curtains.

"Get weez me, Johnny," she'd say. "You damn fool dogface, you!"

"I am weez you, baby. You know that."

"I mean weez zee curtains, you damn fool! You no good G.I. Dogface!"

She'd get all excited, you know? Only made it worse. And the thing was, there was a time when she could hang the curtains, only she'd wait too long. It kept going on. You know?

"How long we going to stay here?" she said, rolling over and looking at me, her breasts mushing out, black hair snarled around her shoulders, and that pixie red mouth, and those sly dark eyes watching. "How long, Johnny?"

"I told you a hundred times. Till I find Jeff, and break him loose from those bastards."

She squirmed closer. It was getting dark, but a slant of stale light came in the bottom of the window, where we had some dead infantryman's shirt nailed up for blackout. The light spread on her bare body and it kind of choked me. I mean, Marie was so damned beautiful. I'd picked her up in St. Mère-Église, and now look.

"Johnny?" Her voice was softly inquisitive. "You don't even know maybe thees Jeff he is dead."

"He's not dead."

"But—you don't know."

"He's alive. They've got him. They'll stick him in some Goddamned barbed wire camp, or shoot him. He's my brother. I got to get him."

I looked at her and reached out and ground the cigarette into the dirt floor, then slapped her thigh. Her thigh was hot.

"Try and understand," I said. "Jeff and I—we made a pact. Agreed on something. Even before I took off. If I hadn't met that guy from my outfit, I wouldn't have known. Understand?"

"I don't zeenk I do, Johnny."

I hauled her over and kissed her hard on the mouth. I rolled over, waiting. She started ruffling my hair.

"I keep *trying* to understand, Johnny."

"Yeah, O.K. We said, if one of us gets captured then the other's gotta get to him—*somehow,* any damned how—and help him escape. And eff everything. See?"

"What ees thees eff?"

"You oughta know. Understand, now?"

"Non!"

I started to give her a shove. Hell, I was nuts about the babe. She'd got to me deep. It was bad, knowing I had to leave her. There was nothing else to do. And I was worried all over again. A machine gun rattled off across the bombed-out town. I whapped her behind and rolled out of the sack, and stood up.

"No *amour?*"

I walked back past the big old wine barrels the Germans had shot holes in, and on through the tunnel to the section of cellar under the hospital where I kept the Jeep hid. What was left of the hospital. I was plenty nervous. It was dark in the tunnel and something rolled under my foot. I remembered the hand, lying there. Whose hand? Somehow you just let them lay.

I had the Jeep fixed up comfortable. Tore out the back seat, fixed a pad, and had it stashed with Ten-in-One, and a few Ks, and some French bread and wine. Whoever had lost the Jeep had built plywood sides, doors and all, and it was right nice. Small, but home.

"What's up, soldier?"

I stood still. A damned M.P. He had on a white helmet, and he was standing just under the blanket draped across the blown-out place where I drove the Jeep in. Trouble. He was a big bastard. M.P.s usually are.

"Nothing's up."

"Out here a sec."

He had a Tommy-gun. His straps shined and creaked a little. His boots were shined. No telling what kind of guy he was. With my luck, a mucker.

He ripped the blanket down, big as life, and motioned with the barrel of the machine gun. He had an evil face in the dusky light coming across the bombed-out streets of rubble.

I got a little crazy. This had to happen.

"Stand there, soldier."

I had to get rolling. Nothing was going to stop me. A bunch of M.P.s had pulled into town the day before.

"What's all this?" he said.

"All what?"

One look and he'd know I was AWOL. I hoped he was green. He gestured toward the Jeep. I had scraped the back bumper so you couldn't read the outfit anymore. I started praying Marie wouldn't run out here naked. That would be fine. All this, and me not even sure where Jeff was located by now. They could have him clear to Heidelberg, and I'd been holding my breath all day.

"I pulled in for a nap. Just taking off again."

"Yeah? Where to? Where's your outfit at?"

"I'm a courier."

"Let's see your pass."

"You couldn't read it in here. Let's go on outside."

"You first."

I walked past him and got a good look, and it was lousy. He wasn't green. He was having fun.

"Watch it," he said.

I got into the twilight, and he laughed. My stomach began to hurt where I'd caught a ricochet at Anzio.

"Courier, my naked ass," he said. "Courier to what?"

"Outfit's spread all over hell," I said. "Clear to Barfleur. Here's my damned pass. You guys all the time think—" I walked up to him, handing out an old card and it kind of stopped him and the gun sagged and I let him have it with everything.

Not the card, boy. The fist. I brought the gun down with my left and caught him hard in the face with my right. His helmet flew off and rattled around. He shook his head and looked at me, red-eyed. Then he began yanking at the gun. I hung onto the gun, trying to get at him again, and dodge right.

The gun went off, raising hell. St. Lô echoed. He had a drum on, and pieces of wall splattered down, and dust spurted around my feet. Close. He kept swearing like a fool, gripping the trigger, the gun bucking like crazy between us. I dove at him and the hell with the gun. We went down and I saw Marie running naked out behind the Jeep, her mouth wide open, holding her breasts.

He started yelling.

"Dugan! Dugan—for Christ's sake! Dugan!"

I beat the living hell out of him.

There was nothing else to do. He was hard, but I had to get away. I wrecked him. Then I got up and looked at him, feeling sorry, breathing hard, and the indigestion starting fine now. I figured maybe he'd ripped open the bayonet slice in my side. Blood trickled, hot.

"Dugan," he muttered, out cold.

He moved. I was mad about the indigestion. I got down and beat his head on the ground, then stood up. Marie was over by the Jeep.

"Johnny. *Il est mort!*"

"He's not dead. I'm taking off." I walked past her and on through the tunnel. My stomach hurt like hell. It was barb-wire and busted glass inside. I leaned against the tunnel, and she came running through toward me. I went on into the cellar, and grabbed my helmet, and strapped on my .45. My canteen was full. I put the helmet on. Every time, it was the same. You feel: here we go again.

"Une minute."

"What?"

"I be ready—very quickly."

"I'm going alone, Marie. You'll wait here for me."

"Johnny."

She walked slowly over to me and stopped and just looked. The hell. She held her hair back along the sides of her head with both hands.

"I'll go weez you, Johnny. Yes—*oui!*"

"Nope."

I took her in my arms; all that lovely, wonderful, gorgeous hunk of France, and kissed her, and it was worse than anything.

"See you. You wait here. I'll be back. I'm not walking out on you."

I started for the tunnel. I couldn't look at her again. She had no right getting into my fouled-up life, but there she was. For a second I hoped I wouldn't get back for her. For her sake.

I checked the M.P. He was still out. I tossed the Tommy-gun into the Jeep, put my M-1 up front, got the blanket and threw that back there. Then I moved through the darkness, feeling walls, until I made the racked bottles by the hospital stairs. I found four litres of Cognac the Germans hadn't smashed, and took them back to the Jeep. Marie would be safe here; as safe as anyone could possibly be safe.

I went back and got another bottle and cracked the Goddamned neck off and poured it down. Onto the mess in my stomach. The only thing that helped—Calvados, and Armagnac, too—but Cognac was the best. I kept pouring it down, then choked a little, and poured again, remembering how wonderful the morphine was in that hospital when they flew me to England. And the way that nurse had kept sneaking me a shot in the night. I went back to the Jeep, drinking from the busted neck, and got the engine started.

No sign of Marie.

Well, she knew how I felt. She knew I wasn't bulling her; we had that much between us. A lot, I figured. More than most people had, even married back in the States.

Christ, Christ. . . .

I drove past the cold M.P. and damned near drove over his legs, my gut hurt that bad. Then the Cognac began to work.

I headed up past the church. The engineers had cleared the roads pretty well, but the town was knocked to hell and gone, laid flat. Nothing left but a few houses up on the hill past the Vire. The moon was up bright, and you could see the red front line in the north, and on the horizon, blurring, and I heard the guns rumble. Must have been a Goddamned strategic withdrawal again. St. Lô stank bad. I held the gas pedal to the floor, drinking the Cognac, and passed two groups of frogs digging in piles of rubble and broken debris.

Their homes. Piles.

One old woman stood weeping in the moonlight, holding up a bent spoon.

I cut out of there. The Red Ball went through, and I got jammed behind a truck convoy, rolling about seventy, then took to the shoulder and began passing. It was a bitch. Those drivers went through hell, and they were all half shot, and wild men at the wheel.

I got past, and let her roll. You could hear the guns. You could see it up there—spotty—but there, all right, O.K.

I wished I hadn't left her back there.

The guy said he and Jeff had been on patrol, and he was the only one got away. They gunned the others, but they took Jeff. They had him in with another bunch of PWs and if they hadn't killed him, he'd be in a town I knew of. If we hadn't taken the town, and it didn't look like we had.

I came through some place called Haircut-for-Tired-Braces, or something. A British M.P. was on the corner and he flagged me. Hell, I stopped.

"Perhaps you might have a bottle?" he said. "I've been standing here for two days."

I handed him what was left, and gunned out of there. The moon was gone and it was black. It kept on stinking till I got into the country again. I started watching for a truckload of gas. I stopped twice to check Jerry cans, but they were empty. Finally I spotted a ditched truck, and went over. The Negro driver was lying sprawled dead out the door, his head shot mostly off. The windshield was shot up. He'd run it into a mine field. I crawled up over the gate, and checked. There was a cat in there, a spotty one, huddled down under a torn tarp, and it didn't even meow. I dropped three cans of gas off, went over the side, filled the Jeep and took off again.

I tried not to worry about Jeff. But after all, he was my brother. He was always in a jam, somehow or other. He had to get caught. Only, thinking like that wasn't any good, either.

I got on Marie again, and tried not to think about her, and began on St. Lô, and how our planes had bombed the living hell out of the 30th in mid-July. The whole sector was rotten with gore, and the Nazis had crawled in deep.

A sputtering to my right brought me to. It was a German machine pistol off in the woods. I rammed the gas to the floor.

A week and a half I'd been away from my outfit, and it seemed like years. Four days I'd been with Marie, and it was like we'd been married and had known each other a long time. Last night, off on the St. Lô-Périers Road, I'd run into another AWOL, and it was an old buddy. He'd told about Jeff, and where he thought he was.

I braked the Jeep. Tanks in the road up ahead. I backed, turned, and took a cut-off. Knowing the country a little, I remembered a dirt road off toward the town I wanted.

It was wild. The Nazis were laying everything down but the guns themselves. The sector was crawling with GIs trying to load on trucks. German artillery and mortar was really ripping things apart.

"Hey, you!"

I kept going. Some Second Looie ran after the Jeep. I pushed it hard but had to keep it fairly slow because the road was streaming with men. A truck got a square hit two hundred yards in front of me. In the flash, I saw pieces of men flying. I turned into the woods, seeing white faces and the dull flash of helmets. Everybody was yelling. Why in hell didn't they crawl in?

I hit a country road again, and it was quiet for a time with sporadic firing and machine pistols, and rifles up ahead and to the right. Then that quit and I heard planes droning overhead, stuck my head outside, but couldn't see anything.

A Kraut yelled something, and I knew I was in it. Like that. The same old feeling, everything blanked out, and running like hell. I pushed on the gas pedal, and knew I couldn't head back now. A tank lurched off the road in front of me, and I turned left off the shoulder into woods again. The trees weren't thick.

The tank belched. Trees ripped and blew up.

I kept going, headed for the road again to make time, Nazis or no Nazis. You get dizzy, and I knew I was near where I wanted to go, and in the middle of some mucked up offensive by God only knew which side.

On the road, I hit the town. It was as mad here as it had been a mile or two back. There was going to be hell tonight, and it started raining—a steady, rotten downpour. But I was glad of that.

The guy from my outfit'd said they had the American PWs located in an old building to the East of town. I hit a side street, and a fat German officer rumbled out of a house and started flagging me. I gunned the Jeep. I'd been running with the lights off, and I turned them on in his eyes, and went straight at him. He started trying to unbuckle his silly Luger holster and the snap was caught. His gut was strapped in twin bulges. I hit him and he went sprawling.

The thud wasn't too loud. I rode over him and he kept on screaming after I'd made two blocks. Our artillery was laying it in here, and I thought about the men in the building on the East of town.

I was drunk as hell. I got another bottle out and uncorked, and drank. It was some stuff, right enough. The sky was shooting with tracers. A plane came out of nowhere and laid an egg. Fritzie's chickens.

I had a flash, and knew I'd been drunk for a long time now. I drank some more. It was a bitch. Nazis were running all over the place. There was a great similarity to the confusion I'd gone through on our side, everybody yelling and running back and forth.

A building to my right went.

I took the road down along the river, and saw the building the guy'd told me about. A five-hundred pounder landed in the river, and it was gorgeous.

It kept on raining.

I ran the Jeep up an alley, and parked it, and got out running.

"*Kamarad!*"

"The hell with you!"

He was a big one, with helmet down to his ears, and shoulders like an ox-yoke. I let him have one .45 slug in the chest, and ran over him. They had trucks lined up in front of the building by the river, and another fat German officer was brandishing both arms, screaming at a tired-looking handful of SS men. Another plane came down. I wondered if it were theirs or ours? It laid another in the river. The German officer flipped and went bulling at the men, trying to argue them into something. The truck drivers kept gunning their engines.

There was a double front door, and no lights showing, and I came up along the side in the mud. Another plane began screaming. The Nazis bolted and started hitting dirt. The fat officer took out his Luger and started shooting at them, swearing in Kraut. They weren't *Gott im Himmel's,* either. The plane laid the egg, and cut off down the river.

I could hear guys yelling inside the building, battering at doors and walls. I went down along the side of the building, and around back over a wall.

I never saw him till he had me. He was a short, stocky, thrust-jawed bird, and he slammed at me with the stock of his rifle. It caught the Cognac bottle and smashed it. I had my .45 in my left hand. I dove at him with the broken neck of the bottle, and he started firing the damned rifle wild. He ducked and I felt the bayonet slice that same Goddamned place in my side, and somebody rammed a rifle into my other side, and the first one knocked the .45 out of my hand. I went sprawling.

I was on my knees. I tried to run that way, coming to my feet, and my helmet came off, and one of them smashed me in the head.

They were gobbling and grunting. I couldn't tell how many there were. The world swam and sank and reeled around, maybe Cognac, maybe not.

"American, eh?"

Somebody hauled me to my feet.

"What are you doing here?"

I fell down, and somebody hauled me to my feet. Everything was mud. A building down the street went and I remembered the Jeep parked in the alley. If they got that, I was sunk. I was sunk, any way you looked at it.

"I asked you question!"

He smashed me in the face. It was the fat Nazi officer, with one of those peaked caps cocked over one eye, and ribbons down to here, with a damned riding crop. He had that crazed look everybody gets at night during a bombardment. Everything was going to hell everyplace.

"Throw him in with the rest."

"Like hell."

"No! Put him in the truck."

They started to drag me. I began laughing. One of them smashed me in the face again. I was bleeding all over, and somehow I was going to get into that building where Jeff was. I started yelling Jeff's name. Two Nazis came running down the side of the building, and one of them carried a potato-masher grenade. He yelled something and the fat officer took offense and fired at him with the Luger. They were a dandy crew.

The one yanked the string, and flung the grenade. I was loose, standing there. I ran as hard as I could and hit dirt, and the thing went off, white in the night, guys running and yelling, and the fat officer crawling and weeping now.

I snaked along the side of the building to the wall again, and went over again, wondering how I'd get back on the other side. They were setting up a holler inside. My stomach was a mess. I lay there and puked in the mud, and a plane came down, and all hell erupted about seventy-five yards to the rear, in an apartment building of some damned kind, glass splattering, and dirt flying. There was no door that I could see.

"*Ach-tung!*"

It was the fat officer. He was on his feet again, bleeding in the chest all over his ribbons. He was determined. He started firing at me, but he was wild. I ran right at him, and he died firing at me, and his chest wasn't even there. Hunks of lung bellowed pinkly in the scattered white light, and you could see the mushed-up insides, and a corner of his ticker still throbbing, and quivering, and then that quit.

I went running, and vaulted the wall, and came up the side again. The trucks were out there, still running, but nobody in them. The side of the street by the river was caved in, and planes were thick up there now. The whole Goddamned night was one insane clattering and banging and slamming, with pieces flying through the air, and white, blue, and red light, like smashed neon.

I made the door, and machine-gun slugs ripped the wood, driving in a slant toward me, so I hit dirt off to the side again.

"Jeff!" I yelled. "Jeff Williams!"

The machine gun cut loose, rattling from across the street. I saw the grenade loop through the light and dove crawling again, and it went off like a handful of mud in the Mississippi.

And I felt my right leg go. Down by the ankle. It just went, like a stick of wood, and you knew it was gone. But knowing it doesn't help, always. Because you don't want to believe it, and I didn't want to look at it. The pain wasn't anything at all. I knew about that, too, and decided to use the advantage of what few minutes I had.

I got up and my foot crackled as I ran, and some white pain got into my knee, but it still wasn't all there, and I could use the leg.

"Johnny!"

I stopped and looked at her. She came running up the river bank, just this side of the bridge with the machine gun going it from down the street. You could see the street rocks and water spattering at her heels as she ran toward me.

I just stood there. Watching it. What could you do. She kept running, with her hands out and her hair flying, in that thin gray cotton dress she had, and the lights were so bright her hair looked white. Maybe it was. I don't know.

"Johnny," she said, and they hadn't got her and I could even smell her in the middle of it.

I tried to ask her how she'd got here. All I could get out of the frog talk was the word Jeep. She'd stowed away in the back, somehow, under the blanket.

We held each other, and the machine gun quit.

A gentleman. I let her go and made a dive for the door again, and the pain struck. I went flat with it, like somebody took my leg and rammed a hot iron straight up the shinbone to the knee-cap.

"Get the door open," I told her. "Get the door! Hurry up!"

She looked at me, then ran for the door. The planes came back. I lay there in a sea of pain, watching them in the pink-lined clouds, like slow files of kids' toys marching through the heavens.

She kept working on the damned door. It was locked, and she couldn't do any good. I crawled over to where she was, and pulled myself up and had a look. It was barred with steel.

"Jeff's in there," I said to her.

"Damnfool dogface!"

She turned, plastered against the door in the light, soaking wet, and the rain pouring down, and them inside really clamoring now. I half-walked, half-dragged myself to the trucks, and fished around inside by the front seats. I found a Luger, only that wasn't any good for what I wanted. Then I felt the grenade box, and got three of them and started back for the building. Some more trucks came running down the street, past the building. I triggered the Luger, and felt it jam, and threw the Luger at the first truck. It bounced off the hood, and splashed into the river. The trucks stopped, and I ran for the door again, with my leg crackling with bright pain now. The blood sucked in my shoe.

"Get out of the way, baby!"

She just stood there.

"Away from the door—*la porte,* whatever the hell!"

She ran toward me and I heard them yelling from the trucks. I found the loop and yanked the string on the potato-masher, and threw it up by the door. Then I did the same with the other, and grabbed Marie and knocked her into the mud, hugging her close. She kept spouting French, and I didn't get a word of it.

All I could think was Jeff and those guys in there.

"You shouldn't have come," I told her.

The grenades went. I watched the door go, too, and it was a big white sheet of light. I looked around at the trucks, and a guy was standing on the running board shouting orders. Helmeted men poured over the sides, and then I heard them shouting from the building.

"Jeff!"

"Yeah man! What you want?"

He came running out of that door.

"I heard you," he called.

"Johnny, quick!"

I was watching them come out of the building, a stream of men. Marie kept pulling at me. I couldn't do much about that, and she was pulling me through the mud.

I saw them get it.

The Krauts had a machine gun set up in one of the truck beds, and they laid that on them. I saw Jeff get it running, across the chest, and again, before he hit the ground in the light, across the legs.

She kept pulling me. I couldn't do anything about that. They all got it, as far as I could tell.

"Lie still, Johnny."

"Sure."

We lay there in the pouring rain at the corner of the building, and watched the Krauts. They went over and looked at the guys, lying dead in the wet street under all the crazy lights.

"Don't move, Johnny."

"Sure."

We lay there like that. After a while the trucks went away and things got quiet again. Pretty soon, I heard more trucks, and they were G.I. You could tell by the sound of the engines.

It was no good. It was just no good at all.

Love Me, Baby

True Men Stories
April 1957

The old man turned stiffly in the wicker chair, and wrinkled his faded eyes at the girl. She was a dazzlingly lush blonde in a black Bikini, seated cross-legged on the thick green turf of lawn above the lagoon. To the left, just around the point, the Mediterranean town of Cassis nestled rainbow-roofed under a cerulean blue sky.

"Well, baby," the old man said, his voice cracking. "I hear your Frenchie coming in his toy car."

"God!" the girl said. "I wish you wouldn't talk that way. It's filthy, the way you talk!"

The old man laughed a dry, withered laugh. It sounded like leaves rustling around a cellar casement window, and above the laughter an open-mufflered car spluttered to a stop beside the villa.

"You two going swimming again?" the old man said.

"We might. Maybe down where the wreck is. Do you begrudge me that?"

"Not as long as I can see you, my dear."

The girl's face was filmed very faintly with perspiration, and a certain curious agitation was revealed in the way she breathed. There was an eagerness, an urgency just in the way she sat there.

"You've dragged me half way around the world," the girl said. "Clear to France, now—keeping me away from everybody. You're scared you'll lose me."

"No, my dear—it's not exactly that."

"Yes, it is! I've told you, I just want to be with you. After all, I'm your wife. Only, sometimes I *do* like seeing other people."

"Other *men*, darling. Let's be specific. It's my money you like. You're a lovely liar, and a glorious cheat—but let's speak truth between each other."

"Oh, my God," the girl said, standing up.

"How about Marie Reclamer, over there—next door?" the old man said, gesturing toward a pink and blue vine-twined, sprawling house, separated from his villa by a waist-high hedge. "Your Frenchie was her lover, until he grazed over here and spotted you. Can you imagine what she might think—down inside—seeing him with you every day? They were to be married, remember?"

"It isn't like that at all," the girl snapped. "Henri simply didn't care for her anymore. Henri and I are merely friends. She *understands*—she doesn't think the disgusting things you do."

"Ah," the old man said. "Disgusting, eh?"

The girl turned her rigid back.

• • •

A tall, broad-shouldered and very handsome man moved languidly down across the slope of lawn toward them. He wore white swimming trunks, and a white terry cloth jacket. As he neared, the girl turned and waved to him and she seemed to shiver just beneath her skin.

The old man noticed everything.

"Excited, my dear?"

"You're filthy!" she said, whispering.

He sighed, drew a brown metal medallion of some kind from his pocket and sat there rubbing it with his thumb. He had on a pair of ragged khaki shorts, his stick-like knees and legs inert. His sparse gray head and neck jutted from the collar of a blue woolen turtle-neck sweater obscenely, bringing to mind buzzards perched in skeletal trees on autumn afternoons.

"Henri," the girl said. "I'm so glad you came."

"*Jour*," Henri said. "*Ça va?*" He nodded to the old man. "Hallo, M'sieu Hallister, ça va bien?"

"*Merde*," the old man said. "I'm fine, thanks."

Henri stared at the old man for a moment, shrugged, and looked at the girl. She bridled, avoiding his eyes. Henri spoke with gestures, and was on the bouncy side.

"It is one glorious day," Henri said.

"It stinks," the old man said. "But I rather imagine it's all in one's perspective."

"*Oui*," Henri said. "This is possible." He looked at the girl, and she winked slyly, careful that the old man did not see. Her mildly tanned creamy flesh seemed almost over-ripe, even juicy, in the strangely saffron sunlight of the *Côte d'Azur*. It was very obvious that she wanted to get away with Henri and, looking at him, one busy hand on her side where her husband could not see, she pushed her fingers under the scant Bikini shorts and pulled them taut, her red lips damply parted. Henri tensed nervously and cleared his throat.

• • •

The old man's tone was sarcastic. "Why don't you two go swimming? I hate to detain you."

"Oh, *mais*—but you're not detaining *me*," Henri said. "I like talking with you."

"*Merde*," the old man said. "I'd like to get drunk."

"You know what the doctor said about that," the girl told him. "You've drunk enough for ten men. You stick to your coffee."

Henri beamed suddenly. "But the swimming—it is an excellent idea. We could, Janie—if you like—swimming, I mean. For a little."

"The water looks good," the old man said.

Henri said, "Of course, I must rush back to town soon, you know?" He raised his eyebrows at the old man. "I do like you to know how much I appreciate being allow' to come here and swim." He made a face of deep disgust and stretched his palms. "The beach at Cassis, it is so, 'ow you say? Crowded. *Pas gentil*."

"By all means," the old man said.

Henri nodded. "Ah, *oui*."

• • •

The girl's voice was a shade hoarse with excitement. "We could maybe look around the shipwreck again," she said. "Wouldn't that be good, Charles?" She glared at her husband, then smiled at Henri. "Charles has been telling me more about the wreck, where we swim. He thinks we haven't searched in the right spot. He says he has checked the records and knows for a fact the Germans never recovered the treasure. Very few people even know of it, Henri. It's in a steel box, nearly half a million dollars in American currency. The box was listed as water tight, and Charles says since the bottom is rocky, and since the ship's hull was ruined so, perhaps it just sits there. He thinks we should look well. The Americans sank the ship in '45, you know? That's not so terribly long, when you consider...."

"It's true," the old man said, interrupting. "I've tried to look myself. It would be an amazing thing. Think of it—but"—he moved spiked shoulders—"I'm much too old, even though the water isn't deep."

"We'll go have a look!" Henri said.

"Yes!" the girl said. "Let's look real hard today, Henri. Let's go!"

The old man coughed dryly. "My dear? I realize how young and energetic you are. But, please—be sure to keep in sight, so I can watch you?"

"Yes," the girl said.

"Oh, we will, *certainement*!" Henri said.

"It gives me a modicum of enjoyment," the old man said, his faded eyes wrinkled as he stared at the girl.

"We'll call to you," Henri said. "We'll wave!"

"*Merde*," the old man muttered.

"You can see us plainly down there," the girl said. "And perhaps Marie will come over from next door—visit with you, bring you afternoon *café au lait*, like she's done before."

The old man's eyes twinkled lewdly. "True," he said.

"We won't be long."

Henri and the girl moved down the slope toward the lagoon, and the urgency was in both of them now, very obviously.

• • •

The green lawn met a stretch of sand which led to the water. On either side of the lagoon, pastel-hued cliffs reared jaggedly. Far out on the water, a smack heeled limberly. Close in, just to the right of the small sand beach, out perhaps twenty feet, among rocks, the old German hull lay on its beams ends, rusting in little more than fifteen feet of water.

As soon as they were beyond earshot, the girl's voice became throaty with delight. "Henri, darling—I could hardly wait. I'm burning up for you—half mad with waiting! Where were you? You took so long today."

"*Cherie*," he said. "I am the same weez you. My palms itch for you. I cannot contain myself, true. I wanted to come at dawn. Be with you all the time. But I 'ave been trying to figure a way, *Cherie—some way*. All of the time I think of you with that ancient. In bed, at night." He put both hands to his head. "It drives me crazy! What are we going to do? Always in the water—it is not enough."

"Lord, Henri. I know. We'll think of something. But we've got to be careful, you know that. We don't want to lose out on his money."

They reached the sand.

"Turn and wave," the girl said.

• • •

They turned and waved at the slope. The old man waved back to them, and over across the waist-high hedge. Marie Reclamer, wearing a tight canary yellow dress over her full-curved body, watched. Marie Reclamer's usually pouting red lower lip was clenched tightly between even, glistening white teeth, and her dark eyes seemed abnormally bright.

"*Pah!*" she said, spitting toward the hedge. She turned and ran up the slope to her home, across the patio, and inside to the kitchen. She ran well-shaped hands through a thick wealth of black hair, then smoothed her palms across plump hips. "Henri," she whispered almost sadly, then more bitterly, "Henri."

Her hands moved quickly, adjusting a steaming silver pot filled with coffee, another of hot milk, cups and saucers of delicate chinaware, and a single brandy glass on a silver tray. From a cupboard, she withdrew a bottle of cognac, uncorked it, and humming harshly brought another small bottle down. She uncapped this small bottle, glanced at the label, which read: *Cyanide—Faire Attention—Empoisonne!*—and dumped a liberal stream of white crystals into the bottle of cognac. She put the poison away, corked the brandy, shook it, checked to see that the crystals were dissolved, then set it on the tray.

Still humming, she picked up the tray, and started across toward where the old man was seated on the lawn, watching Henri and the girl.

"Hurry," the girl said, as Henri and she moved across the sand. "Let's get in the water."

"Better go over by the wreck, make it look good," Henri said. "He can see us plainly, as it is. He'll think we're looking for his damned treasure." He made as if to spit.

"Suppose there *was* treasure and we found it."

"To dream," Henri said. "*Vite, cherie.*"

. . .

Their hands brushed. The girl grabbed his fingers and squeezed hard, then they stepped into the water, among the rocks, beyond the sand. They were in full view of the old man, and not far away. He could see them clearly, though he couldn't hear them speak.

"What did the ancient do to make all that money?"

"He was in the army, long ago," the girl said. "That's all I know. His people were rich, of course. He was quite a goat in his day."

"He is an old goat now."

They were in water up to their necks. Henri's arms went out and his fingers touched her shoulders. She seemed to cringe into herself.

"Oh, darling," she said. "I've waited for you for so long . . ."

Their lips touched for a moment.

"Not yet, *cherie*," Henri murmured. "The old goat can still see us. Splash a little. Make it look as if we were swimming and move to the shadow of the boat's hull."

"Come to me, my darling," Henri whispered in the shadows.

She moved silently, swiftly into his arms, her lips pressed to his. And then slowly, with their mouths glued together, they sank into the water.

. . .

On the shore, the old man looked at his wife and then turned to Marie. "Young people think a man ages all over. It is true that some of the senses dull—hearing perhaps, taste, smell—but the eyes grow sharper. Do your young eyes see what mine old ones see?"

"Pah! He is only a man—and not a very good one at that."

"Aren't you jealous?" The old man's eyes twinkled.

"I am never jealous—men come and go in my life." Marie shrugged her pretty shoulders. "I do not know if it is a blessing or a curse."

"In this case," murmured the old man, "it is a blessing for you—a curse for me."

In the water the girl tore her lips away from Henri. "Wait," she whispered. "It's Marie with my husband."

"Never mind them, my darling."

But she looked at them. The old man wasn't much nearer. He was speaking with the woman in the yellow dress. They both waved. Henri waved. The girl closed her eyes—fastening her lips to Henri's, and slowly they sunk out of sight.

• • •

In a while, they laughed and began diving again, being careful not to come far out of the water.

"Stay with me all afternoon," the girl said. "Don't leave me, darling. I couldn't bear it. It's so short as it is. Please?"

"Yes. We will try to zeenk of something. But, first, let us dive and swim and make it look good." He winked at her, and splashed her. "Then we can rest again. *Bon?*"

She dove deeply. They swam down and down into the sunny blue-green depths along the ship's side. Their naked bodies shimmered, and suddenly the girl bubbled furiously from the mouth, pointing, grabbing for her lover. They swam quickly upward, burst surface, and began talking in excited whispers.

"Did you see it?"

"*Oui*! Yes! It is fantastic, *cherie*! It cannot be! The box—I swear it does look like the very box the ancient said was listed on the records."

"Oh, good Lord, it is," she said. "I know it. Charles is so seldom wrong. He knows of these things. It's all he has time to do—paw through dusty records, like that. Do you suppose?"

"Let's look again. Dive deep, *cherie*! Then come up and we'll see if we can figure out a way to get it to dry land." He drew her carelessly to him, now, and quickly kissed her throat. "Be calm," he said. "It might be nothing."

"Wave!"

• • •

They turned and waved to the old man and the woman up on the lawn. The old man and the woman waved back, calling to them.

"Hurry up, you two!" the woman called. "There's hot coffee for M'sieu Hallister, and Janie and me—and Henri? I have your favorite brandy—Henri, all for you!"

Henri and the girl laughed, clinging with their bodies underwater. Then they took deep breaths and dove deeply again, down and down through the swirling silvery blue depths, their bodies flashing in vagrant sunlight. They clung to the rust- and barnacle-covered sides of the exploded ship's hull, then hovered above the rocky bottom.

All sorts of junk littered the bottom around the ship's stove-in sides. Old chains, and girders and beams, and rusting iron fixtures—and resting in half-shadow sat a steel box, perhaps a yard square. Strands of filmy green sea-weed rose from the box, and it was rough with rust. A loop handle showed on either side.

Henri and the girl surfaced again.

"I believe it ees it," Henri said.

"Kiss me," the girl said. "I don't give a damn!" She clutched at him. "We don't need his filthy money."

Their mouths came together and the girl moaned and moaned with pleasure. They parted, breathing heavily. "We cannot rest now," Henri said. "We must go see. Look," he said. "We will dive down. You take one handle, I will take the other. It will be heavy, but not too heavy. We will move it along the bottom a little, then come up for air. We can keep doing this, until it is near shore. Then we will leave it in the water, and when it ees night—we will come and take it out—and go!"

"How can we be sure it *is* the money?"

Henry shook his head. "I think it is, *cherie.* But we cannot be certain until dark. We must take the chance. Are you weez me?"

"*Am I!*"

"Wave to the ancient."

• • •

They waved, not even bothering to look up across the lawn now. "*Chou-chou!*" Henri said. "Let's go—take a good breath—a big breath."

They grinned at each other, breathed deeply, and dove hard. They went full to the bottom this time, and clung to a narrow steel beam that arched across the rocks near the steel box. They moved in watery slow-motion toward the box, bubbling and motioning to each other. Just where the box was, the sunlight sliced goldenly through the water, and the half-shadow over the box was as clear as daylight.

They looked at each other, and Henri signaled, motioning toward the slope of bottom toward shore. They braced themselves on either side of the box. They leaned down and grasped the handles. . . .

• • •

Up on the lawn, Marie Reclamer, in the tight yellow dress, screamed and ran down toward the beach.

A noise like thunder roared in the afternoon. Down in the water, a great seething and bubbling took place, the lagoon lifted and lifted, ballooning higher into the air, and the old shipwreck heaved gigantically. Then, with a terrible explosion, the water broke and showered skyward, the hull splintering and tearing. Wreckage and sheets of water rose amid blinding light, hovered, then began to rain down. Water and pieces of steel splattered nearly up to where the old man sat in his wicker chair, holding a withered and twig-like hand over his thin, pale lips—coughing. He quietly eyed the lushly curved legs of the young woman in the yellow dress, standing down the slope a way, her back to him. He nodded his head.

Down there the water still seethed.

The old man sat, watching, rubbing the brown metal medallion between his fingers. Then he tipped his ancient head and read an inscription to himself!

> *FOR VALOR AND EXCEPTIONAL BRAVERY ABOVE AND BEYOND THE CALL OF DUTY, PRESENTED TO CHARLES HALLISTER, CAPTAIN 2nd EXPLOSIVES & DETONATIONS BATTALION. MASTER OF CONTACT DETONATION. FRANCE—1917*

• • •

The old man coughed a very gentle cough.

"The hell with coffee," he said. "This is an occasion, isn't it?"

He reached to the silver tray on a table near his chair, picked up the brimming glass of brandy Marie Reclamer had poured moments before, and, as old men will, gulped it to the dregs.

Stop Off

Man's Life
May 1957

Outside it was raining. It was night. In the three-room apartment just off the court, the slim, dark-haired girl moved quietly. First she settled herself in a comfortable lounge chair beside the empty fireplace, her head tilted toward her lap. She was an extremely pretty girl, her hair done just so in careful braids that nestled against the brushed sheen of hair, pulled back into a sort of bun, tied with white ribbon. Her lips were full and red. Her eyes were very black, almost as if they were all pupil, and they were lazy, disinterested eyes. She wore thin white lounging pajamas. The pajamas did not conceal the fact that her body was young, vital, lushly contoured. She was a tall girl, full-breasted, and vigorous. She seemed worried—harried.

Rising from the chair, she moved directly across the small sitting room past the apartment door by the fireplace, and on into the kitchen. She stood by the sink, staring at the rain-drenched window.

A footstep sounded in the court.

She listened. From the living room, a china clock on the mantel chimed twelve times. She listened to that, too. There was something at once delicate and certain about the way she listened.

Again there was a footstep in the court.

The footsteps came nearer, then suddenly broke into a run as a car's headlights washed through the street beyond. The girl turned, both hands pressed to her face as the feet pounded onto the small outside porch, and the kitchen door swung inward.

• • •

Rain lashed the dimly lighted room, and a man leaped inside, slammed the door shut and stood there panting, staring at her.

"Don't move," he said. "Don't take a damned step!"

"I wouldn't think of it," the girl said.

The man scowled. He stood there, pressed against the door, breathing that way, waiting for something. Nothing happened. Outside in the street, the car hissed past, headlights glaring momentarily, and vanished.

"You make a sound, you'll be sorry," the man said.

The girl said nothing. She had not moved from her position by the sink. The man watched her closely, and his hand slipped along the door to the catch, lifted the bolt into place. He was listening. Rain came down. It drummed on roofs and the tops of garbage cans.

"Would you care to come in and sit down?" the girl said.

"What're you trying?"

"I'm not trying anything. I simply asked if you wouldn't care to come in and sit down."

"Yeah? I'm all wet."

She shrugged. "Anybody would be wet."

He muttered hoarsely. "Don't play with me!"

She turned abruptly and started toward the living room, into the brighter wash of saffron light from a lamp near the chair by the fireplace.

He made a sound in his throat, came across the floor fast, grabbed her, pushed a dripping, rain-soaked face close to hers. His fingers bit into her arms. His pale hair hung limply wet down the sides of his head, and his suit was torn and dirty, wet through.

• • •

His eyes were very bright, and he nodded faintly. He moved his hands down along her arms, clasped her waist. He squeezed her waist, his palms moving to her hips, then, and her lips parted.

There was something careful about his tone now.

"Lonely?"

She did not answer him.

"Sure—don't matter who I am. Don't matter a damn about anything. A babe like you, lonely—just sitting here. Waiting for a guy to come along an' take her to bed."

She still did not speak, nor did she move. It seemed to worry him. He suddenly pulled her hips toward him, and the firm flesh met his body, pressed, her back arched, her breasts coning up toward him.

His scowl held, and even though his arms were around her, his attention seemingly upon only her, it was obvious he was listening more intently than ever. There was no sound now, from outside—other than the steadied and belligerent downpour.

He was a young man. He watched her suspiciously, looking into the dark eyes, then staring at the parted red lips. Her arms hung at her sides.

"Okay," he said wisely. He leaned and tasted of her lips, moving his mouth gently upon hers, then more harshly, and her arms lifted, snaking around his neck, and her body curved to him. His fingers grasped at the full flesh under the pajamas. He yanked his face away.

"Damn! What's your game?"

• • •

He broke free of her, breathing a bit heavily now, watching her, puzzled, suspicious.

"Game?" she said. She smiled a lazy, promise-laden smile. There was something almost sly in her expression. It seemed obvious that she was scheming something.

"I killed a man tonight," he said, his voice rising. "They're after me—the cops are after me." He watched her but there was no reaction. "You heard it over the radio," he snapped. "You know there's a reward for me. You're trying to trap me—that it? Trying to sex me—so you maybe can get me off guard an' make a phone call? Something like that?"

"I've never heard of you."

"I bet," he said. He looked rapidly around the room, spotted the telephone on a stand. He stepped over and violently ripped the wire from the wall. "There," he blurted out.

"Is there anything I can do for you?" she said, very seriously.

"What are you trying to put over?"

"Nothing."

His voice held a wise nastiness. "Then what's a dame like you—with those looks"—he gestured with a flip of his fingers, encompassing her body—"doing cooped up here—acting the way you act?"

"I was just going to bed."

"I don't mean that!" He had shouted in that soft way, harsh, arrogant—with maybe a trace of fear in it now. "I mean the way you're all sexed-up. Ain't it obvious? Listen, dish," he said, stepping close to her again. "It's obvious to me. I can smell it on you, hear that? I speak plain."

• • •

She grinned at him, turned away, moved to the chair by the fireplace and sat down. She crossed her legs. The fine white cloth stretched tightly over round thighs and calves and it seemed as if she did not wear anything under the smooth-fitting pajamas top that hugged her.

The man stared at her body, wet his lips with his tongue. A car turned into the street out back. The man waited, breathing harshly, listening.

"Something I could do for you?" she said again.

"Damn you!" He seemed confused. He leaned toward her. "Somebody live here with you? Maybe they're coming home? That it?"

"I'm all alone. Honestly."

"Because I got a gun," he said. "See it? You think I won't use it on you?" He snatched a gun from his waist, under his shirt, held it out. "I said I killed a man. I killed two men. I shot them in the guts, you hear that?"

"I'm not interested in that. Neither are you."

He placed the gun on a chair across the room, then stepped back to her, smiling gently now, wisely. He reached down and grabbed her, yanked her from the chair, pulled her to him. He unbuttoned the top button on her pajamas top, slipped his hand inside, watching her eyes. Her lips opened.

"Why don't you try to stop me?"

She smiled faintly.

His voice changed, questive. "You a whore, babe? This your stash?"

"No."

He snapped her to arms' length and shook her savagely. "What *are* you then?"

She colored her eyes. "You had it right—when you first said it. I'm lonely. That's all. Just lonely."

"You're a liar!"

"No."

"Don't kid me, bitch—don't try it. You're trying to pull *something*. Here, hell— I'm soaking wet—you like to get wet, too?"

"Yes—maybe I would."

• • •

Her body moved, thrusting at the thin pajamas, and he sucked in his breath.

"Think you can kid me along," he said, and yanked her to him, his hands rough on her body now, exploring without care, deliberate, and vicious. Perspiration showed in a film across his face. The girl moaned softly, pressing against him, and he began to breathe rapidly.

"Ain't you got a boy friend?" His voice was hoarse.

She shook her head, her eyes still closed.

"Why ain't you got a boy friend?"

"Some—sometimes that's the way it is."

He spoke through clenched teeth. "Maybe you expect him along about now?"

"No," she whispered.

"You think I won't give you what you're asking for, baby?" He roughly thrust both hands around her, pressing her to him.

"Oh that feels good," she said. "Yes."

"God," he said, holding her tightly. Her body moved against him and he seemed to be trying to restrain himself. "A gorgeous hunk like you," he said. "With no boy friend. The world gone bats?"

"No," she said, moving. "It's not that—"

His gaze traveled the room anxiously.

"You're lying!" he said again.

• • •

Her pajamas were plastered tightly to her flesh now, wet where she touched him, the plump outlines of her thighs plainly revealed. Abruptly he pushed his mouth against hers and she moaned softly in her throat, her arms coming up around his neck again.

"Damn you!" he said. He started to release her, his expression still suspicious, his voice shaky. He stared at her, his hands on her, and suddenly he pulled her close again, kissing her all over her mouth, then down on the neck, and her ears, and her hair with a hot excitement. She clung to him wildly.

"Love me, Larry," she said. "Please—please love me. Don't stop—just love me, Larry. I don't care *who* you are. *But just don't stop!*"

• • •

She cleaved to him, urgent, open.

He swore softly, lifted her under the knees, picking her easily up, and started carrying her swiftly toward the bedroom.

"Oh, my darling," she whispered. "Don't ever stop—don't ever . . ."

The door beside the fireplace crashed open, slammed back against the wall, the lock splintered. Two cops burst into the room.

"It's him!"

The young man dropped the girl. She landed on her side, came to her knees, sobbing, half fell, then gained her feet, staggering against a table.

"Get him!" a cop yelled.

Two more harnessed, rain-soaked, uniformed men ran into the room. The young man leaped running for the window. The room rocked with explosions, thunderous, as the night was abused with discordant sound. The girl screamed once, then just stood there.

• • •

The young man sprawled against the window, held for a moment, then slowly folded to the floor, his throat and wet-shirted back torn and bloody. He gasped twice and died.

"You all right, Miss Sloan?" one of the cops said. "Lady next door, she said something was going on. Said you never had visitors. We were checking this neighborhood."

"I'm all right. He's dead, isn't he?"

"Yes."

Two other cops, wearing dripping slickers, hunkered over the body of the young man. They whispered:

"Terrible thing. We saved her just in time, I guess."

"Yeah. It would have been awful—her blind, and all."

I'll Be in the Bedroom

Trapped Detective Story Magazine
June 1957

Lunch hour, and *The Coffee Pot* was jammed. My place. The sweet green was rolling in, and the world was a bright place with only one exception—Helen's husband. True, we managed to be together pretty often, but the fat boy was always lurking around the corner, and with Helen, sometimes would never be enough.

"Johnny?" she said, calling me to the end of the counter. I went over to her. The men in the place weren't tending to their beans. How could you blame them, the way she looked? Black hair, big brown eyes, soft red lips, one of *those* bodies under tight green—and a big curl smack in the middle of her forehead that said she was horrid. "Johnny, I only have a minute."

She leaned across the counter, smiling for me. I reached out and flicked that springy curl with my finger, and she brushed my hand with her lips.

"Cut it out," she said. "You know what that does to me! Listen, I just stopped by to tell you something." Only that was as far as she got right then. We both heard the harsh bite of tires on gravel from out front, and turned to look through the plate glass. I heard her breathing stop.

"It's Hurd," she said.

"Christ—you better skin out the back way, fast!"

Her husband was already by the door. It never occurred to either of us that she might have stopped in for coffee, or something. Just that I'd been fooling around with that guy's wife.

She came off the stool fast, and I held the door open through the kitchen.

"What was it you wanted to tell me?"

"Later," she said. "I've got to get out of here. Hurd's no dumbbell."

Her full hip brushed me, and I took her hand. "Where'll I see you?"

She was trembling. "Let you know, Johnny."

I watched the slimly-curved silken calves scissor across the kitchen and out the back door. Archie, my cook, eyed me dourly and shook his head above the steaming grille.

"Connelly? Where the hell you at?"

• • •

I opened the dividing door, and stepped back into the dining area. Hurd Temple, hugely fat, red-faced, pig-eyed, wearing a three-hundred-dollar dust gray gabardine and a flamingo tie, lunged toward me around the counter. Everybody in the place stopped eating.

"Easy," I said. "What can I do for you?"

He shouted it. "You gadamned wife meddler! I'll tell you what you can do! Where is she?"

"Where is who?" I said as quietly as I could.

Somebody down the counter snickered. I didn't bother looking to see who it was. Temple was smoking through the ears, he was that hot. He was a lot of money behind those pig-eyes, and somehow that worried me, too. Maybe that's what held me back from slugging him—that and the fact that I had to keep things quiet, because this man's wife had me nuts, and nobody was going to take that away from me. I wanted her every minute so bad I couldn't think.

He stood in front of me with that big gut of his jouncing up and down under the expensive cloth. It might have been comical; it often was when Helen and I discussed him.

"Connelly," he said, as loud as he could speak. "I want you to get this—and get it straight—"

"Come into the kitchen."

"Kitchen, hell. Don't want your customers to hear what a mucker you are? That it?" He turned and faced the room, one hand on top of the cash register. "Yeah," he said. "Pay you folks to listen. You're patronizing a gigolo's restaurant, a dirty . . ."

I grabbed his arm. "Better shut it off, Temple."

He whirled on me. "Connelly," he said. "I'm telling you, once and for all. Stay away from my wife—don't go near her. You do, I won't sic the cops on you—I'll kill you!"

His face was a twisted red furnace of emotion.

• • •

It was all I could do to stand there. Thing was, he had all the points on his side. He'd made an ass out of himself, but that didn't matter. A couple of my regular noon customers came up to pay their checks, avoiding my eyes. Sally, a red-haired waitress, stepped to the register, and she didn't look at me, either.

"Get out," I said to Temple, fighting to keep a hold on myself. "Before I throw you out."

He stood there a moment, rocking on his fat.

"Just remember what I said, Connelly." He turned and bulled out fast, heavy, each step jarring the room. Some dishes came loose where they were stacked in the sink, rattling, as he slammed the door.

"Take care of things," I told Sally, and gave the dividing door a shove, heading for the kitchen.

"Ain't none of my business," Archie said, not looking at me. "But if I was you, Johnny, I'd sure as hell quit. . . ."

"Keep it that way," I said, and pushed out the back door. My car was parked under the billboard.

"Honey! Johnny, here I am."

It was Helen. She showed her face above the rim of my car door, her eyes alight with that sly wickedness that had me crazy inside; that had dropped me into a maelstrom ever since she and her husband had rented that place out on the beach a little over a month before.

• • •

I went to the car, shoved in behind the wheel, started the engine and gunned out of there. She sat tight up against me, plump round thigh and firm breast pushing against me as her damp lips brushed my jaw. Her skirt was up over round silken knees, the taut green of her dress shimmering.

"Johnny, baby—I've got to get home. He raised hell, didn't he?"

I didn't speak. I drove like crazy through town, and out along the causeway, then drew up off the road under some palms. Every bit of me was tight up, I was that mad. I began to wish I'd sunk one into his fat gut, customers or no. Then I began to cool a little. *The Coffee Pot* was everything I had, and it was making money. Sure, only what was *The Coffee Pot* beside Helen?

"Johnny?"

"Yeah?"

She squirmed closer, her left arm snaking around my neck, her right hand working up under my shirt, hot palmed, and the red lips whispering. I turned and grabbed her, holding her tight. Her soft body wriggled still closer, the shimmering green sliding up across her legs to above sheer, gartered nylons.

"Calm down, Johnny. Never mind that fat crud. He's a lot of hot air—know why?"

I looked down at her smiling lips, the lidded eyes.

"He's going away," she said. "For a whole week!"

Everything vanished. Right away all I could think was what she'd said. We'd been waiting too long for just this. A chance to be together without dodging behind corners. Going away for a week?

"But, listen," I said. "The way he acted in there?"

"You played it just right. He thinks he scared you. He's going home now and pick up his luggage, then I'm driving him to the airport. He's leaving for the coast. For a whole week. You know what that means?"

• • •

I knew, but she tried to show me. We'd never had the time we wanted together. Everything had always been hurried, like right now. A week was a wild dream.

"I'll be back from the airport by two," she said. "You come over at two. I'll be waiting, Johnny. I'll be in the bedroom."

She had me going, right then. I kissed her lips, her throat, and the springy black curl on her forehead. She clung to me, then pulled away.

"No, baby—not now. Wait, honey! Easy—it'll be better for the waiting, I tell you!"

"Okay." I managed to stop somehow. We looked at each other, breathing like a couple of steam engines. "Okay," I said. "I'll drive you home."

"Not home, you nutty lover—my car's parked at a gas station up the road. I took a taxi to your place."

I dropped her off, kissed her goodbye, and watched the luscious way she walked over to her Lincoln collapsible. She dusted me a juicy kiss.

Driving back to the restaurant, I thought about how really lucky I was. She would somehow work a divorce from Hurd Temple, it had to be. Because the way we loved each other was something you don't often get with. We'd have enough money when I opened a couple more eating places, started the chain I planned.

• • •

So by one o'clock I was strung up tight as Elvis' guitar, and I didn't give a damn if *The Coffee Pot* burned to the ground. I figured I'd head out there and wait for her to return from *Tampa International*, maybe warm up the bedroom. Just the same, I took it easy coming down the beach road, and easier still across the dunes till I made sure Hurd the Fat One wasn't outside pruning his rosebushes, wised up to the game. He'd brought Helen to the Florida Golf Coast for a peaceful vacation—she was getting just what she wanted.

The place was quiet; a ritzy layout—money. I walked through the glassed garden, across the sunny patio, and inside. It was cool. A bird sang someplace. The Gulf caressed the beach out there. I headed for the bedroom, feeling good.

It was dark and cool in there, too, only it smelled a little strange—and then I just stood there in the gloom, staring at the mountain of fat on the bed. At the beady eyes, watching me.

"Temple," I said. "I was just—" Then I stopped, and went over there, and I could see the knife still stuck in his side, the six other places where he'd been stabbed. The trickles of blood on the expensive spread. And I heard the racing hiss of tires on sand, too—and the sudden whispered shouts—the quick running pound of feet. Temple was doubled a little on the bed, his hands fisted. I whirled and ran through the house, my heart rocking. She'd done me in—as sure as hell. Fright wormed through me, and I leaped for the rear door.

I leaped straight into a cop's arms.

"Hold it, Jack!"

He rammed a thirty-eight into my chest. For half a second, I thought of trying to take him, but his eyes were a little gone, and he was plenty nervous.

"Cartwright," he called. "Get the men. He's here, all right. We didn't have to wait for him!" Then to me, "Come on—let's look around."

"What for? I'm waiting for somebody."

"Sure. Move."

• • •

We drifted around the house. I kept watching for an opening. We walked into the bedroom, and we stood there looking at Hurd Temple, wearing his leopard-skin swimming trunks, his ballooned gut poked full of holes, and the knife hilt sticking up that way.

"Hey!" another cop ran through the house. "There's a car stuck up the beach a ways. Spinning tires—a convertible."

"Go check," the one with the gun said.

Two plainclothes men came into the bedroom and glanced at Hurd Temple, then at me. One of them went over and flicked the blinds open.

"Well, Connelly," the other said, a lean, long-nosed character with an edged voice. "Couldn't stand it, could you? Had to kill him. What gets into you guys? His wife got away in time, eh? She said you were trying to kill her, too, after you got through with her—only she got away."

• • •

I heard my voice, wild—nearly insane. "You've got to listen to me! It's not like that at all." I told them everything, knowing none of it was any good—knowing I was caught square in the middle. They had even run a check at *The Coffee Pot*, and Sally told them about Hurd coming in this noon.

"It was Mrs. Temple," a cop said, coming in the door, and Helen was with him. "She was trying to get away from him—car stuck down the beach. Poor kid's scared out of her wits."

She watched me with frightened eyes. She was wearing a snug and meagre two-piece white swim suit, and a rubber bathing cap. Her lushly curved body leaned blatantly in the doorway, then she cringed toward the cop.

"Keep him away from me!" she said. "Please, keep him away!" Then she seemed to see the bed for the first time, and covered her face with her hands, shuddering. "Thank God you're here—thank God you caught him."

"It's all right, Mrs. Temple," the one with the long nose said. "Better step into the other room."

"Wait!" I said. "She's lying—will you listen?"

He looked at me, blinked. Helen uncovered her face.

Her voice was beautiful acting. "He would've killed me, too. I was out swimming when my husband cried for me, and that's when I noticed Mr. Connelly's car. I came up to the house, and saw him stabbing Hurd—through the window. It was awful." She paused, then said, "I took the chance and used the kitchen phone. He didn't hear me. He never realized I was around till just before you policemen came. He would have killed me, too—I was stuck in the sand. I didn't dare use the driveway to get to the road."

The long-nosed cop spoke softly. "You're a little to blame, Mrs. Temple. You *were* running around with him."

"No!" she said. "He kept after me. Today I went to his restaurant, trying to reason with him again—it didn't do any good. My husband went there, too—you know about that."

"Well, Connelly?" the cop said. "We may as well head for headquarters." He shook his head. "It's pretty pat, isn't it?"

• • •

I'd told them everything I could. They wouldn't listen. I was in the bag, and this was it for good. And I could read it in her eyes, too—the mockery, for only me to see. And I could picture the words in her mind, "Too bad, Johnny, you fool. Hurd had money—you haven't got anything. You're just a sucker for a hot dame, don't you think I realized that? I picked you carefully." Because that's what she would be thinking. I knew that now. I knew a lot of things, and I made a leap for her. I wanted to get my hands on her, just once—in a new way.

"Hold it!"

But I was free, and I reached her. She twisted in my arms, fighting, and her cap rubbed off against my shoulder. I knew right off there was something wrong, but I couldn't tell what. Then I knew, and let her go as they jumped me.

"Wait," I said. "One thing—just one thing. Let me look at the body—at Temple!"

They finally allowed me to step over by the bed.

"Please," she kept saying. "Get him out of here!"

I spotted what I was looking for, clenched in Herd Temple's stiffening left fist. I freed the fingers, and held it up to them—a brush of black.

Helen's eyes went wild.

"This hair is hers," I said. "He tore it from her scalp, probably as he died—she couldn't find it in her hurry. It belongs in the middle of her forehead."

She whirled running. One of the cops grabbed her arm. She fought like a cat, claws out, spitting. A different Helen now. She knew it was all up with her. The naked white scalp showed across the front of her hairline, where Hurd Temple had ripped loose that spit curl—and a good deal more besides.

"Don't listen to him!" she yelled, fighting.

"I came a bit too early, Helen," I said. "Right? I nearly caught you in the act. So that's when you phoned the cops and staged your getaway."

It was quiet in the room. There was no further need for talk. I dropped Helen's spit-curl on the floor and got out of there.

The Price of Pride

Triple Western
Summer 1957

Ed Tunstall stood in the afternoon shadows of the aspen beside his cabin and stared at his son, Rick. The look in the twelve-year-old boy's eyes told him he didn't measure up. Somehow, as a father, he had failed. It was such a damned little thing, only right now it loomed mountainous—maybe because of something else that rode inside him; something he had carried too long. He knew Martha was listening behind the woodshed door. He knew she would be understanding, but thought it would be better if she cursed him.

"Tom Greenbaugh's got a buckskin he'll let me have for sixty dollars," Rick said. "Darn, Pa—I like buckskins best of all. He's not busted, but I could do it. I'd want to bust him, bein' that he'd be my horse."

Ed recognized hope in Rick's face. He looked at the dark, unruly hair, the shoulders already broadening against the seams of his blue homespun shirt. That face might have been his, twenty years ago. But the blue eyes were Martha's, patient, wistful.

"A man *should* have a horse," Ed said. He fumbled around for the right thing to say, but nothing came. Rangy, raw-boned, he hunched his shoulders. He felt old and wished he were drunk. Last year it had been a Sharp's rifle. This year it was a horse. He couldn't even keep his own horse and cow fed right, let alone think of buying another.

Only there was more to it than that.

"Yes, Pa?"

"You can use mine any time you want," Ed said. "Take him right now."

Rick's eyes held steady. "Sure, Pa, but I didn't mean like that."

Ed watched Rick go to the well and drink deeply of the icy water from the tin cup that hung on the nail he'd whacked into a stump four years ago. There had been no new nails. He heard Martha sigh and the door creaked shut as she left the woodshed, and went into the cabin.

Rick stood by the well, swiping water from his chin with a stretched sleeve. "School begins next week, Pa," he said. "Most of the fellows livin' out of Clayhorn will ride."

"You can ride my horse, Rick."

His son nodded, turned slowly, and walked off across the road, toward the barn. Ed frowned. "Rick? Wait up."

Rick didn't seem to hear. Ed stood there another moment, then turned and walked through the woodshed into the kitchen of his home.

Clayhorn was going to appoint a new sheriff. Old Tim Matthews had bought a small spread and sworn he intended to resign. Ed knew he was well liked in Clayhorn, even if he was poor, taking odd jobs tending bar at the Tumbleweed on Saturday nights, and part-time work at the blacksmith's shop. If he could get the Citizens' Committee behind him, with Matthews putting in a word, he might get that star—only he'd never had a chance to show his colors with his guns.

Something sick and all too familiar touched him and went away. A sheriff's gun counted big in town, what with Clayhorn being a stop for Texas men on their way to Kansas with cattle. Trail drives meant gambling, sharpers, hell-hot times, camp-followers of all kinds.

• • •

He watched Martha over by the stove, thinking, if they ever find out about four years ago—if they ever get to know why I come to Clayhorn from Abilene—I'll never even snatch a job shoveling manure in the livery barn.

Thinking like that brought the scarlet picture of a white-hot noon once more back to mind. The vicious roar of guns, his brother Will screaming with three lead slugs ripped into his stomach—yelling, "Get him, Ed! Get that dirty son!"

Only he hadn't gotten him. He hadn't even tried. And he would never forget it, either.

He had ducked plenty fast into his brother's barn, pressed his eyes to a crack and watched the lithe killer with the gold-flecked eyes ride off laughing. The man had also stolen Ed's horse. He didn't do anything about that, either.

He'd been afraid. How many times had he told himself that he hadn't been afraid for himself? He had feared for Rick, and Martha. Who would take care of them if he were killed?

Nobody believed that in Abilene. For a long time now he hadn't believed it himself. In the long nights he sometimes whispered in the dark if only I had the chance to do it over again. And saying that, he would lie there and wonder if it would be the same. . . .

They had left Abilene the next morning, after burying Will, everything they owned piled on a single battered wagon. Rick didn't know why they left, but Martha did. And sometimes, lately, she looked at him queerly.

He cleared his throat now. "I've got to get Rick a horse," he said. "If I don't, I stand to lose my son."

Martha smiled. "I understand, Ed." Her fading yellow hair clung to her shoulders, and in her pale blue eyes Ed saw the same expression he'd seen in Rick's.

He turned his back. Beyond the kitchen windows, mountains loomed, the grandfathers of the earth.

"You mustn't feel bad, Ed. He knows we can't afford to buy a horse, special. When we can, he'll have one. He knows that."

He turned and looked at her.

She hesitated, smoothed the pale blue gingham dress over her hip. "I wish you'd ride into Clayhorn. We're all out of salt."

He knew she wasn't through. "Where's the money?"

She moved up to him, touched his arm. "Ed, why don't you speak to Matthews again? I mean—we can't live out here the way we are like—like jackrabbits, forever. It's not right for Rick."

Ed bit off what he started to say. The most he had ever saved in these four years of scrounging was twelve dollars. It was in his war-bag, in the fireplace closet. He went and got the twelve dollars. A man needed a good drink at a time like this.

He buckled on his gunbelt in the kitchen, jammed his black-butted .44 into the holster with a savage thrust of his palm. He sensed Martha watching him quietly.

"Go ahead," he said. "Say it. What'll I do with it, now I got one on?" His boots scraped as he strode toward the door, hat in hand.

"Ed?"

He paused, turned.

"You forgot the salt money. It's on the shelf as you go out."

• • •

He rode down Clayhorn's dusty main street between grey-weathered buildings. The hot sun of late afternoon slanted into his eyes.

He hitched up in front of Furlow's general store. He would get the salt first, then have a look around and maybe talk with Matthews. Talk wouldn't hurt, though he doubted it would do any good. He could show Matthews, or anybody else, how to knock tin cans off a stump with his gun. But Clayhorn wanted a sheriff of proved courage, good nerve, and the necessary ability to think some first, shoot first, then mull it over and find out he had thought right to begin with. They wanted a sheriff with a trail behind him of honor and pride; a clear trail. He had a trail, all right, but it was as dim and as much without honor or pride as the worst owlhoot.

Rick stood at the end of that trail, calling him a failure as a father, who had brawn and brains enough to raise his own bacon, but who didn't actually earn anything but October beans.

Inside Jake Furlow's store, he blinked against the shadows.

"Ed Tunstall!"

Tom Greenbaugh, the last man on earth he wanted to see, turned away from the counter, holding a sack of coffee.

"Hello, Tom. Just talked with Rick about you."

Greenbaugh nodded, smiled good-naturedly with his beefy red face and hitched at sagging jeans below a barrel chest. "Yeah. That buckskin. Your kid sure wanted that horse."

Hope rose in him for an instant. Maybe it was Tom's cheerful face. "Could we work some kind of deal, Tom? Rick's dead set on a horse, and it looks like the buckskin's it."

Greenbaugh shook his head. "You couldn't buy him, trade for him, or steal him—he ain't to be had."

Jake Furlow moved up behind the counter and smiled a quick greeting, his spectacles glinting.

Ed said to Greenbaugh, "Thought maybe I could work something out."

"Two hours ago, you might have. I don't own the horse no more, Ed. Sold him, in a way." Greenbaugh's gaze left Ed, rested on a sack of spuds.

Ed slacked against the counter. "Where's the horse now?"

"Yonder." Greenbaugh pointed across the street.

• • •

Ed turned. Hitched to the rail in front of the Tumbleweed Saloon, stood the buckskin, its glistening black mane and tail stark in the failing afternoon. Even in the distance, Ed saw it was a fine horse. Silver studs gleamed on an expensive saddle.

"Why'd you go and sell him, Tom?" He scowled, wondering at Greenbaugh's averted eyes. "How much did you get?"

Greenbaugh abruptly looked squarely at him. "You may as well know. It'll come out, anyways." He fished in his pocket, flipped a silver dollar, let it slap into his palm. "Just that."

"Tom! For hell's sake—my kid—"

Greenbaugh waved a thick hand. "You don't know who bought 'im, Ed. I'm not young no more, an' besides, one horse don't seem to mean so much under the circumstances. I wish it'd been you."

Jake Furlow spoke for the first time, his voice thin.

"It was Nick Blazer who bought Tom's horse, Ed. Must of heard of him. He's an outlaw, done time in the pen. He was born in Clayhorn. Said he was passin' through on his way to Mexico and took a likin' to Tom's buckskin. Said he figgered Clayhorn owed him somethin' for bringing him into the world. He gave Tom a dollar to make it proper."

"Blazer's got a price on his head," Greenbaugh said quietly. "He'd kill at a batted eye, bad clean through. He's wanted from here to hell an' gone for everything from horse stealing to woman snatching. Ain't a soul in town that will cross his path."

Ed had heard of Blazer, but he'd never seen the man. The outlaw's savage exploits were almost legendary, or as legendary as a man could get in a country of untampered blood.

"What about Sheriff Matthews? Why don't he bust down on him? Somebody's got to—some time."

Greenbaugh turned away, started out of the store. "Ask Matthews," he said. "Sorry about your kid, Ed."

Ed stared across the stretch of sun-blasted street toward the slatted bat-wing doors of the Tumbleweed Saloon.

Jake Furlow scratched a whiskered chin. "Was there somethin' you was needin', Ed?"

"It'll wait."

Ed walked on out of the store and turned down the plank walk toward the sheriff's office. His heart rocked in rhythm with the determined pound of his boots.

• • •

Tim Matthews looked as tired as Ed felt. The sheriff of Clayhorn yanked his feet off the old roll-top desk, slammed them to the floor. He ruffled his white mane of hair and squinted up at Ed.

"Tim," Ed said. "There's a ranny named Nick Blazer in town."

Matthews bit down once on the chew of tobacco in his cheek, squeezed a spurt of amber between thin lips straight in to a brass gaboon on the floor.

"So," he said. "You're here to ask me why don't I go ask him to come along quiet-like, while I collect reward money and maybe get written up in the *Gazette?*"

"Something like that," Ed said.

Matthews' eyes lost their humor. "Yes," he said softly. "Reckon I'd of felt the same, once." He looked up again. "But not no more. I bought me a ranch. I'm a rancher, and I aim—"

"You're still sheriff," Ed said, sorry at once that he'd spoken. He saw the tiny flash of embarrassment in old Tim's eyes. Matthews had been a hard-shooting man in his day. He wasn't too old to live, but he reckoned he was too old not to care about *wanting* to live. "Sorry, Tim," Ed said.

"That's all right. But I still ain't going to do it. Blazer's drinking quiet, minding his own. I'm alive, and I've got a good record. I want to think about that record while I wrastle yearlings."

"Your wrastlin' days are over, Tim—you know that." He stood there another moment, wishing deep breaths alone could do something about the hollow feeling inside him. "I want you to deputize me. Give me a star, for one hour."

Matthews just sat there looking at him for a time. When he spoke, it was with a serious drawl, the words pointed.

"Ed, what's troubling you? You been in Clayhorn four years, by my count, livin' not much better than a buzzard. Now you're asking me to let you get yourself gunned in the face. Are you loco?"

"Maybe. I hope not."

Matthews lashed a string of amber at the gaboon, spoke a whispered epithet. "In that case, Ed Tunstall, you're an officer of the law." His face still sober, he added, "I'll have Jake fix a couple packin' cases together right away."

"What for?"

"Your coffin, Ed." Matthews clawed around in the desk, flipped a piece of tin into the air and Ed caught it. "Pin it on," the sheriff said. "I done my share."

Ed forced a grin.

"Ain't fooling," Matthews said. "Blazer's a dead shot an' quick as a split-tailed flea. He's said he'll never be taken alive. He don't hanker to being caged."

"Go see Jake about that box," Ed said. "Get it off your mind. But, listen, he's head of the Citizens' Committee. You might put in a word for me about taking over your job."

"So that's it."

"Wish me luck?"

"Take my curse," Matthews said.

• • •

Ed walked slowly in a diagonal line from the sheriff's office, toward the Tumbleweed Saloon. He wanted a smoke, but he didn't take one. He wanted to run the other way, but he didn't do that, either. He felt a little like more of a fool than he had been feeling for four years. He felt four years was long enough, one way or the other. He wanted to feel clean again. It had been a long time—so long he wondered maybe it was too late to feel any other way. His hand touched the butt of his gun, snapped away as if it were hot. That didn't help.

You're scared, he thought. You went and hid in a barn. What the hell are you doing, crossing the street, carrying a gun as if you meant it? There ain't no barn to hide behind.

He glanced at the big buckskin horse standing by the hitch rail. Blazer must have broken him some already. He swallowed something that got in his throat, and paused just outside the Tumbleweed's doors to loosen his gun in the holster.

He was surprised to find himself doing it without thinking about it beforehand. It was jammed so tight he had to hold the holster down with his left hand in order to draw the gun free.

And he remembered Martha's face as he'd rammed the gun in there. Maybe he was loco, like Matthews had said. He thought of the packing cases in Jake Furlow's store, and he thought of Rick, standing by the well with the tin cup in his hand, looking at him that way.

"Most of the fellows livin' out of Clayhorn will ride."

Well, he was afraid. Who was he afraid for now? If he didn't go back home, Rick and Martha would make out all right. Nobody was going to shoot them down. The town liked them.

A rough shoulder pushed against him. Ed turned to recognize one of the townsmen. "Well, Tunstall? You goin' inside or you goin' to stand here an' block the door?"

Ed looked into the smoky, bloodshot eyes of the man, and knew him as a bar lounger. He saw the amused expression, and the sudden blunt disdain on the other's face as the man glimpsed the star hanging on his shirt pocket.

"Well, I'll be damned," the man said.

Ed said nothing. The man turned and walked hurriedly off down the plank walk, his boots stumping in the sunny silence of the afternoon.

He pushed open the bat-wings, stepped inside the saloon and headed for the bar. One man stood at the bar, his back turned to Ed. The man was dressed in freshly washed and ironed range-clothes, and twin ivory-butted guns were lashed low with yellow-new thong on narrow hips. He heard Ed enter, wheeled slowly around, and leaned against the bar, elbows braced.

"Hello, stranger," the man said. "I been listening."

Ed stopped walking. He watched the slim man thrust his hat back on his head, and he saw the lean and unchanged face, the bold gold-flecked eyes.

He had seen those eyes once before. The sickness of four years flushed through him, right then, and he couldn't have run if he'd tried. There was only memory, like black armor—only a man can't hide behind a memory.

"Sorry," Blazer said. "I kind of got the jump on you. Been waiting. It's better than whisky. Fellow name of Greenbaugh spilled it that a man called Tunstall wanted to buy the horse I bought." Blazer reached up and rubbed fingertips across his forehead. "Put me to mind of another Tunstall up in Abilene a while back. I knew him for a few minutes one August afternoon." He paused, watching Ed, but Ed did not speak. "Then, darned if I didn't see you heading from across the street with your law-badge shinin', an' the barkeep told me who you are." Nick Blazer did not move and his gaze was level and steady.

The silence was like water in a glass.

"Barkeep went away," Blazer said. "Told him he should hang around—but he just went away."

"You killed my brother," Ed said.

• • •

It was crazy, how words came out. Wrong words. He hadn't meant to say that. He'd wanted to say something hard and cutting, only the sickness was inside him now, inside him to stay—so bad that maybe he couldn't even go home if he was able to walk.

"Your brother wasn't yellow, was he, Tunstall? He stood right there with a damn fool pitchfork—trying to shoot me with a pitchfork." Blazer moved his head from side to side. "You could have killed me, Tunstall. I'd just escaped jail. Only had those three bullets in my gun, and I used them on your brother."

Ed knew where the barkeep was. Right now, Clayhorn probably knew everything about him. Rick and Martha would have to travel far and fast to escape the brand he'd leave on them.

"You owe me a horse," he said, the words coming that crazy way again.

"Huh," Blazer said. "Back to Abilene, after you skidaddled, they allowed as how maybe you weren't really scared, Tunstall. Some said you didn't try for me 'cause of your wife an' kid." Blazer lowered his voice. "You an' me, we know different, don't we?"

"Do we?"

Blazer closed his eyes, then opened them. "I killed your brother, and I stole your horse. I always knew we'd cross someday, Tunstall. I wanted it that way. Never liked a fyce. Back home in Louisiana, we had a fyce-hound. Did you ever watch one run with his tail wrapped up under?" Blazer paused, his elbows never leaving the bar. "What are you going to do, tinstar?"

He heard his own strange voice, speaking not because of what Blazer had said, but only because there is a time when all men must speak.

"I said you owed me a horse."

"That what you call it, Tunstall?"

"You see that barrel of whisky, last one at the end of the bar? The spout's dripping."

Blazer nodded.

"Draw when the next drop hits the canister."

Blazer's elbows did not move.

Ed waited, remembering, watching the other man's eyes, and suddenly the blur of Blazer's hands and guns a split second after the tinkle of the whisky dropping into the canister confounded him. All he knew was that his own gun was in his hand, bucking, and Nick Blazer's guns were firing wild.

The hammer on Ed's gun clicked against an empty shell.

Blazer grinned, standing against the bar, his gun hands slowly drooping until they dangled at his sides. Ed watched as the guns clattered to the sawdust-covered floor. Blazer twisted and knelt down, then stretched out on his back. There were five holes in the front of his freshly washed shirt.

Ed stabbed his gun at the holster three times before it stuck where it belonged. He felt a hand on his shoulder. It was Sheriff Tim Matthews.

"I told Jake Furlow about the packin' cases, Ed." Matthews saw a thread of amber flowing across Blazer's dead body into the bar trough. "Reckon we can still use 'em, hey?"

Ed wanted to grin. He saw Tom Greenbaugh and several other men crowding into the saloon.

"We was watching," Greenbaugh said. "Let's have a drink."

Men crowded toward the bar. Ed heard quiet words that were very pleasant to his ears, but he turned to Greenbaugh.

"Tom," he said. "About that buckskin . . ."

• • •

It was just sunset when he entered the kitchen. Martha and Rick were seated at the supper table. Rick stared silently at his plate. Martha looked up, her eyes worried.

"You've been gone a long while," she said. "Supper's on."

Ed jammed one hand into the pocket of his jeans. "Rick," he said. "Would you step over to the barn with me a minute? I'd like a word with you."

Martha searched his eyes. He knew she wondered if he had been drinking.

Rick stood up. "What about, Pa?"

"Just come on."

They walked across the road toward the barn. Ed wondered how long it would take before Rick opened his eyes, looked toward the corral. He heard Martha following them.

The boy paused, his eyes bewildered.

In the corral a large buckskin peered over the fence, pricked his ears, and whinnied. His black mane flared in the fresh evening breeze.

"He's your horse, son. Go take him."

The boy started running, stopped, started off again, then skidded to a halt. His eyes were round and bright. Over the corral fence, hand-tooled, and brand-new, was slung a fine silver-studded saddle.

"Durn, Pa!" Rick said. "Gosh durn!"

The boy ran on ahead. Martha came up and Ed gruffly explained as best he could. Then, avoiding her eyes, he rolled a cigarette, lit it, and drew smoke deep into his lungs.

"You used your gun, didn't you?" Martha said.

"Yes." He fished in his pocket, brought out the thing that had burned a hole in his palm ever since he'd left Clayhorn for home. "Tim Matthews gave me his star," he said, and the words were coming as crazy as ever. "It isn't fixed proper yet, but it looks like I'm sheriff now."

Rick ran up to them from the corral. He stood there, obviously unable to speak.

"Don't say anything," Ed told him with a grin.

"Well, I'll say something," Martha said. "There's no salt on the potatoes, Ed Tunstall. And that's what you went to town for."

Ed looked at her. "Almost forgot," he said. He reached into his hip pocket, handed her the bag of salt. "A man can't think of everything at once."

That Damned Piper

Pursued
June 1957

That's what Mr. Jeffries always said. It would get under your skin—nothing against Mr. Jeffries, understand. Only you'd think it would be his turn sometime. But it never was anybody's turn but mine. None of the other guys had my kind of luck. Even Pranti, with the big nose, you know? We called him "Nose," and he wasn't too bright. Mr. Jeffries would say to Pranti: "How much change you got up there, right now?"

"What?" Pranti would say. "Where?"

"That's where you keep your nickels, don't you?" Mr. Jeffries would say. "Up your nose, Nose?"

Old Nose Pranti. He would stand there with his mouth hanging, feeling his beak. You could tell he was wondering maybe there was a couple stray coins up there.

But what Mr. Jeffries always said to me. *"You'll always have to pay the piper, Chuck. No matter which way the ball bounces. Life is like that."*

Then he would laugh.

That damned Piper. How I'd like to get my hands on him just once. Only you can't, because he's not real, see? I mean, he is real—but he's what you call nebulous, or something—like a ghost. He can turn up anyplace, and it's no joke. The thing is, you always got to pay him. Mr. Jeffries told me that the first time, and hundreds of times since, and Mr. Jeffries was right.

"Then why you always laughing about it?" I asked him. "What's so funny?"

"You have to treat it with humor, Chuck."

That damned Piper. What I mean is, O. K., so you got to pay him. But I always got to pay him on time, see? He never waits for me, like Mr. Jeffries, and the other guys. And he cleans you out. Oh, all right, so Fingers John fell in Jersey City on that Insurance safe job. And Scars Lyttle got himself smithereened when he tried to plant that bomb in never-mind-who's car, that time last Christmas. But that's the big go, understand . . . what I'm talking about is the ready gelt. I mean, you got to live—a little wine, a little spaghetti, maybe even mignon, necessary dames—how you going to live if you're all the time paying that damned Piper?

Can you answer me that?

Listen, if I grab six bits off a stack of newspapers when Blind Brownie isn't listening, you know what happens? I probably trip and lose it down a grating. Or say maybe I do something for Mr. Jeffries and he flips me a C note. So I go and find some dame and maybe we kill a pint in her pad, then head out for a ball. I come to maybe in an alley with nothing but my underwear—or worse yet, the tank. I been rolled, and the snatch went South, and Mr. Jeffries is mad, and maybe I got to grub, grub, grub for two weeks, or spread hot tar on the county highways along with the rest of them, some fat screw yawning under a tree babying his shotgun. I don't blame the dame, understand . . . it's *that damned Piper!*

Mr. Jeffries always gets peeved when it happens. I tell him he should know, he put it into my head. Finally he says it's all right, only you can see it peeves him.

Only he won't pry you out of a corner. I mean, he will and he won't. He won't get a lawyer to spring you, or stand bail, if you get slapped in the tank, anything like that. Only if it's a bum rap, like something bigger—then he'll send over the Pig. The Pig's Mr. Jefferies' mouthpiece.

I'm telling you this so you'll understand. I mean, just this one time, like it was when Tuesday Mr. Jefferies said: "Chuck, you're ready. I know I can depend on you. It's time you began to grow and I earnestly believe you have grasped the ropes to an extent where I can expect something better. You want to move to a better apartment, and buy some good clothes, maybe even find a worthy girl for yourself—one that won't always go South when things get rough." So then we all got together there and Mr. Jefferies explained it. "And here's the road map, Chuck, and the keys to the car. All you have to do is drive down Sixteenth until you reach the ice house, and park. Be there at ten on the nose. Willy will come by and toss you the suitcase. Then you follow the road map, Chuck, and bring the suitcase to me. We'll all be up at Spider Lake, I got a new place up there. We'll have a real ball. Plenty of girls, the works, Chuck—everything. Only one thing to remember, Chuck—one big point—when you hit Oakville be careful, drive like you're traveling over eggs, because the sheriff in that town's hot as they come. And you've got to go through Oakville to reach Spider Lake—where we'll all be waiting. Check?"

"Check, Mr. Jefferies. Absolutely."

So, you see, Friday night I nailed the suitcase when Willy tossed it. I followed the road map. And at noon Saturday I breezed into Oakville, driving the Buick like there was eggs all over the road, thinking about the lake and all, and this burnt-face cop stops me on his bike and says: "Where's your license?"

"What did I do?"

He took my license and nodded, and said: "Can't you read the speed-limit signs? Or is it you just don't want to?"

"Hey, take it easy. I was only doing fifteen miles per hour, officer, sir."

"You admit it, then."

"Admit? Who's admitting?"

"There's a sign on that elm tree over there. Read it off to me, Mister."

So I did. "Kindly reduce speed. Maximum speed 40 miles, minimum speed 35. Through highway. Keep moving."

"Follow me," the cop said.

So I followed him to this red brick building across from the park and you could smell jail the second you laid eyes on it.

"Come on," the cop said.

Well, I had the suitcase jammed in under the front seat where Mr. Jefferies had the fans taken out for just such an emergency. But I was sweating, let me tell you, because at the split over to Spider Lake I was supposed to get 5 G's. Count 'em! I don't know what Mr. Jefferies would get, but I didn't care.

"You want to be drug?" the cop said.

I got out and we went in.

It was empty in there. A single-story building, red brick, bars on all the windows, and three private cells and a bull-pen. Across from the cells was one of these old roll-top desks and a swivel chair. It was pretty hot, and a fan was going on top of the desk, ruffling some papers.

"Look," I said. "I got to make a phone call. I'm entitled to a phone call." Because you could tell how he was acting, he was in a groove—one thing at a time.

He went to the desk and picked up a fistful of keys and went over and unlocked the cell by the bull-pen and opened the door.

"Inside."

We watched each other for a minute, and I went into the cell. He slammed the door and locked it, then tossed the keys back on the desk.

"Wait," I said. "Listen, here. You don't even—hey, wait! I'm not—I wasn't—"

He was gone. Then I stood there sweating, listening for him to open the car door out there by the curb. Then the motorcycle started up, roaring, and he gunned her off down the street.

It was a small cell. There was an iron cot, a john without any seat, one barred window, a wash basin, and a galvanized pail. I went over to the window and hung my chin on chipped cement, looking toward Spider Lake.

Mr. Jefferies would be peeved.

I laid my forehead on the chipped cement.

Nothing happened for over a half hour. I just stood there, then finally I went over and sat on the cot, thinking about the suitcase and Mr. Jefferies waiting at Spider Lake.

On the roll-top desk was one of these desk-signs, with gold letters behind glass, you know? *Sheriff B. Snow.* The fan hummed. The papers ruffled. Outside a bird sang, and a car rolled along the street.

That damned Piper. Only it was too early to start paying. . . .

I jumped up and went to the window and grabbed the bars, trying to yank them out. For a minute there, I was pure nuts. I raged around the cell, then sat down on the cot again.

Like the street was eggs. . . .

I didn't hear anybody come in, but when I looked up, she was standing there. I mean. She could've stepped right up on the bar in a strip-joint and gone into her act, right then and there.

"Who are you?" I said. "Listen, will you go?—"

"I'm Sheriff Snow," she said.

I stood up and went to the bars and she smiled at me, then waltzed over to the desk. She had on this tight tan skirt, and a white blouse, nylons, and low white cowboy boots. She wore a white Stetson on top of long ash-blonde hair, and her hips ground it out, man. Around her hips she wore a big fat leather gunbelt, and a holstered pearl-handled .45 bounced on her right thigh. She had a waist you could wrap your hands around so the fingers would meet. This gunbelt was tight, biting into her hips, see?—so they bunched out every time she moved.

And nothing under that skirt to say so.

She turned and grinned at me again. Big bright blue eyes, and red lips, and she didn't jiggle, understand? She jounced—just once or twice every time she moved. Her tin star was pinned on the left one.

"Sheriff?" I said. "You're a sheriff?"

She didn't say anything. She sat down in the swivel-chair and crossed her legs, not giving a damn. She took her hat off and tossed it on her desk, then pushed at her hair, watching me.

"No kidding?" I said.

She didn't speak.

I told her about being picked up for not-speeding. "I've got an appointment. Can't you just tell me what the fine is—I'll pay it, be on my way. No use me hanging around here."

She just watched me, still grinning, only not quite so much. Like the grin was wearing out because something else was behind it. I don't know.

"Don't you see?" I said.

She just watched me.

"Don't you?" I said.

We stared at each other. She scratched her leg with long red nails, slid down in the chair and crossed her legs the other way.

"I've gotta get out of here!" I yelled. "God damn it. What are you trying to do? What the hell kind of a town is this?"

"Take it easy, Honey-bun," she said.

"What?"

"Honey-bun. Easy does it."

"What the hell, you making talk like that?"

"I make all kinds of talk."

"Let me out of here."

"Easy, now—steady."

"Listen, if you're Sheriff Snow, you know damned well you can't hold me like this."

"I can hold you any way I like."

"I got a right to use the phone."

"Not if I don't say so."

"I want a lawyer."

"Honey-bun, relax."

"Get off that stuff."

"Don't you like it here?"

"I got to be someplace. Right away. I'm late."

"You're here, now. You've got things to do."

"What?"

"Things to do. Things I want you to do."

"Listen, Sheriff—"

"That's better, Honey-bun."

"Sheriff, I can't hang around here. I didn't do anything, for chrissakes. I've got to get going. Don't you understand? I'll pay your fine. Sheriff, ma'am."

"Miss."

"I've got to get going. It's business."

"What kind?"

"Private. Personal business."

She uncrossed her legs, as careless as ever, and stood up and walked over to my cell. She stood about two feet away. We watched each other. I moved back into the cell a little. She moved up to the bars and pushed against them, watching me.

"Miss Sheriff," I said. "Honest and truly, I've really got to get going. I'm willing to pay my fine."

"Don't worry."

"Huh?"

"You'll pay your fine. But Honey-bun, you simply must relax. The more you carry on, like you are, the longer it'll be."

She was nuts. The whole thing was screwy. I didn't understand it. I knew there was no use trying to understand it.

"Just stay like that a while, Honey-bun."

"Quit calling me that."

She grinned and pushed against the bars, bulging through the bars. I don't want to give the impression she was fat, anything like that. She wasn't. She was perfect, but she had so much of everything that when she shoved against the bars things had to find a way, see?

"All right," I said. "I'm calm, I'm relaxed. Now, you tell me how much the fine will be, I'll pay it. I got enough to cover it, I think."

"Let's hope so."

The way she said that made me look at her closer. All I saw was the usual, and nothing you'd miss the first time. It all hit you in the eyes *wham*.

"It's crazy," I said. "Getting picked up for driving too slow."

"Feel better, now?"

"Yeah, I'm all right."

"Want to come out now?"

"Sure."

She went over to the desk and picked up the bunch of keys, and came back, her face real quiet, and worked the key in the lock.

"Open the door, Honey-bun—and come out here."

I did that. I got out my wallet. I had thirty-three dollars. It shouldn't be that much of a fine.

She laid one hand on the wallet and pushed it toward me. "Not that way," she said. "Put the money away."

"What?"

"Hurry up."

"I've got to get out of here!"

She waited and I put the money away. I had ditched my rod under the seat along with the suitcase, just if anything happened, like this.

"Now, come along, Honey-bun."

I put the wallet away, sweating to beat the band, now—because Mr. Jefferies would be ready to flip. The only thing I could do was go along with her, and see what happened.

"You're just kidding, aren't you?" I said. "The whole thing's just kidding, ain't it? I mean, I heard of things like this. What you having, some kind of convention, or something?"

"I'm not kidding. Follow me."

I followed her outside into the sunlight. We stood on the sidewalk by the Buick and she looked at me. She hadn't brought her hat along and the sun shone in her hair, and she was a beauty. A positive beauty.

"You drive," she said. "Let's get going."

"You mean—my car? Drive?"

She opened the door on the driver's side, motioned me in. I slid under the wheel. She went around and got in beside me and slammed her door.

"Go ahead," she said. "Start driving. I'll tell you where to turn."

I sat there. Then I looked at her. "Shouldn't there be some kind of explanation, Sheriff? I mean, what the hell—fun's fun."

"You're exactly right." She slid that pearl-handled .45 out of its holster and prodded me in the ribs with it. "Now, let's go."

We drove on out of town, and along a wooded road, and she finally had me turn in and park beside a cabin just above a small lake.

"Is that Spider Lake?" I said.

She shook her head. "No, Honey-bun. Spider Lake's the other side of town." She shoved the gun into my ribs again. "Get out, now."

"Sheriff, I'll gladly pay your fine."

"I know it. I always exact a certain toll, you see?"

"What?"

"Out."

We got out and went inside the cabin. If Mr. Jefferies could only see me now, I thought. And I was beginning to get real worried, because she looked terrific and all, only she had to be nuts. She had to be.

Mr. Jefferies would kill me if I didn't get to him inside the hour. I mean, literally, kill me. I began to know that for true, you see? It was a lousy feeling—real bad. I'd seen him do it. They gunned Slim Dagget with .22 rifles, set him up, and used him for target practice. He lasted over two hours, the way they did it. Mr. Jefferies wasn't a man for excuses when so much dough was tied up in it.

"What'd you mean—'exact a toll'?" I asked her.

"Let's go inside. You'll find out."

We went up on the porch and into the cabin. It was cozy in there, heavy furniture, built for comfort. There was this great big studio couch covered with a leopard-skin rug and some red pillows. The couch was the important thing in the big room.

I turned and looked at her.

She was grinning, closing the door.

"Seems to me this is a funny way for a sheriff to be acting," I said.

"Another election coming up," she said. "I won't even be here to run, though. Besides," she said, jamming the .45 back into the holster, watching me. "It was just a crazy fool thing I got elected in the first place. I'll tell you about it sometime."

"You will?"

"You bet."

"Then what you want with me?"

"I want you to pay your fine, Honey-bun."

She stepped up to me and shoved her hips forward and slid her arms around my neck. "Haven't you a sneaking suspicion what that fine might be? Don't you think you might like it?"

"Hell—well, I—"

"That's the idea. That's better."

It was like kissing a bonfire, not that you'd ever try that. I mean, after all!

She said, "Oh," and stepped back a little, looking at me. Then she began to strip, like I told you; it would have been a slick act in a joint to slow jazz.

"It's just it's better this way, somehow," she said. "Being I'm sheriff, I have to be pretty careful in town, you know?" She plopped the gun and gunbelt on a chair, unzipped the skirt, slacked her hips and the skirt puddled around her feet on the floor. "So I exact my toll," she said. "I'm not married, you see?"

"You probably should get married," I told her.

"Someday I will. Come on, you, too."

"Me what too?"

"Undress, silly."

Pretty soon, then, she came up to me like that, breathing kind of hard and her eyes glazed a little. "Sometimes I wear the gunbelt when I'm undressed," she said. "I'll show you afterwards."

"I'll bet it's a picture," I said.

"Honey-bun."

. . .

"You want a receipt?"

"What?"

"I asked if you'd like a receipt?" she said. "You know, for paying your fine so nicely and without kicking up a fuss." She rolled over onto her elbows, and cupped her chin in her palms, watching me, all that wonderful soft hair like sea-foam on her shoulders. "Only I was just kidding, Chuck," she said very softly. "Because I know you don't want a receipt."

I half set up, grabbing her arm. "How did you know my name? I never said my name!"

She just grinned a little, lazily, with pleasure in her eyes. "I'm psychic."

"You're sick? Damn you—if you—why don't you tell . . . ?"

"Here, darling—not sick—*psychic.*" She chuckled. It was something to hear, and she was something, the very most, all the way, up and down and sideways. "Psychic means I know what you're thinking, I know all about you. Your name's Chuck Armbruster and there's one hundred and eighty-three thousand dollars in that suitcase under the front seat of your car. Enough to last a lifetime, if you spread it out in the right places."

We watched each other. I didn't move.

"I'll go get the suitcase," she said. "My name's Betty—I never told you."

"What? You'll what—wait!"

She slid off the couch and waggled across the floor to the front door. I was kneeling on the couch, watching her. She turned at the door and blew me a kiss. "Relax, Chuck—I'll bring it right in."

"You're naked."

"I know it."

She went outside and slammed the door. I came off the couch and went over to the window, yanked the curtain aside. The sun glinted off her lush bare body as she dragged the suitcase out from under the seat. I groaned, thinking about Mr. Jefferies.

She was a doll. But I was a dead duck unless I got the hell out of here and over to Spider Lake. I remembered her .45, and jumped for the chair where she'd dropped it. I found it, started taking it out of the holster when she came in the door.

"Drop it, Honey-bun," she said. "I've got your gun—you left it under the seat."

I dropped her .45 back on the chair and turned.

She shoved the door closed with her foot, and carried the suitcase over to the couch. She tossed the gun down and unsnapped the snaps on the suitcase. "You might have ruined everything," she said. "That's the trouble with you. You're too impressionable."

"Come off it."

"My name's Betty, I told you."

"All right."

"Of course, maybe being impressionable will come in handy—look at that!"

She had the suitcase open. I went over and we both stood there and ogled the loot. It was hell. It was beautiful. It was green and neat, in bundles.

She leaned down and picked some of it up, and rubbed it on her. She stood there with bundles of it, some of the paper wraps breaking, rubbing the money all over her bare flesh. She threw her head back, rubbing herself with the money—hundreds and fifties drifted to the floor around her feet. Then she stopped. She scooped it all up and put it back in the suitcase, breathing as hard as she had on the couch, and closed the suitcase and clicked the snaps. Then she looked at me, and her face was quiet as hell.

"It's going to be ours, Chuck. Ours. Understand?"

I knew right then I had a real honest-to-god bat to deal with.

. . .

"So, you see?" she said. "That's all you've got to do. Now, let's lie down here again and wait. I mean—wait, anyway." She chuckled softly, watching me, and pulled me back toward her on the couch. Then she said, "Wait!"

I was dizzy, the way she'd been going.

She knelt beside the suitcase, opened it, reached in and brought out a pack of hundreds, then snapped it shut again.

"What's that for?" I said.

She squinched up against me. "I just want to hold it in my hand," she said. "That's all."

I reached around her and clawed for my gun. I got it and straightened up and the cabin door opened. In walked Mr. Jefferies.

"Betty, baby," he said. "You got everything in order?"

She lay there with that bundle of money and watched him. Then she turned her face a little and whispered to me. "Go ahead, Chuck—do it. Kill him. Like I told you—kill him, or he'll kill you—which do you want?"

"Hello, Mr. Jefferies," I said. I had the gun between Betty and me, so he couldn't see it. "Ran into a little mix-up."

He stood there. "I know, Chuck—I know." He was nervous, and his eyes were bloodshot. He didn't look good at all—tight all over, you know? "Betty," he said. "Get off the bed—get away, you know what I had to do. And you, Chuck—come on—stand up over there. Hurry up, Chuck—I don't have all night. You've had your fun—now you've got to pay the Piper. Ha-ha."

"What about the others?" Betty said. "Did you take care of them?"

"What do you think I've been doing? I took care of them," Mr. Jefferies said. "And I buried them—all by myself. And I'm tired. I've been thinking and thinking about you and me, baby."

She started to get off the bed, knocking me with her hand, telling me to come on—*do it, Chuck.* . . .

"Betty?" he said.

"What?"

"Never mind getting off the bed."

"What?"

He reached up and pulled a gun off his shoulder, a snub-nosed .38, nickel-plated. Hell, I used to clean that damned gun for him.

"What do you mean, Honey-bun?" Betty said to Mr. Jefferies. "What's on your mind?"

"A clean sweep," he said, levelling the gun, and I lifted my own gun and began squeezing. I shot him four time straight in the face. It was like the cabin blew up. Mr. Jefferies frowned and dropped his .38 and it clattered on the floor. He was dead, still standing there, frowning. Then he fell down like somebody knocked him flat. Then he was laid out on the floor.

"Oh, Chuck!" She came around and started kissing me all over, saying my name. The way she wanted me to pay some more of the fine off, right then and there, should have warned me, I suppose. I talked her out of that, hard as it was—because there was something about Mr. Jefferies lying there bleeding on the floor, you know?

"It's all ours, now."

"How long've you known Mr. Jefferies?" I said.

"A long time. We worked it all out. He had all you guys working for him, and he had to be rid of all of you—every one, Chuck. And still he had to be sure of getting the money from that payroll robbery. He was sure he could depend on you—he's been building you up for this for over a year. That's why he said meet at Spider Lake. Nobody ever goes out there. He killed the others, Chuck—and I was supposed to keep you here until he came. Then he'd kill you, and bury you, and he and I would go away together." She paused. "Only, Honey-bun—I was kind of tired of him. And, anyway, he couldn't be depended on."

"But I can."

"Yes, darling—yes, yes, yes." She kissed me. "Now, we've got to bury him."

"Then what?"

"Then we'll just go away together."

I looked at her balancing everything against everything. I mean, this Betty was something—you couldn't want anything more than what she was. Nobody could.

"Something's wrong, though," I said.

"What?"

"Oh, nothing. Forget it."

She frowned. "Now, Chuck—*what is it?*"

"Nothing—let's bury Mr. Jefferies."

• • •

Well, we drove the two cars—the Buick, and Mr. Jefferies' big black Caddy, right on through Oakville and back to the city. I parked the Cad in front of Mr. Jefferies' place, and wiped it clean, and then Betty and I lit out across the country, looking for a place to settle down.

But it bothered me. It bothered the hell out of me. I mean, paying the Piper. You got to, that's all. And here I was with everything. All the money in the world, all the witnesses buried underground where nobody would ever find them, and living with the sweetest little sheriff that ever pinned on a star. What I mean.

Even Mr. Jefferies had said that *"the sheriff in that town was as hot as they come."*

Well, he was right.

But it bothered me. I told Betty all about it, too, and how it always worked that way with me. You had to pay, that's all.

"You're full of it," she said. "Honestly, Chuck—you're a scream, sometimes."

"You don't understand. There's nothing you can do about it."

"Pooh!"

"Yeah. O. K. Pooh. Just the same—"

We were in a little place in Mississippi, then. And that same night she began calling me Honey-bun again, for the first time since the afternoon we'd buried Mr. Jefferies and left the cabin.

We took our time. Then we got to St. Louis, in a really swell apartment, and I woke up on a warm Sunday morning with a hangover. There was no sign of Betty. I didn't even get nervous. There was no suitcase, and no car.

Just a note on her pillow.

"You were right, Honey-bun. No matter what you do, you simply have to pay the Piper. Because I just want to go away from you now, so you're really paying because I'm taking all the money and there's nothing you can do about it. Who knows, maybe I'll pay sometime, myself. But fun's fun, and I like fun. G'by."

So, you see? She was just a dame, like all the times I'd wake up in the alley or the drunk tank. And he always cleaned me out. No half-ways about it. What can you do about it?

Of course, I'm looking for her. I always look for her, because what else is there to do? And they'll be looking for me, because Mr. Jefferies wasn't buried too deep, see—and somebody will dig around that cabin, sure as hell. And anyway, I got to pay for that, too.

I know I got to pay for everything.

Like as not Mr. Jefferies will pop his head up and yell, "Chuck—Chuck Armbruster—you got to pay. You know you got to pay!"

That damned Piper.

Old Timers

Murder!
July 1957

Malleck shifted heavily in the lawn chair, snatched a white handkerchief from the frayed breast pocket of his worn gray sport jacket and mopped his fierce old face. White afternoon sun boiled on the rolling green lawn, shimmered across the pool, danced blurringly along the edges of limber palm fronds.

"I had to come to you, Dan," Malleck said. "It's damned important."

The large, gray-haired man in the chair opposite him gave the sash of his terry-cloth robe a harsh yank. Light glared on the glass wall of the patio, and, beyond them, under the shade of cedars and palms, the sprawling white house lay quiet.

"Been a long time," Packard said. He was perhaps fifty, or slightly over, well cared for, trimmed as neatly as the lawn. "Been over seven years, hasn't it?"

"Does it matter?"

Malleck carefully folded the handkerchief and still more carefully fitted it back in the pocket. The furrowed mahogany of his forehead fed ubiquitous canals of sweat. Sweat beaded and dripped from his hawkish nose, pearled on his chin, puddled around the too-tight collar of his yellow shirt.

"Drink, old man?" Packard said, reaching toward a glass cocktail table twinkling with bottles and ice.

Malleck shook his head.

Packard grinned, showing white teeth that were not his by blood and nerve, and there was a trace of amusement in his somber brown eyes.

"Sure a surprise seeing you," Packard said. "Walking in on me like this, after all these years. How's Grace?"

"She's fine."

"I call her that. Never met her, but I always think about her. Wish you'd bring her around—but I understand. Think about Helen, too—you and Helen. But Helen was different—more like us. In her own way, of course."

"Yes."

"Think about you two a lot. The old days, Joe. Helen was a wild one, but there was so much about her—fire. Somebody you'd never forget. They don't make that kind of beauty often these days. Something's gone out of it." He moved his hands out, dropped them into his lap. "Maybe I'm getting old." He paused. "I have three young beauties running around here someplace—but they'd never stand a chance against Helen." He paused. "As I say, I never met Grace."

Malleck frowned. "Dan, I . . ."

Packard talked on: "Thinking yesterday about the parties. Remember?" He paused again, closed his eyes, opened them. "Makes me want to cry sometimes. Hell—it was the day, that's all. Everything was bright. Even at midnight. Something about the way the leaves used to rattle in the streets in fall, you know? Everybody busy—I mean, going—going someplace. Different down here now, too." He drew a long breath, let it out slowly. "Everything was better. I mean it."

"I know."

"One great big wonderful party." He shrugged. "Parties got to end. Everybody knows that. We just didn't think it would. Keep trying to bring it back." He lifted his right hand, waved it, let it drop to his lap. He leaned back, shoved both hands into the pockets of his robe. "All the young punks. Moving fast—faster than we ever used to move, I guess, Joe. You know that. Ideas, they've got—big." He brought his right hand from the pocket, twirled it at his temple, put it back in the pocket. "Ideas—all the time. Buzz-buzz. Gee at the front door, you saw him—strictly a BB gun. Plotting, though." Packard nodded to himself. "Hard to believe. My God, it's different now."

"I know."

"And you." Packard looked down at his feet, talking. "Why did you ever get the way you did? You could have had everything, yet you just wanted—I'll never know. Not old enough yet for us to sit so you can tell me."

Malleck said nothing.

"No," Packard said. "Not yet. Helen never knew?"

"No."

"Grace?"

Malleck just sat there.

Packard sighed. "Well, we still try to throw the parties, but they're not the same. Wish you'd bring Grace around. I know you won't. What're you hear for?"

"A job."

"Oh?"

"I've got to have a job, Dan."

"Well, there's plenty openings, even with all the bucking and the politics. But I never figured you'd come around to that. Where would you like to be placed?"

"You don't understand, Dan."

"A job . . . *oh*—" Packard sat there.

"The biggest you've got. It's got to be big."

"You're talking about money?"

"It's got to pay."

"I can let you have whatever you—" Packard stopped. "This is rough, Joe. In seven years things have changed, believe me. It's a long time."

"That's one thing never changes," Malleck said. "I've got to have a job."

"Absolutely anything but that."

"It's all I know. I'm an old dog."

"Oh, come off it. How much do you need?"

Malleck said nothing.

"It's not a question of not knowing anything else, these days," Packard said. "Not even when you quit, like you did—went away. I can fix you up with anything you want."

"Do it, then."

"Hell, Joe . . . all right—twenty thousand's tops."

Malleck leaned forward. "That's not good enough."

Packard took his hands out of the pockets of his robe and straightened in the chair. He reached down beside his chair, picked up a frosted glass, drained it. "Sure you won't have one? No." He set the empty glass down.

"I've got to have it," Malleck said. "Grace doesn't know about me. She thinks I've made my pile, see? I love her—get that—*get it straight.* She's never going to find out. We don't live big, but she's always had what she wanted. I've got to have it, Dan. I'm flat—I'm broke. Try to understand that. It's difficult, with all this you—

" Malleck moved his fist tightly on his knee. "That's the way it is," he said quietly. "I'm not going to go on explaining why. I want in and out, one last one—and it's got to be at least fifty grand. I *know* you can do it. I know who you are. I don't give a damn who it is, or what it is, or who's filling tops now. Think back—you know how I work."

"Worked," Packard said. "Good God, man. You're not young anymore. Said so yourself."

"Everything's the same," Malleck said. "I can make the fifty grow right, I know it."

"Why didn't you think that seven years ago?"

Malleck did not answer.

"There's nothing like that now," Packard said.

"Don't fool with me, Dan." Malleck's voice changed subtly, coarsened. "There's got to be. I mean it."

"You haven't changed."

"Who changes?"

"You're right. But you never fell—you never slipped—not once. What is it inside you?"

Malleck said, "I don't know. If I knew I would have told you. At least, I don't know with me."

"How many is it, Joe?"

"Forget that."

"No. We were kids together. We grew up—we've been friends a long time. I want to know. Did I ever ask you?"

"You're not asking now."

Packard sat there. "Maybe I'll never figure you."

"Grace is all I've got," Malleck said. "Maybe I don't deserve her. But, damn it—it's not going to blow up now. I'm in debt—"

"I can't do it."

"You've got to."

"Only I can't."

Malleck came fast out of the chair, his fist sank into the robe across Packard's chest, the fingers clamped, and Packard was lifted halfway from his chair. Malleck moved his head down, looking into Packard's eyes, and his voice was quiet. "I want the job. *I've got to have it!*"

He released his hold on the robe and Packard dropped into the chair. Malleck went back and sat down.

"The only reason you're not dead now is because I saved you," Packard said. "There've been three meetings, Joe. That and your rep, of course. You'd gun anybody, wouldn't you?"

"Anybody."

"Three times I've saved your life," Packard said. "For seven years you've been out—and alive. What do you want? You think I don't know how many and who?"

"I know you know."

"They'll kick about your age." Packard leaned toward Malleck and said mildly, "They'll rub you, Joe." He cleared his throat, said: "Fifty thousand to you is fifty from some other guy's pocket. It won't ride."

Malleck said nothing.

"All right," Packard said. He stood up, scowling. "Wait here. No, come on inside. I want to check."

"I'll wait here," Malleck said. "It's nice out here."

Packard shook his head and walked slowly along the patio toward the house. Malleck watched him go, watched the consciously squared shoulders, the stiffly held back.

"There goes old Dan Packard," he said softly.

• • •

"It's syndicate," Packard said. "And it's tender. They'll do it. All I know is you report to Klinger in Chicago. I had to talk to get you this, how it's your last, and all. The old years. How you're my best friend, from way back."

"Thanks, Dan."

"They all remember you."

They shook hands. Neither spoke now. Malleck turned and walked down by the pool, looked at the water, then took a sloping series of flag steps over a knoll. Atop the knoll, he paused, glanced back. Three young girls in colorful Bikinis were running laughing down to the pool from the house.

Dan Packard was slouched in his chair.

• • •

Late the following afternoon, in from Chicago, Malleck picked up his car—a black two-door sedan—at the airport and drove into the town where he lived. He parked in front of a small but nicely landscaped dwelling, went up the front walk and in the front door.

"Grace?"

An extremely attractive woman with light blonde hair, very happy eyes, and a red-lipped mouth, hurried toward him through the front hall. She wore a white peasant blouse, and a black furling skirt. She was younger than Malleck, perhaps in her early thirties, and he hulked like a great old work horse beside her light litheness.

"I was worried, Joe."

He caught her in his arms, lifted her into the air, and for a moment it was quiet as they kissed. He let her down slowly, but seemed unable to release her. Then, finally, he did, with deep reluctance.

"Had to stay away last night," he said. "And I've got to run again now. Wanted to let you know." He paused and for a moment it was as if he searched with clumsy desperateness for out-of-reach words. "I might be a little late—but I'll be back sometime tonight. Something's come up—it's a chance to . . ."

"You don't have to tell me," she said.

"What?" His voice was faintly sharp.

For only a part of a moment the bright light in her eyes dimmed. "Just hurry back," she said, smiling. "That's all."

He stilled. "Is something the matter?"

"No—no, Joe. I just don't like to be alone."

He watched her for a moment, lightly frowning. Her gaze was direct, but it was as if she willed it that way, against some strong and curious compulsion. He took her in his arms and kissed her again, then turned and walked on out the front door.

Twilight combed the streets with pale amber. He got into the car and sat there. His big brown hands tightened on the wheel and he stared for some time at the windshield.

Again there was that hidden quality of desperation as he spoke:

"She couldn't possibly know. Not possibly."

He started the car and drove off.

• • •

Malleck stood in the dark shadows beside the house, dropped the small jimmy into his jacket pocket, then finished opening the window. He climbed into a dark room, waited, then moved among shadowed furnishings along a wall toward dim light.

He reached a door, pushed it slowly open, then stepped out into a large marble hall. It was the entrance hall to the house, cool and quiet. Soft saffron light shone from somewhere, a quiet suffusion, and suddenly Dan Packard was walking toward him through the light.

"Joe? What the hell—I didn't hear you come in. Did you ring?"

"No."

"What now?"

"This," Malleck said. He drew a gun and two explosions thundered in the marble hall. The front of Dan Packard's white dinner jacket tucked twice. Packard continued to walk until his legs buckled, and then he walked on his knees, saying gruffly: "You rotten . . ." And then he fell flat out, dead.

Malleck stood like that for a brief interval, his face expressionless, then turned back through the doorway of the room he'd just left, and ran through the darkness.

Deep in the house, somewhere, a woman called.

"Dan? Dan?"

Malleck leaped from the window down onto the soft grass of the lawn.

"Joe? Joe?"

He stopped short, the gun held slightly forward in his hand, listening. Then he began to run again.

"Joe?"

A woman ran quickly toward Malleck up across the sloping lawn, her blonde hair touched with pale light from streetlamps.

"Grace." The word was something broken. "Go back."

She reached him.

"I followed you." Quick despair walled them close. "What did you do, Joe—what did you do? I had to follow you. I've suspected for too long." Then she stared down at the gun in her husband's hand. "I had to know," she said.

Grief lived between them.

"Run," Malleck said. He grabbed her arm, thrusting at her. "For God's sake, run. We've got to get away from here."

They vanished, stumbling into the dark shadows of trees, and from the house a woman screamed.

High Heels and Kisses

True Men Stories
August 1957

He turned the ignition off, set the brake, and looked out across the old wooden pier at the calm waters of the bay. The girl beside him opened the door and swiftly got out of the car.

"I don't see why in hell we had to come out here," she said. She slammed the door, and strode out onto the pier. Her high heels echoed on the wooden planks. Tall, shapely, blonde, she seemed very nervous.

"What's the difference?" he called, climbing from his side of the car. "I just wanted to show you where we'll meet tonight."

"You could have told me."

He sighed. He had disliked her from the start. Yet, from the moment he met her, he had known she'd be perfect for the job he had in mind. And she was perfect.

She turned. Afternoon sunlight haloed around her head, brightening her powder-blue dress, gleaming on the fine curve of her hips.

"We shouldn't be seen together at all—not now. Not with tonight." Her voice was strained and quite sharp.

"Nobody's going to see us, honey."

She watched him quietly, turned her back, and strode over to the railing. She leaned on the railing, looking out across the bay. He stepped up behind her, put his arms around her, pressing against her, his lips against the back of her hair.

"You're sweet," he said. "I like being with you as much as possible."

"After tonight you're going to be with me a lot. And to tell you the truth," she said, turning in his arms, facing him, "I still don't understand what you're going to tell your wife."

He forced himself to keep the grin plastered on his face. Just having her mention his wife made him hate her more. He loved his wife, and that would never change.

"Not going to tell her anything, Jean," he said, thinking of how this girl in his arms would be dead on this very spot a few hours from now. And Meg and he would have everything they'd ever wanted. He wished it were over with. "Why should I tell her anything? She doesn't suspect anything. We'll just go away, that's all—you and me. With the money."

"With the money." She did not smile. "Well, God knows how much I want that money."

• • •

He kissed her. He had known her for three months. He couldn't say he hadn't enjoyed some of the time they had spent together. Jean was very much woman. All a man could ask. Yet, he had slowly come to hate her. On top of that, she was as weak as himself. He could easily visualize what would happen if he went along with the plan as she thought they would. In a year or two, the fifty grand would be gone. Then there'd be another job, similar to this one. Other jobs after that. Or something would happen. They'd get caught, because how many times can you pull a thing like this? Or she'd find another guy. He'd be left flat. He could never work things alone, either. And how many Jeans does a man run across in a lifetime? How long is a lifetime?

With Meg it was altogether different. They would have the fifty thousand dollars, and it would last them the rest of their lives, properly invested. Which Meg would see to. And they'd be happy, because Meg would never know he'd stolen the money and was a murderer.

• • •

Actually, he wouldn't be a murderer, or a thief. It wasn't really in his make-up. It was just this one time, and that was all. Just the one chance he had to take. And it would be easy.

"Thinking, thinking, thinking," she said. "Man, the way you grind it up is real crazy."

"Yeah. Now, look, honey—you sure you got Adams sold on you—all the way down the line?"

"He's for me—," she grinned. "Don't worry about my part. We know for a fact he'll have the money with him when he comes home. In the briefcase. I'll get him in the kitchen, all right—don't worry about that. All I worry about is your timing, Doug." She shrugged out of his arms, frowning. "I'll make sure the door's unlatched. But you've got to be there at exactly eight-thirty. That's when I'll get him into the kitchen. The briefcase'll be on the hall stand. From there on it's up to you."

He took her in his arms, holding her against him, grinning at her. He didn't have to force the grin this time. He was thinking of what Meg and he would have.

"You may have to go along with him," he said. "I mean, after. He'll see the money's gone. It's a big deal to him, selling Abercrombie on that deal. He'll flip."

"Let him," she said quietly, her face buried against his shoulder. "I'll meet you right here at ten—just like we planned."

"He'll probably call the cops."

"Let him."

"What'll you tell them?"

"He won't even want me there. Look, he wouldn't want me mixed up in it in any way, Doug. He's got a wife in Detroit. He'll shoo me out, but fast."

"There's nothing to worry about, then," he said. He kissed her, thinking of Meg. He wouldn't have to lie to Meg anymore after tonight. He would be in the clear, straight up and straight down. All the way.

"I don't have to see him for quite a while yet," she purred. "Should we just stand here?"

He grinned at her again, appeasing her.

"I think we'd better break up right now," he told her. "We'll be together tonight—and from then on it'll be just the two of us."

"I keep worrying about your wife," she said.

"Well, cut it out, honey!"

"I can't help it. It just doesn't ring right, Doug. She's not just going to sit there and wonder where you've gone, and do nothing about it. After all, you've been married for a long time."

"Let me take care of that." He couldn't keep the harshness out of his voice. "O.K.?"

She tightened her lips. "O.K. But, I'll tell you, Doug. Again, and again—I don't like it."

• • •

He fisted her chin up, looking straight into her eyes. "You will, baby," he said softly. "You'll like it. I'll see to that."

She shook her head away, and broke clear.

He watched her stride over to the car and slide in across the seat, flipping her skirt over her knees. It wasn't going to be easy, killing Jean. He knew that. He shouldn't think about it.

"Come on," she called.

He got into the car and drove back to town. He let her off on a suburban corner, so she could catch a bus. No use taking any chances.

He drove around for a time. He didn't want to go home. Not yet. Not until it was all done, all off his mind—so Meg and he could be together—free—completely free, and at ease. He shouldn't have anything on his mind. He wouldn't—after ten tonight.

• • •

It was so perfect. So absolutely smooth. This guy Adams was a set-up. He had located Adams through a friend of his who worked in a branch office of the company Adams traveled for. They'd arranged for a meeting with Jean, without the friend's knowledge of any particular of what they were doing. Adams went for her. He couldn't help himself. He always went for some Doll on trips like this, they'd discovered that. Adams thought he was having fun on a business trip. Even if he suspected anything, they were still pretty certain to be in the clear.

With Jean out of the way—dead certain.

He had to laugh at that—quietly, but with great mirth. He kept on driving around, had a few drinks at an outskirts bar, then drove into the country and got the .38 revolver he'd buried under a hickory stump. He hadn't taken any chances, other than the ones necessary.

He parked the car down the block from the old apartment house, where Adams was staying. At twenty after eight, he was on the stoop. He slipped into the hall, headed for the shadows under the rear stairs, and found Adams' rooms. It was the first time he'd been here. But Jean had checked him out on everything.

He glanced at his watch, standing by the door.

He could hear nothing from inside. He thought how it would be if she couldn't get him into the kitchen. He dismissed that. She would.

He heard a footstep near the door, dodged back toward the stairs. If the door opened, he was caught. It didn't open. He heard the footsteps going away.

Suppose Adams opened the door? Then he grinned to himself, his face stolidly composed. Adams didn't know him, so what could he say?

His watch read eight-thirty.

He tried the door, lifting against it as he turned the knob, as Jean had told him to. At first he thought it was locked. His heart socked into his throat. Then the door clicked softly, and swung inward.

• • •

He opened it cautiously, looking through the dimly lighted interior. He could hear them talking in whispers from another room of the apartment.

The kitchen. He could see the glowing saffron through the partially open kitchen door. He heard Jean speaking.

"Mm-m-m-m, honey," she said. "No one can mix a drink the way you can."

He heard the ice clink, and a shadow passed momentarily across the yellowed light, then the shaker beat out a tattoo. He tried to accustom his eyes to the faint gloom of the foyer. He saw the table beside a hall closet. The briefcase wasn't there.

Something inside him screamed, but he held on tightly. He slipped past the door. The briefcase was resting on the arm of an easy chair, just inside the room. He stepped to it, grabbed it.

"God, you're nice," a man said from the kitchen. "God, you're beautiful," he said. "I love you, Jeannie. God, you're beautiful!"

Jean made comforting sounds.

He made it back to the door, eased it shut. He wanted to check the briefcase right there. He knew he should get outside. There was always the chance somebody might enter the apartment house, see him. It could be bad.

• • •

He hurried down the hall, the briefcase like some sort of living thing, warm against his side, under his arm.

Outside, he saw no one. As soon as he was on the sidewalk, he worked the fasteners on the case. It wouldn't open. It was locked. There was no key. He stepped into the shadows of a tree, hooked his heel in the top of the leather case, stomped it into the ground, and yanked. The lid tore open. He grabbed it up, staring in at the packed currency.

He ran for the car. Elation coursed through him. He'd never felt so wildly happy in his life. And it was all for Meg. All the endless years of worry, and grubbing for a buck would be gone. She'd have everything she'd ever wanted. There would be no single grain of suspicion on them. He would quit his job at the brokerage office, where he was little more than a hambone, anyway, and they'd leave town.

He would tell her he'd made a killing.

He didn't bother to laugh at that one.

He drove out of town. He let his thoughts play back toward what Jean and Adams were doing now. He hoped she would find some real pleasure with Adams. It would be her last really happy time with anyone.

Then he cut her from his mind and dwelt on Meg. He had never loved another woman, not really. She was his world, and always would be. She knew, too. She knew how much she meant to him. He couldn't ever let her know, in any way, what had happened—how he'd really gotten this money.

• • •

He reached the wooden pier by the bay. He'd made repeated nightly visits here. He knew the place. Nobody ever came around the spot. There was only the one place to park, and it wasn't the location for lovers.

He put the briefcase under the front seat, took the gun, went out onto the pier and stood by the railing—waiting.

He found it bad to think of what he would do to Jean. Even if he had always really disliked her, they had been very close. They had shared each other's thoughts—all of hers—all of his, up to a point.

He refused to think about her. Just kill her, toss her into the bay, and get out of here—that was all.

He forced his mind to Meg; her thick black hair, the way she had of speaking his name, the shape of her lips, the shape of her hands—the shape of her. Of Meg. The woman he loved. His wife.

• • •

At ten o'clock, he began sweating. He'd thought before of just leaving town with Meg, and letting Jean take her chances. But that would mean he'd forever after have to take chances himself. He'd never know when she might be right behind him.

He saw the car coming, saw it slow, saw it stop just behind his own. Jean's Ford convertible.

He watched her step from the car. He stood with his back to the railing and waited, listening to the click of her heels.

She stepped onto the pier and moved toward him, then hesitated. For a scant instant he didn't want to kill her. Then he squeezed the trigger. Three times. Pumping them into her.

• • •

She fell without noise. The sound of the shots echoed sharply through the night.

"So long, Jean," he said. He hurled the gun backward, over the railing, and stepped over to her.

Leaning down, he caught her by the shoulders. Raised her high above his head and was about to heave her over the railing when the other car's lights flooded the pier, blinding him. He let the body drop.

He crouched, stunned, seeing his wife, Meg, lying dead there at his feet, her rich black hair fanned out on the pier.

He said her name, kneeling above her, choking on her name. He heard the clicking of heels moving toward him across the wooden planks.

Jean stood in the light, holding the gun.

Her voice was very soft. Almost gentle. "I wasn't born yesterday, Doug," she said. "I tagged you around a little. I saw you buy that gun, and hide it out there under that stump. I finally figured what it was for. So I told your wife you were in trouble, that you wanted to see her out here. I brought her along." She laughed quietly. "And now look. Look what you planned for me. Doug, Doug—you must have really loved her. And she loved you—coming out here, like this, with a stranger—like me. I hoped I was wrong, Doug—"

"Damn you!" He came to his feet.

"I take it the money's in the car?"

He started for her. Her shadow was outlined against the car's headlights. She shot him several times, and once again the night echoed to the staccato sound. Then there was silence, broken only by a woman weeping.

The Glass Eye

Guilty Detective Story Magazine
September 1957

Rain drove like hail through the police spotlight beam that was trained across the reedy slope of empty lot to the ditch where the crumpled figure of a man lay. Cruiser headlights glared here on the windy outskirts of town. Slickered men wandered and grouped. A tall man in a trenchcoat listened as a stocky man in a drenched dark suit talked against the quiet confusion.

"You're sure it's Art, Lieutenant?" the stocky man said. "What would Art be doing out here?"

"It's your brother, all right. But we'd like you to take a look. He was dropped out here by somebody, Tom. Besides, his eye's gone."

The stocky man wore no tie. His dark hair streamed. His face was pale, the mouth calm.

"He's the only man I know with a glass eye," the lieutenant said. "After all, Tom, he and I worked together on the force. I was with him when he lost the eye."

The stocky man turned away. The lieutenant said something unintelligible into the rain. The stocky man slogged down the slope of field past a billboard illumined with sickly purple light. He reached the edge of the ditch and stood there. The rain began to let up. It came in angry bursts with the wind.

A thin stream of water trickled in the ditch, forming a small puddle around the body. The body lay on its back, an angled clutter of cramped and grotesquely positioned limbs. It was clothed in trousers, a stained white shirt, and a twisted jacket. The neck was arched, head caught back, face soaked and pale, mouth gaping inhumanly, one eye drowsy, the other an empty hole.

"We been looking for the eye," the lieutenant said. "Could be it's lost in the mud. Could be he lost it wherever it happened."

The stocky man's voice was flat. "It didn't happen here?"

"No. He was dragged from over by the curb, then pitched into the ditch."

"How did he get it?"

"Now, relax, Tom. I knew how you'd be, that's why I wanted to talk to you first."

"How did he get it?"

• • •

The lieutenant sighed shortly. "Coroner's not here yet, so I haven't checked everything. There's a slug in his throat." The officer paused. "From the back. You going to have a look?"

"That's all right," the stocky man said. The curiously flat tone of his voice did not change. "Did you find the gun?"

The lieutenant moved his head from side to side, then said, "No," softly. Then he said more loudly, "Sorry to drag you out of bed to this, Tom. It's a Christ of a thing. Will you see his wife?"

"Yeah."

"Any ideas? You know what I mean."

The stocky man stared at the body in the ditch.

"There were two guys he was worried about," he said. "Think I'll do a little checking."

The lieutenant's voice hardened faintly. "We didn't bring you out here for that, Tom. That's our job. You're not a cop anymore, either."

"What do you mean, 'either'?"

"You're a businessman." The lieutenant quietly watched the other, concern in his eyes. "If I'd thought for a minute—"

"My name's Dolan, the same as his—don't forget that."

"God damn it, Tom. If you got any ideas, let me have them."

"Go to hell," Dolan said.

"Oh, Jesus," the lieutenant said. "Don't be that way."

They watched each other. The stocky man looked down into the ditch again. "That's Art Dolan," he said. Turning, he started walking swiftly back up the soggy slope.

"Tom!" the lieutenant called. "God damn it, Tom! Listen to me—don't try anything on your own." He ran a few steps up the slope, his trenchcoat slapping against his legs, the cords in his neck standing out whitely in the glare of the spotlight. "Tom! I mean it—I want the names of those men!"

Dolan paused and turned atop the slope, nearly to the weed-grown sidewalk. Wind buffeted him. Wet newspaper lifted at his feet.

"Go to hell, lieutenant," he said.

The lieutenant took another step, one arm up.

"Tom, damn you! Don't mess around. I'll be forced to take you in, can't you understand?"

Dolan turned and walked across the sidewalk to his car.

• • •

Dolan waited in the phone booth, receiver to his ear. He smeared his right hand across soaked hair, wiped it on his thigh. "Hello? . . . Yeah, honey, it's me. . . . Listen, something's come up. . . . Yes, it has to do with Art. . . . No, not here. Take it easy, will you? I said, take it easy, please, baby. Was Art home tonight? Not? . . . Didn't he come home at all? . . . No. Phone? . . . All right, I'll be right over, as soon as I . . . Yes, right along. Just hold the fort. . . . You know I do."

He stood outside the booth, felt for cigarettes. The package was soaked. He threw them into the street, climbed back under the wheel of his car. For a moment, he sat there. Then he abruptly started the engine and drove the small sedan viciously away from the curb and down the wind-shot canyons of city streets. A block back, a clock on a corner by a bank chimed twice, but Dolan didn't hear it.

• • •

Dolan pounded on the door. The hallway was dim. A small red bulb glowed at the far end above a sign reading EXIT. He pounded harder now.

"Cotelli!" he shouted. "Open up! Cotelli!"

He beat his fist against the panels, rattled the knob, shouting in the dead silence.

"Cotelli! Damn you, open up!"

A door behind him cracked, then widened and a sleepy-eyed, dark-haired woman looked out. She clutched a thin wisp of sleazy blue silk about her body, but it was inadequate covering. She was slightly drunk, and her mouth was redly smeared.

"What the hell's up?" she said.

Dolan turned, breathing heavily.

"Where are the Cotellis?"

"They moved, for God's sake."

The blue cloth parted and a long, plump, white thigh showed. Her breasts were heavy under the cloth, the swell of round flesh bare. Her hand moved down and more of her breasts were revealed as the gown parted.

"Moved? When?"

"Weeks ago. I'm trying to sleep. Go away, or something." She began to leer faintly.

"Where did they move?"

"To Chicago."

"You're sure?"

"Positive. Weeks ago. I got a card—" she motioned him to her door, clicked a light, and reeled slightly across the exposed bedroom to a littered dresser. She pawed, came up with a bent card, returned to the doorway, the blue cloth held only by a single snap at the waist now, her body undulant and bold. She yawned, handed the card to Dolan. He read it, handed it back, looking at her.

"I'm awake now," she said. "I live alone, honey. For a price, I can do anything Marie Cotelli could."

Dolan turned and started down the hall.

"Don't you believe me?" the woman called.

He said nothing. She cursed him and slammed the door.

• • •

Dolan turned on the light in the hotel room, and closed the door. The heavy-shouldered, bull-headed man in the bed shot to a sitting position, eyes wide.

"Just lie there, Bruno," Dolan said.

"How—how'd you get in here? Get the hell out of here. What the hell's going—?"

"Shut up."

Dolan walked to a closet. He turned savagely, leaped to the bed and grabbed the big man's right wrist as it moved to a night-stand. He cracked the drawer of the night-stand, took out a revolver, smashed it against the man's wrist twice.

"Just don't," Dolan said.

The man lay there grimacing with pain.

Dolan returned to the closet with the gun. He opened the door, checked clothes. He hurled a wet raincoat on the floor. A suit jacket, brown with thin yellow stripes, was on the same hanger inside the raincoat. He stepped to the bed.

"Where were you tonight, Bruno? Don't lie."

"My mother's. Brooklyn. Jesus Christ, man."

"I can check."

"Check. Check. Check!"

"When did you get in?"

"Midnight. I got caught in the first of the rain. Please, what's the matter?"

"Nothing."

The man called Bruno seemed to strengthen, lying there. He sat half up. "Believe me," he said. "I been to my mother's. The whole clan was out there. Sister's birthday. You can check it out, believe me."

Dolan stared at him, frowning.

"I mean it," Bruno said. "Now, what happened?"

Dolan continued to frown. His lips moved. "Art's dead. Somebody killed him."

Bruno's voice was a whisper. "Christ. I'm sorry."

"I'll bet. He checked you in for ten. You hated his guts."

Bruno nodded soberly, watching Dolan. "Sure. I hated his guts. But not enough to pull the big one. Not me."

Dolan's scowl was gone. He handed the gun to Bruno. Bruno said, "Thank you," replaced it in the night-stand drawer, and sat there in bed, rubbing his wrist. Dolan looked at the raincoat and the brown and yellow-striped jacket on the floor.

"I hope you're telling me the goods," he said.

"You can check it out," Bruno said. "Know how you feel. But it wasn't me, O. K.?"

"You almost had a right, even," Dolan said. "The way he treated you. Beat you up, that time."

Bruno half-smiled. "It hurt."

"All right," Dolan said. He walked to the door, paused, looked back. "All right, Bruno," he said. He turned the light off, stepped outside, and closed the door.

• • •

"Darling," Irene Dolan said. "Tell me—tell me quick. What is it?"

"Your husband's dead."

She stared at him. She was a blonde woman, tall, and with a front-line shape tightly confined in black satin lounging pajamas. They stood in her living room, but the bedroom door was open, and a rumpled bed showed pinkly beyond a white shag-rug. She stood there for a long moment staring at Dolan. Then she lifted one hand to her face, turned and took two steps toward a couch, then stopped and moved her hand down. The fingers crimped into the taut satin covering her right thigh. The jacket of the pajamas was waist-high, and her round hips swelled and bunched when she moved. She whirled, eyes wide, watching Dolan, and looked momentarily as if she might cry.

"Just don't do that," Dolan said. "What point? You're glad, and I should be."

She moved quickly to him, thrust against him, put her arms around his neck. "Hold me, darling. Hold me hard. Hold me, hold me!"

They kissed, mouths working together. The woman's hips moved in a slow tight rhythm against Dolan. Her hands tightened, working on his shoulders. Dolan's hands tightened on her waist, then moved to her buttocks with a kind of automatic movement and they strained against each other, kissing, like that. The woman slightly lifted one leg, pressing the thigh against Dolan, and he slipped his hand down and gripped the thigh up higher.

"Oh, God!" she gasped. "We're free—free, Tom!"

He was breathing heavily, his face sheened with perspiration. He held her away, her body arching from the waist, the long beautifully shaped legs against him, the swollen breasts peaked against the black satin, firm white flesh revealed in the throat sash.

"He was murdered," Dolan said.

"Don't, Tom," the woman said, tipping her head down. "Please, please, don't. It—it just doesn't do anything to me, knowing he's dead. It couldn't. I didn't love him. He wouldn't let me go." She paused, looked up at him.

Dolan's eyes were vacant. "He was my brother."

"It just makes me feel wonderfully free," she said. "God, Tom—I want you. It makes me want you like I've never wanted you before. I'm crazy with it. I feel filthy and obscene—and that's how I want to feel."

"Irene."

・・・

She began to move herself against him again, slowly, tightly, with a harshness that showed in her face. A kind of savage wantonness, of greed and earnestly fired passion. There was sleep in it, and brutality, and it began to affect Dolan.

"He was my brother."

"I was his wife. But I'm your woman."

"Are you thinking about his money?" Dolan said.

"No. No, no. You have enough for us, forever."

He pulled her to him, and they both were breathing heavily now, looking into each other's eyes.

"We're animals," he said. "We're doomed and damned, Irene. You see that?"

"I want to sin with you. That's how I love you."

"He's not cold yet."

"That's how I love you," she gasped. "It had to happen. I knew something had to happen. Jesus, Tom—love me!"

Holding each other, they walked staggering into the bedroom, eager. She fell back on the bed, her golden hair fanning on the pillows.

"Who did it, Tom?"

"I don't know."

He told her where he had been, what he'd been trying to do. She held his hand against her, obviously not listening now, guiding his hand, her plump lips very red, her eyes half-lidded with desire.

"Please, Tom—before I go crazy!"

He came up onto the bed, then hesitated, frowned, looking at something on the floor under the bed.

"Christ," he whispered.

"Jesus, Tom!"

He left the bed, noises coming from his throat. He leaned, came up clutching a soaking pair of brown trousers that had been balled under the bed.

"Irene!" he shouted, turning to her.

He shook the trousers. Something glasslike, gleaming blue, leaped from the right pants cuff, spiraled through the air. It winked. It bounced to the floor. It rattled skidding off along the baseboard, and Dolan dropped the soaking brown trousers with the yellow stripes, snatched his hand out.

He held up a blue glass eye.

The eye winked in the pink light of the bedroom.

"Bruno," he said. "Bruno and you!" he shouted.

"Now, Tom—it's nothing. It's nothing, Tom!"

He moved stolidly toward the bed, holding the eye.

"Christ," he said. "He was my brother!"

She watched fascinated. Then she screamed.

The glass eye winked as it rattled on the floor.

This Petty Pace

Mystery Tales
June 1959

It was night. Hunched by tall shrubbery, he watched the house, very careful about how he moved. There was an odor of damp earth and sweetly flowered summer. He wanted to see Norma. He wished he didn't have to enter that house when she gave the word. He had never before robbed. He was not at heart a thief. But the plan would bring them everything they wanted.

"Jimmy?"

Fear lightly touched him as Norma's whisper carried across the rear lawn. He did not move. He was debating. Not consciously, but in the hidden place where it counted, and it made him hesitate.

Norma was the maid in that house. He loved her.

"Jim?"

He straightened. Norma was moving toward him, across the yard, from the back porch. Moonlight sheened her face, drenched her shapely body under the black cloth of her dress, glowed in her dark hair. He watched the way she walked, her high heels twin twinkles across shadow.

"Over here," he whispered.

"Come on, Jimmy!"

"Yeah, all right. I'm coming."

He drew away from the shrubbery. The thick carpet of lawn munched beneath his feet.

"She's asleep, now. She took her pill and she's out cold."

"Norma! What about the kid?"

"He's sleeping, too—in his room."

She moved to him and pressed against him, her body tight. He tasted her breath, her tender lips.

"Norma? Baby?"

"Yes?"

"You still want to go through with this?"

She said nothing. She just looked at him in that sly way. He buried his hands in her hair.

"All right," he said. "We'll do it."

"You scared?"

"I just keep wondering if it's the thing to do."

• • •

She pushed against him and he felt the tensing of her flesh. He couldn't deny what she did to him. That's what had got him this far.

"Now, listen," Norma said, whispering hoarsely. "I'll tell you again. Listen good! You go straight to her room. She'll be asleep. The money's in the top drawer of her dressing table, left side. Behind the make-up kit. The jewelry's in two boxes. One's on the dressing table. The other's on the second closet shelf, behind all those hats." She paused. "All those gorgeous hats." Her face was pale. He half felt like running out toward the streetlights, but he just stood there, watching her lips. "You got it all straight, now, honey?" she asked.

"Yeah."

"Remember, Jimmy—be bold."

"Be bold?"

"Yes. Bold as hell—it's our chance!"

"Suppose her husband comes home?"

He watched the house now, as though wires were attached to his eyeballs, pulling tautly from the house.

"Listen, Jimmy. He *won't* come home. From right now, you've got an hour. In an hour, you'll meet me in the room downtown."

"You're leaving now?"

"I'm through with work. I'll drive to the corner, stop at the drugstore, pick up Jean." She prodded him with her finger. "Jean's my alibi."

His throat felt dry.

She drew close. "You won't need an alibi, honey. But I've *got* to have somebody know I left the house on time, see? They'll probably question me."

He felt doomed. "Suppose she wakes up?"

"She won't, I tell you. Not with those pills she takes every night. Just walk in and get the stuff, and walk out."

• • •

She stepped away, yanked up her skirt, flipped her hips, and skinned out of a pair of tight black nylon panties. She handed them to him.

"Wrap the stuff in these."

He stood there holding the panties.

"You sure we should meet tonight?" he said.

"Scared somebody might see us together?" she said. "Nobody will, nobody has yet. Besides, I'm all excited—" She clung to him, her lips moist, her hands soft against his face.

He wanted her so badly he couldn't stand it. So he would do it. A movie usher's pay envelope would never be enough for Norma, and he had to have Norma.

"Get going," she said.

"Okay."

She patted his cheek. "What a time we'll have!"

"Yeah—I guess."

"Now, be bold," she said. "Act like it's your house. Walk in there and do your business."

A moment later she was gone. He heard her car start up in the drive, roll on the gravel, turn into the street. Then she was gone. He was alone.

He started toward the house, thrusting the soft black nylon panties into his jacket pocket. Tall, thin, his moonlit shadow was a jagged slat across the lawn.

He paused on the back porch, peering into the dimly lighted kitchen. It had taken Norma weeks to get him this far. He still didn't know if he wanted to go through with it. He would, though. Only he was scared.

He was an usher at the *State*. That's where he'd met her. She had come regularly to the movies, alone, and he'd watched her come seven times and sit in the same seat, before he asked her to go out with him. He had always wondered why she never wanted to go around people. It was all right, though, parking some place out of town, the way they did. It was more than all right.

She had everything planned. They would let things cool, then go away together. Visioning this spurred him.

He opened the door, stepped inside, closed it carefully. He moved swiftly through the house. He knew every step of the way. She had taught him.

• • •

An old grandfather's clock in the richly carpeted hallway solemnly ticked, fingering the hour of ten.

"It'll be easy, honey. I leave at ten and the kid's asleep by then. She takes her pills and her husband never gets home till eleven. See?"

He was halfway up the winding stairs. It was a rich-smelling place, big and what you dream about.

Reaching the landing, he glanced at the kid's closed door, then started down the hall. He passed a huge, gold-framed mirror, and saw dim pink light spreading from the open doorway of her room. Norma had said she always slept with a light on.

He looked inside.

The room was pink. It was a palace. She was lying on the big bed, her golden hair spread on the pillows, the soft pink covers only to her waist. She was the most beautiful woman he'd ever seen. For a moment he just stood there staring.

• • •

The grandfather's clock bonged ten. His shirt was suddenly soaking wet with sweat. He stepped into the room.

He saw the dressing table, its sable-tinted mirror reflecting his pale features. Over there was the closet. He fumbled quickly in his jacket pocket, squeezing the panties, remembering Norma, watching the sleeping woman. He moved to the foot of the bed. The windows were open, curtains pinkly billowing.

The woman slept half spread out on her side and back, one arm flung out, the other curled in her thick hair. Her gown was like pink smoke. He pulled his gaze from her, started toward the dressing table.

But she was so beautiful, he had to look at her again. And she was looking at him.

Rooted to the floor, he watched her begin to sit up, her mouth opening, and he saw her tongue and remembered the open windows. She was going to scream, coming up out of sleep.

He dove across the bed and grabbed her.

"Shut up!" he said. "Shut up!"

He lashed one hand across her mouth. She squealed against his palm, thrashing. She was very strong, throwing herself all over the bed, trying to get free and scream. He didn't know what to do. Her fingernails raked his wrists.

He thought frantically of the pills she was supposed to have taken. He crawled over her, holding her tightly, and abruptly she bit him, her teeth sinking into the side of his hand. He jerked his hand free, saw her suck wildly for a scream.

"No!" He grabbed the fluffy pink pillow and stuffed it over her face, one knee on her, holding her down. Her gown was stripped over her shoulders, her eyes agonized and wild upon him over the pillow's edge. Her body convulsed in savage anger. He smashed the pillow over her face, watching her, pleading with her—out of his mind.

"Please, be still—you got to be still!" He heard his shrill whisper, like the wind through the curtains. "Don't scream—please, please—be still!"

Her big round eyes watched him. They were so brightly blue. He turned his face away, pressing with the pillow, sobbing, sweating, not knowing what to do. On the night table he saw a book, a glass of water, two red capsules. She hadn't taken the pills—he mashed the pillow as she struggled.

Her hands clawed and scratched. Her hands were suddenly monstrous—like an eagle's claws. Blood purled from scratches.

He fought her in panic. He rode her furiously bucking body, feeling the big round eyes.

"Oh, please!" he begged. "Please, don't—don't scream!"

She became absolutely still. He lifted the pillow and she sucked air like a machine. He slammed the pillow down again in a frightened fury. He arched his face to the ceiling, straddling her. What could he do?

If she screamed, they'd hear her clear downtown.

Sweat dripped from his face onto her forehead.

"I'll go," he whispered, begging her. "I'll leave the house. I won't hurt you—just let me go—let me go—be quiet—"

. . .

She writhed under him.

"Please, lady!" He began talking crazily, speaking to her in a furious, tender whisper, with the awful fright inside him. He talked like a phonograph record, imploring her, trying to explain the unexplainable.

He was still talking when he realized she hadn't moved for some moments. He jerked the pillow wildly away.

She stared at him, her eyes half-lidded. Her mouth was wide open, mashed in, the lips caught dryly back away from her teeth, her color dark.

"Stop it!"

He came off the bed, dropped the pillow, grabbed her fiercely and shook her. She rattled loosely on the bed, her head flopping around. Her lip plopped back over her upper teeth with a small noise.

He went a little crazy, kneeling on the bed, holding her face in his hands. He rocked her back and forth. He mashed his head into her breasts, listening, not breathing. Nothing to hear from her, either; no thumping, no nothing.

. . .

He flung himself off the bed, tore the covers off her, rolled her onto the floor on her stomach, fell on her. He knelt, then, trying to give her artificial respiration, trying to recall how it was done from his old Boy Scout Handbook.

He was so nervous, he couldn't get the rhythm.

He rolled her onto her back. Someplace he'd heard you could blow the breath back into them. He pressed his lips against hers, gusting air into her, filling her lungs—imagining her lungs filling and releasing.

Life was gone. Nothing happened.

Finally he just knelt there, staring at her.

He began to sob and cry a little. Then that ceased and he just knelt there. He could hear himself breathe, but that was all. The curtains moved. He hadn't meant to do it.

Why had she tried to get away? She was so beautiful and he would never have hurt her. He had killed her. They killed so easily. Something between sobs and laughter worked in his throat.

"You kissed Mom. What you doing to Mom?"

He whirled. A young boy stood in the bedroom doorway, looking at him.

The boy was maybe nine or ten years old, dressed in blue and white polka-dot pajamas, rubbing his eyes. He had big round blue eyes and his sandy hair stood on end.

"I'm gonna tell Daddy," the boy said. "You aren't supposed to be here."

The boy stood there a moment longer, then ran into the room and over to his mother. He looked down at her and then at Jimmy. They stared at each other across the woman's body.

The boy's face was suddenly a thing of fright. He edged backward toward the door.

"Now, now," Jimmy said, coming to his feet. "Here, here—"

"No," the boy said.

"Wait, now."

"I'm gonna tell Dad!"

"Wait."

"I saw you kiss her. What's the matter with her? You aren't my Daddy!" He turned and ran.

Jimmy ran violently after him, caught him at the head of the stairs. He tried to hold him. The kid fought like a savage, not yelling, just grunting.

"You let me go!"

"Now, wait—please, wait."

"Daddy'll be home."

The kid made a wild rush. Jimmy held to the pajamas jacket, but the boy snapped it free and ran down the hall. He got inside a bedroom, slammed the door in Jimmy's face.

The door was locked. He could hear the boy on the other side, listening, breathing.

"Open the door," he said. "Come on, kid—open the door."

The boy did not reply.

He stood there, shaken, and half crazy. The kid had seen him, and that was all he could think. The kid could describe him, and that fact was like some kind of ignited bomb inside him. He flung himself desperately at the door. But it was locked and solid.

• • •

Turning, he dimly saw a bathroom at the end of the hall. He raced down there, and found a door leading from the bathroom to a bedroom. Another door was on the far wall of the bedroom. He crossed fast, panting, snatched it open. He was in a dark closet. There was a door on the other side of the closet. He snatched that open and was in the bedroom with the boy.

Lights from a streetlight shone brightly into the room. The boy was by a bed, watching him, fright in his eyes. The eyes that had seen him do this thing.

He had killed a woman and the kid had seen him.

Jimmy moved toward him. The boy turned and ran at the hall door, trying to unlock it.

"Daddy-Daddy-Daddy!"

• • •

Jimmy grabbed him. He flung him across the room. The boy slammed from his grasp, tripped and sprawled headlong, sliding on the waxed, hardwood floor. The kid's head banged against the rock-hard base of a huge old chest of drawers. The crack of skull striking wood was like a shot.

"Oh, no," Jimmy said. "Jesus, please, no!"

The boy didn't move.

He went over and rattled the boy around. He wasn't dead, just unconscious.

The boy began to come to, softly crying. Then he began to yell. Jimmy whipped one hand over the yelling mouth. He couldn't strike the kid. He couldn't kill him. He grabbed the kid up in his arms, holding one hand across his mouth. The kid wriggled and fought, and Jimmy carried him out through the hall door into the hall.

At the foot of the stairs, the front door opened. The house wasn't lighted and he ran and turned running, and the hall lights came on.

"What's going on—stop!" a man shouted.

Jimmy ran through the hall into the kitchen, carrying the wriggling kid. He ran out of the kitchen door.

"Stop!"

The man pounded after him, shouting.

Jimmy ran across the lawn with the man shouting behind him. Lights blinked on in nearby windows. He knew he should drop the boy, but he couldn't. It was as if his arms were frozen. All he could think was he had to find Norma. She would know what to do.

He ran through a thick hedge into an alley where his car was parked, an old Ford coupe. Inside the car, he pushed the boy across the seat, started the engine and gunned away.

The boy was yelling. He grabbed him, holding his hand across his mouth.

The man ran after him, nearly up to the car, shouting at him. The man struck at the car with his hands. The sound was like a beating drum.

He came out of the alley and headed downtown.

He slid the car to a halt in the alley where Norma's room was. She rented a room at the back of a store, in the downtown business section. He slid out quickly, yanking the kid with him, one hand across the boy's mouth. It had been a crazy ride across town. The boy kept yelling in his throat.

He half-dragged, half-carried the boy to Norma's door and beat on the panels. The kid kicked him in the shins, struggling like a trapped animal.

The door opened and Norma stood there.

"What's—Jimmy!"

"Look out, for God's sake!"

He rushed inside, kicking the door back with his foot. It partly closed, arrested by the night latch. Norma had a tiny living room and bedroom, combined, with a minute kitchenette to the left. She stood there in a red shorty nightgown, wide-eyed.

Jimmy's hand slipped. The boy yelled.

"Norma! Norma—help me—Mommy—"

• • •

Jimmy caught him again, brutally covering his mouth.

"What have you done?" Norma said, shrinking back.

He tried to explain, but it was crazy. It sounded crazy even to him. "He saw me, don't you see? Now he's seen you! What'll we do?"

"You fool," Norma said. "Did you get the money?"

"How could I?"

She turned and hurried into the bedroom. He watched her strip off the nightgown, and quickly start to dress.

"What you doing?"

"I'm getting out of here," she said. "Fast."

He saw two suitcases on the floor under the bed. Half-dressed, she dragged them out.

"You damned fool!" she said, buttoning her blouse. "You deserve it. I was going to leave you flat, anyway, soon as I got my hands on the money. You hear that? I was leaving tonight, after I sent you home. I quit work tonight, for good." She slipped into her shoes, grabbed the two suitcases.

"Norma!"

"Out of my way."

"Norma!" he yelled. He let go the boy and grabbed for her. The boy turned and ran at the door, flung it open, running out into the alley, yelling.

"Get him," Norma said. "For God's sake, get him!"

"Norma—"

• • •

Whirling, he ran into the alley. The kid was halfway down, running and stumbling in the semi-darkness. Jimmy ran after him. The kid was yelling for his mother.

Jimmy stopped, looking back. Norma had just come out of her doorway, carrying the two suitcases.

"Norma!"

She didn't answer, vanishing into the shadows beyond her room, where he knew her car was parked.

The kid had reached the end of the alley, on the street. He was yelling and screaming. Jimmy turned and ran hard after him, came onto the sidewalk.

The kid was pounding along the sidewalk in his pajamas, yelling.

"Stop—damn you!" Jimmy shouted. "You hear me?"

The distance between him and the boy shortened. A car in the street slowed and stopped. Then another. Two men ran toward him. He heard the shrill sound of a cop's whistle.

"Mommy!" the kid yelled.

Two men piled into him and he went down, his face burning across the cement. He fought them, looking toward where the kid was, trying to run after him. One of the men kept hitting him in the face. They both kept saying things, but he didn't know what they were saying.

"What's up?"

"Guy chasing that kid, officer."

"Let him go."

Jimmy struggled to his feet. The kid had halted a half block down, turning to watch.

"Listen, you—what . . . ?" the big cop said.

Jimmy wheeled, running.

"Stop," the cop said.

Jimmy kept running, back toward the alley, now. He had to stop Norma.

Something smashed brutally into his back and knocked him flat and he heard the shot echo through the night streets. Then another.

He crawled bleeding along the sidewalk, with the god-awful pain in his back, something broken in there, working his way toward the alley.

"Chasing that kid," a man said.

Feet pounded along the sidewalk toward him. He heard the sound of a car coming out of the alley.

"Stop her," he said weakly. "That's Norma—"

• • •

He forced his head up and saw her as she drove past. She saw him, too. Then she turned her car into the street. He watched the taillight wink back at him like a red eye. Then the eye shut.

Blood mirrored on the sidewalk under a streetlight.

"He's dead," the cop said. "Go pick up that kid, will you?"

Complete Index of Gil Brewer's Short Stories

This index lists all short stories by Gil Brewer known to exist. As well, it lists all known print publications of these stories in English with the exception of appearances in the omnibus *Giant Manhunt* collections, as individual issues of *Giant Manhunt* may vary in their contents. Manuscripts held at the University of Wyoming's American Heritage Center are listed only if not yet published. Scans of these manuscripts may be purchased at the center's website.

Abbreviations:
    DCL = *Death Comes Last: The Rest of the 1950s* (Stark House Press, 2021)
    DIAPE = *Death Is a Private Eye: Unpublished Stories* (Stark House Press, 2019)
    DODT = *Die Once, Die Twice: More Unpublished Stories* (Stark House Press, 2020)
    GBP = Gil Brewer Papers, American Heritage Center, University of Wyoming, Collection 8187
    RDQ = *Redheads Die Quickly and Other Stories* (University Press of Florida, 2012)
    RDQEE = *Redheads Die Quickly and Other Stories: Expanded Edition* (Stark House Press, 2019)

"Alligator." Published under the pseudonym Eric Fitzgerald. *Hunted Detective Story Magazine* 9 (April 1956): 48–56. Reprinted in *DCL*, 128–134.
"The Axe Is Ready." *Trapped Detective Story Magazine* 1.4 (December 1956): 39–50. Reprinted in *RDQ*, 209–219; and *RDQEE*, 169–176.
"Backwoods Tease." *Men* 13.2 (February 1964): 19–21, 92–101. Condensed from *The Brat* (Gold Medal, 1957).
"The Bargain." GBP, Box 4, 22 pages.
"Beach House Tramp." *Male Annual* 5.5 (1967): 12–15, 113–129. Condensed from *The Tease* (Banner, 1967).
"'Beeg Fool.'" *Salvo: Finest Foxhole Fiction—The Blood, Lust, Terror of Combat* 1.1 (January 1957): 14–21, 92–98. Reprinted in *DCL*, 189–197.
"Beetle's Bottle." GBP, Box 7, 17 pages.
"Beyond the Vineyard." *Swank* 12.1 (March 1965): 50–52, 54.
"The Black Suitcase." Published under the pseudonym Eric Fitzgerald. *Hunted Detective Story Magazine* 8 (February 1956): 50–66. Reprinted in *RDQ*, 113–129; and *RDQEE*, 93–103.
"Blue Moon." *Mike Shayne Mystery Magazine* 34.5 (April 1974): 67–73.
"Bothered." GBP, Box 6, 12 pages. Different version of "Bothered" (*Manhunt*, July 1957).
"Bothered." *Manhunt* 5.7 (July 1957): 9–11. Reprinted in *American Pulp*, ed. Ed Gorman, Bill Pronzini, and Martin H. Greenberg (New York: Carroll & Graf, 1997), 409–415; *RDQ*, 244–250; and *RDQEE*, 199–203.
"Brother Bill." As by Jim Beard on table of contents. *Don Pendleton's The Executioner Mystery Magazine* 1.4 (April 1975): 88–94.
"Candy." *DODT*, 107–112.

"Caprice." *DODT*, 165–171.
"Cave in the Rain." *Ed McBaines* [sic] *87th Precinct Mystery Magazine* 1.4 (April 1975): 99–105.
"Cave in the Rain." GBP, Box 6, 12 pages. Different version of "Cave in the Rain" (*Ed McBaines* [sic] *87th Precinct Mystery Magazine*, April 1975).
"Clean Sweep." *DODT*, 30–43.
"The Closed Room." *Alfred Hitchcock's Mystery Magazine* 24.4 (April 1979): 88–96.
"Come Across." *Manhunt* 4.4 (April 1956): 52–61. Reprinted in *RDQ*, 178–188; and *RDQEE*, 136–143.
"Cop." *Mike Shayne Mystery Magazine* 17.2 (July 1965): 40–58.
"A Curious Bird." GBP, Box 6, 8 pages.
"Cut Bait." Published under the pseudonym Eric Fitzgerald. *Pursuit Detective Story Magazine* 15 (May 1956): 75–83. Reprinted in *RDQ*, 189–197; and *RDQEE*, 144–149.
"Daylight Dynasty." *DODT*, 147–154.
"Deadly Little Green Eyes." *Mike Shayne Mystery Magazine* 36.2 (February 1975): 54–83.
"Death Comes Last." Published under the pseudonym Eric Fitzgerald. *Hunted Detective Story Magazine* 6 (October 1955): 92–117. Reprinted in *DCL*, 78–96.
"Death Is a Private Eye." *DIAPE*, 175–226.
"Death Is the Sweetest Thing." GBP, Box 6, 17 pages.
"Death of a Prowler." *Trapped Detective Story Magazine* 2.6 (April 1958): 48–56. Reprinted in *RDQ*, 259–267; and *RDQEE*, 227–232.
"Death Window." *DIAPE*, 159–166.
"Death with a Ten Foot Pole." GBP, Box 7, 20 pages. Different version of "With a Ten Foot Pole" and "With a Ten Foot Pole You."
"Decision." *DIAPE*, 227–230.
"Devotion." GBP, Box 7, 17 pages.
"Die, Darling, Die." *Justice: Amazing Detective Mysteries* 2.1 (January 1956): 57–77. Reprinted in *The Hardboiled Lineup*, ed. Harry Widmer (New York: Lion Books, 1956), 84–103; *RDQ*, 91–112; and *RDQEE*, 59–74.
"Die Once—Die Twice." *DODT*, 186–196.
"The Doll." GBP, Box 8, 17 pages.
"Don't Do That." Published under the pseudonym Bailey Morgan. *Hunted Detective Story Magazine* 7 (December 1955): 93–100. Reprinted in *RDQ*, 82–90; *RDQEE*, 53–58; and *Black Cat Mystery Magazine #5* 2.1 (2019): 139–146.
"Encore." *DODT*, 144–146.
"Errors." GBP, Box 7, 12 pages.
"Escape to Never." *DODT*, 89–98.
"Escape to Never." GBP, Box 6, 15 pages. Shorter version of "Escape to Never" (*DODT*, 89–98).
"Exchange." GBP, Box 8, 10 pages.
"The Explanation." GBP, Box 7, 10 pages.
"Family." *Alfred Hitchcock's Mystery Magazine* 23.3 (March 1978): 54–61.
"Fiasco." GBP, Box 8, 17 pages.

"Final Appearance." *Detective Tales* 48.3 (October 1951): 54–62. Reprinted in *Black Mask Detective: A Magazine of Gripping, Smashing Detective Stories* [UK] 9.2 (January 1952): 36–41, 54; and *DCL*, 21–30.
"Final Gesture." GBP, Box 6, 8 pages.
"Fog." *Manhunt Detective Story Monthly* 4.2 (February 1956): 50–57. Reprinted in *DCL*, 113–119.
"Fool's Gold." *Alfred Hitchcock's Mortal Errors*, ed. Cathleen Jordan (New York: Dial, 1983), 156–160.
"Friendly Persuasion." *DODT*, 59–62.
"Friendship." GBP, Box 6, 17 pages.
"The Gentle Touch." *Don Pendleton's The Executioner Mystery Magazine* 1.5 (May 1975): 40–48.
"The Gesture." *The Saint Detective Magazine* 5.3 (March 1956): 104–109. Reprinted in *The Saint Detective Magazine* [UK] 2.7 (May 1956): 91–96; *The Saint Detective Magazine* [UK] 4.5 (March 1958): 108–112; *101 Mystery Stories*, ed. Bill Pronzini and Martin H. Greenberg (New York: Avenel, 1986), 37–41; *A Century of Noir: Thirty-two Classic Crime Stories*, ed. Mickey Spillane and Max Allan Collins (New York: New American Library, 2002), 169–173; *RDQ*, 135–140; and *RDQEE*, 107–110.
"The Getaway." *Mystery Monthly* 1.1 (June 1976): 58–66. Reprinted in *The Mammoth Book of Pulp Fiction*, ed. Maxim Jakubowski (New York: Carroll & Graf, 1996), 138–145; this collection was reprinted as *Pulp Fiction* by Castle Books in 2002.
"Getaway Money." *Guilty Detective Story Magazine* 3.3 (November 1958): 67–74. Reprinted in *RDQ*, 268–274; and *RDQEE*, 233–237.
"The Ghost of Hermit Key." GBP, Box 7, 13 pages.
"Gigolo." Published under the pseudonym Bailey Morgan. *Pursuit Detective Story Magazine* 10 (July 1955): 67–78. Reprinted in *DCL*, 37–45.
"The Glass Eye." *Guilty Detective Story Magazine* 2.2 (September 1957): 79–86. Reprinted in *DCL*, 245–250.
"The Golden Scheme." *DCL*, 152–165.
"Goodbye, Jeannie." *Accused Detective Story Magazine* 1.3 (May 1956): 81–84. Reprinted in *DCL*, 135–137.
"Good-Bye Now." *Alfred Hitchcock's Mystery Magazine* 13.7 (July 1968): 86–93. Reprinted in *Get Me to the Wake on Time*, ed. Alfred Hitchcock (New York: Dell, 1970), 11–19.
"Harlot House." *Mystery Tales* 1.5 (August 1959): 23–33. Reprinted in *RDQ*, 286–297; and *RDQEE*, 245–252.
"He Wouldn't Believe." GBP, Box 6, 18 pages. Unfinished?
"Hell House." *DIAPE*, 115–123.
"High Heels and Kisses." *True Men Stories* 1.6 (August 1957): 38–39, 58, 60. Reprinted in *DCL*, 239–244.
"Hit." *Alfred Hitchcock's Mystery Magazine* 22.6 (June 1977): 28–32.
"Home." *Accused Detective Story Magazine* 1.2 (March 1956): 122–128. Reprinted in *Hard-Boiled: An Anthology of American Crime Stories*, ed. Bill Pronzini and Jack Adrian (New York: Oxford UP, 1995), 341–347; *RDQ*, 141–148; and *RDQEE*, 111–115.

"Home-Again Blues." Published under the pseudonym Eric Fitzgerald. *Pursuit Detective Story Magazine* 14 (March 1956): 108–128. Reprinted in *RDQ*, 149–170; and *RDQEE*, 116–130.

"House of Captive Women." *Male* 7.1 (January 1957): 20–23, 86–97. Condensed from *A Killer Is Loose* (Gold Medal, 1954).

"House of Rage." GBP, Box 7, 41 pages. Pages 4–8 missing.

"Hung Up." *DODT*, 63–70.

"I Apologize." *Mike Shayne Mystery Magazine* 34.3 (February 1974): 45–49.

"I Couldn't Tell You." GBP, Box 8, 13 pages.

"I Had Sex with a Martian." *DODT*, 44–50.

"I Saw Her Die." *Manhunt Detective Story Monthly* (October 1955): 37–43. Reprinted in *DCL*, 97–102.

"I Was a Teaser for the Cops." Uncredited. Romantic Secrets 1.1 (December 1976): 44–47.

"The Idols' Secret." GBP, Box 8, 15 pages.

"I'll Be in the Bedroom." *Trapped Detective Story Magazine* 2.1 (June 1957): 70–78. Reprinted in *DCL*, 210–215.

"I'll Never Tell." *Swank* 18.5 (June 1971): 12, 14, 44.

"Incident at Snake River." GBP, Box 8, 14 pages.

"Indiscretion." *Swank* 13.2 (March 1966): 12–14, 76. Reprinted in *A Devil for O'Shaugnessy/The Three-Way Split* (Eureka, CA: Stark House, 2008), 173–176.

"Inheritance." GBP, Box 6, 7 pages.

"The Intruder." GBP, Box 6, 8 pages.

"The Invalid." *DODT*, 71–78.

"Investment." *Mike Shayne Mystery Magazine* 34.4 (March 1974): 58–65.

"It's Always Too Late." *Detective Fiction* 156.1 (April 1951): 27–35. Reprinted in *RDQ*, 39–50; and *RDQEE*, 25–32.

"The Journal." GBP, Box 8, 6 pages.

"Junk Yard Blues." *DIAPE*, 130–135.

"Kill Crazy." *Posse: Virile Stories of the Old West* 1.2 (April 1957): 61–65. Reprinted in *RDQEE*, 188–194.

"The Killer." *DODT*, 178–185.

"Killer's Love Slave." *Men* 15.9 (September 1966): 20–23, 86–97. Condensed from *The Hungry One* (Gold Medal, 1966).

"The King." GBP, Box 8, 14 pages.

"The Knife." GBP, Box 4, two incomplete versions, both 9 pages.

"Knife-Job." GBP, Box 4, 8 pages.

"Lady for Rent." *Playtime: The New Fun Magazine for Males!* 1.1 (1965?): 38–42.

"Lapse." *DIAPE*, 99–106.

"Let Me Be First." *Swank* 14.10 (December 1967): 13–15, 74.

"Lion-Eyed Moon Girl." *DODT*, 99–106.

"Live Bait." *Don Pendleton's The Executioner Mystery Magazine* 1.6 (June 1975): 105–110.

"Long." *DIAPE*, 97–98.

"Looking Around." GBP, Box 6, two versions, 8 pages and 9 pages.

"Love . . . and Luck." *Cavalier* 21.9 (July 1971): 66–67, 69–70. Reprinted in *Cavalier Yearbook* ("1973 edition"), 66–68, 74; and *A Devil for O'Shaugnessy/The Three-Way Split* (Eureka, CA: Stark House, 2008), 166–172.
"Love Me, Baby." *True Men Stories* 1.4 (April 1957): 24–25, 52, 54, 56, 58. Reprinted in *DCL*, 198–204.
"Love-Lark." *Don Pendleton's The Executioner Mystery Magazine* 1.4 (April 1975): 49–56.
"Lover." GBP, Box 6, 8 pages. Different story than "Lover (I)" and "Lover (II)."
"Lover (I)." *DODT*, 155–160.
"Lover (II)." *DODT*, 161–164.
"Love's Weekend." *DIAPE*, 149–158.
"Luna Caprice." GBP, Box 6, 10 pages. Manuscript incomplete.
"Mantis 36." *DODT*, 128–136.
"Mantis 36." GBP, Box 6, 16 pages. Earlier version of "Mantis 36" (*DODT*, 128–136).
"The Mark." GBP, Box 8, 9 pages.
"The Mask." GBP, Box 8, 6 pages.
"Matinee." *Manhunt* 4.10 (October 1956): 47–56. Reprinted in *RDQ*, 198–208; and *RDQEE*, 150–156.
"Meet Me in Hades." *DODT*, 79–88.
"Meet Me in the Dark." *Manhunt* 6.2 (February 1958): 13–23. Reprinted in *RDQEE*, 209–226.
"Meeting." GBP, Box 8, 7 pages.
"Memento." *DIAPE*, 76–80.
"Memory of a Hanging Man." *Topper* (September 1966): 32–34, 74–76.
"Midnight." Published under the pseudonym Jack Holland. *Hunted Detective Story Magazine* 8 (February 1956): 67–78. Reprinted in *DCL*, 120–127. Different story than "Midnight" (*Sportsman*, August 1967).
"Midnight." *Sportsman* (August 1967): 26–28, 72–73. Different story than "Midnight" (*Hunted Detective Story Magazine*, February 1956).
"The Milkman." *DIAPE*, 71–75.
"Moment." GBP, Box 8, 9 pages.
"Moment in Gehenna." GBP, Box 6, 27 pages.
"The Monster." GBP, Box 7, 20 pages.
"Moonshine." *Manhunt Detective Story Monthly* 3.3 (March 1955): 42–50. Reprinted in *My Favorite Crime Story* (Derby, CT: Charlton Publications, Inc., n.d.), 44–48; *RDQ*, 51–61; *RDQEE*, 33–39; and *The Best of* Manhunt: *A Collection of the Best Stories from* Manhunt *Magazine*, ed. Jeff Vorzimmer (Eureka, CA: Stark House, 2019), 282–289.
"Mother." *Mike Shayne Mystery Magazine* 35.2 (July 1974): 91–97.
"Motive for Murder." *Man to Man: The Stag Magazine* 6.2 (June 1955): 26–27, 44, 46–47. Reprinted in *DCL*, 31–36.
"The Mountain Kid." *Zane Grey Western Magazine* 1.1 (October 1969): 113–119.
"Mow the Green Grass." Published under the pseudonym Jack Holland. *Pursuit Detective Story Magazine* 14 (March 1956): 101–107. Reprinted in *RDQ*, 171–177; and *RDQEE*, 131–135.
"My Bloody Hands and I." GBP, Box 6, 60 pages.
"My Husband Wanted Evil Sex with Me." *DODT*, 172–177.

"My Jeannie." GBP, Box 8, 10 pages.

"My Lady Is a Tramp." Published under the pseudonym Bailey Morgan. *Pursuit Detective Story Magazine* 9 (May 1955): 1–15. Reprinted in *Pursuit—The Phantom Mystery Magazine* [Australia] 1.9 (1955?): 13–25; *Bad Girls*, ed. Leo Margulies (New York: Crest, 1958), 80–94; *RDQ*, 62–76; and *RDQEE*, 40–49.

"My Murderer, My Lover." *Men: The Adventure and Entertainment Magazine* 9.8 (August 1960): 19–21, 88–97. Condensed from *Angel* (Avon, 1960).

"Nepenthe." *DODT*, 19–29.

"Nethra." *DODT*, 51–58.

"Number One." *DIAPE*, 63–66.

"Oh Wow." *GBP*, Box 6, 14 pages.

"Old Timers." *Murder!* 1.4 (July 1957): 15–17. Reprinted in *DCL*, 234–238. *Note:* When published, this story's title was given as "Old Timers" on the magazine's table of contents and "Old Times" on the layout of the story itself. In Brewer's handwritten log of story sales, he listed the story as "Old Timers."

"On a Sunday Afternoon." *Manhunt* 5.1 (January 1957): 128–141. Reprinted in *The Young Punks*, ed. Leo Margulies (New York: Pyramid Books, 1957), 98–114; abridged in *Man's Magazine* 5.7 (July 1957): 14–15, 54–59; *The Violent Ones*, ed. Brant House (New York: Ace Books, 1958), 150–167; abridged in *Man's* [Magazine] *Annual 1968* (1968): 50–51, 97–101; *RDQ*, 220–236; and *RDQEE*, 177–187.

"One More Look." GBP, Box 7, 16 pages.

"Pain Is a Four-Letter Word." GBP, Box 7, 22 pages.

"Pawnee." *Zane Grey Western Magazine* 1.3 (December 1969): 112–124.

"Peccadillo." GBP, Box 8, 10 pages. Different story than "Peccadillo" (*Mike Shayne Mystery Magazine*, May 1973).

"Peccadillo." *Mike Shayne Mystery Magazine* 32.6 (May 1973): 47–53.

"The Peeper." *DIAPE*, 55–62.

"Phone Call." *Adam Bedside Reader* 1.30 (August 1967): 70–73.

"Pig in a Blanket." GBP, Box 8, 7 pages.

"Pigeon." GBP, Box 7, 13 pages.

"Pillow Face" (incomplete). *DODT*, 197–200.

"The Present." GBP, Box 7, 9 pages.

"A Present for Cleo." *DIAPE*, 13–54.

"The Price of Pride." *Triple Western* 18.3 (Summer 1957): 81–87. Reprinted in *DCL*, 216–223.

"Prowler!" *Manhunt* 5.5 (May 1957): 1–3. Reprinted as "Prowler" in *Challenge for Men* 5.6 (September 1959): 12–13, 74, 76; as "The Prowler" in *Guy* 5.5 (October 1967): 14–15, 66, 68; *RDQ*, 237–243; and *RDQEE*, 195–198.

"Ransom for a Hot-Blooded Hooker." *Complete Man Magazine* 6.5 (December 1966): 18–19, 70–81. Condensed from *Wild to Possess* (Monarch, 1959).

"Red Scarf." *Mercury Mystery Book-Magazine* 1.3 (November 1955): 3–97. Reprinted in revised form as *The Red Scarf* (Crest, 1959).

"Red Twilight." Published under the pseudonym Frank Sebastian. *Hunted Detective Story Magazine* 6 (October 1955): 87–91. Reprinted in *RDQ*, 77–81; and *RDQEE*, 50–52.

"Redheads Die Quickly." *Mystery Tales* 1.3 (April 1959): 117–128. Reprinted in *RDQ,* 275–285; and *RDQEE,* 238–244.
"Renegade." *Blazing Guns Western Story Magazine* 2 (December 1956): 103–119. Reprinted in *The Horse Soldiers,* ed. Bill Pronzini and Martin H. Greenberg (New York: Fawcett Gold Medal, 1987), 62–78; and *DCL,* 177–188.
"Return to Yesterday." Published under the pseudonym Eric Fitzgerald. *Pursuit Detective Story Magazine* 16 (July 1956): 62–72. Reprinted in *DCL,* 145–151.
"Reunion." GBP, Box 8, 12 pages.
"Rope Enough." GBP, Box 8, 13 pages.
"Sara's Place." GBP, Box 6, 5 pages.
"Satisfaction." *DIAPE,* 136–140.
"Sauce for the Goose." Published under the pseudonym Eric Fitzgerald. *Pursuit Detective Story Magazine* 13 (January 1956): 94–107. Reprinted in *Bad Girls,* ed. Leo Margulies (New York: Crest, 1958), 112–126; and *RDQEE,* 75–84.
"The Screamer." Published under the pseudonym Eric Fitzgerald. *Pursuit Detective Story Magazine* 11 (September 1955): 1–44. Reprinted in *DCL,* 46–77. Reprinted in expanded form as —*And the Girl Screamed* (Crest, 1956).
"A Season of Change." GBP, Box 8, 7 pages.
"The Secret." GBP, Box 6, 13 pages.
"Shalimar." *DIAPE,* 147–148.
"She Opened the Door to Murder." See "Stop Off."
"Short Go." Published under the pseudonym Jack Holland. *Hunted Detective Story Magazine* 10 (June 1956): 111–120. Reprinted in *DCL,* 138–144.
"Shot." Published under the pseudonym Roy Carroll. *Manhunt Detective Story Monthly* 4.2 (February 1956): 140–144. Reprinted in *RDQ,* 130–134; and *RDQEE,* 104–106.
"Should a Body Cry." GBP, Box 8, 15 pages.
"The Sickness." GBP, Box 7, 17 pages.
"Small Bite." *Alfred Hitchcock's Mystery Magazine* 15.2 (February 1970): 110–115.
"Smelling Like a Rose." *Mr.* 1.6 (July 1957): 38–40, 48–50. Reprinted in *RDQ,* 251–258; and *RDQEE,* 204–208.
"Soap, Suds and Sable." GBP, Box 6, 6 pages.
"Somebody Knew Her." Published under the pseudonym Barry Miles. *Pursuit Detective Story Magazine* 18 (November 1956): 110–116. Reprinted in *DCL,* 166–169.
"Someone Is Listening." GBP, Box 6, 9 pages.
"Something Special for Benny." GBP, Box 8, 19 pages.
"Sometimes I Love You—Sometimes I Hate You." *DODT,* 121–127.
"Southbound." *DIAPE,* 67–70.
"Southern Comfort." *DIAPE,* 107–114.
"Spaghetti." As by John Harding on table of contents. *Don Pendleton's The Executioner Mystery Magazine* 1.4 (April 1975): 70–75.
"Stop Off." *Man's Life* 5.3 (May 1957): 30–31, 72–74. Reprinted as "She Opened the Door to Murder" in *Real Men* 12.10 (February 1969): 34–35, 42, 44–46. Reprinted in *DCL,* 205-209.
"Summer's Lease." *DODT,* 137–143.
"Sunflower." *DIAPE,* 141–146.

"Sunrise." GBP, Box 4, 8 pages.
"Sunset." *Gallery* 5.8 (July 1977): 56–58, 122, 124, 126, 128–129.
"Sunset." GBP, Box 7, two versions, 25 pages and 27 pages, of story that appeared in *Gallery* (July 1977).
"Suppertime." GBP, Box 8, 13 pages.
"Swamp Tale." *Mystery Monthly* 1.7 (December 1976): 40–47.
"Sweet Amy." *Needle: A Magazine of Noir* 2.2 (Fall 2011): 64–72.
"Swing with Me." *Caper* 13.12 (October 1969): 36–37, 68–69, 71–72.
"Sympathy." *Mike Shayne Mystery Magazine* 25.1 (June 1969): 125–128.
"The Take." GBP, Box 8, 11 pages.
"The Taking of Cherry." *Stag* 28.2 (February 1977): 58–59, 70, 72–73. Reprinted in *Man's Epic* [Australia] 7 (1978): 24–26, 66.
"Teen-Age Casanova." *Justice: Amazing Detective Mysteries* 1.3 (October 1955): 55–68. Reprinted in *Young and Deadly*, ed. Leo Margulies (New York: Crest, 1959), 44–58; and *DCL*, 103–112.
"Tell Me." GBP, Box 8, 7 pages.
"The Test." GBP, Box 8, 14 pages.
"That Damned Piper." *Pursued: Exciting Crime Fiction* 1.4 (July 1957): 37–42. Reprinted in *DCL*, 224–233.
"That French St. Woman." *Man's World* 10.1 (February 1964): 14–15, 88–97. Condensed from *13 French Street* (Gold Medal, 1951).
"That Night in Jinny's Bed." *Men* 26.6 (June 1977): 56–61.
"They'll Find Us." *Accused Detective Story Magazine* 1.1 (January 1956): 27–35. Reprinted in *RDQEE*, 85–92.
"The Thinking Child." *Mystery Monthly* 1.4 (September 1976): 38–50.
"This Petty Pace." *Mystery Tales* 1.4 (June 1959): 66–77. Reprinted in *DCL*, 251–258.
"Time." GBP, Box 8, 14 pages.
"Token." *Mike Shayne Mystery Magazine* 31.1 (June 1972): 121–125.
"Too Long." GBP, Box 8, 7 pages.
"The Tormentors." *Manhunt* 4.11 (November 1956): 19–26. Reprinted in *DCL*, 170–176.
"Trick." *Alfred Hitchcock's Mystery Magazine* 14.11 (November 1969): 115–120. Reprinted in *Coffin Break*, ed. Alfred Hitchcock (1974; New York: Dell, 1985), 31–38.
"True Love." GBP, Box 7, 9 pages.
"Tryout." GBP, Box 8, 13 pages.
"The Tube." GBP, Box 6, 22 pages.
"Tweak." *DODT*, 113–120.
"Twilight." GBP, Box 6, 7 pages.
"Ugly." *DIAPE*, 167–174.
"Upriver." *Ed McBain's 87th Precinct Mystery Magazine* 1.6 (June 1975): 97–105.
"Venuto's Castle." GBP, Box 8, 15 pages.
"A Visit from Morse." *DIAPE*, 124–129.
"Vote for Me!" GBP, Box 6, 8 pages. Unfinished?
"Waiting." GBP, Box 6, 9 pages.

"A Waking Dream." *Ed McBain's 87th Precinct Mystery Magazine* 1.5 (May 1975): 98–104.
"A Water-Bed for Marlene." GBP, Box 8, 15 pages.
"Whiskey." Published under the pseudonym Bailey Morgan. *Pursuit Detective Story Magazine* 18 (November 1956): 45–62. Reprinted in *RDQEE*, 157–168.
"Whittle Whittle." *DIAPE*, 91–96.
"Window of Deceit." *DIAPE*, 81–90.
"With a Ten Foot Pole." GBP, Box 6, 20 pages. Manuscript heavily revised in pencil. Different version of "Death with a Ten Foot Pole" and "With a Ten Foot Pole You."
"With a Ten Foot Pole You." GBP, Box 7, 20 pages. Different version of "Death with a Ten Foot Pole" and "With a Ten Foot Pole."
"With this Gun—." *Detective Tales* 47.3 (March 1951): 46–55. Reprinted in *Detective Tales* [UK] 2.9 (July 1954): 18–24; *RDQ*, 27–38; and *RDQEE*, 17–24.
"'You Got So Much—I Want a Piece!'" *Escapade* 14.9 (September 1969): 13–15. Reprinted in *Caper* 14.3 (July 1970): 51–53.
"The Zoo." GBP, Box 8, 8 pages.

From the Master of Obsessive Noir. . . .

Gil Brewer

1-933586-10-9 Wild to Possess / A Taste for Sin $19.95
"Permeated with sweaty desperation."—James Reasoner, *Rough Edges*

1-933586-20-6 A Devil for O'Shaugnessy / The Three-Way Split $14.95
"Brewer's insights into the psychology of sexual enthrallment and obsession still resonate."—David Rachels, *Punk Noir Magazine*

1-933586-53-2 Nude on Thin Ice / Memory of Passion $19.95
"His entire livelihood came from writing works in which lurid narratives were rendered in a punchy, unadorned prose style."— Chris Morgan, *Los Angeles Review of Books*

1-933586-88-5 The Erotics / Gun the Dame Down / Angry Arnold $20.95
"Showcases the impressive storytelling talents of Gil Brewer, a true master of the noir mystery genre . . . strongly recommended."—*Midwest Book Review*

978-1-944520-58-8 Flight to Darkness / 77 Rue Paradis $19.95
"Murder, madness, swamps, gators, a savagely beautiful woman . . . it doesn't get much better than this for noir fans . . . crazed and breakneck."—James Reasoner, *Rough Edges*

978-1-944520-55-7 The Red Scarf / A Killer is Loose $19.95
"There are some neat plot turns, the various components mesh smoothly, the characterization is flawless, and the prose is Brewer's sharpest and most controlled."—Bill Pronzini, *Big Book of Noir*

978-1-944520-76-2 Redheads Die Quickly and Other Stories: Expanded Ed. $19.95
Edited and introduced by David Rachels. A reprint of the 2012 edition with five new stories, including the novelette "Meet Me in the Dark."

978-1-944520-77-9 Death is a Private Eye: Unpublished Stories $17.95
Editor David Rachels has assembled another essential noir collection, 22 previously unpublished stories, including two classic novellas from the early 1950s.

978-1-944520-88-5 Die Once—Die Twice: More Unpublished Stories $15.95
Twenty-four previously unpublished stories from the noir master, including some of his 1970s erotic fiction. Edited and with a new introduction by David Rachels.

978-1-951473-04-4 The Tease / Sin for Me $19.95
"Brewer packs each novel with plenty of unexpected twists to keep the suspense taut and our interest maintained to the very end . . ."—Alan Cranis, *Bookgasm*

Stark House Press, 1315 H Street, Eureka, CA 95501
griffinskye3@sbcglobal.net / www.StarkHousePress.com
Available from your local bookstore, or order direct or via our website.

www.ingramcontent.com/pod-product-compliance
Lightning Source LLC
LaVergne TN
LVHW011023080526
R19377900001B/R193779PG838202LVX00001B/1